A Harvest of Hope

Books by Lauraine Snelling

Song of Blessing

To Everything a Season
A Harvest of Hope

An Untamed Heart

Red River of the North

An Untamed Land
A New Day Rising
A Land to Call Home
The Reapers' Song
Tender Mercies
Blessing in Disguise

Return to Red River

A Dream to Follow
Believing the Dream
More Than a Dream

Daughters of Blessing

A Promise for Ellie
Sophie's Dilemma
A Touch of Grace
Rebecca's Reward

Home to Blessing

A Measure of Mercy
No Distance Too Far
A Heart for Home

Wild West Wind

Valley of Dreams
Whispers in the Wind
A Place to Belong

Dakotah Treasures

Ruby
Pearl
Opal
Amethyst

Secret Refuge

Daughter of Twin Oaks
Sisters of the Confederacy
The Long Way Home
A Secret Refuge 3-in-1

Song of Blessing • Book 2

A Harvest of Hope

LAURAINE SNELLING

BethanyHouse
a division of Baker Publishing Group
Minneapolis, Minnesota

© 2015 by Lauraine Snelling

Published by Bethany House Publishers
11400 Hampshire Avenue South
Bloomington, Minnesota 55438
www.bethanyhouse.com

Bethany House Publishers is a division of
Baker Publishing Group, Grand Rapids, Michigan

Printed in the United States of America

Library of Congress Cataloging-in-Publication Data
Snelling, Lauraine.
    A harvest of hope / Lauraine Snelling.
        pages ; cm. — (Song of Blessing ; 2)
    Summary: "In the early 1900s, Miriam Hastings leaves Chicago after bury-
ing her mother and returns to Blessing, North Dakota, to carry on her nursing
studies. Despite her continued resistance, Trygve Knutson continues his pursuit
of her heart"—Provided by publisher.
        ISBN 978-0-7642-1310-6 (hard cover : alk. paper) — ISBN 978-0-7642-1105-8
(softcover) — ISBN 978-0-7642-1311-3 (large print : softcover)
    I. Title.
    PS3569.N39H37 2015
    813'.54—dc23   2014045338

Scripture quotations are taken from the King James Version of the Bible.

Cover design by Jennifer Parker
Cover photography by Mike Habermann Photography, LLC

Author is represented by Books & Such Literary Agency.

15 16 17 18 19 20 21   7 6 5 4 3 2 1

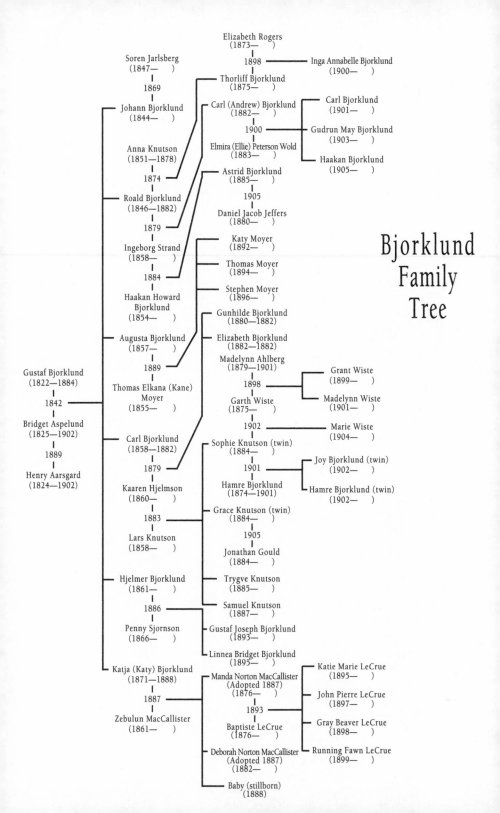

Bjorklund Family Tree

Gustaf Bjorklund
(1822—1884)

1842

Bridget Aspelund
(1825—1902)

1889

Henry Aarsgard
(1824—1902)

Johann Bjorklund
(1844—)

Soren Jarlsberg
(1847—)

1869

Anna Knutson
(1851—1878)

1874

Roald Bjorklund
(1846—1882)

1879

Ingeborg Strand
(1858—)

1884

Haakan Howard
Bjorklund
(1854—)

Augusta Bjorklund
(1857—)

1889

Thomas Elkana (Kane)
Moyer
(1855—)

Carl Bjorklund
(1858—1882)

1879

Kaaren Hjelmson
(1860—)

1883

Lars Knutson
(1858—)

Hjelmer Bjorklund
(1861—)

1886

Penny Sjornson
(1866—)

Katja (Katy) Bjorklund
(1871—1888)

1887

Zebulun MacCallister
(1861—)

Elizabeth Rogers
(1873—)

1898

Thorliff Bjorklund
(1875—)

Carl (Andrew) Bjorklund
(1882—)

1900

Elmira (Ellie) Peterson Wold
(1883—)

Astrid Bjorklund
(1885—)

1905

Daniel Jacob Jeffers
(1880—)

Katy Moyer
(1892—)

Thomas Moyer
(1894—)

Stephen Moyer
(1896—)

Gunhilde Bjorklund
(1880—1882)

Elizabeth Bjorklund
(1882—1882)

Madelynn Ahlberg
(1879—1901)

1898

Garth Wiste
(1875—)

1902

Sophie Knutson (twin)
(1884—)

1901

Hamre Bjorklund
(1874—1901)

Grace Knutson (twin)
(1884—)

1905

Jonathan Gould
(1884—)

Trygve Knutson
(1885—)

Samuel Knutson
(1887—)

Gustaf Joseph Bjorklund
(1893—)

Linnea Bridget Bjorklund
(1895—)

Manda Norton MacCallister
(Adopted 1887)
(1876—)

1893

Baptiste LeCrue
(1876—)

Deborah Norton MacCallister
(Adopted 1887)
(1882—)

Baby (stillborn)
(1888)

Inga Annabelle Bjorklund
(1900—)

Carl Bjorklund
(1901—)

Gudrun May Bjorklund
(1903—)

Haakan Bjorklund
(1905—)

Grant Wiste
(1899—)

Madelynn Wiste
(1901—)

Marie Wiste
(1904—)

Joy Bjorklund (twin)
(1902—)

Hamre Bjorklund (twin)
(1902—)

Katie Marie LeCrue
(1895—)

John Pierre LeCrue
(1897—)

Gray Beaver LeCrue
(1898—)

Running Fawn LeCrue
(1899—)

CHAPTER 1

BLESSING, NORTH DAKOTA
MID-SEPTEMBER 1905

Be careful, pay attention were the only thoughts to have when sitting down to milk this particular cow. Trygve Knutson had learned that the hard way, and the bucket had been nearly full. "Easy, old girl." He used the same words with her whenever he had the bad luck to get her. Forehead planted firmly in her flank and milk streaming into the bucket, he fought to keep his mind on what he was doing.

"But I don't need to go to school." Manny sounded determined, not that it would do him any good.

"Pay attention to this cow," Trygve muttered aloud to help him focus.

"Sorry, but all children here go to school until they are graduated from the high school." Andrew Bjorklund spoke calmly, as if they'd never had this conversation before.

Trygve inhaled the good smells of warm milk and cow, overlaid with grain and the always present taint of fresh manure.

7

Thoughts of Miriam tried sneaking past his resolve, but he shut that door too. He heard one of the cow's four stomachs rumble. This time he reacted instinctively, even before the shift of her feet, and pulled the bucket away. "That's it. I am putting kickers on you from now on!"

"That was quick," Andrew commended his cousin.

"Does she do this with everyone?" Trygve nestled the bucket back in place and returned to the squeeze-and-pull hand motions that had been part of his life since he was six years old. The reprieve of his years building windmills for his Onkel Hjelmer's well-drilling company had been a good thing, but now he knew he was needed at home. Whether milking cows was his favorite job or not.

When he dumped his full bucket into the strainer, he went back and picked up Manny's. Since the boy was still on crutches, due to a badly broken leg, carrying a bucket of milk was not possible. No matter how he tried to do everything.

"You better hustle. We'll finish here. You go get washed up and on the way to the schoolhouse." He motioned the boy toward the door, ignoring the dagger-sharp glare.

Manny swiveled and handed him the half-full bucket, picked up his crutches lying beside him, and maneuvered himself to his feet, an awkward and scary process in its own right, and then stumped out the door.

Half smiling, Trygve watched the boy head for the house. "I remember when I was that age. I argued I didn't want to go to school too. And I love learning. I just didn't want to do it there."

Andrew, also smiling, nodded. "Me too. You know, Manny is finally acting like a normal boy his age. He's going to turn out just fine. I'm sure of it."

"So am I." No doubt Manny would be in jail now, just like his bank-robbing brothers, if Tante Ingeborg and Onkel Haakan had not taken him in. The boy's brothers had been arrested trying to rob the bank right in Blessing. Manny was so sullen and uncooperative at first, on the defensive. Then for a while he was almost too nice. But you could tell when he finally figured out that he was loved and those who loved him didn't need a special reason. He did not have to earn love or even earn his way. Now, at last, he was blossoming. Soaring, if one can soar on crutches.

Andrew walked past with another bucket. "Finish that one, and I'll let them out."

Trygve stripped the final cow and, after hanging his three-legged stool on one of the barn posts, emptied his bucket into the strainer. While that drained, he lugged the first of three milk cans to the wagon waiting outside. Morning chores, other than milking that one ornery cow, could pretty much be done without much concentration. George McBride, Ilse's deaf husband, loaded the final can and took the handle to pull the wagon to the springhouse, where the milk cooled until they could skim off the cream and send that up to the cheese house. The Blessing Cheese Company shipped cheese to many cities around the country.

This morning's milking crew included Trygve, Andrew, Manny, and two of the returning students to the deaf school run by Trygve's mor, Kaaren Knutson. George had been one of their students in the early years. Then he married Ilse Gustafson, who was and remained Kaaren's main assistant.

When they all headed home to eat breakfast, Trygve stopped at his tante Ingeborg's house. He could hear Manny grumbling when he stepped up onto the porch. Ingeborg was speaking.

"Takk for wanting to help me, Manny, but school is the most important thing you can do now, and that is how you help me."

"Ain't no help in that." Manny straight-armed the screen door, nearly smacking Trygve with the frame. The boy clumped down the steps, his lunch bucket looped over his hand gripping the crutch.

Emmy, Ingeborg's adopted granddaughter who was raised on the northern Indian reservation, smiled an apology as she passed him and darted out the door. At age eight, she was several years younger than Manny, but she still treated him more as if she were a mother instead of a schoolmate. Manny didn't seem to care. Trygve knew Manny had a grandmother, but the boy had never talked to Trygve about his mother. It could be he needed one now, even if she were a saucy little girl.

Trygve entered and crossed the kitchen. "Tante Ingeborg? Good morning."

His aunt turned away from her woodstove to smile at him. She had her silvering hair braided this morning, the braid twisted into a figure eight at the back of her head. That pleased Trygve. Some days she felt so sad she didn't bother with the braid. Still, it was obvious—and quite logical—that losing her beloved Haakan had been an absolutely crushing blow to her.

"The milk is on its way to the springhouse, and Andrew talked about going over to Thorliff's for something. I am leaving for breakfast. Can I get you anything?"

"Takk, Trygve. I can't think of anything. How is Manny doing with the farm chores?"

"Just fine. I sent him up here for his books and lunch pail before he had finished, so I stripped his last cow for him. He's a good worker."

She nodded. "Say hello to Kaaren for me."

"I shall." Trygve walked outside and stood for a few moments on his tante's porch. One thing for sure about this part of North Dakota, you could draw the horizon with a ruler. Still, it was a warm and lively place. Pastures and wheat fields stretched out almost forever, shimmering in the sunlight. The windbreak Tante Ingeborg had planted had grown into a robust row of trees now, and an orchard provided inviting shade out there.

A yellow-headed blackbird popped up out of the tall grass in the near pasture and perched on a fence post. It threw its head back and tried to sing. By no means was his song something you could dance to—coarse and harsh, no melody at all—yet he sang anyway. Like Manny coping with a new world, usually not too effectively, at least until he could get rid of the crutches, but he was coping anyway. And like Trygve's tante, floored by her loss, yet soldiering on anyway. One could do worse than learn from a yellow-headed blackbird.

Garonnk cree cree cree.

Whistling in the morning sun, Trygve stepped off the porch and headed home to breakfast. In a way, he felt a twinge of guilt for not having anything particularly burdensome to cope with just now. And that was silly. Still—there it was. Certainly he mourned Onkel Haakan's passing, as did everyone else. But everyone died eventually, and Onkel Haakan had led a long rich life, filled with love and accomplishment. Mourn, yes, but Trygve did not really have to cope the way his aunt had to. Was he being too callous, not caring enough? Others seemed to care more than he did.

And, like always, Miriam sprang to mind. Talk about coping. She was in Chicago now with her family. A student nurse from Chicago training for a year in the Blessing hospital, she had been called home because her mother was fading, growing weak to the point of death. How was the lady doing? Rallying? She had the best of medical care. Maybe she could pull through. But what a heavy burden for Miriam! And her younger brothers and sisters had to cope just as much. Perhaps Trygve should go back there to help, to be with her. But he was needed here just as much, easing Tante Ingeborg's life as best he could. What to do? What to do?

His mor, Kaaren, was putting a big bowl of fried potatoes in the middle of the breakfast table as Trygve strode up the back stoop and into the Knutson house.

"How is Ingeborg doing, Trygve?" she asked, setting out a basket mounded high with buttermilk biscuits, butter, and a new glass of blackberry jam.

He stepped to the sink to wash his hands. "Holding on. She still weeps easily and often. I really ought to lime her outhouse. I could smell it as I left, and I left by the *front* door."

Trygve's father, Lars, sitting at his place at the head of the table, nodded. "Probably a lot to do over there. Haakan didn't move fast during his last months, but he moved steadily and kept up with a lot of the necessary things."

"I want to winterize her place too. Maybe Thorliff and I can get to that this next week." Trygve plopped into his chair.

Mor set out her delicious baked-eggs-and-cheese dish and a platter piled high with rashers of bacon.

Trygve looked at the bounty. "Whose army is visiting, and why are we feeding them?"

Far raised his voice. "Carl! Come on, boy. Breakfast!"

"Ah." Trygve picked up his napkin. "That's who we're feeding. Why is Carl here?"

"Ellie said he could stay with us a few days and help me with the garden," Kaaren answered.

Carl came thundering down the stairs. He climbed up onto his chair, Far rattled off the standard grace, and Carl reached for the biscuits.

"Ahem!" Trygve stared at him and then looked pointedly at Mor.

The boy got the hint. He picked up the basket of biscuits and handed it to Kaaren.

She put two on her plate. "I remember when you were about this age, Trygve. You were always hungry. For a few years there, we practically shoveled the food into you and still couldn't keep you satisfied. But you outgrew it. So will Carl." She handed the basket back to Carl.

Lars served himself some bacon and passed the platter across. "I wasn't much older than you are now when you were born, Trygve." He took a bite of bacon. "How're you and that little nurse doing?" Trygve's far was not a subtle person.

He smiled. "She's still in Chicago. She's supposed to return Sunday."

"Seems like a sweet girl."

Trygve picked up the bowl of eggs and served himself. "Astrid says that as student nurses go, Miriam is the best she's ever seen. I count that more important than being sweet." He passed the eggs on to Far.

Mor asked, "Ready for coffee?"

Ilse got up and fetched the coffeepot. Trygve held up his mug and smiled when Ilse reached him. Sitting next to him, Carl held up his cup.

"You're kind of little for coffee." She took the cup, filled it half full of milk, and added just enough coffee to color it. "There."

"Takk." The little boy's blue eyes twinkled as he took a sip.

Trygve watched the exchange. They'd all learned to drink coffee that same way, the love of coffee passing on from generation to generation. It would probably be the same when his kids . . . For the millionth time already this morning, his thoughts went to Miriam. Sweet. Yes! Responsible. Capable. Wise. And so pretty, even with that unruly mop of black hair she tried so hard to keep pinned down.

I love you, Miriam. Return to Blessing soon.

CHAPTER 2

CHICAGO, ILLINOIS

How come God didn't make our mother better? I prayed so hard."

If only I knew. But Miriam couldn't tell Truth, her baby sister, that. As their mother had said so frequently, *"God's will be done."* Instead, Miriam held her close and let her cry. It seemed as if the tears would never stop—for her too. Tonio had taken time off from his job at the railroad for the funeral and burial. Perhaps that was the best way to get through, just keep on working so one did not have time to think.

Besides, she had heard her mother pray to be released from the pain and uselessness. She didn't blame her a bit, but oh, how she, they all, hurt. This was far worse than when their father died those three, or was it four, years ago. She laid her cheek on top of Truth's head and rocked them both.

They had all made it through the funeral and burial without collapsing. The few mourners had gathered in the church after the burial, and several had brought memories of their earlier life, the life before their father died. And now both of their

LAURAINE SNELLING

parents were gone—together again, but leaving their children bereft. That evening they were all gathered in the rooms they called home, if one could call the tenements of Chicago home. But it had been before their mother left. She had been able to make anything a home, just with her presence.

"My job is going real good," Tonio said as he paced the room. "They say I've been doing a good job, so that's encouraging." He turned and continued to pace. "We can continue to pay the rent here."

"I wish I could stay." Miriam watched her brother, who had become the man of the house in the last year. Having a steady job had made such a difference.

"But you can't, Miriam. You know you signed a contract, and you have to honor that. Mother would not want anything else. She got her wish, to be able to see all of us together again before she died. We've been managing so far, and I don't see any reason to think we can't continue as we have."

Joy dabbed at her eyes, a continuing action of all of them. "I can get some of the mending done tonight."

"You are becoming a good seamstress too," Mercy said. She now did all the mending and sewing for the hospital and brought much of it home. She'd been teaching ten-year-old Joy to help on some of the easier pieces, and even eight-year-old Truth was learning how to sew. Mercy occasionally helped with the evening meal at the hospital too.

Miriam nodded. The plan Mrs. Korsheski had put into place seemed to be working. She looked to Este, who at fourteen seemed to have grown a foot since she'd left for North Dakota. He still could have hidden behind one of the bean poles out in the garden at the hospital, where he spent half of his time. He also worked with the cook in the hospital kitchen.

"I used to bring Mother fresh vegetables from the hospital garden. One day we carried her outside to sit in the shade and watch us working. I wish we had done that more."

15

"But she was so weak." Mercy rolled her lips together. "I wish you could have seen her face, Miriam. She seemed to absorb the sun and glowed. I hope there are gardens for her to enjoy in paradise."

Este straightened up and gritted his teeth. While his eyes were swimming in tears, they did not fall. He sniffed them back. "Tonio and me, we'll take care of our sisters."

Miriam thought about her life in Blessing, so different from their life in Chicago as to be almost unbelievable. The clean air, for one. Here, her nose burned from the rank stench of the tenement. Clean houses, green trees, and vast horizon-ending fields, children laughing while they played and people who visited together. The hammering and sawing could not begin to compare with the cacophony of the city. It was like a whisper to a whirlwind.

"How will you keep warm this winter?"

"We can buy coal. And besides, we're not here most of the day, so it will take a lot less."

Tonio had an answer for everything. Clearly he'd been thinking on the same things she had. Pride in her brothers and sisters edged out the burning grief, or at least dulled it for the moment.

"Will you stay here with us tonight?" Mercy asked.

"Yes." Nurse Korsheski had given her the guest room at the hospital, since her former room now housed another nursing student. But tonight she'd stay at home with her siblings. "I have a meeting with Nurse Korsheski in the morning and will be speaking to the nursing students in the afternoon. She says if you come at lunch, you can listen if you want."

"We have school," Truth reminded her.

"Perhaps you can get out a little early."

"You can help me in the garden," Este offered with a grin.

"Or me in the kitchen at dinner. Cook likes little girls a whole lot." Mercy settled on the floor by Miriam's knees. "Cook really likes you too. She says you're the best nursing student they have ever had."

Miriam started to refute the comment but decided not to. Cook did her best to take care of all the student nurses and future doctors from that program. Between the two schools, the hospital was well served. Not like the paucity of help in Blessing. If they ever had an accident or epidemic of some kind, that little hospital would be in serious difficulty.

"Tell us more about Blessing." Truth prodded her sister. "You wrote about a little girl named Inga."

"She's younger than you are—she's only five—but what a mind that child has. I always thought you asked a lot of questions, but Inga is a never-ending fount of whys and whats. She loves her grandma Ingeborg, and I know she must be crushed that her grandfather died. She spends a lot of time at their house."

"Her grandma lives on a farm?"

"Yes, and lots of calves were born this summer. She has a little dog named Scooter, and her best friend is Benny, a boy with no legs below his knees. He used to live here in Chicago, but after he was injured, Dr. Bjorklund found a family in Blessing to adopt him. He gets around on a low wagon with wheels."

"By himself?"

She nodded. "Or the other children pull him."

"You said there is a school for the deaf there too?"

"There is. I left before all the students returned from summer vacation. But all the children in Blessing know how to talk in sign language. The students from the deaf school go to the regular school during the day once they've learned signing."

The sun had set while they visited. Mercy and Joy brought out their hand sewing and handed Truth a dish towel to hem.

"I could help, you know," Miriam said, nudging her sister.

"But you are a guest."

"I think not." Miriam felt like she'd stepped back in time, to before she started nursing school, when they'd sit like this. But their mother, when she was healthier, had occupied this chair.

No one ever wasted a moment. There was always more mending to do, or hemming. Their mother and Mercy did most of the sewing on the fine dresses they'd been hired to create.

By the time they went to bed, Miriam in their mother's bed with Truth snuggled up at her side, life in Blessing seemed as far away and as gossamer as the clouds playing hide-and-seek with the moon. Except for a certain young man who had insisted he had fallen in love with her. Could she possibly ever love him in return?

Resolutely she forced herself to concentrate on life here in Chicago and how she could help provide for her brothers and sisters. As the oldest, that was her job.

The next morning, Miriam greeted Mrs. Korsheski right on the mark at nine thirty. "Thank you for making such provisions for my family. I know Mother died in peace, knowing they are provided for."

"You are welcome. Your mother is missed here too. So often I would find someone sitting by her bed, even ambulatory patients. She had a peace about her. You couldn't pass by her bed or when she was sitting in a chair, which didn't happen too often, without feeling that sense of comfort. I've never seen anything like it."

Miriam rolled her lips together, sniffed, and blinked. She would not cry again. "Th-thank you. And thank you for bringing me back so I could say good-bye to her. I will never forget those last days we had together."

"She wanted to see you again so terribly. I would see her staring at the wall, and it was like she'd already had a glimpse of glory. I moved her to a bed where she could look out the window, and it was like I had given her a new life, she was so overjoyed. I often wonder what she saw on that brick wall out there."

"I think she was living in her memories. She used to tell us stories of her life before coming to this country. How she loved

England and then she fell in love with my father, who was from near London, and he taught her all about gardens. She always had at least one thing growing until she became so weak last year." Miriam blinked and mopped at her eyes with her handkerchief. "Thank you for reminding me of the good parts. I won't forget your kindness to her."

"She left a legacy here too. We won't forget her." Mrs. Korsheski cleared her throat and blinked. "Now, I want a full report on your time in Blessing." She nodded to a paper in front of her. "I have a list of questions here, so I will go down it."

Miriam used her handkerchief again and heaved a sigh. "The first thing—student nurses are desperately needed there. With the three of us, that doubled their staff. The two Indian women are not much help yet, and part of our responsibility has been to help train them in simple basics of patient care, along with our regular nursing duties. Dr. Elizabeth is no longer able to be part of the active staff. Due to her health, she has had to assume more clerical duties that she can do from home. Dr. Astrid has put her on bed rest—while not on strict, close to it."

"And do you know the problem?"

"Dr. Elizabeth is pregnant, and I have a feeling, based solely on my observations, that she had trouble before and has lost several babies."

"She nearly died giving birth to Inga."

"I see." That explained a lot. No wonder everyone was so protective of her.

"Do you know when the baby is due?"

"After the new year—February, I think." Interesting what one could learn just by paying attention and thinking things through. While no one had laid out all the facts to the students, rumors ran rampant. She watched as Mrs. Korsheski wrote herself a note.

"What do you think would help them the most?"

The question caught Miriam by surprise. She repeated it to herself, shaking her head. "Barring a major crisis . . ." She started to say they could use a more experienced nurse, but stopped. "I think Dr. Astrid can handle either the teaching or the patients, and maybe the way things are, she won't have to do so much administrative work. But they were strapped having two doctors, and now with just one . . . I know I'm rambling but . . ."

"Ramble on. This is what I want to know—your observations."

"The biggest problem is surgery. We had a young boy there with a compound fracture, a really bad one, of the femur. Dr. Astrid knew most doctors would have taken the leg off, but she decided to try something unusual. She tried to nail the two bones together. We kept the infection out for a few days, and then we had to go in again and remove the nail and dead bone, so his right leg is shorter than the other. But the leg finally healed, and Manny gets around real well on crutches. We are hoping he can start using just a cane pretty soon."

"That is quite an accomplishment. I wish Astrid could work in a big hospital where research is going on. She has unusual insight for such a young woman. I'm convinced that someday there will be a way to hold bones in place to heal."

"She devised a traction device that kept the muscles from contracting and stabilized the bone. Said she'd seen a picture of one."

"I wonder if we should send one of our final-year residents out there."

"You know, their only student nurse before the three of us arrived was Annika Nilsson. Annika has since returned home, so it is now only we three. I am certain both doctors would say they need all the help they can get."

"Astrid told me Annika has an excellent position in Minnesota now, a rural area with limited medical resources, much like Blessing before the hospital was established. How are our other two nurses doing there?"

"You were so right that we'd have new experiences not available here. We are expected to do whatever needs to be done, including scrubbing down a room and disinfecting it when needed by a patient. Or translating. An Irish man was speaking Gaelic, and I know a bit of the language, so I was able to translate for him." She didn't mention her part in assisting the priest.

"Corabell was on duty when a woman was at the hospital for something else, and her baby decided to come right then. Dr. Astrid got there as Corabell caught the baby and waited while Vera followed the entire routine. And did well." *Even though she was shaking for a long time after.*

They continued their discussion until the bell announced the noon hour and dinner being served in the dining room.

"Thank you, Miriam. If there is anything else . . . ?"

"An X-ray machine would be a big help, since so many we treat there have broken a bone or two. One of the workers died shortly after his arrival due to consumption. We all wore masks and followed quarantine procedures. The people who live in Blessing are remarkably healthy, including the pregnant mothers. Maybe it is all the fresh air and good food."

"And teaching. Astrid's mother, Ingeborg, has been providing medical care and information to the people there for years. Have you met her?"

"Oh yes. She has invited us to her house several times, and she and the pastor there show up at the hospital whenever prayer is needed. They believe in the power of prayer in that town."

Mrs. Korsheski stood, so Miriam did too. "You are ready for your presentation this afternoon?"

"Yes. As much as I can be. I thought to let them ask questions too."

"Good."

Should she say this next thought? Mrs. Korsheski had told her to be candid. "You know, I think one thing is very different from here."

"What is that?"

21

"Out there, the doctors treat us all as part of the team. They expect us nurses to think and act when and however needed."

Mrs. Korsheski rolled her lips together, but her eyes twinkled. She dropped her voice. "Are you saying some of the doctors here can be . . . uh . . . overbearing?"

Miriam paused. *Be diplomatic.* "That would be one way of putting it. That is why I see training in situations like Blessing is invaluable. You said that before we left, and you were right."

"Thank you. By the way, are all three of you keeping some kind of journal or diary of your experiences there?"

"We keep careful notes on patient charts and in the day log, if that is what you mean."

"Good. That is necessary, but I'm talking about notes of a personal kind, more observations, I guess, than facts. I find it sharpens my insight and gives me a place to go back and check when my memory gets shady."

"About nursing?"

"About nursing in a small hospital, in an unfamiliar town, and things that might help others to prepare for the life."

Miriam stared at the older woman for a moment, questions playing tag in her mind. "Can we talk more about this?"

"Of course. You have another day here before you board the westbound train. We'll make time. I'd be very interested in reading such a memoir."

CHAPTER 3

BLESSING, NORTH DAKOTA

Ingeborg woke to damp sheets and pillowcase and a soaked nightdress.

She blinked in the dimness of early dawn, listening to the whispering of the curtain with the breeze and a bird trying out its vocal cords to greet the new day. Blowing out a breath, she forced herself to turn her head to the empty pillow. The pillow with no indentation, the sheets still pristine from the wash line.

Haakan had not returned in the night, the only gift she pleaded for every night before falling into the well of sleep. To see his face one more time, to hear his voice calling her *My Ingy*, to feel the warmth of his body in the bed beside her.

She sat up, afraid of slipping back into sleep. The pit. That was what woke her. She'd not been that close to the edge of depression since those many months after Roald died before she had finally returned to the land of the living, the land where she no longer needed to nearly kill herself to keep the land, the precious land they had sweated and bled for, the free land for their children. The land was secure now, owned by her and her sons and daughter.

But Haakan was gone. She'd read and reread the verses where

23

Jesus talked about going to prepare a place for us in his Father's house of many mansions. Perhaps good farmland too, a place for the farmers who wouldn't know how to sit still, even though she was sure that singing heavenly praises was a wonderful thing.

Lord, am I going crazy? You'd think I'd not see the pit again. I know you've promised to never leave me nor forsake me. You will not allow me to fall over the edge, but I beg of you, remove the horror of it altogether. All these years I've trusted you, as you said, and I know you are never changing and you will not go back on your word now.

But, God, I hurt so bad. I am so tired of crying. The tears drain me, then attack again like a swarm of bees. Only there is no honey here, only pain that has attacked every part of me, but mostly my soul. Can one's soul be destroyed by pain and tears?

She waited in the silence. The bird outside in the tree burst into song with all his chorus mates, welcoming, heralding the rising sun, the rooster from the chicken coop joining in, playing his own song, but all of them together sang of morning.

Another day. She could hear her Freda rattling the stove lids. Her cousin now had her own house a short distance from Ingeborg's, but she still got up long before dawn and always arrived at Ingeborg's early in the morning. Now Manny's crutches were beating their own tattoo on the floor, and the screen door screeched when the boy went out to join the milkers. Haakan had always oiled the screen door. So many things Haakan did that she had taken for granted, or probably not even recognized until they were left undone.

A man's whistling fluted up through the tree branches. Probably Trygve. He whistled a lot. The men were on their way to milking. A cow bellowed, followed by two more.

Ingeborg reached for her wrapper and, ignoring the slippers by the bed, headed for the outhouse. The dew cushioned her steps, the wet grass squeezing up between her toes. Ah, another blessing. When she opened the privy door, she realized no one had sprinkled lime down the holes. Automatically she started breathing through her mouth. A tear meandered this time rather than rained down her cheek. She brushed it away and gritted her teeth. The incongruity of the verse that tickled her mind made her forget and breathe through her nose. *This is the day which the Lord hath made; we will rejoice and be glad in it.*

Patches scratched at the door and whined.

"I'm coming." *Lord, this is indeed a sacrifice of praise. I will praise you when my heart is broken, the outhouse reeks, the other side of the bed is empty . . .* Stepping outside and away from the little building that wore a shawl of honeysuckle, which she could now smell, she stopped and blew out a long breath. The shorn wheat fields went clear to the western horizon, the corn stalks in the garden barely showed any green, instead browning to a fall color. They should be chopped down and fed to the cows. The ears on the stalks in the cornfield all hung at half-mast, awaiting the picking, while the cleaned-out corncrib awaited the dried and shucked corncobs.

Other years they'd had a corn-shucking party. The thought of having a party made her eyes fill yet again.

"Oh good." She pulled open the screen door to hear the sizzle of turkey frying in leftover bacon grease. Since they were out of hams and bacon, Freda had smoked the turkeys that Trygve brought her. He'd shot several when he and Johnny Solberg had gone hunting. Soon the skies would darken with the southbound flocks of ducks and geese, and the smoker would be going steadily again.

Getting dressed, Ingeborg remembered the year she'd challenged her sons to a hunting contest and she had brought down the first deer. Haakan had not been pleased that she'd reverted to her early days of hunting, farming, and chores, all done in britches. While she'd shot the deer, she had been wearing a dress and apron, just to please him. Wouldn't her family be surprised, or rather shocked, if she took out the rifle and did some hunting just to find out if she could still aim well?

She braided her hair and coiled it in a figure eight at the back of her head before putting on a clean apron for the day. Maybe today would be the day Manny would not try to talk her out of forcing him to go to school.

Last night they had sat out on the porch, and he'd read to her from his textbook. He was doing better in reading and had easily remembered the sums, as he called adding and subtracting, one skill his mother had taught him.

Her mind wandered, trying to see mountains clad in trees that should be donning their fall garments about now. Manny had spoken of maple and various nut trees, of apple trees laden with fruit, and of growing tobacco, or "tabaccy," as he called it. Kentucky, far enough away that he should never have to see his bank-robbing brothers again. But it was still in his heart.

He'd not mentioned leaving, in spite of not wanting to go to school. At first he'd threatened often. He took his chores here on the farm very seriously, even to fixing a harness so he could pull the wagon to haul the buckets to feed the hogs in spite of his crutches. Soon the calves would be weaned, and he wouldn't have to feed them.

Ingeborg went out to the kitchen to find that Gray Cloud and Dawn Breaking, their two Indian nursing students, had already arrived to help Freda with the early-morning chores. One was thumping the churn and the other was hauling hot water to the washing machine and the raised tub for rinse water.

"Thank you," Ingeborg said, forcing a smile. Just because she didn't feel like smiling was no reason to take it out on others.

"You are welcome. We enjoy helping you. You help the hospital. Freda put biscuits in the oven." Dawn still spoke carefully, but she was doing so much better in the nearly two weeks they had been there. Every evening they attended the classes in English that Amelia Jeffers offered at the schoolhouse.

When the machine was full, she watched Gray Cloud put in the first load of sheets and other white things. She'd only needed to show these students something one time, and they would do it, both at the hospital and here, even though they didn't yet understand the necessity of all the washing and cleaning.

"Do you know what your class is on today?"

"More bandaging." Neither of the women wasted words.

The banging from down at the barn announced that the milking was finished, and soon she could hear Manny's crutches on the porch floor. She set his bowl of oatmeal on the table, and Freda cracked two eggs into the grease in the frying pan. His lunch already waited in the lard pail on the counter.

As soon as he washed his hands and sat down, she took her chair across from him. "Manny, I'm thinking you and I and Carl and Inga, oh, and Emmy too, should go fishing when you get home from school. Do you think you can make it down the riverbank?"

His eyes lit up. "'Course. Or scoot down on my rear."

"Good. I'll call to make sure the others can go. A fish fry tonight sounds mighty good to me."

"I could stay home and we could go earlier."

She started to answer firmly and then, catching the glint in his eye, realized he was teasing her. She and Freda swapped astonished looks. She looked to Emmy, who was sitting quietly as usual. "Do you want to go fishing?"

Her grin said more than her nod.

Hanging the wet sheets on the line was one of the chores Ingeborg loved, but even better would be taking them down later, smelling only like sheets dried in the wind could smell—fresh and perfumed by God's own breath. With the sheets flapping around her, she stared toward the garden. They would bring in the squash and pumpkins today and maybe get the onions dug so they could be braided and hung in the cellar. Good thing Haakan had dug them a large cellar, as big as the entire house. He'd dreamed of someday putting a furnace in the basement.

So many dreams buried in the box along with the dreamer.

At nine o'clock the two Indian women left for the hospital,

and while Freda washed a couple more loads, Ingeborg washed the butter, filled the molds, and set them in the icebox. Then taking out eggs, she gathered the ingredients for a cake and set to mixing up the batter. After that she would bake cookies. If Inga was coming, there had to be gingerbread men in the cookie jar. Maybe they wouldn't get to the squash today after all.

"I'll send Inga out as soon as she changes clothes after school," Elizabeth said when Ingeborg telephoned.

Ever since summer, Inga had walked to the farm by herself, something she had pleaded to do some time before permission had been granted.

"How are you feeling?"

"About the same. Some days are better than others. Ingeborg, have you given any thought to helping more at the hospital? I hate to ask, because you are always so generous, but if you taught some of the nursing classes—like you and Kaaren did, was it last summer?—that would make it easier on Astrid."

"Ja, I can do that."

"I hate to ask that right now, but . . ."

Ingeborg shook her head. "You don't understand. Trying to make things easier for me is kind of you, but the busier I am the less time I have to feel sorry for myself. Grief will take over your life if you let it, so I believe more work is the best medicine, and helping others makes it even better. Does that make any sense?"

"You must be related to Thorliff. I hardly see him lately."

"How is he?"

"Taking his pa's death hard, but then we all are. Coupled with his concern for me and the baby, he is riding himself with whip and spurs."

"Ja, making himself too tired at night to do anything but fall into bed. I know." She'd seen the black circles under her son's eyes, and he had lost weight, enough so that it showed. He and Astrid were quite a pair.

And what kind of example am I to my children? The thought struck like a lightning bolt.

"Ingeborg! Are you there?"

Ingeborg blinked and stared at the black mouthpiece. "Uh, ja, I am. Just got lost in a thought is all. Did I ask you if Inga can go fishing after school? After all, that was my main reason for telephoning you."

"Of course, and I hope you know you do not have to have a reason."

"Takk. Tusen takk. You are doing what the doctor ordered?"

"Yes. But the days I feel like myself again . . . well, let's just say, Thelma would make an excellent prison warden or general."

"We could call her General Thelma." Ingeborg smiled when she heard a slight chuckle. Good. They all needed to be laughing more. She was counting on Inga and the others to help her laugh. *Lord, please take away my sad eyes in time for Inga to come.*

"We will try to bring home enough fish for all three houses."

"I'll tell Thelma to be ready."

"Just in case."

"Ja, just in case."

When they hung up, Ingeborg stared out the window at a world with a sheer covering. She saw Patches leap off the porch and go running toward the barn, then Andrew leaning over to pet him.

"I'm going up to the cheese house," Freda announced from the back porch. "Your cake should be done soon."

And I better get the cookie dough mixed. She stopped long enough to make the call to Ellie to ask if Carl could go fishing. Her chuckle still clung around Ingeborg's shoulders.

❧

A platter of gingerbread men with raisins for eyes, a smile, and a button nose was waiting on the counter when she heard Manny's crutches thumping on the porch floor. For a change she heard Manny's and Emmy's voices too. Words were never wasted between the two of them.

"Something sure smells good," Manny announced as he sniffed his way in the door. His eyes lit up when he saw the mound of cookies. "Is Inga coming?"

"Manny McCrary, you are getting too smart for your britches. But yes. As soon as she gets here, we will go. There is buttermilk in the icebox or plain milk to go with the cookies. Carl is already down at the barn digging worms. He didn't even come up to the house, just got out the manure fork." She had seen him with his bucket and dragging the fork that was taller than he. When that grandson of hers was born, God gave him an extra dose of determination.

Emmy fetched the glasses and the pitcher of buttermilk without asking Manny what he preferred, set them on the table, and then ran up the stairs to change to her home clothes, as she called them.

Patches' yipping of delight announced Inga before she called, "Grandma, I am here." She burst through the door, Carl and his worm bucket right behind her. She threw her arms around Ingeborg and squeezed. "Oh, I have missed you so much."

"Ja, me too."

Inga looked up, not releasing her hold, a grin splitting her face. "You miss you too?"

Ingeborg shook her head. "You caught me again." One had to be careful around Inga; she picked up every nuance.

After another squeeze Inga danced over to the table. "You made gingerbread men without me."

"I sure missed my raisin stickers."

Carl looked up at her with a slight frown. "I coulda helped you."

She bent over and kissed his nose. "Next time I will call for you. Did you get lots of worms?"

"I did, so we can catch lots of fish." He pulled out his chair at the table and climbed up. "Goodie wanted to come too, but I told her she was still too little. Can I take her a cookie after?"

CHAPTER 4

"You let me sleep!" Dr. Astrid Bjorklund Jeffers accused when she found her husband on the porch.

"I know. I checked with the hospital, and there was nothing there they couldn't handle, so I didn't call you." Daniel Jeffers watched his wife carefully, trying not to be obvious.

"But I had a class to teach at one."

"Deborah took that over. She said she knew the information well enough."

Astrid sank down on the settee, and instantly her mother-in-law, Amelia Jeffers, set a cup of coffee beside her along with a sandwich.

"You'll feel better once you get something in your stomach."

Astrid sucked in a deep breath and reminded her jaw to unclench. Wagging her head, which still twinged with the headache that had forced her to lie down for just a few minutes but ended up well over two hours, she muttered something unintelligible.

"Now eat. If they need you, well, that's why we have a telephone."

Knowing he was right didn't make it any easier. After a bite of sandwich, she cradled her coffee cup with both hands.

"Can I warm up your coffee?" Amelia arrived with the coffeepot and filled her son's cup. "Astrid?"

"Just started on it. Thanks for the lunch."

"It's good to see you sitting down for a change." She filled a cup for herself and returned the pot to the kitchen. Before sitting down on the porch, she set a plate of cookies on the table.

Astrid inhaled the aroma of molasses. "I wonder how long it has been since I baked cookies, or anything for that matter."

"I can't count that far." Daniel flopped the corner of his paper forward enough to wink at her. "Good thing there are others who take good care of your poor neglected husband."

"Really?" Astrid lowered her cup but relaxed again when he winked at her. "I do worry about that, you know."

"Haven't you enough to worry about with the hospital, training the nurses, caring for patients? Do you have to borrow trouble?"

Amelia rolled her eyes this time and tapped Daniel on the arm. "You should talk. Let's see, creating a training program for new workers, overseeing the ones you have, fixing the machinery when it breaks, selling the machinery you have produced—"

"Don't forget turning Pa's plans into reality," Daniel interjected.

"Oh, and helping whoever needs something." Astrid joined the game.

"Do you mind if I read my paper in peace?"

"Not at all. What does Thorliff have to say this week?" Astrid watched her husband over the top of her cup. Was he looking tired too, or was it the shadows on the porch? She finished her sandwich and reached for a cookie at the same moment the telephone rang the two times for their house. One ring was Thorliff's. She motioned Amelia to stay seated and strode back into the house.

"They need you at the hospital," reported Gerald Valders, who was now the manager for the telephone company as well as taking the switchboard when needed. "Deborah said it wasn't a critical emergency. One of the construction workers got a bad slice on the arm."

"Thanks. I'll get right over there." Astrid hung up, grabbed her bag, and waved to the others as she left the porch. "I'll do rounds too before I come home."

"Supper will be waiting."

"I have a meeting at seven," Daniel called, raising his voice to make sure she heard.

She waved an acknowledgment and continued her fast walk. Jogging didn't seem necessary. If the man was bleeding dangerously, the nurse would have said so. They needed to attach numbers to the word *emergency*, but they all understood *stat*.

She pushed open the hospital door to be greeted by the fragrance of red and yellow blooming roses, a bouquet that always adorned the desk, thanks to Amelia's rose garden. She renewed it as needed. Roses smelled better than disinfectant any day. She could hear the nurses in the first examining room. Stopping in the doorway, she watched them at work. Nurse Vera was cleaning the wound, Gray Cloud arranging the tray, Dawn Breaking with her fingers pressed on the inner side of his elbow, and Deborah supervising, making suggestions as needed.

She turned to smile at Astrid. "This one needs stitches." She raised her hands. "I know I could have done it, but we are working with protocol, right?"

Astrid nodded. "Do you have a name for our patient, and does he speak English?"

"Mr. Buchmeister and yes." Deborah smiled at the man on the table watching their every move.

Astrid smiled at him. "You are in good hands, Mr. Buchmeister. We'll get you fixed up right away. By the way, I am Dr. Bjorklund." With that she stepped to the basin to scrub. "Everyone scrubbed before touching the patient?" They all nodded. Astrid shook her hands and walked over to Vera to look over her shoulder. "Good. Have you examined it closely for any remaining detritus?" After a nod, she added, "and irrigated it with sterile water?"

"We had to stop the bleeding first." She nodded to Dawn Breaking, who was pressing against the artery to stop the flow.

"Is the blood coagulating?"

Vera nodded. Gray Cloud shot Astrid a questioning look.

Deborah explained the term, and the Indian woman nodded.

"All right, Dawn. Release the pressure slowly." When the blood started flowing again, Astrid asked. "Is the flow less now than in the beginning?"

They all nodded.

"Good. Vera, will you check to make sure the tray is supplied?"

When she started to say, "But we . . ." Astrid continued. "Always double and even triple check. Mistakes are far too easy to make, and when you are under a lot of pressure, even easier. Establish good habits, and that will save a patient's life at some point."

"Now irrigate the wound again with carbolic acid, and we'll close it up." She turned to their patient. "I'm sorry, sir, but this is going to sting pretty bad."

"Yoost get it done. Danke." Though his accent was heavy, at least he could understand them.

While Astrid closed the wound with small, perfectly spaced stitches, she explained each step to her nurses, then asked Vera, "Have you ever sutured a wound before?"

"No."

"Then come here beside me. Do you know how to sew and tie knots?"

"Well, yes. We covered that in training, just never on a patient."

"Remember what you did." Astrid demonstrated on one more stitch and then, after cutting the silk, handed her the needle. "Now you do the next one."

Vera sucked in a deep breath. "I'd never get a chance to do this in Chicago."

"Probably not." Astrid watched carefully. "Good, good. Now see, that wasn't so hard. I suggest you take one of our needles, since they are different than those used in fabric, and practice. Let's see, how many more stitches do you think we need?"

"Uh, two maybe?" Vera looked to Deborah, who nodded, and then to Astrid, who did the same. "You want me to do them?"

Mr. Buchmeister cleared his throat.

Astrid turned to him. "Don't worry. I'd never let her make a mistake."

When the stitches were in, she nodded to Deborah. "This next is what you covered today and yesterday, right?" At her nod, she turned to the two Indian women. "Now, I want you to tell me what to do, step by step." She smiled when their eyes widened. "Dr. Red Hawk will be very proud of you."

When they were finished, their patient sat up and grabbed his shirt. "No money to pay you until payday."

"You were injured on the job?" At his nod, she smiled. "I'll send the bill to the company. Please don't go rolling in the dirt, and try to keep it clean. We'll change the dressing in a couple of days and see how it is doing."

"Danke. Thank you." Out the door he hustled, as if they might run after him and do something else.

After the shift change, when Corabell replaced Vera, Astrid conducted evening rounds, checking each of their patients and asking the nurses what they had seen during the day regarding each one. While the nurses served the supper trays, Astrid stopped in the office to see what absolutely required her attention. She picked up the list of needed supplies and sent the two Indian women home for the night, leaving Corabell on duty. Astrid went to Elizabeth's to drop off some papers, said goodnight, and headed home. Sure enough, it was seven thirty. But that was earlier than some other nights.

The sun was setting, with a fine line glowing on the western horizon. The evening star, holding back the true dark of night, was already smiling down at her. A bullfrog announced his availability, while the others sang the melody, and a mosquito whined in her ear. Somewhere over in the tents, a baby cried and was hushed, a dog barked twice, and she could see the kerosene light on her front porch, backed up by the lighted windows.

Their house did look friendly, one of Astrid's requirements when she and Daniel had discussed the plans. She mounted the steps to the back porch, the lamp flickering in a slight breeze. A nip in the air reminded her that fall might be a bit late this year, but it was coming soon. Even the air smelled like fall, a tang to it that summer didn't have.

"I'm home."

"I'll be right there." Amelia bustled through the door into the kitchen. "I have your supper in the warming oven."

Astrid had given up saying "You needn't do that." Amelia, like her son, would do what she felt was right, and she saw her place in Blessing as taking care of her son and his doctor wife. And her rose garden, which was known and admired far and wide. The work of her hands graced the registration counter at the boardinghouse, Penny's mercantile, the church on Sunday morning, and Thorliff's house.

Astrid set her bag in its appointed place by the door and, after washing her hands at the sink, allowed herself to finally sink down in a chair at the table.

"You look tired."

"I shouldn't after a nap like I had."

"One nap can't make up for all the short nights." Amelia set a plate with baked squash, potatoes, and baked chicken in front of her. "Would you like a roll? I'll warm it for you, since it was baked yesterday."

Astrid stretched her neck, tilting her head from side to side. "Thanks, but this is plenty." Amelia was already slicing two rolls. Astrid shook her head for what little good her opinion counted. Amelia buttered them and laid them in a frying pan, then pulled it to the hotter section of the stove.

"That's okay. I wanted one too. All of a sudden that just sounded good. I thought tea might be good too." She fetched two mugs from the cupboard and set them on the cooler end of the stove, then poured water from the steaming kettle into the rose-trimmed teapot. The fragrances of tea and hot butter waltzed across to the table.

Astrid smashed her potatoes and added butter, all the while shaking her head. She and Daniel would certainly not be this well cared for without Amelia. And the lady had worried she would not be useful.

"How are your English classes going?" she asked.

Amelia smiled. "I think I'll add one on Saturday afternoon for some of the men who are too tired in the evening and for any of the wives who want to come. I have ten, no, eleven pupils in the class during school. Two hours every morning is not really enough to catch them up with the others. We need people to tutor those who are so far behind in school."

"That's an interesting thought. Like my two Indian nurses. Mor is helping them with English, and while they can read, just barely, she is helping with that too." Astrid paused. "Perhaps that is too much for her right now." Just the thought of her mother's grief brought her own crashing back down on her. Far was gone and the tears sprang out of nowhere and cascaded down her face.

"I know." Amelia set the rolls on the table, along with the steaming teapot, and settled into her chair. She stroked Astrid's hand and arm. "Oh, I so know how it hits you again like that. Grief waits and pounces when you least expect it." She handed Astrid a handkerchief from her apron pocket. "And that is why you must let Ingeborg help any way she can. Doing for others is one of the best comforts when you are suffering like she is, like all of you are."

She checked the tea and poured it into their cups. "I remember one day when your pa came to help me with the garden. He insisted on spading up an area along the fence that the weeds were trying to take over. While I pulled weeds and raked, he told me what it was like when he first came to Blessing. What a great storyteller he was, and such a memory. Did you know that little Andrew got lost in the grass and a wolf found him?"

Astrid sniffed. "I've heard the story so often. Metiz' Wolf. Even wild animals remember the good a person does for them. Metiz freed him from a trap and doctored his foot, and Wolf never forgot that. He even brought his family back to visit one year, but after Metiz died, we never saw him again." She reached for one of the toasted half buns and sniffed again.

"Mor always said Metiz helped keep them alive those first years. She taught them how to live on this land like the Indians did, harvesting more than wheat and hay from the land. That is where Mor got her fund of knowledge of natural medicines, although she and her mother learned that in Norway too." She glanced down, surprised to see that her plate was empty.

"Someone needs to write these stories down. They are the history of this valley."

"Thorliff is the writer in the family. I'll suggest it." A tiny head shake accompanied her words. Thorliff was worse off than she, and he wouldn't talk about it. He just drove himself onward.

A few minutes later, she thanked Amelia and pushed herself away from the table.

"You leave those dishes alone. I have to have something to do."

"Of course you do." She inhaled. "What is that I smell?"

"Oh, I have rose petals drying for potpourri. I'm going to mix a bit of mint in too for an unusual touch. By the way, I hung plenty of mint, so we have it for tea too. Your mother and I are going to dig sarsaparilla roots. She said she knows of a place with plenty of them. Her knowledge of natural remedies is fascinating."

"I know. That's where I got my love of medicine." A yawn caught her midword. "Good night."

Good thing she could get ready for bed while half asleep. She didn't even hear Daniel crawl in beside her.

Her shoulder being shaken dragged her up from the dream she'd been having. "What?"

It was Daniel. "Astrid, there is a man at the back door. His wife is having trouble birthing a baby. I'll help you."

"Where?"

"In the tent camp."

"He can't get her to the hospital?" She threw on her clothes while asking him.

"He says she is too far along."

"Tell him I'll be right there."

"I did." Daniel hesitated. "Do you want me to come along?"

"Yes." She threw the answer over her shoulder, not sure why he'd asked. *Please, Lord, I didn't even know someone was pregnant there. Protect her and the baby, please.*

CHAPTER 5

I lost another baby!" Astrid slammed the palm of her hand on Ingeborg's table.

"No you didn't! The baby was born dead, and there was nothing you could do about that!" Ingeborg shook her head.

"Had I gotten there earlier . . . Why, oh why, did they wait so long? Another baby gone and, O God, I hate this part of what I do." She hollered this last at the ceiling. Even the rain ran like tears down the windows, the water from the roof clattering into the rain barrel beside Ingeborg's porch. "So much death lately. Oh, Mor, I cannot stand this."

"I know. Oh, how I know."

"I don't know why I came visiting you when I'm such a mess." Astrid dug in her pocket for a handkerchief, shaking her head as she tried to wipe her eyes and blow her nose. She tipped her head back. "It was their first baby, and he seemed to be fully formed, so why did he die? Mrs. Sorvito was in no condition to answer questions, even if I could have asked them. And her husband was in no shape to talk either. He was too frantic about possibly losing her."

"But she is at the hospital now?"

"Daniel and I carried her to the hospital, lifting her by the corners of the sheet, once I got the bleeding stopped. I wasn't taking any chances. Another man finally helped us. I think they were too afraid of the hospital to go there when she went into labor. No money probably."

"Or women aren't usually taken to a hospital to have a baby, you know. They are supposed to have it at home. Was there a midwife there?"

"No. You know, there aren't many women in that camp." She sniffed and blew her nose again. The worst seemed to be over. "I think they speak Italian. It's a shame Miriam isn't here. She speaks both Italian and Gaelic. The man went to find Father Devlin, one reason he was unwilling for us to take her. I assured him that Father Devlin would come to the hospital. He must have been dead asleep to not have heard all the commotion."

"I believe he is away."

Astrid stared out the window. "Do you want to go dance in the rain?"

"Not today. It's a bit chilly for that."

"Do you remember when we did? Tante Kaaren and Sophie and Grace and us?" Astrid got up to stand beside her mother.

"More than once. There is nothing like rain-washed hair." Ingeborg finished her coffee. "Freda is out in the cheese house. I should be helping her."

"Instead, you are helping your daughter." Astrid leaned her head on her mother's shoulder.

"Does Elizabeth know?"

Astrid shrugged. "I got the woman stabilized, left orders, and went home for breakfast. Then I just grabbed the umbrella and came out here." She blew out a breath. "I sure wish Miriam would get back here."

"Trygve said she is coming on Sunday's train."

"How come I didn't know that?" Why did Ingeborg know this and Astrid did not? Had they called Elizabeth and she forgot to tell Astrid? "I better get back to the hospital." She paused.

43

"I miss the nurses no longer staying at our house. It has been delightful to see Corabell adjust to life so far from home, but I think living in a home rather than the boardinghouse was a good thing. At least at first."

Ingeborg nodded. "I like having Gray Cloud and Dawn Breaking drop by now and then. They are a great help, and they're learning things that will serve them well when they go home to their tribe." She adjusted Astrid's shawl around her shoulders.

Astrid paused in opening the door. "Mor, why don't you come with me? You could be a mother to that poor Mrs. Sorvito today."

"All right. I will. I'll leave a note for Freda. There is nothing pressing here today."

"Do you want the buggy?"

Ingeborg made a face and shook her head. "Outside in a rain-washed world is a great place to be."

The telephone rang, and they paused and counted rings. Ingeborg returned to the box on the wall.

"Is Astrid still there?" It sounded like Rachel, Goodie Wold's niece, on the switchboard.

"Ja. We are just going out the door."

"Tell her to go to the hospital. It's not critical, but she's needed."

"I will." She rushed out the door. "We need to hurry."

The two women broke into the half run, half walk they had used for years when a patient needed them. They were both puffing by the time they arrived at the hospital, and Deborah pointed them in the direction of the patient.

Vera met them at the door. "The bleeding has slowed way down."

"Good. What have you done?"

"Changed the packing as often as needed. What else is there to do?"

Astrid headed into the room. "Massage her lower belly. The

44

afterbirth looked to be intact, but the light was poor there. Does anyone here speak Italian?"

They all shook their heads.

"And she doesn't speak English. Although her husband does some. I want to know if she carried any other babies to term or lost them early."

Vera shook her head. "If only Miriam were here, she could ask those things."

"She'll be back on Sunday," Deborah Norton said softly.

There it was again. Deborah knew and Astrid did not. "When did you learn that?"

Their most experienced nurse hesitated. "Why, I think there was a written message that Mrs. Korsheski had telephoned from Chicago to say Miriam was coming on the Sunday train. I think it is still on the desk."

"Do you know when it came?"

"Early this morning, I think."

"Then how did Trygve know she was coming?"

Deborah shrugged. "Maybe she wrote to him."

"And we have no idea who took the message?"

"Corabell was on duty. She must have forgotten to mention it in all that was going on this morning. They had a boy in here with projectile vomiting shortly after you left. It was a real mess. He is sleeping in the ward. His mother is with him. Poor woman was up all night with him." She paused then added before Astrid could ask, "We put him way at the end in case he is contagious."

"I see." But all Astrid really saw right now was that an important message had been nearly lost. However, all the patients were as well cared for as possible. Her resolve strengthened. They needed more training for emergencies so that no matter how severe the pressure, no one panicked and forgot what they were to do. Astrid thought back to her experience at the Indian village that had been so decimated by measles. How she had gone from tipi to tipi to see who could possibly be saved and then stipulated care. They'd not managed to save all the sick ones, but those who lived would have died without their care. Her father had been there with them. She kept from looking at her mother by sheer will. While that trip sometimes seemed far in the distance, other times it seemed like it had happened last week.

An epidemic was not beyond possibilities right here in Blessing. Or some other catastrophe. While these thoughts had been racing through her mind, another track focused on the woman with the bleeding. The good old trick of pressure on an artery could stop bleeding, but not in this case. There were several possible vessels involved and located too deep in the abdomen to reach.

She returned her attention to the patient. Her mother was sitting by the young woman's bedside, gently washing her face, murmuring softly, and with her came a sense of peace that made even her daughter relax. Color had begun to return to the woman's face. Ingeborg washed and dried the limp hands and arms, then began on the upper torso, her croon continuing.

Astrid knew for certain her mother was praying all the time, perhaps singing her favorite Bible verses. All the nurses needed lessons from her mor in how to care for a patient, especially those who were unconscious. She moved silently to the opposite side of the bed and checked her patient's vitals. Her pulse was fast, which wasn't surprising with the blood loss. The woman was breathing easily. She was so young and thin. Still, nothing told her why the baby had died. Not that they could always pinpoint reasons anyway. Perhaps this woman had not had sufficient food, and from the looks of her, that could well be the case. She'd seen cases like this at the hospital in Chicago, women from the tenements, where people sometimes starved. Was Miriam's family in bad shape? she wondered.

"I'll be in the office. Thelma will send any patients over here that show up at the door. Thank you for mothering her."

"You are welcome." The bath finished, Ingeborg took out

some lotion that smelled like Amelia's roses and began smoothing it into the patient's skin.

Later that night, the Jeffers family had just finished eating supper, all together for a change, when a knock on the door brought Daniel to his feet.

"Why, Father Devlin, come in!" Daniel stepped back and motioned their guest inside. "Have you had supper?"

"No, but when I returned late this afternoon, I heard about the sad happenings in the camp." He smiled at Astrid. "I am muckle sorry for yer day."

"Thank you. Did you go to the hospital to see her?"

"I did, and while Mrs. Sorvito is still as weak as a baby bird, thanks to ye she still be alive."

"She knows the baby was born dead?"

"Aye, she told me. I went to the wee thing and baptized it straightway, of course, in her presence. She asked if I would celebrate a proper funeral for it, and that I will."

"You can talk with her, then?"

Father Devlin chuckled. Despite how many miles he had traveled today, his eyes twinkled. "Aye, Latin be close enough to Italian that we could converse. To a degree and with lots of gestures, of course. Sure and I'd not want to preach a sermon in it, but I understand more than I can speak it."

"Tomorrow, could you ask her some questions for me?"

"That I could. Ah, and thank ye for yer insistence that she go to the hospital. Too many of the poor are afraid of both doctors and hospitals. Of the money and the unknown." He smiled at Astrid. "But then other places don't have a hospital like this one. I suspect ye'll never make a dime from it, not the way ye neglect to charge people."

"How can one charge when there is no money to be had? When they can, people will pay, and often they pay with their labor, or whatever they have. One woman is doing the laundry to help pay after we cared for her."

"Never fear. God himself will bless ye." He started to leave, but Daniel pointed to the table where Amelia was setting a full plate down.

"Sit, man. Anything can wait while my mother feeds you. If you don't, she'll feel she failed in her duty."

Amelia tsked and shook her head. "Pay no attention to him, but it would be a shame to waste this good food. I know it is good, because Daniel had thirds tonight."

Father Devlin raised his hands, and Astrid motioned to the sink. Hands washed, the priest sat down, said a brief grace, and cleaned his plate, mopping the gravy with the last of the sliced bread.

"More?" Amelia hovered by his shoulder.

"Ah no. Thank ye. I be—"

"As big as you are, you can eat more. We do not stand on politeness here." She brought the pan over and dished up what was left. "You wouldn't want to waste this last bit, now, would you?"

"Well, since ye put it that way." He smiled up at her. "I never be one to waste God's good gifts."

"So how was your trip?" Daniel asked. "Your horse held up?"

"That he did. Like everyone else, life in Blessing brings health to the broken."

"What a thing to say." Astrid stared at him.

"Well, ye have but to look about. A hospital, a church where people truly believe in our God and His power to bring healing, people who treat outsiders as family from the beginning. Not my church, not exactly, but close enough." He laid his fork by the plate.

Daniel studied him closely. "What exactly is your church? Catholic?"

Father Devlin licked his lips and paused for a long moment. A simple question. Why did he hesitate? He smiled. "I know not how much ye ken of the liturgical church, that is, the Roman Catholics, the Orthodox, the Anglicans, the Copts. A few other groups. Nor how much ye're aware of Ireland's troubles. 'Tis a long and tangled history since the seventeenth century. Basically, we've two sets of folks in Ireland."

Daniel frowned. "Is this the green and the orange?"

Father Devlin shrugged. "It be infinitely more than that, but the idea's there. I be of the orange sort and an ordained priest of the Anglican communion rather than Roman Catholic, as ye call it."

Astrid wagged her head. "You did several Catholic rites, Father."

"Aye." He paused again, as if he were marshaling his thoughts. "But not exactly. The old Anglican and present Roman rites be very close. When a dying man be wanting to reconcile with his God, I doubt he'd quibble much. Ye'll recall, yer nurse Miriam assisted. In a truly Roman rite, a woman would never be permitted to do that. Nor would I, in the Roman tradition, be allowed to set foot in yer Protestant church. It simply cannot be done. Rules, ye know."

Daniel stared at his coffee mug. "Now I'm confused. Ma, may I have some more coffee?"

"Are you sure you'll sleep tonight with all this coffee?"

"Believe me. I'll sleep."

"This is all new to me." Astrid propped her head in her hands.

"There is a hymn from around 1800, from Ireland's blessed St. Brigit, and I translate roughly:

'I would have an ale-feast for the king of kings,
And the heavenly host to be drinking it for all eternity.
I should like there to be hospitality for their sake;
I should like Jesus to be here forever.'

"Now I ask ye: Can ye fault a faith and a devotion that expresses itself as a grand party hosted by a woman?"

Daniel laughed out loud, and it was the first in a long time that Astrid had heard him do that. He nodded.

"Exactly! And I be thus torn. How to reconcile it all and serve the risen Christ as well? Now in St. Brendan's day, if ye needed to sort things out, ye became a white martyr. Ye cast yerself asea in a boat, wandered into a foreign land, or some such. 'Tis a means of the getting of wisdom. So I am, as ye see, a vagabond, a white martyr, seeking a true faith that all me heritages and training might embrace."

Astrid nodded. "I remember the peace in that patient's face. You gave him exactly what he needed, what he hoped for. It was a gift from God."

"To me, that is serving Christ. It's what I pledged to do. And in me Celtic heritage 'twould be warmly welcomed. So ye see how torn."

"I see." Amelia was listening just as intently. "So have you gotten any wisdom yet?"

Father Devlin laughed. "Nay. But I see a real need for me services here in Blessing. Although I fear I strike a divisive note."

"It's not you." Daniel's voice was hard, bitter. "It's others."

"I shall qualify that. Like any big family, there are some who think they know best for everyone, and they can get a bit uppity over one thing or another. But well ye know, they usually come around when they decide to let the good Lord be the Lord and not try to take over His job themselves." He leaned forward. "John and I have been talking, and we have an idea or two. Ye know ye cannot put two clerics together without getting more than two ideas out of it. But when we keep the faith, good will come about." He looked at the three around the table. "Ye believe that, aye?"

"Well, yes." Astrid looked to Daniel, who looked to his mother, who was nodding emphatically.

"Meself detects a note of hesitation, and I understand that. But God promises to bring good out of evil and bad things, and I think we are going to have a chance to see Him in action. We will all agree to pray and praise God for the answers before we see them, for that be what faith is about. Then we wait and see." He nodded and kept right on nodding before he pushed his chair back and stood.

"And now, I thank ye all for this fine dinner, the company, and letting this chatty priest bend yer ear." He stopped at the door. "Tomorrow John and I will bury that baby right in the churchyard, the place for God's children, no matter the age or faith." He set his hat back on his head, touched the brim, and out the door he went.

Astrid and Daniel sat looking at each other, slowly wagging their heads.

"Now, he is a force to be reckoned with."

Amelia was wagging her head too. "No, son, he is not the force. It's the God he serves. Why, I feel like a whirlwind just blew through here, all in the guise of a man. I think I will make him a new shirt so I can wash that one he is wearing."

CHAPTER 6

How could forty-eight hours last a week?

If Trygve Knutson never milked another cow, it might be too soon. At least he'd not drawn the troublemaker this time. He stripped out the last drops and picked up both stool and bucket at the same time. On his way to the milk can, he stopped by Manny.

"You said you had a favor to ask."

"Mister Trygve, you think Benny could ride a horse?"

Trygve looked back to the boy, who was just stripping out the cow he was on. The smile Manny sent him made all the doubts worthwhile. The boy was indeed fitting into life in Blessing. "Well, I don't know. Never thought about it."

"If someone helped him on, we could strap his legs to the saddle. Use a couple belts, y'know?" Manny handed Trygve the bucket and went through the gyrations he used to get upright.

Trygve dumped both buckets in the strainer, waiting with the second until the first had gone through. *What a thought!*

On the way up to the house, Manny continued. "I been thinking on how to help him walk too. Did you read Moby Dick?"

"I did, years ago. Why?"

"Well, that Captain Ahab gets a peg leg after he loses the leg, right?"

"True."

"Why can't we carve Benny two pegs? He'd prob'ly have to use crutches, but he has such strong arms." He turned to Trygve. "Worth a try, ain't it?"

"Isn't it."

"Isn't it? We could make the crutches adjustable for when he grows. Or make him longer ones. And the pegs too. Pad the stump ends with sheep's wool and leather, like we did my crutches. How come no one thought of this before?"

"We've been trying to design a chair for him, with wheels like one we saw in a catalogue." Trygve stopped and stared at Manny. "Are you reading Moby Dick or—?"

"Grandma reads part and I read part. Emmy can read real good."

Trygve clapped the boy on the shoulder. "Well, I'll be. I am so proud of you."

"'Twarn't nothin'. I ain't—er, am not stupid."

"That I know for sure, but you are learning mighty fast. Reverend Solberg must be happy as can be."

"Mrs. Jeffers is helping me too." Together they clumped up the steps to the porch.

Emmy looked up from setting the table when they came into the kitchen. "Wash your hands."

"Good morning. Breakfast will be on the table as soon as you sit, Manny." Ingeborg turned from the stove, pancake turner in hand.

Freda slammed the dough over on the floured counter. "Trygve, do you have time to wax the cheese wheels today?"

"Can I help with that?" Manny asked, pumping the handle to run water into the washbasin.

"Sure. You can build crates. That's a sitting-down job but a very necessary one. Can't ship wheels without crates." Trygve smiled at Freda. "I'll come by when Manny gets home."

"Takk."

Trygve left, thinking all the way home about putting Benny on a horse. And about Miriam, of course. Always thinking about her. He climbed the familiar stoop into the Knutson kitchen.

His mor was putting the fried potatoes out. "Are you working for Thorliff today?"

"Ja." He stepped to the sink to wash his hands. "The boarding-house is coming along well. I'm helping with the roof. They're going to have some extra shingles, 'cause we won't use most of our last bale. Do you need any patching at the school?"

"No one has reported a wet ceiling, but I haven't looked at the roof. Go up and look if you would."

"I shall."

His father stomped into the kitchen and plopped into his chair. He lowered his head and started rattling off grace so quickly, Trygve almost didn't get his head bowed in time. Far reached for the potatoes even as his head came up. "I'll want your help caulking the windows this afternoon."

"I'm helping Thorliff pretty much full time. Can Lemuel help you?"

"He's got a new job besides delivering the papers. Butchering or something. Or putting up chickens."

Trygve smiled. "He is not fond of dressing chickens."

"Money is money. Hjelmer is managing Lyme's farm now and wants to get rid of the chickens."

His mor sat down and helped herself to the scrambled eggs. "Your little lady comes in tomorrow, you say?"

"Ja. She should be boarding the train today. This train is the one that stops at every single little whistle-stop on the route. And they change engines at least once, she says. Takes forever."

Kaaren nodded. "If you're helping Ingeborg and working on the boardinghouse and building your own house, when are you going to go courting? I assume you want to."

Trygve paused to study her. Where was she going with this? "Ja, I do."

"Please don't forget to make time for her. With all you're committed to, it will be very easy to get too busy."

What could he say? "Takk, Mor." That's what he always replied to her unsolicited advice. Of course, her advice was usually very good. Could he get too busy for Miriam? Never! But as he thought about it, *never* became *maybe*. It was something to watch out for.

Wax the cheese wheels. Trygve shouldn't have said he'd do that, but he did, so he would. That afternoon he laid shingles until he saw the school let out, then picked up Manny in the buggy and drove out to the cheese house.

While Trygve and Freda coated the big clumsy cheese wheels with the wax to keep them fresh, Manny sat down with the stack of one-by-three precut boards and, with hammer and nails, assembled the crates. The stack grew beside him.

"Good job," Freda said. "You're getting faster and faster."

"It helps to not waste time hitting your thumb." Manny stuck the offended member in his mouth. He eyed the lumber pile and the stack. "We'll need to cut more."

"I'm sure we have enough for this shipment. I'll crate the wheels first thing tomorrow. You were a big help, Manny." Freda shut the door behind them as they stepped out into the sunshine. "It could freeze any time," she mused, apparently talking to no one in particular. Manny crawled up into Trygve's buggy.

What did Trygve hear? He looked to the northwest. Sure enough, that was the steam engine he had heard. "Here comes the threshing crew."

"Uff da!" Freda hiked her skirts and clambered up into the buggy. "We'd better get more dinner ready."

Trygve drove into Tante Ingeborg's front yard and left the two to get out of his buggy by themselves. He rapped at the door and entered. "Threshing crew."

"Ja, I heard." Already, Tante Ingeborg was stuffing more stovewood into the firebox.

Trygve crossed to the telephone, lifted the receiver off the hook, and asked the operator to call the deaf school. His mother answered. "Mor, the threshing crew is crossing the river."

"Oh good." She paused. "Tell Ingeborg and Freda I'll send some food over. That'll be easier than feeding them all here today."

He gave the message and headed outside to set up the trestle table benches that were leaning against the house. Emmy ran to help him.

"What can I do?" Manny asked.

"Slice the bread."

"It's a good thing I baked bread today." Freda brought a pot of soup from the icebox and then headed to the cellar. "We can add more vegetables." The extended soup was heating on the stove by the time they heard a horse and wagon pull up.

Ingeborg glanced out the window. "From Kaaren. We can set all the food on the table in here."

Emmy appeared at the door, so she gave her instructions. By the time they had the food all set up on the table, they could hear the racket of two steam engines pulling the separators, the cook wagon and team, and five teams pulling wagons. Grace and Kaaren both came running over from the deaf school, and they all welcomed the returning crews.

The wagons drove in first, with Jonathan in the lead. Grace met him at the barn and greeted him with open arms. Trygve was sure she was crying. She'd not looked at him since they met on the way to the barn. Joseph Geddick leaped to the ground, and one by one, the others arrived, with Solem Brunderson driving the steam engine that Haakan used to drive. Trygve went to stand by Ingeborg. The steam engines shut down, and the sudden silence almost hurt one's ears.

Kaaren put an arm around Ingeborg's shoulders, but she stood tall, ignoring the tears streaming down her face. At the sight of her tears, Trygve fought the burning in his throat and eyes. Surely grief was contagious.

After the crew had eaten and everyone had headed off to their own homes, Trygve finally got over to his basement, or what would one day be a basement or cellar. Right now it was just a hole. He'd been digging a short while when two men peered over the side.

"Could you use some help?" Reverend Solberg asked. "Tommy and I here need some physical work for a change. Our brains are tired."

Father Devlin threw a shovel down into the hole. "Or would you rather we started up here?"

"Anywhere you want. As you can see, there is plenty of opportunity for all." Trygve slammed his shovel into the ground and trundled the wheelbarrow up the ramp. He'd dug deep enough that he could no longer just throw the dirt over the side as he had several weeks earlier.

Devlin stared down into the hole. "There's not room there for three shovels. I'll start here."

Trygve saw Samuel, hands in his pockets, whistling his way across the field toward them. When he got close enough, he studied the hole. "You didn't get very far. We've been gone what, a month?"

"Somehow I had lots of other things that demanded doing."

Samuel grinned at Solberg. "I'll stay up here with Father Devlin."

Within the hour, Andrew showed up, as he'd said he would, and the dirt flew out of the rapidly expanding hole. A while later, Emmy appeared with a bucket and dipper, offering a drink, and Inga carried a basket with cookies.

"Grandma sent these."

The men climbed out of the hole and gathered around.

Inga peered down into the hole. "Still lots to go, huh?"

"You'd better be glad we didn't ask you to come help," Samuel teased.

"We didn't have to bring the cookies."

Several of the men chuckled. Andrew took the last cookie. "Is Carl at Knutsons' or over at Grandma's?"

"Grandma's. He and Manny are hauling more pumpkins and squash in from the garden. But they'd rather be fishing."

"Who wouldn't?" Andrew heaved a sigh. "Better get back at it. Takk, ladies."

The girls headed back toward the house, and the men returned to work. They stopped when the cows began lining up at the barn.

"They're as good as an alarm clock." Andrew stuck his shovel upright back in the dirt.

"Thanks for the help." Trygve was the last to climb out. With Samuel back, he could bypass the milking, but right now milking sounded like a nice reprieve.

The triangle rang at Tante Ingeborg's. Her voice carried faintly across the field: "Coffee's ready."

As if under orders all five men made a direct line across the field to the Bjorklund house. The fragrance of apple pie welcomed them to the porch.

"Have a seat and we'll bring it out." Ingeborg, with the two little girls, returned with plates of apple pie topped by slices of cheese and cups and coffee. "I figured the cows could wait a few more minutes."

Andrew raised his plate. "You're so right." One of the cows bellowed as if on cue, making them all laugh.

"How come I wasn't invited to the party?" Lars, on his way down to the barn, stopped at the first step.

"Didn't see you out there, that's why." Andrew drained his coffee cup. "I'll go let 'em in. Onkel Lars, you can have my seat." He stood up and laid his empty dish aside.

"Takk, but I'll go get milking. Someone has to take pity on the poor cows." He ambled off toward the barn.

Trygve watched him go. Work. These men knew hard work, and the women did too, just as much. Would Miriam, a city girl, fit into this life of constant work?

She would, he was certain. She would be a fine addition to the family.

Now to convince her.

CHAPTER 7

Tomorrow she would be back in Blessing.

Miriam stared out at the blackness broken up by small towns and dotted by farms. Trygve's last letter, which came just before she was to leave, said the wheat harvest was finishing and the threshing crew would disband. He said Ingeborg had "sad eyes," as Inga called them. Tears were close to the surface for many in Blessing. Haakan was terribly missed.

Miriam leaned her head back against the seat. Oh, she understood tears. Would they ever cease? Would the hole in her heart eventually heal? On one hand, she knew it would, and on the other . . . But when? Mrs. Korsheski had reminded her that healing would take time, and hard work would help. Miriam knew the woman understood whereof she spoke. She had lost both mother and husband in the last couple of years. Her children were grown. She dreamed of going to visit them all one day, since many of them lived other places.

The thought of someday having children of her own reminded her again of the man who insisted he loved her. How could someone really know love as quickly as he'd said he did? With the clacking wheels, her mind wandered back to the early years when her father was still alive and they lived in a real house, not a tenement. Back to the days of laughter, with their father teasing his wife and throwing whatever child was a baby up in the air, and them all laughing. Laughing! Had the latter years killed the laughter, or was it the unrelenting poverty?

She, at least, had been ahead in school and was able to finish. But Tonio hadn't. As each of them reached an age where they could find work that brought in money, they'd quit school. Now, finally, the two youngest ones were back in school. Now that Tonio and Mercy and Este had steady jobs so they could support the family. How could Mercy go into nurses' training without finishing high school?

If I married Trygve, my family could come to Blessing, and they could all go to school. She slammed her head back against the seat. Where had that thought come from? That would be a terrible reason to marry a man. She could feel her drooping eyes widen and reminded herself to close her mouth. Glancing around at the other passengers near her, she was gratified to see no one was staring at her. She had a job promised at the hospital in Chicago. Then her younger sisters at least could go back to school.

But what about Mercy and Tonio and Este? Now guilt had names.

Go to sleep! Somehow her mind refused to obey the order and instead rampaged ahead. Blessing, the people there, the clean air, the hospital that was so in need of good help, the training of new nurses, the dreams of the Bjorklund women and others for the hospital and the town. A house of her own. That one stopped the parade!

She pulled the last letter out of her reticule again and held it up to the dim light. Trygve Knutson wrote a good letter, and he lived up to his word. He cared about the people around him. She could feel the grief. Haakan, Mr. Bjorklund, was a fine man. How was Ingeborg bearing up? Probably like she was. You do what you have to do and cry into your pillow.

At least in Blessing she would be as busy as she could handle. And then some.

Miriam and Mrs. Korsheski had talked about the little hospital and how she could help the most. Her mind drifted back to that conversation, safer than the visions of a certain broad-shouldered, very good-looking young man. Would he be at the train?

Oops, back to Mrs. Korsheski and their talk.

❦

"We are dreaming that one day soon we can send our interns out there for experience also," Mrs. Korsheski had said in her office the other day. "If we can develop that as a true arm of our hospital, our program will be so much more beneficial to both our doctors and our nurses. That Blessing hospital is going to need someone to run it, an administrator to take the burden off the doctors Bjorklund. I wish I could send one with you now.

"I've even thought of bringing Astrid's mother, Ingeborg, back here to teach a few weeks on the uses of the ancient healing ways she is so versed in. Our medical world likes to think the new is always better, but I have seen too much to put all my confidence in the new." She'd leaned forward in her chair. "Enough about my dreams. I have here some things for you to take with you—some for the hospital, and a packet for each of the Indian nurses. Dr. Bjorklund's letter says their names are Dawn Breaking and Gray Cloud. Also, I haven't had any reports from that hospital since you left, so when you get there, please let me know what has gone on."

"I will." The idea of adding to their fund of knowledge appealed to Miriam. During her time in Blessing, she had come to respect and admire Ingeborg and had gotten only a glimpse of her wisdom. "I think a lot about how quickly our young patient Manny healed. It was due in large part to Ingeborg's dedication to both his mental and physical ability. You should have seen how she worked with him. He did not have time to lie around and feel sorry for himself. She made him work, and sometimes when I went in his room, he was dripping with sweat from his

couple waited too long to call me, and she'd not been eating enough—all the problems we are talking about. Mor reminded me that is why education is so important. And the only way we can educate most women is to go directly to them."

"Like you did to the reservation?"

"Yes, and now we are on our second pair of Indian nurses, who are getting minimal training, for sure, but it will make a difference. Tomorrow you will meet Gray Cloud and Dawn Breaking. I think you'll like them very much. I certainly do."

They stopped at Astrid's gate. "Thank you, Trygve. The walk has done me good."

"Thank you for letting me, uh . . ." Miriam rolled her lips together and blinked.

"I know. I know." Dr. Astrid opened her gate. "You are welcome. I do love to be part of life-changing experiences. And there are a lot of them in medicine. Good night."

Miriam and Trygve strolled over to the boardinghouse. What in the world was her hand wanting to do? Take his? What a preposterous thought. They mounted the steps, the moonlight supplemented by the lamps on the porch.

"Thank you for walking me to town."

"You're welcome. Perhaps I'll see you again tomorrow."

"Perhaps. Good night." Why did she feel as if she were fleeing as she entered the door he opened for her and headed for the stairs?

His "good-night" floated behind her.

She climbed the stairs to her room, about as weary as a body can get. Her room. Her own room!

I will not peek out the window.

Miriam sank down on the edge of the bed. Good thing she had unpacked earlier, her carpetbag now in the closet, and had taken a bath, because right now, all that sounded possible was her bed. She stared at the window. Was that whistling she heard?

efforts. His muscles did not atrophy, as happens to so many with severe breaks and surgery like that." She didn't mention all the hours she had known Ingeborg and others spent praying for the boy, since she herself doubted the efficacy of prayer.

And she told Mrs. Korsheski, "I'm afraid I feel torn in two directions."

"Oh, and how is that?"

"Between here and there."

⁂

The train whistle blew and the train slowed for a stop, bringing her back to the present. She had actually voiced her concern to Mrs. Korsheski, when she'd not even admitted it to herself. What was it the nurse had said? Her exact words?

"You will do well either way. Or both ways. Sometimes we can have our cake and eat it too. And keep in mind that what God plans for you is far better than what you can plan for yourself."

It was the last part she'd tried to put aside. Her mother had believed that too, and look what it got her.

An early trip to heaven to be with her beloved? What is so wrong with that?

But she had wanted to stay with her children. She'd heard her say so.

Tears flooded her eyes again. What had her mother seen, known, to be able to smile like that? *Oh, Mama, I miss you so, and I sure do hope you were right about heaven.* After the stop and two passengers had settled into seats, she wrapped her coat around her and, settling her head on the windowsill, fell into a light sleep that broke every time they stopped. She had known there would be many stops, but she'd never imagined there'd be this many.

⁂

Early Sunday morning she woke to find a little boy standing in front of her, staring. She shook herself awake and sat up.

"Bertie, don't bother the lady." The woman across the aisle smiled apologetically. "I'm sorry, miss."

"He startled me is all." Miriam watched the boy throw himself against his mother's lap, as if she'd scolded him, and then peer at her from his safe place. "How old is he?"

"Bertie is three. Show the nice lady how old you are." The little man's tongue came out and he stared at his hand, seeming to will his fingers to obey. When he got three up, he grinned at his mother. "Very good." From the looks of the woman, it wouldn't be terribly long before Bertie had either a new baby brother or sister in his life.

"Where are you going?"

"To Blessing, just west of Grand Forks, North Dakota. What about you?"

"We are going farther, to Bismarck. Have you been there?"

"No, Blessing is the farthest west I've been." Not that she'd been east of Chicago either. "Will you be staying there?"

"Yes. Bertie's papa is already there. He says I will love the town and the people. But I've never been away from my family before, and this is so far away."

"From where? I mean, where was home?" She smiled at the little boy, which sent him burying his face in his mother's skirt again.

"We live in Rochester, south of the Twin Cities. Or rather, we lived there." She sniffed as if she were about to cry.

"Leaving is hard."

Just then the whistle blew again, and Bertie covered his ears with both hands.

While his mother comforted him, Miriam looked out the window.

"Grand Forks. Next stop Grand Forks." The conductor made his way through the car and stopped beside her. "Not too far to Blessing now, miss. You ever eaten at the boardinghouse there?"

"That is where I'll be living."

"Fine place, Blessing." He wagged his head. "That little town sure is growing."

Miriam watched him sway on down the aisle. Funny he should mention the boardinghouse. She wondered if the others had moved her things over to the new wing yet. Soon she would be there again. Was she feeling anticipation or dread?

Blessing did indeed come soon, as the conductor had promised. The train jolted and wheezed to a stop.

"Thank you for traveling with us, miss," the conductor said with a smile as he helped her down. "I think there is a young man waiting for you." He nodded over his shoulder. "I know him. Trygve Knutson. He's a good man, a real fine young man." He tipped his hat to her and reached back for her carpetbag. "You had a couple of larger boxes too, right?"

"Yes, sir. They went in the baggage car."

"They'll be unloading them with the other supplies for here."

Miriam smiled back at the conductor and hoped she'd said thank-you. It was like her gaze was locked on the man coming toward her, and she found that she couldn't look away. Smile, don't smile. But her lips knew better than her mind as the smile stretched. He was even better looking than she'd remembered.

He stopped in front of her, his smile taking up his whole face. But about the time she thought he was going to lock her in his arms, just before she could take a step back, if she could take a step back, he nodded. "Welcome home." Then he offered her his bent arm. "Let's go make sure your other things are here." Picking up her bag with the free hand, he strolled off with her as if they'd seen each other just yesterday.

The sigh she heaved came clear from her toes.

"Are you all right?"

"I'm just grateful to be walking on a floor that doesn't move."

He squeezed her hand against his side. "I was beginning to think you would not return, but my tante Ingeborg assured me that you had given your word and you would keep it."

Be honest. "Actually, I tried not to come, but Nurse Korsheski would not allow it."

"I'm sorry to hear about your mother."

The burn started instantly. "Thank you."

"The rest of your family is all right?"

"Yes. Sad, but I think since they saw our mother suffering more than I did, they were grateful she's no longer suffering. I am too, but . . . I . . . I wanted more time with her. But not so terribly weak like she was." She heaved another sigh. "There are no easy answers is one lesson I am learning."

She pointed to the boxes piled to the side. "Those go to the hospital. They are medical supplies. I packed a couple of personal things in them, but I can get them when I go on duty."

Why was it that whenever he looked at her, her heart rate picked up?

"Your things are all at the boardinghouse. Miss Nester packed them for you. They moved over early last week. Others wanted to come too. I think Miss Wells is on duty."

She kept looking around, anywhere, so she wouldn't have to look at Trygve. "Everyone in Blessing must be at church."

"Well, not everyone. Dr. Elizabeth is not allowed to go anywhere. Astrid is afraid if she catches anything—"

"Is there something going around?" Their steps kept slowing as they neared the boardinghouse.

"Not that I know of. Oh, I nearly forgot. Tante Ingeborg has invited you to dinner at the farm." He stopped. "Please. I know you are exhausted, but it would mean a lot to her."

I just want to take a bath and go to bed.

He did not wait for an answer. "I'll come back and get you." Together they climbed the three steps to the boardinghouse porch. "I'll take your bag to your room." He opened the door and motioned her in.

"Why, Nurse Hastings, you're back at last. How good to see you. Good morning, Trygve!" Mrs. Wiste came from be-

hind the desk, her smile of greeting lighting the dimness of the vestibule.

Trygve was grinning too. "'Morning, Sophie. Where shall I put this?"

"The lady or the bag?"

"Both."

Miriam was poised to be aghast at the banter when she remembered that Trygve and Sophie Wiste were brother and sister. Was that perhaps why she liked Mrs. Wiste so much? It was going to take some time before she got all the family connections in Blessing straightened out.

Mrs. Wiste led the way to the stairs. "Your room is all ready. The other two chose to share a room, but I hated to put three of you in together. Especially since you will all be on such different schedules. Will this be agreeable with you?"

"Of course, and thank you." Miriam had to hurry to keep up. "I see they've gotten most of the outside done."

"They have, and there is not a lot left to do inside anymore either. You nurses will be able to sleep during the day here now. At least I hope so. Neither of the others has lodged a complaint. Dr. Deming, the dentist, is in the same wing. Funny to think of wings here at our boardinghouse. Dinner will be at noon and supper is served at six. Breakfast starts at five thirty, so that should not be a problem." Mrs. Wiste marched toward the end of the hall.

"There's going to be a little hammering, though." Trygve pointed upward. "The ceiling moldings aren't in yet. I'll try to finish that tomorrow morning."

"Here we are." Mrs. Wiste stopped. "Miss Wells and Miss Nester are in that room next to yours. They wanted to be here to greet you, but Mrs. Jeffers talked Corabell into accompanying her to church, and Vera is on duty." She opened a door and stepped aside. "There are towels on your bed and a list of meal times on the door. You will have morning sun in your room. Here is your closet." She opened a narrow door where Miriam's aprons and extra things hung.

67

"They even unpacked for me. I am so touched. Mrs. Wiste, this is lovely. Look at the quilt and the braided rug, even a rocking chair and a dressing table. Are all the rooms like this?"

Trygve was grinning again. "Sophie, here, is very proud of her new addition, but I know she did some extra things for her nurses, as she calls you. Sophie has a very proprietary interest in anything to do with the hospital. As you will hear, she is forming a volunteer hospital society. I have a feeling the society will become a rival of the quilting circle. Or maybe not." His grin made her smile back.

"We have a society like that in Chicago. They do a lot of good to help both the hospital and the patients. But in Blessing too?"

Mrs. Wiste was grinning as well. "Right. We will have a party when the boardinghouse is truly finished, and I have a feeling from the bits I've heard, it will in some way become '*a benefit for the hospital.*' Those are the words you will hear bandied about."

Miriam leaned closer and dropped her voice. "Do you think I could take a bath now, and then a nap?"

"Of course you can. There's sufficient time for that. We have shared bathrooms in this addition, so you and the other nurses will share this bathroom between your two rooms, not like down the hall." She opened a second door. "This is your bath."

"Oh my." Miriam's cheeks flamed. Now Trygve knew what she had asked.

Trygve half bowed. "As I said, things are changing here. Welcome home." He paused at the door. "You will come to dinner? Please?"

Miriam could not refuse. "What time?"

"I'll come for you at one."

"If I am not downstairs, please send someone up for me."

His grin nearly cracked his face. "Rest well."

I sure hope I am not making a mistake. She wasn't sure if that meant accepting the dinner invitation or agreeing to go with Trygve.

CHAPTER 8

Mor, are you sure you want to do this?" The voice on the other end of the line sounded worried. "We can easily move dinner from your house to ours."

"Astrid, I cannot live in a cocoon. Life needs to return to as normal as possible. So ja. I want everyone to come to my house like usual. It won't be long before it's too cold to be outside. Freda has chickens in the oven, and we made bread yesterday. Everyone will bring what they want, and we'll have plenty of food and laughter. Besides, we need to welcome Miriam and the threshing crew back. Maybe we can even have a ball game."

"All right. Amelia said you really wanted this, so I won't say anything to change it."

"You are coming?"

"Of course, unless there is an emergency. See you soon."

Ingeborg hung the earpiece back on the prong and heaved a sigh.

"Astrid?" Freda asked.

"Ja. Life has to go on with whatever we can do to make it like always. Fall is here; winter will come. I will miss Haakan forever. Sometimes I will cry, and right now I thank God for laughter, even more than usual." She looked over to Emmy, who was watching her carefully, her dark eyes so sober. Ingeborg opened her arms. "Come here, little one. Hugs are the best thing for sad eyes." She hugged Emmy close. "Don't you be worrying about me. We'll just get through it all."

Freda asked, "Where is Manny?"

Emmy stepped back. "Out with his horse. He took Joker a treat. He said maybe the little kids would like to ride this afternoon."

"How thoughtful of him." Freda sounded surprised. She was always less accepting than Ingeborg.

"Then he was going to harness the horse for the buggy." Emmy looked from one woman to the other.

Ingeborg shook her head. "That boy."

"He doesn't like to see you cry. He hopes you will smile when he drives up."

Please, Lord, protect that boy. He is trying so hard. "I will make sure to smile. Thank you."

Emmy hugged her one more time and returned to clearing the table.

Lord, please fill my eyes with smiles for the sake of these children, who are trying so hard to cheer me up. Remind me that joy comes with the morning. I sometimes forget that when the bed is empty beside me.

She really looked at Emmy. The dress and pinafore she was wearing were woefully small, too short and tight too. "Emmy, I think we need to make you some new clothes. Those are too small for you." Besides being so worn and faded. "I will go to-morrow while you are in school and get us some fabric. What color would you like?"

Emmy turned, her wide-eyed look so endearing that Ingeborg felt like whirling her around like she did Inga at times. "I like red and blue." She looked down at her dress. "No holes."

"True." Ingeborg glanced at the clock. Ten thirty now and church was at eleven. "We'd better get a move on. Freda, are you coming?" She gave the invitation every Sunday and, as usual, was gently refused. One of these days they would have to have a talk about that. What was keeping Freda from attending church?

The jingle of harness caught her attention. Sure enough, there was Manny with the buggy. "Will you look at that? Uff da, what determination." She turned to Emmy. "You go tell him I will be out in a minute."

"I will put the squash in to bake as soon as the pies come out." Freda looked up from scooping the seeds out of the inside of the big green squash she had taken the hatchet to because it was so hard. "Good thing the tables are still out."

Ingeborg gathered her shawl and draped it around her shoulders. "I wish you would come."

"Maybe next Sunday."

When Ingeborg descended the porch steps, Manny started to get out, but she waved him back. "I'll be fine." She climbed up into the buggy and settled herself on the seat beside him as Emmy clambered up into the back. "You have done wonderfully well. Far more than anyone expected or even hoped." She didn't bother to say he scared her at times.

He smiled, backed the horse, and they trotted down the lane. "I was thinking, will Benny be here this afternoon?"

"I have no idea who all is coming."

"Well, I figured we could help him ride the horse by belting his legs down to the saddle so he can't fall off."

Ingeborg stared at him. Was this the boy who, a couple short months earlier, didn't even want to talk to those little kids? *Lord God, oh, the miracles you are always at work on.* "I don't know why not. I'll make sure they are coming."

As usual, she cried her way through the service. Astrid sat on one side of her and Emmy on the other, then Manny. It started when they stood to sing "Holy, Holy, Holy." Oh how she missed Haakan's baritone voice beside her, the warmth that radiated from him, his sheer presence. Even the last year, when he had diminished in both size and energy, he was still Haakan. She could hear Anner behind her mumbling about something and looked to see that Father Devlin had joined them. What was the matter with Anner that he couldn't let go of his anger?

Then Reverend Solberg preached on the gospel for the day, where Jesus had talked about loving one another. John 13:33 to the end of the chapter had always been one of Haakan's favorite passages. He more than once commented that when Jesus called his disciples *little children*, he knew human nature well. Some of the adults in Blessing acted like children too.

More tears. Would this never stop? She felt Emmy's hand sneak into hers. On one hand God had taken away a part of her life, but here He'd given her two more children. Inga sat with her father right in front of Ingeborg and turned around to smile at her grandma. Her smile dimmed when she saw the tears. She sighed, and Thorliff nudged his little girl to turn around.

"But Grandma's crying." Her whisper could be heard to the back of the church at least, if not clear to the boardinghouse.

Ingeborg mopped her eyes and sniffed. When they all stood for the benediction, she cleared her throat. She'd made it through another service, and at least this time she didn't feel like bolting out the door and running until the pain stopped.

As they filed out the door where Reverend Solberg was greeting everyone, she felt another little hand on her other side.

"Grandma, you okay now?"

"Ja, I am."

"I miss Grandpa too. Ma says it will get better, but he can't come back. I sure hope he likes it in heaven. Do you think he can see us?"

Ingeborg shared a look with Thorliff, who raised his eyebrows. "Your turn," he mouthed.

She knew exactly what he meant. She squeezed Inga's hand and then Emmy's before whispering to them. "If you want to go outside with the other kids, you go. I'll be fine."

They beamed at her, giggled, and headed for the door.

Penny stopped beside her. "I wanted to remind you we have quilting on Thursday. It will be good to get back together again. It seems like forever since we met."

"Has anyone invited Amelia Jeffers?"

"I did, and two of the new ladies too. Some of the women from Tent Town are starting to take part in community activities. That is so good to see."

"It'll get easier," Reverend Solberg said when she reached him.

"I know, but that was one of Haakan's favorite Scripture passages. And I so cherished when he sang the bass line of 'Holy, Holy, Holy.' She glanced over to where a group of the men were visiting. Anner's voice could be heard above the others.

She turned to Thorliff. "Please go make sure Father Devlin knows he is invited to the farm for dinner."

Thorliff nodded. "Ja, I will." He stopped for a moment. "Did Manny really harness that horse and hitch it to the buggy?"

"He did. And wait until you hear his idea." When she heard Anner say something about "those people," she wanted to go over and join the group, but instead she looked around for Hildegunn. Where was she?

When Kaaren joined her, Ingeborg asked, "Have you seen Hildegunn?"

"No, and that's strange. I wonder if she is sick. I've not heard." She turned to ask Penny, who said the same.

"I'll go ask Anner." Penny strode over to the men's group and returned shaking her head. "He said she has a touch of the grippe, but he didn't seem too concerned."

"Too busy causing trouble to think about his wife," Kaaren muttered under her breath.

Sophie joined them. "That was some sermon. I have an idea that I am hoping we can seriously discuss at quilting."

"We have to wait until then?"

Sophie grabbed for one of her three-year-old twins. "No, you stay right by your ma."

Penny asked, "Does anyone know if Nurse Hastings came in on the train?"

Kaaren snickered. "She must have. We've not seen Trygve. He was planning to meet her. He says they'll come this afternoon."

"Well, I sure hope she realizes how lucky she is to have a good man like Trygve. Smitten, I think, is the word I heard." Penny smiled at Ingeborg and then Kaaren. "We need a romance in Blessing. Are they really planning to play ball this afternoon?"

"That's what Far says." Sophie smiled. "Not that he's that rousing a ball player."

"I need to get home. I'll see you in an hour or so." Ingeborg headed for the buggy, where Manny already sat waiting.

"Can I ride with Grandma?" Inga pleaded.

Thorliff looked a question at his mother, who nodded. With the two little girls giggling in the back seat, Thorliff helped his mother into the front. "I'll be out later. Elizabeth wants to come too, but she's afraid Astrid will have a fit. She is getting real tired of being housebound."

"Good. That must mean she is feeling better."

"I think so."

Oh, Lord, I hope so.

❧

Sometime later at Ingeborg's, after everyone had eaten all they could hold, the women were putting away the few leftovers as the men chose teams for the ball game, along with plenty of heckling from those not playing. Lars agreed to umpire, assisted by Reverend Solberg.

"You playing?" Thorliff asked Father Devlin.

"I'm not sure. I've not played for a long time."

"You'll do fine. You can be on my team, if you would."

Trygve stepped up to them grinning. "Looks like we're going to have the old guys against the kids." He motioned to Jonathan's team, where Andrew and the other young sprouts had gathered, as his father was wont to call them.

"Hey, watch who you're calling an old guy," Thorliff teased. "I don't exactly qualify."

"Close enough," Trygve said with a grin.

Ingeborg realized where the game would be played when the men hazed the cows out into the other pasture and picked up the piles in the near pasture. Perfect. The enthusiastic fans could sit on the fence rails.

She was especially pleased that quite a few people from Tent Town were gathering here. Penny had mentioned that more workers were becoming involved in the community. What better place than here? They settled onto blankets just inside the fence and leaned against it, a part of the crowd and yet not exactly. Ingeborg noticed that one of the wives was pregnant. Good and pregnant. She laughed and chattered with who was probably her husband as she opened a folded towel and laid out a fried bread of some sort.

The men worked together to position the sandbags for the bases, measuring off the proper distances. With the game ready to begin, Lars raised his hands, and eventually silence fell.

"I want us to dedicate this game to Haakan. He enjoyed the game like we all do. I don't know if they play baseball in heaven, but we sure miss him here."

Someone started clapping, another cheered, and the clapping and cheering lasted for several minutes.

Ingeborg, settled in a chair near the gate, smiled through her tears, a little girl on either side of her as if her guardians.

"Play ball!" Lars hollered, and the pitcher for the old men, Daniel Jeffers, threw the first pitch past Andrew to Toby Valders, the catcher.

"Strike one." The game had indeed begun.

After a bit Manny headed to the back pasture and whistled for his horse. Joker trotted over and accepted carrots from his admiring public. Inga and Emmy pulled Benny on his cart down to the barn, where Manny had brought his horse.

Trygve left off sitting on the bench and motioned for Miriam to come with him.

Ingeborg watched them go. She knew what Manny was planning and thought it a great idea. "I'll be back," she told Kaaren.

"Where you going?"

"Down to the barn with the little ones."

Kaaren turned back to the ball game, and Ingeborg joined the others at the barn.

She stopped beside Miriam. "I am so glad you are back. I realize you are needed and missed in Chicago, but you are sorely needed and missed here too. Not just what you offer the community, but you. Yourself. Miriam Hastings."

"What a lovely thing to say. Thank you. Is this really Manny's horse?"

"It is."

"Well admired, I see."

Ingeborg laughed. For Manny's bay, Joker, stood serenely inside a cloud of children, looking regal, nonchalant. Obviously the horse was convinced that it was fully worthy of all this admiration as the children patted him and fed him chunks of carrot. She decided she must put in at least one extra row of carrots next spring, just for Joker.

Benny sat in his wagon off to the side, watching.

Leaning on a crutch, Manny swung his saddle up onto Joker's back and then ducked under the horse's neck to adjust the other side.

"Look at him negotiate those crutches!" Miriam wagged her head. "It isn't that long ago that he could hardly walk. Is there some magic or something in the air here that people get well so quickly?"

Now Manny was back on this side, cinching his saddle down firmly. Clearly Manny was a good hand with horses.

Trygve brought out a box and plunked it down beside Joker. "One at a time, line up. Carl is the youngest, so he can go first. Here, Carl. Even with the box you won't be able to get up there. Let me help." And he swept Carl up and plunked him in the saddle. "I'm going to walk beside you in case you start to slide."

Carl gave Trygve a disgusted look. "I ride the big horses with Inga."

Manny grinned at Ingeborg. His delight was obvious. If he'd been a puppy, he'd have been wagging his tail to beat all get out. Ingeborg grinned right back, as wide as she could muster. He laid Joker's reins over his shoulder and hobbled off, the horse casually and obediently ambling along behind him.

Inga wormed in between Ingeborg and Miriam, but it was Miriam's hand she grasped in hers. "We need two ponies, Grandma, one for Carl and one for me. Then we could ride and not have to have help getting up on them. I asked Grandpa, but he went and died."

Miriam smiled down at Inga. "You *need* a pony?"

"Yes! Two of them. It's not nearly as much fun to ride double on one."

"Need." Miriam was smiling. Ingeborg laughed.

Inga ran off to join Emmy, who stood beside Benny. Out in the side pasture, Manny started back their way.

"She reminds me so much of my little sister," Miriam mused. "At their age, needs are completely different from ours. Sometimes it's nothing more than a new pencil."

"Ja, so true."

Miriam licked her lips. "Perhaps I am speaking out of turn, but . . . you are my hero."

Ingeborg's mouth dropped open. Their eyes met.

Miriam explained. "I have suffered a grievous loss, and so have you. But here you are hosting a dinner for the whole community, being a blessing to others, carrying on. You are loved by all because you have earned that love by loving others. I want to follow your example. It is what I want to do."

What could she say? Not often was Ingeborg at such a loss for words. "Takk. Tusen takk."

Manny and Joker arrived, and Trygve lifted Carl off. He pushed the wooden crate closer beside Joker. Inga hopped up on the crate, stuffed her foot into the stirrup with a little help, and swung up . . . well, not quite all the way. Trygve boosted her the rest of the way into the saddle.

"See what I mean, Grandma?" Inga called over her shoulder as Joker rambled off. "A shorter horse! A pony!"

"Ja, I see. Hold on tight."

Trygve turned to Emmy. "You'll be next."

Emmy shook her head. "Let me be last, or not at all. I rode horses all the time when I was little. Everyone did."

"Then, Benny, you're next."

"What?" Benny looked startled. His face softened. "Oh, I almost didn't get your joke there."

Manny took Inga out through the side pasture, the same route he had taken with Carl. As they started back, Ingeborg had to smile. She could see Inga talking a mile a minute.

Manny brought the horse back, and Inga slid off by herself.

"You want to ride?" Manny asked Benny, holding his horse by one rein.

Benny made a face. "Did you ever notice I don't have legs?"

Trygve stopped beside the boy. "Would you like to try? Manny has an idea that might work. All we can do is try."

Benny looked from Manny with the horse to the horse's back and then to Trygve. He looked just plain scared. But then his grin rivaled the sun.

"I'll tell you how we're going to do this. I don't think I can throw you up there like I did Carl, but we can do it in stages. First sit on my knee and reach for the latigos. These." Trygve showed Benny the leather straps that pulled the cinch tight.

"Then you haul yourself up, and I will help you swing one leg over."

"Might ye use some help here?" Thomas Devlin stopped beside Ingeborg.

"Good. Thanks. Together we can lift him up and slide him in place, then we are going to tie him to the saddle."

Between the two of them, they hoisted Benny into the saddle and, using the belts Trygve had brought, buckled Benny's upper legs to the stirrup leathers.

Trygve looked up at him. "What do you think? Are you comfortable?"

Benny's eyes were as round as saucers. "I am on a horse. A real big horse."

"Now, you hang on. You have plenty of strength in your arms, and probably good balance. Manny, lead him out slowly, and we'll walk beside."

With Father Devlin on one side and Trygve on the other, Manny clumped away. But he did not use his usual route. Instead, he took Benny to the edge of the baseball field, along the outfield.

Inga beamed up at Ingeborg. "Look at him, Grandma. Benny is riding! If we had a pony, he could ride easy. The pony could be his legs."

Applause started at the ball field, and pretty soon everyone was on their feet, cheering and clapping. The game came to a halt.

Grinning wildly, Benny waved to his admiring fans. The triumphant rider and his entourage returned to the barn.

Ingeborg laughed inside and out. It was the first time since Haakan died.

All was well. No, wait. Benny was slipping, his right leg sliding out from under its belt.

"Oh no!" His mother, Rebecca, started toward them with determination, her slightly swollen abdomen now evident, her husband right behind. She was due to deliver after the new year.

But Trygve had grabbed Benny's left leg and shoved him back to upright. Gerald and Rebecca walked over and stared up at their son.

"Ma, Pa, Manny made it so I could ride."

"I'm so proud of you, Benny. I never thought you could ride." Rebecca turned to Manny. "You sure know how to be a friend."

"Benny and Inga helped me when I was so sick."

Ingeborg listened to the exchange, sure her smile was as wide as theirs. She looked up to see Father Devlin smiling and nodding.

Trygve was not smiling anymore. "And to think Anner demanded we sell the boy's horse."

Ingeborg saw his jaw tighten. Somehow Anner Valders needed some wind taken out of his sails.

"Hey, let's play ball," Lars called.

Father Devlin turned to Trygve. "You can get him down by yourself, right?"

"Ja, that will be easy. Just give him a shove and splat, he's down."

"Hey!" But then Benny got the joke and laughed. Trygve and Benny undid the belt buckles. Benny slid off into Trygve's arms and got settled back in his wagon.

"Trygve," Kaaren called, "it is almost your turn to bat!"

"Coming, Mor!"

Ingeborg locked her arm through Miriam's. "If we stand right here, we can see both the children and the ball game."

"I've never been to anything like this before. Everyone is having such a good time. Wait, Ingeborg, look. There may be a problem."

Ingeborg turned to look where Miriam was pointing.

The pregnant woman from Tent Town was wagging her head and holding her swollen belly. Her husband knelt close beside her, their heads together. Miriam hastened over to them with Ingeborg right behind.

"Inga, you go find Tante Astrid!"

Inga ran off.

Miriam was kneeling with them, speaking softly.

Ingeborg settled onto the blanket also. Uff da. The man was speaking rapidly, and Ingeborg could not understand a word he was saying.

But apparently Miriam could. She straightened. "Her water just broke, and contractions are already severe. Her name is Isobel. He calls her Izzie, and this is Diarmid Munro. They are Scots. Mr. and Mrs. Munro, this is Ingeborg Bjorklund."

"Pleased to meet you," Mr. Munro said, and Ingeborg realized that they were speaking English, but with a brogue thick enough to walk on.

"How do you do." She smiled at Mrs. Munro. "I think you'd better come into the house."

Thwock!

The onlookers cheered lustily. Ingeborg and Miriam looked up to see Trygve toss his bat aside and head for first base. There went the ball, flying, flying down the pasture. The two runners ahead of him made it home and then Trygve did too. People cheered and jeered.

Trygve came trotting over to Miriam, grinning from ear to ear. He swelled his chest and arched his back. "Youth will triumph!"

Miriam made a strange noise, and it did not sound complimentary.

Trygve looked at Mrs. Munro and instantly turned serious. "Uh-oh. I'll go get the buggy."

"No." Ingeborg waved toward her front door. "This baby isn't going to wait for that jolting ride to the hospital. Mrs. Munro, come inside, please."

Mr. Munro's eyes went wide. "Oh no! We daren't do that. I'll see her to the—"

Miriam broke in, "Aye, you'll dare! Mrs. Bjorklund here has delivered hundreds of babies. She is very good at it. *Very* good! You need her help and knowledge just now, and well, I attest that her home is always open to those who need it. For your wife's sake, Mr. Munro."

He opened his mouth, closed it again. "Aye. Whatever ye say." He helped his wife to her feet and started her for the house, holding her close.

"Thank you." Ingeborg smiled at Mr. Munro. She couldn't quit smiling. "It won't be the first baby born in this house, and I hope not the last."

A life had departed this house.

A life was arriving.

Sudden tears almost buried the smile, but the smile won out.

Mrs. Munro cried out a long groan, stopped, and doubled over. Her knees buckled to the grass.

Trygve stepped forward and scooped her up into his arms. She made a startled noise and flung an arm tightly around his neck.

And Miriam felt a sudden, violent stab of jealousy. Jealousy! How ridiculous! There was absolutely no affection in the gesture, of course. Here was a woman in extremity, hanging on for dear life, being hauled into the unknown. And Miriam was jealous? For shame!

But she could not make the silly jealousy go away.

Trygve marched smartly toward the door, double time. Miriam hiked her skirts and ran ahead to hold the door for him as he carried the woman inside. Ingeborg hustled after them.

As he passed through the door, he muttered, "You know her skirts are wet, don't you?"

"Aye."

Ingeborg called, "Here comes Astrid!" She hurried inside and turned toward the kitchen.

Miriam continued holding the door as the doctor strode up onto the porch. Good! With two fine baby deliverers here, Isobel Munro had the best care possible.

Miriam followed Dr. Astrid down the hall to the main bedroom.

Trygve came out. "I'll be just outside. Let me know when you need something."

Dr. Astrid failed to say thank-you, so Miriam did. He smiled at her and left.

Miriam helped Dr. Astrid remove the skirts and petticoat. Mr. Munro knelt beside the head of the bed, and his wife clutched his arm tightly. He looked terrified.

"Have you ever assisted with a home delivery before?" Dr. Astrid asked as she completed her examination.

Miriam shook her head. "That would have been this year, but I am here instead."

"Tell me what you see." Dr. Astrid stepped back, so Miriam moved down and made her own examination. "The perineum is bulging. The baby is in the birth canal."

Ingeborg entered with an armful of sheets and pads and set them on a chair. "I'm putting my instruments on to sterilize. Want me to add yours?"

Dr. Astrid smiled to her mother. "Takk. And would you please set the tea to steeping?"

"It already is."

Dr. Astrid nodded to Miriam. "Take over."

Take over! *Who would ever have dreamed my day would go from riding the train to handling a delivery?* Nurse Korsheski had been right. She was getting experiences here like she wouldn't have anywhere else. And besides, the doctors here didn't order the nurses around like some of the others, especially Dr. Gutenheimer of Harvard, in Chicago. She'd heard even some slaves were treated better than he did the nurses.

A long throaty groan. The tiny wet-haired head presented. Good! A normal birth.

"Breathe!" Dr. Astrid stroked the woman's shoulder. "Good. Panting is good.

"Miriam, make certain that the pads are positioned properly under her. Good."

Miriam focused on the emerging baby.

"Massage the perineal tissue to help it stretch. Stroke it outward. You have seen it done. You don't want the perineum to tear. Mrs. Munro, rest as you can, and when it is time to push, breathe and push hard with the contraction."

"Ah, ah . . ." Mrs. Munro tried to stifle the scream, but it came as a drawn-out wail.

The tiny head emerged and flopped down instantly. Miriam gasped. Did the neck break? Izzie Munro gave one more agonizing push, and the baby slid into Miriam's waiting hands.

"It's a girl. You have a baby girl. Oh, she is so perfect." Miriam held up the baby by its tiny ankles, her fingers looped tightly, for the infant was so slippery. She patted the soles of her feet smartly.

The baby rattled, sucked in air, and belted out a yell fit to call cows. They all laughed through their tears, and Miriam tenderly laid the squalling infant on her mother's chest while the umbilical cord slowly stopped pumping and lay flaccid.

"Such a wee one," Izzie Munro purred. She stroked the tiny head, the minute fingers, the cheek. "Diarmid, sae tiny."

"And sae beautiful," he murmured. Tears streamed down his cheeks.

Miriam tied off the cord and cut it, watching for a moment to make certain there was no leakage.

Dr. Astrid was deeply kneading Mrs. Munro's lower abdomen. "We do this to help the uterus contract more quickly so we have less bleeding and help expel the afterbirth."

Ingeborg picked up the newborn. "Would you like to wash her?"

"Could I?" Miriam blinked back tears. "I helped birth a baby, and now I get to wash and dress her. I remember when my baby sister, Truth, was born. She was like a doll, she was so tiny. But I took care of her because my mother was too weak." She looked at Dr. Astrid.

The doctor smiled. "I'll attend the afterbirth and cleaning up."

Gently Miriam carried the tiny thing to the kitchen. The towels were waiting, the basin filled and ready, the water temperature just right.

Memories rolled over her as she gently washed each tiny finger and toe in the basin of warm water. What was her sister Truth's destiny? What course would her life take? And what would this tiny one achieve? Perhaps they would be great things, magnificent things. After the baby was diapered and fitted with a belly band, then wrapped snugly in a sheet, Miriam brought her back to the bed and nestled her in close beside her mother.

Ingeborg asked, "Mr. Munro, would you like to come to the kitchen for some tea and biscuits?"

"We must be leaving, so ye can have yer peace back."

"No. She must rest here tonight. Tomorrow, perhaps."

Miriam smiled. "Believe me, Mr. Munro, you'd be doing Mrs. Bjorklund a great favor in staying. There be more to this than you know."

He looked at his wife, and their eyes said silent volumes. He stretched over to kiss her forehead and stood erect. "Tea would be lovely."

He followed Ingeborg to the kitchen.

Dr. Astrid was smiling. "Miriam, you handled the situation perfectly. You're an old hand already."

"Surely not an old hand, but oh, I got to help my first baby into this world. And that wee one wasn't waiting on anyone. How can I thank you?"

"Believe me, we have all been there, and the awe of this miracle never goes away. I am so grateful there were no problems. Join them and have some tea. Get the details from Mr. Munro for your report."

Miriam smiled and nodded. "Thank you again." She walked out to the kitchen.

Mr. Munro looked like a wagon had run over him. Trygve, across the table from him, looked none too happy, and neither did Manny beside him. Trygve was hard at work on a wedge of apple pie—a quarter of a pie, actually—and Manny was wolfing down a sandwich. Somewhere, Mr. Munro had found the energy to split a biscuit and butter it. He poured a little milk into his tea and added a big spoonful of sugar.

Miriam sat down beside him. "Mr. Munro, this is not your wife's first birthing, is it?"

"Our fourth. Three boys, now this girl."

"Are the boys here with you?"

"Nay." He looked infinitely sad. "Our eldest died in a fishing accident two summers ago. He was out in a dory with my cousin Arvid when a squall came up and dashed them on the rocks. Both drowned. This last winter, the fever went through our town with a vengeance. We're from Stornoway, about as far north as ye get in the Outer Hebrides, and we lost the other two, as well as my mother and sister-in-law. Now it was just the two of us again, so I said, 'It's got to be better than this somewhere, aye?' And we emigrated. First to Nova Scotia, then out to here to find work."

Manny looked stunned. Miriam felt stunned. To lose his mother, sister-in-law, cousin, and all three children in two years, and to be uprooted, and . . .

Trygve smiled. "Welcome to North Dakota. I hope Blessing gives you rest and prosperity."

The man smiled suddenly, sat up a little straighter. "Things 're lookin' up already, aye?"

"They sure are."

Dr. Astrid came out and sat down. "Did Daniel take his mother home?" She poured herself a glass of water.

Ingeborg nodded. "He said he'd come back for you if you wanted." She put a wedge of pie in front of her daughter without being asked.

"Takk, Mor. No, I'll walk with Trygve and Miriam. Who won the game?"

"The old guys did." Manny shuddered and shook his head. "Can you believe that?"

"And the final score?"

"Five to three." Trygve, glum as a grave digger, wagged his head. "We had three innings with no scoring, tied up. And then Father Devlin hit a homer with one on base. End of game. Unbelievable."

"Who woulda thought some duffer that old could hit so hard?" Manny took the final bite of his sandwich. "And that cow kicked the bucket over for Andrew tonight. I think she was getting even for us being late."

Ingeborg looked at Dr. Astrid in amazement. "All that was going on when we were in there? I never heard a thing."

Dr. Astrid smiled. "We were busy, Mor."

"If there is nothing else to be done, I should probably get back to the boardinghouse." Miriam fought back a yawn. "I know I'm not on regular duty tomorrow, but I would like to go in and catch up on things, if that is all right."

"Did you sleep on the train?" Dr. Astrid asked.

"Some, but I think it is catching up with me."

"Well, the milking is done, so I'm sure Trygve won't mind walking you back, unless you want a buggy ride."

"Oh no. Walking sounds wonderful. Are the mosquitoes still around?" Miriam tried to hide another yawn. "Sorry."

Trygve pushed back his chair. "Are you sure you can walk that far?" His grin said he was teasing.

"I'll check our patient first and then I'll be ready."

"I'll set Mr. Munro up with the cot and check your patient. I'm going to sleep upstairs, so we don't have to disturb them. You go ahead." Ingeborg gave Astrid and Miriam each a hug. "Just think, we had another baby born here, like you said. We are so very blessed."

Miriam smiled back. "I'll never forget this."

"No, you won't. Your first baby will always hold a special

place in your heart. I remember mine, and it was clear back in Norway. Oh, so many years ago. I was in training to be a midwife. That's all I ever really wanted to do."

"Good night, Tante Ingeborg. Thank you for insisting we have dinner here and the ball game. Some things will never be forgotten."

"Like Benny riding the horse?" She smiled at Manny. "All thanks to you."

Manny ducked his chin. "'Twarn't nothin'." He frowned and his head kept on wagging. "We gotta help that boy."

Trygve gave Ingeborg a raised-eyebrow look.

Ingeborg asked, "Do you want a lantern?"

"No. There's plenty of moonlight." He stood up.

"I'd almost forgotten what the moon looked like when I was back in Chicago. You just never notice it much. Or maybe I'm just not usually outside after dark." Miriam accepted the shawl Ingeborg handed to her. "It's that cold out?"

"The sun goes down and it cools off fast. I'll see you tomorrow. I have errands in town." Ingeborg paused. "You do a lot of sewing, Miriam. Right?"

"I have, but not lately. At least not since I started nursing school, other than the dress I sewed for myself when I was here. Mrs. Jeffers has a very nice sewing machine."

"I thought so. Would you like to help me pick out some fabric for Emmy? All her clothes are way too small."

"I want to go over to the hospital for a while but I would be pleased to help you. I've done a lot of sewing for my sisters." She paused. "That's what I could do for Christmas—sew a dress for each of them. Surely Mrs. Jeffers would let me use her machine again."

"If not hers, you are welcome to mine. And since you like to sew, perhaps you might join our quilters. We are meeting this Thursday."

"Let me see if I'm on days or nights."

"Of course." Ingeborg patted her arm. "I hope you enjoy your room at the boardinghouse. I know Sophie and Maisie were fussing to get the furniture in those rooms right away. You know, Sophie thinks the world of you nurses. Maisie too."

"Maisie . . . Ah. You mean Mrs. Landsverk. See you tomorrow." A yawn tried to break her jaw again, so Trygve hustled her and Dr. Astrid out the door and made sure they navigated the steps safely. Patches rose from his bed on the porch, stretched, and escorted them partway down the lane before turning back.

Miriam listened as Astrid and Trygve discussed local events before her mind returned to the birthing room and seeing that baby slip right into her hands, hearing her first cry, waving her fists in the water. That baby had studied her face as intently as if memorizing her.

"Can I ask you a question, Dr. Astrid? Trygve, I know this isn't appropriate, but—"

"But things are different here, aren't they?"

She could feel the heat of his arm as he strolled beside her. "Yes, they are." *Don't think about him. Think about what you observed.* "The baby seems alert and strong. I don't remember infants being like that in Chicago."

"You're right. They aren't usually. But think how the women there live. Lack of good food, dirty air, close quarters. Many of the women who come from better districts than the tenements wear corsets, which of course should never be worn by pregnant women. There is no room for the baby to grow the way it should. They are not outside in fresh air, and the more wealth, the more they are encouraged to be fashionable." She took a deep breath. "Sorry, you got me going."

"But that makes such good sense. We try to get them to come for checkups, and even though we don't charge if they are poor, it's like . . . like . . . ." Miriam raised and dropped her hands. "They don't understand we are trying to help them, I guess."

"I lost a baby a few days ago over in the tent camp. The

couple waited too long to call me, and she'd not been eating enough—all the problems we are talking about. Mor reminded me that is why education is so important. And the only way we can educate most women is to go directly to them."

"Like you did to the reservation?"

"Yes, and now we are on our second pair of Indian nurses, who are getting minimal training, for sure, but it will make a difference. Tomorrow you will meet Gray Cloud and Dawn Breaking. I think you'll like them very much. I certainly do."

They stopped at Astrid's gate. "Thank you, Trygve. The walk has done me good."

"Thank you for letting me, uh . . ." Miriam rolled her lips together and blinked.

"I know. I know." Dr. Astrid opened her gate. "You are welcome. I do love to be part of life-changing experiences. And there are a lot of them in medicine. Good night."

Miriam and Trygve strolled over to the boardinghouse. What in the world was her hand wanting to do? Take his? What a preposterous thought. They mounted the steps, the moonlight supplemented by the lamps on the porch.

"Thank you for walking me to town."

"You're welcome. Perhaps I'll see you again tomorrow."

"Perhaps. Good night." Why did she feel as if she were fleeing as she entered the door he opened for her and headed for the stairs?

His "good-night" floated behind her.

She climbed the stairs to her room, about as weary as a body can get. Her room. Her own room!

Peek out the window.

I will not peek out the window.

Miriam sank down on the edge of the bed. Good thing she had unpacked earlier, her carpetbag now in the closet, and had taken a bath, because right now, all that sounded possible was her bed. She stared at the window. Was that whistling she heard?

Go see.

I will not!

She'd heard him whistling before. Trygve had waited to make sure her light was on. A buzzing feeling started in her toes and, like a spring flower, bloomed on her face. Hands to her cheeks, she could feel the heat of it. Her upper arm could still sense the nearness of his.

She had promised herself years ago that she would not tell lies, either to herself or to other people. The hard one was for herself. Surely she could laugh this off and pretend this attraction, for that's all it was, did not exist. Temporary puppy love.

A knock at her door brought her to her feet. She heard a giggle and smiled.

"Miriam, it's me, Corabell. Are you decent?"

"I most assuredly hope so." Blinking away her exhaustion, Miriam crossed to the door and swung it open.

Corabell threw herself into the open arms. "I was beginning to think you were going to stay in Chicago."

"You and everyone else, and I was hoping so too." Miriam drew her inside and closed the door. "How have you been?" She stepped back. "You look so much better. Where did Miss Mouse go?"

"Oh, I don't have time for her here." She drew out a covered plate. "Mrs. Landsverk said you might like a little something before bed."

Corabell never talked this much, or this fast. At least not the Corabell she knew. Vera yes, but not Miss Mouse. Miriam asked, "What has happened to you?"

"I don't think anything. I am just so glad to see you. So tell me the news from home, and where have you been?"

"When I got off the train, Trygve insisted I go to the Bjorklunds' for dinner today. There were all kinds of good things happening and a baseball game. And I got to catch a baby, and Benny—"

"Wait a minute." Corabell held up her hand. "Repeat that!"

"The mother is from Tent Town. She went into fast labor at the ball game, and Dr. Bjorklund let me do it all. Oh, Corabell, I've never had such an experience in my whole life. When that little girl slid into my hands, I held her when she took her first breath, and then she hollered like you would not believe. She is the smartest, most beautiful baby I have ever seen. I'm surprised she did not get up and walk. I got to bathe her. Oh, and I cut the cord."

Corabell leaned forward to hug Miriam. "Oh my. Only in Blessing."

"Things are indeed different here."

Corabell unwrapped the plate of bite-sized pieces of yellow cake with chocolate frosting. "The food here is divine."

"You like it better than at the Jeffers'?" Miriam popped one of the pieces into her mouth. "Oh, that is good."

"Even without coffee." Corabell took a second. "Not better. Mrs. Jeffers was so good to us there, but different. Eating in the dining room is always a treat." A grin lit her eyes, and she leaned forward to whisper. "Vera has met a man."

Miriam could feel her eyes pop wide open. "Already?"

Corabell nodded, vigorously enough to set the wisps of hair around her face to fluttering. "Dr. Deming, the dentist. He has an office at the hospital, or he will have. Right now he sees patients, not very many, at the surgery, as they call the Bjorklund house. That is Dr. Elizabeth's house, you know."

Miriam nodded. "And how is she?"

"Getting stronger, I think, but Dr. Astrid has forbidden her to come to the hospital. She has caught up on ordering supplies, and several big crates arrived last week." Corabell sat down on the edge of the bed, so Miriam did too and put the plate between them.

"And I brought more supplies from Chicago." Miriam caught a yawn, but strangling it nearly dislocated her jaw.

"Oh, I'm so sorry. You need to go to bed."

Miriam laid a hand on her arm to keep her from fleeing. "Soon, but we have so much to catch up on."

Corabell leaned over and hugged Miriam again. "I am so sorry about your mother. We all are."

Miriam blinked but failed to keep the tears from falling. "Thank you. She rallied after I got there, and I was hoping . . . but Mrs. Korsheski was right. The rally did not last." The tears took to running instead of creeping, and she cried into Corabell's shoulder. "I . . . I had the craziest dream; I dreamed she came to Blessing and danced and sang in Mrs. Jeffers' rose garden. Ma used to dance and sing."

"And now she is doing it again, only this time in heaven. She has lots to sing about there."

"I know. If I didn't have that knowledge, that hope, I think I would shut myself away in a box. I can see her and Father dancing like they did before life got so hard." *Does heaven really exist? Will God really take care of my mother?*

They visited for a few more minutes before Corabell returned to her room and Miriam prepared for bed. When she turned back the covers, she found a sachet of rose petals on the pillow. "Oh, Ma, how you would have loved it here." She carefully set the little net bag in one of her dresser drawers, where whoever unpacked her belongings had placed her unmentionables. She'd never had a closet and a chest of drawers, and a bathroom on the other side of a door. Such luxury.

CHAPTER 10

How could his world change so drastically just because a certain young woman had returned to Blessing? Trygve whistled his way back to the Gould house, Jonathan and Grace's. He liked having a room there—it was far different from his former one at the deaf school. A kerosene lamp on the table cast a welcome glow in the window when he mounted the steps.

He stopped on the porch and looked out toward where the mounds of dirt, barely visible in the moonlight, attested to his labors on the cellar. All the help he'd received made such a difference. He thought about lighting a lantern and going over to dig for another hour or so, but then thought the better of it. Getting up before daylight would be wiser.

But even when he was in bed, his mind did not want to shut down, instead replaying every moment, from the time he saw Miriam at the top of the train steps until she bade him goodnight and went to her room. He'd waited until he saw the light from her window and then, hands in his pockets, whistled his way home. She'd surely felt as tired as she looked, yet she had joined the party, which was what it had turned into, and she'd seemed to be having a good time. And then the baby!

She had an easy way with people. Even the children liked her.

During dinner Inga, of course, had asked a million questions, but that was Inga. He'd quickly realized Inga could ask questions he did not dare to, so he'd just listened. Apparently Miriam's own small sister was not much different from Inga. When she spoke of her family, he could tell how much she already missed them. And how much she missed her mother. One could be remedied, and the other would take time.

He thought of Manny. How Benny had beamed as if lit by the sun from the horse's back. Manny had put them all to shame. *I should have been thinking of ways to make things better for Benny.* Everyone was so caught up in building houses they forgot about the people.

His thoughts switched to Anner Valders. He'd heard someone mention that Anner had tried to cause more discord, but one of the other men politely shut him down. What to do about Anner? Besides wanting to plant a fist in his mean mouth. They did not need that kind of talk or feelings in Blessing. Besides, Miriam was one of "those people" Anner had railed about. That simply would not do.

Now that all the milkers were back, he'd not have to show up for milking anymore. He could work on his cellar, but he needed to talk with Thorliff or Daniel. And, of course, there was always work to be done on Jonathan's house to finish it, and to get Ingeborg's ready for winter.

When he finally drifted off, he remembered something Thorliff had said about needing more money to finish the apartment house they had started. But that was Thorliff's problem.

❧

Trygve was careful to move about quietly the next morning, trying not to awaken Jonathan and Grace. He wanted to get some digging in before he went to meet Thorliff. The roosters were crowing as he stepped out to the porch, but he turned when he heard Jonathan call his name.

"Good morning. Didn't expect you up yet."

Jonathan shrugged into a light jacket. "Thought I could help you for a while. Then after breakfast, we could work on the flooring of the back stoop. If that's all right with you?"

"Of course."

At the end of the hour, they climbed back out of the hole and turned to see how much they'd done. They'd made good progress.

"I'll be back to town in time for breakfast," Trygve said as he turned right, heading out to the farms.

Jonathan frowned. "I thought you weren't on the milking crew."

"I can be if they need me, but Lars said they had plenty of help. Samuel is taking my place. I'm going out to make sure Tante Ingeborg doesn't need anything."

Jonathan nodded. "That's where I'm headed too. She's not just in grief. She's slowed down by grief. Doesn't get everything done. Grace said to be back in an hour and a half and she would have breakfast ready."

"Grace is cooking breakfast?"

"Yes. She assures me she has not forgotten how to cook. But I'm thinking of looking for some household help. Do you know anyone?"

Trygve shook his head. "You might ask Ingeborg or Mor. They know just about everybody."

"Gud dag," Ingeborg said when they came through the back door.

"Good morning." Trygve also greeted Freda, who was eating, along with Manny and Emmy.

"I will put two plates on." Emmy looked at them as she stood.

Trygve raised his hand. "Not today. Grace is making breakfast. We're just checking to see if you need anything. Has anyone gotten to caulking your windows yet? And liming the outhouse?"

A whistle came from outside. Ingeborg nodded. "Samuel is here. You better get going, Manny, Emmy."

"I know." Manny pushed back his chair and grabbed his crutches while Emmy picked up both lunch pails, and out the door they went, Manny hollering thank-you over his shoulder.

Trygve stared at Ingeborg. "What happened? He didn't grumble."

Freda shrugged. Ingeborg smiled. "I think he has something up his sleeve. Your question, Trygve. There are always things to do here. Dig the potatoes—the tops are shriveled and ready—and no, I didn't lime the outhouse yet. The windows are caulked, but some gaps in the siding need filling. The wood shrank over the summer."

From out in the lane, Emmy's cheerful voice called, "Good morning, Mr. Munro!"

A gruff Scots brogue replied, "And to yorself, Miss Emmy!" A buggy rattled to a halt out beyond the porch.

Jonathan headed for the door. "I'll get some caulk and shims to patch your siding."

Trygve smiled at Ingeborg. "I'll be by with a bag of lime this afternoon. And then maybe get to the potatoes tomorrow. See you later." He swung the front door open. "Mr. Munro, good morning!"

Mr. Munro beamed. "Good morning!" He looked happy, even elated, and well he should. Last night he had drooped, as glum as Trygve and Manny. Of course, his baseball team had not just lost a game they should have won. "Mr. Valders gave me an hour off to fetch the missus and me wee bairn."

"I see Toby even loaned you his buggy. He's a good man, Toby Valders."

"He is that!"

Why can't Toby's father be so nice?

Mr. Munro continued inside and the two men headed down the lane back to town.

Trygve caught Jonathan up on some of the things that had gone on in Blessing while he was north with the threshing crew.

The boardinghouse was pretty much finished, and fall work would be starting now that threshing was finished. The corn was ready to be picked, shucked, and stored in the corncribs for winter feed. They would feed the stalks to the cattle. Once it turned cold, butchering would come next.

Jonathan and Trygve climbed the stoop to the Gould house.

"I thought you would never get here," Grace said in her slow speech, while her fingers flew in the signs. "Get washed."

Trygve knew Jonathan had been learning sign language ever since he decided he was in love with Grace, but Grace insisted she needed to keep speaking aloud, or her skills would get rusty.

The men sat down at the table in the kitchen, and Grace served scrambled eggs with ham, toasted bread, applesauce, and fried potatoes. She filled their coffee cups and sat down herself. Jonathan said grace, and Trygve marveled that his sister had not forgotten how to cook. Especially after her years at the deaf school on the East Coast, where she taught.

"This is mighty good."

"You are surprised?" she asked.

Trygve shook his head. "No, but you've—"

"I would not pursue that line of thought, if I were you." Jonathan smiled at his wife, who cocked her head, questions parading across her face.

"I will be working with new students at the school today," Grace told the men. She taught the lessons in signing so that the new students, of which there were six this year, could soon attend the Blessing school, where classes were signed as well as spoken. In the afternoon she taught signing to new pupils that could hear, since all the children learned sign language.

Jonathan held out his mug for a refill. "I'll be helping Lars this afternoon after I talk with Thorliff. I'll get to Ingeborg's siding probably tonight or tomorrow. Grace, do you want me to bring you anything from the store?"

She shook her head.

Trygve finished his breakfast. "Thank you. If you tell me what you want done here, I'll help with that in the next day or so."

Grace and Jonathan shared a glance, reminding Trygve what married life could be like. He thought of Miriam. How was her day going? Could they someday have a home and family?

"I'll make a list." Jonathan drained his coffee cup. "Let's go see Thorliff."

The three left the house at the same time. How different from home.

They found Thorliff in the newspaper office, just finishing printing the paper for the week.

"Done. Lemuel will be here any minute to deliver the bundles around town." He wiped his hands on a rag and, taking some twine, started tying the stacks together. Trygve, who had helped before, pulled off a length of twine and started in. They'd just finished when Lemuel, the son of Mr. Sam, the blacksmith, and Mrs. Sam, chief cook for the boardinghouse, arrived pulling a flatbed buckboard. He stacked the bundles of papers on it and, with a grin, headed out.

"Where all does he deliver them?" Jonathan asked.

"Oh, the boardinghouse, the mercantile, the post office, the railroad station, the grocery store . . ." Thorliff rubbed his forehead, leaving a smudge of black ink. "The hospital." He pointed to a rack by the door with a stack of papers on it. "And here, of course."

He looks like he's aged ten years, Trygve thought. Or more.

"Good game yesterday." Thorliff leaned back against the raised counter, rubbing his forehead again.

Both Jonathan and Trygve groaned. "How come no one said Father Devlin could hit like that? We should have won it."

"Let's go have some coffee. Knowing Thelma, cookies or something should be coming out of the oven about now."

"Have you heard anything about those letters to Norway? Is anyone coming?" Jonathan asked.

"No, and I'm surprised."

Scooter, Inga's little dog, barked and wagged a greeting. They sat down on the porch, and like magic, Thelma brought out the coffeepot and a plate of apple cookies.

"How'd you know we were coming?"

"I saw Lemuel haul off the papers. You always come for coffee after that."

"Of course. How is Elizabeth?"

"She's working in the front room. Astrid is here seeing patients."

"She's not overdoing it, is she?"

"No, she is being careful and promised to go lie down if she feels tired."

"Good." Thorliff slumped against the cushion back. "The year's getting old. Won't be much longer we can meet out here."

Trygve prodded. "You were asking earlier about help, Jonathan."

"With Grace spending so much time at the deaf school and me working too, we need some help. Someone who can cook and clean. Do they make replicas of Thelma anywhere?"

"You aren't the first to ask. I'll ask Mor to follow up with another letter to her relatives. It's not like them not to answer." Thorliff set his cup on the table and rubbed his eyes with the heels of his hands. "I had trouble with the press last night, so printing took longer than usual." He reached for one of the still-warm cookies. "I don't think I had breakfast, and I'm not sure about supper last night."

"Ask Thelma. She'll know."

Trygve set his cup on the table. "I need to figure out what I am going to do now that I am done with the milking. Do you need a hand on one of your construction sites?"

"Did the sun come up this morning?" Thorliff reached for his second cookie and took a swig of coffee to wash it down. "Of course I need help. What about your house?"

"I'll have to do that on my own time. I'm trying to help

Tante Ingeborg too, and Sophie needs this and that over at the boardinghouse. She's doing the best she can, but there's just too much with getting the units finished and furnished. I tend to a lot of the little jobs there, but that's all for free. What I need, frankly, is a job that pays money, if I am going to buy a house."

"Have you thought about which model yet?"

"I thought the two-story box one. When I have a family, we'll need the extra room."

"You're thinking ahead."

Trygve smiled. Well, yes, he was. Thanks to Miriam. "I have a good portion of it in the bank, but I will have to get a loan for the remainder. I felt like I was needed here, so I didn't go out for Hjelmer again, you know."

"I know. He was downright angry there for a bit." Thorliff raised his cup when Thelma brought the pot around again.

"I kept a plate warm for you. Do you want it now?"

"I guess so. These guys already ate breakfast." They both nodded.

Trygve asked, "Where is Hjelmer now?"

"Off selling wells and windmills." Thorliff dug into the plate set before him. "I could put you on the crew working on the apartment house, or one of the three individual houses. Which do you prefer? Toby Valders is heading the crew on the apartment house. Those six units have to be done before winter. Six families from the tent camp could live there. How about you report to him tomorrow morning?"

"Standard carpenter's pay?"

"Ja."

"Sounds good. I will."

"And, Jonathan, are you helping Lars, or can I put you to work too?"

"I don't know. I'll be helping with the corn and digging potatoes, and we are finishing up the new dormitory section. So many new students applied we had to turn them away."

He grinned. "I never had any idea how much work still needed to be done in the fall. But then, I always was back to school by now. Funny. Here I have a college education in agriculture, and they never taught about how much plain old work is involved. It was all theories."

Thorliff nodded. "My father brought us over from the old country so that we could build a farm, something we couldn't do in Norway. He too failed to mention how much work that takes. Even when I was very little, I learned to feed animals and chickens and keep the woodbox full. I loved the sheep best back then."

Jonathan grimaced. "And I am just finding out."

The end of the day. At last. Thorliff was ready for it. More than ready for it. He clomped up the back steps to his porch.

Elizabeth was sitting at the table on the porch with an empty coffee cup and a pile of mail. She beamed as he approached. A glorious smile. Glorious woman.

He kissed her and sat down. "You look good. Rosy-cheeked."

"I feel good." She handed him several letters. "These are for you."

He looked at one from the bank. "Ah. Here's the loan extension. Good." He hooked his thumb in a corner and ripped it open.

Thorliff unfolded the single page. There should have been more than one sheet for a loan reset. He read the page again and slammed it down on the table. "That overblown piece of horse manure! Who in the world does he think he is?"

"What is it?" Elizabeth stared at him openmouthed.

"Valders . . . that . . ." Thorliff snatched up the letter and stormed down off the porch, out into the street. Valders was standing at the front door of the bank just locking up.

Thorliff marched double-quick over to him, blocking the man's way. He waved the letter in Anner's face. "What is this?"

"I believe it is clear enough. I'm denying your loan request."

"You can't do that!" Thorliff was yelling. And he didn't care.

"I examined your loan records and repayment schedule. You are overextended. Pay down your existing obligations, and I'll consider giving you more money."

"I remind you that the community owns this bank so that we have a pool of funds to build with. You were hired to manage those funds, not play God, and you cannot—"

"I was hired to take care of that money, and in my considered opinion, giving you more money when you already owe so much would be foolhardy. The matter is closed." He turned away and started walking.

Thorliff was too angry to think. He grabbed Anner's lapel and stopped him, pulling him around to face him. Thorliff realized his fist was drawn back ready to smash this infuriating popinjay in the face, but he hesitated. Anner's eyes widened in terror. The little man shrank aside.

And that terror pleased Thorliff! He wanted Anner to feel some of the intense emotion he felt himself. "The matter is not closed! I filed the request so that you would have a record of it on paper. Anner Valders, you do *not* have the authority to either grant or deny that request! You process it! Period!" He shoved Anner back and let go of the coat. Anner nearly fell.

Anner appeared as frightened as Thorliff wanted him to feel. "F-first you d-d-defend a bank robber c-caught in the act and then you let him off with no consequences at all, and now you threaten me! Thorliff Bjorklund, you will never get another penny from this bank!" He scuttled away so fast he was almost running.

Thorliff desperately wanted to run after him, to punch him, to somehow spend this fury that was boiling up and over.

Jonathan came charging up. "Thorliff! What in heaven . . . ?" He was huffing and puffing. "I saw you from up the street, but

I couldn't get here in time. You nearly beat him up! What's going on?"

"I don't know." Thorliff wagged his head. He wanted to punch somebody. Hit anything. He could not settle his nerves.

What now? They needed that money. Winter was coming quickly, flying at them, like the cold winds that would soon blow fiercely. All those people in the Tent Town—women and children as well as men. They depended on Thorliff, on Blessing. If they could not find shelter, they would leave, go somewhere with warm houses and better chances for survival.

And everything Thorliff and all these others were working for would disappear like smoke in a wind.

CHAPTER 11

Breakfast in the dining room was another experience altogether, with a pretty young girl placing a basket of hot rolls on her table, which had a yellow rose in a small bud vase. Did they have a rose garden out behind the boardinghouse? She should remember the girl's name. *Lily Mae.* That was it. Miriam inhaled the fragrance and smiled at Lily Mae, who set a plate of fried pork chop, eggs, and fried potatoes in front of her.

"All this?"

"Yes, miss." Her smile seemed even brighter next to her dark skin.

"Oh my goodness. This is enough for three people."

"No one goes away hungry from our dining room."

"Please thank the cook."

"Oh, I will. Our cook is my ma. They calls her Mrs. Sam. We been here since Miss Sophie took over the boardinghouse. They's quite a story here, you know." When a man from another table motioned her, she smiled again. "You call if'n you wants somethin' else."

Miriam stared out the front window as she finished her breakfast. She returned to her room, grabbed a sweater, and then left

106

for the hospital. Mrs. Bjorklund would be by later too. What a day this was already turning into.

Stepping into the hospital door was like coming home. The thought made her shake her head. She'd not been there long enough to feel that way, surely not.

"Well, look who's here." Corabell's grin filled her face. "I thought you might sleep until noon."

"Thanks, but I was too excited."

"Excited? To come to work?"

"I guess so. And I was hungry. I thought I'd see Vera in the dining room."

"She was beat. Said she was going straight to bed." Corabell waved a hand apparently at random. "Miriam Hastings, this is Gray Cloud, and this is Dawn Breaking. They came to Blessing while you were gone."

"How do you do." Miriam smiled at Gray Cloud, whose amazing hair was very black and very thick and—to be envied—very straight and looked easy to braid. She nodded and almost smiled. Dawn Breaking, with hair just as straight and lustrous, smiled far more readily and was more fluent in English. She was carrying an armload of sheets from the clothesline, so the two set to folding them. Thanks to the North Dakota breeze, they didn't even need to iron them.

"Has Dr. Astrid been in yet?"

"Oh yes. She always comes before the shift change. We don't have very many patients right now, so Gray Cloud and I have been reviewing the last lessons. She is getting really good at bandaging and taking vitals. Dr. Astrid told us about the new baby. She said you did a really good job."

"I'll never forget it." Miriam looked around. "I thought I'd read through the charts and get acquainted for tomorrow. Is there anything else I should know?"

Corabell shrugged. "Gray Cloud and I are counting medications for the order, and I have to make sure all the charts are up to date. Vera got the last of the crates emptied and put away last night. You're on days tomorrow, right? Dr. Astrid is going to teach the triage process tomorrow right after breakfast so the night shift can stay for it. She insists we have to be ready for any emergency. I'm not sure what kind of emergency we could have here, but we will be ready."

Miriam spent the next hour going through the charts and writing herself notes. She wandered around the hospital, stopping in the kitchen to chat with Mrs. Geddick, who had been the cook ever since the hospital opened.

"It smells so good in here," Miriam said after the greeting.

"Nothing smells as good as bread just out of the oven." Mrs. Geddick tipped the loaf pans on their sides when she set them on the counter, and when all of them were out of the oven, she flipped them over and set the loaves on top of the racks. Then dipping her fingers in the dish of butter, she spread it on the loaves. "I bake bread now for the grocery store too. They say mine is almost as good as Ingeborg's." Her smile showed one missing front tooth.

"From what I hear, that is the best compliment someone can give you. What does she do that is different?"

Mrs. Geddick shrugged. "Will you be here for dinner?"

"No, but I will be tomorrow. I'll be back to work on days for this week."

"Welcome home."

"Thank you." She turned when she heard someone calling her name and returned to the hall.

"Are you ready?" Ingeborg asked.

"I am." She waved good-bye to the others, and the two of them strolled out the door and down Main Street. "What are you planning to make for Emmy?"

"I thought two dresses, two jumpers, a skirt, and a waist. I started knitting her a sweater. The one she has comes just below her elbows. I think someone washed it in hot water."

108

"I never learned to knit. My mother was a beautiful and very popular dressmaker. She sewed for some of the wealthier folks in Chicago. We all learned fine stitching and always helped with the hems. Even with the sewing machine, we spent hours hemming those full skirts on ball gowns and fancy dresses. I knew I wanted to learn to be a nurse, partly, I think, so I wouldn't have to spend the rest of my life hemming."

Ingeborg smiled and patted her arm. "From what I hear, you made a wise choice."

"How are baby Munro and mother doing?"

"Just fine. We can stop and see them if you'd like."

They walked in silence a short while. Then Miriam asked, "The party Sunday. Do people in Blessing always have such a good time together?"

"Well, not everyone was there, of course, but I so enjoyed how many came after dinner for the ball game. I didn't expect that."

"Probably everyone knows winter is coming and there won't be too many more days like that." Together they mounted the steps to Blessing Mercantile and pushed open the door, setting the overhead bell to tinkling.

"Well, look who's here." Penny Bjorklund came around the end of the battle-scarred counter. "How can I help you this morning?" She held out both of her hands, her smile brightening the entire room.

"I realized yesterday that Emmy's clothes are far too short and too tight. How remiss of me not to notice that earlier. So Miriam is here to help me choose materials for some new clothes. Have you two met?"

"Oh yes. Miriam came to visit me not long after they arrived and purchased fabric for a summer dress. She realized shirtwaists and wool skirts were too warm for our summers."

Miriam smiled. "I wore that dress every day. It was so light I could rinse it out at night and wear it again in the morning. Our nurses' aprons cover it all anyway."

Penny nodded and started down an aisle. "Well, come over here. I just got a shipment of corduroy and some wools in—shirt flannel too. I have a blue plaid that will look very nice on Emmy. And I know she loves red. I have that in corduroy for a jumper."

As she spoke, she pulled out the bolts of fabric and set them on the cutting table.

Ingeborg studied them. "I think that blue would be nice for a jumper too and probably the brown for a skirt. If we used the flannel for a dress with long sleeves, that would be warm."

Miriam nodded and fingered the brown wool serge. "This should be warm too. What about a vest?"

"She loves wearing her deerskin dresses with leggings. But they are all small too. I can put a gusset in the things I've made and add a flounce, but I don't have deerskin to add to her other things."

Penny tapped her chin with one finger. "You know, I think I have some things of Linnea's packed away. I know I gave some to . . . hmm, can't think who. I'll see if I can find them. Things got mixed up when we moved back from Bismarck."

"I thought to wash her Indian things and pack them away for her. Someday she might want them."

"Is she really going to be staying with you permanently now?"

"Yes. Isn't our God merciful? Her uncle could have just kept her in the tribe, and we'd not have heard from them again."

"He is a wise man. That's for sure."

Ingeborg turned to Miriam and gave her a very brief history of Emmy's situation while Penny cut the fabrics and they decided on a couple of trims.

They were just finishing up when Mrs. Magron set the bell to tinkling.

"I'll be right there," Penny sang out. She folded all the goods and carried them to the counter to total up the amount.

"I'm going to pay cash today," Ingeborg said. "You needn't put it on credit."

"You sure?"

Ingeborg nodded and turned to the dumpy little lady waiting. "Mrs. Magron, what are you making today?"

"Oh, I started a coat and didn't get enough material. I'm hoping Penny still has some of it left."

"You'll be at quilting on Thursday?"

"Oh ja. It has been too long since we met."

Ingeborg turned to Miriam. "Have you met Mrs. Magron? She and her husband have a farm south of town."

Miriam smiled, but the other woman only nodded, and that a bit stiffly.

"Miriam Hastings is one of our nursing students."

"I know." Mrs. Magron turned to Penny. "I think I will come back later. I forgot . . . I think I need to bring in what I have so we can make sure it matches." She turned and nearly ran out the door.

Ingeborg stared after her. "What was that all about?" She frowned at Penny. "Mrs. Magron is so quiet and sweet, usually a peacemaker. Why the sudden change?"

"Hildegunn and Mr. Valders?" Penny said softly. She emphasized the *mister*.

Miriam felt like she'd been kicked in the shins. Had that really been about her? What was going on?

"We'll see about this," Ingeborg murmured.

"Please, don't pay any attention." Miriam tried to smile. She touched Ingeborg's arm. "Let's go see the Munros." Miriam tried to convince herself the woman was just shy, but somehow that rang false, even to her.

CHAPTER 12

I was so angry. She caught me by surprise."

"Mrs. Magron really acted like that?" Kaaren stared at Ingeborg.

"I know. That was so unlike her." Ingeborg shook her head, sadness weighing her shoulders. "I couldn't even talk to you about it yesterday. I was so upset." She wrapped both hands around her coffee cup. "You know it has to be because of Hildegunn. She's been spreading Mr. Valders' feelings, and division has come to Blessing. Thorliff is so angry at Anner, he won't even talk about it, at least not with me. We have to stop this somehow."

"But how?" Kaaren studied her coffee cup. The chilling rain outside drummed on the porch roof, a cloud that burst after Kaaren had walked over to Ingeborg's. They so rarely had times together like this anymore, especially after classes started at the deaf school. She nodded and looked directly into Ingeborg's eyes. "Reverend Solberg will say our first step is prayer."

"I know, and I have been praying." Ingeborg strangled her coffee cup. "But this one is so hard because Anner went after one of my children. I know Thorliff is a grown man and this is his battle, but he's still my son." The tears welled over. "And he is going through so much right now, even before this." She stared at her fingers, and her voice dropped further. "How can I go to quilting and face Hildegunn?"

"I don't want to go to the post office, let alone the bank. I have a deposit to make, but I *do not* want to see Anner." Kaaren's jaw visibly tightened.

"So what do we do?" Ingeborg knew she was asking God the question at the same time.

Wait.

She stared at Kaaren. "Did you hear that?" The voice had been so clear.

"No. What?"

"I thought maybe you said it, but . . ." Ingeborg shook her head. "I heard *wait*. Just that one word. Wait." She stared at Kaaren, whose eyes must have matched her own, round and astonished. A smile forced its way through her tears. "You know how much I hate to wait."

"And yet, that is the answer we've been given." Kaaren held up a hand, her flat palm toward Ingeborg. "I know. The next questions would be, 'Wait how long and for what?' But we have both learned through the years not to ask those."

"We have?" Ingeborg let her mind travel inward. Waiting. So often lately she was waiting for the tears to dry up, waiting for the promised peace to wrap around her to ease her aching heart. How to praise God and thank Him when she missed Haakan so fiercely. All she could do was teeter on the edge of the pit that yawned at times and scream for Him to help her. "I think I will just stay home."

"I thought you invited Miriam to come with you."

"I did, but she is on the day shift. And Vera will be sleeping, and Corabell will be working with Gray Cloud and Dawn Breaking. Astrid asked if I could go help them too, so I will do that." She blew her nose. "Quit looking at me like that."

"You know Astrid forgot we had quilting."

Ingeborg shook her head, the tears gathering force. "I just can't take any more right now. I can't."

Kaaren patted her hand as the tears flowed, crying right along with her. Ingeborg's hand turned over and gripped Kaaren's as if it were the last resort before the pit sucked her in.

She finally calmed enough to hear Kaaren's gentle voice. "'He maketh me to lie down in green pastures: He leadeth me beside the still waters. He restoreth my soul.'"

One part of her wanted to join in on the gentle words, but another part wanted to leap up and run out the door. Or scream at her to stop. Sometimes she feared the tears would never stop, but she mopped again, realizing the worst had passed.

"You'd think I would be beyond all this."

"Why?"

"I'm older. I should be wiser. When I thought ahead to Haakan leaving me, I figured I would just be able to trust that God has it all in His hands and—"

"You wouldn't feel the horrid pain of grief?"

"I guess. After all, I've been here before. God saved me from the pit before, and I know He will do the same now, again, but then the grief leaps out of nowhere and grabs me, tries to choke me. Sometimes that is what it feels like. I know I am not alone, but it sure feels like it."

"And we know that faith is stronger than feelings. We know the end of the story, we know Jesus is walking right with us, that He already won the war."

"Right. I do know those things. I believe those things. I know God loves me and will not let me go. I know that."

Kaaren stood and wrapped her arms around Ingeborg. "We trust Him and we give Him thanks and praise that He is right here with us, crying with us, laughing with us, giving us good memories."

Ingeborg allowed herself to relax into Kaaren's arms and

against her waist. "Thank you, Father," she whispered, "for my sister Kaaren." She wiped her eyes again. "Thank you for coming over today."

"You are welcome. I see Freda is on her way back from the cheese house."

"Can you stay a while longer?"

"I better get on home before the rain starts again. I need to be there for dinner." She stepped back. "I will stop with the buggy tomorrow to pick you up for quilting."

"I might not go."

"Oh, you will. You know I need someone praying for me when I open the meeting." Kaaren was the elected leader of the quilting group this year, so she had to run the business part of the meetings. "It's probably a good thing I am in charge, or I wouldn't go either. Oh, and if I remember right, you have the devotions."

Ingeborg groaned. "I forgot. O Lord, I can't do that. Not without crying."

"So cry." Kaaren swung her shawl around her shoulders as Freda came in the back door. "See you tomorrow. It sure rained there for a bit, didn't it?"

Freda set her basket on the counter. "Tell Lars that the soft cheese he wanted will be ready tomorrow."

"Good. He's been wanting that for some time. Are you going to make gjetost this fall? I heard someone asking about that."

Freda looked to Ingeborg. "We've not decided for sure. Let me see how many requests we get for that." Ingeborg stood and hugged Kaaren good-bye. "Takk. Tusen takk. I'll let you know about tomorrow."

"Let her know what?" Freda asked.

Kaaren answered. "If she is going to quilting."

Freda frowned and shook her head. "We will see you in the morning. I already have the soup started."

"I was supposed to bring the soup too?" Ingeborg shuddered.

"How much more have I forgotten?" *Yet I remember other things. Truly, how much have I forgotten? Important things? Lord, what do I do now? What if I did forget something really important?* She stepped out onto the back porch and watched Kaaren make her way home, sidestepping puddles in the lane. A breeze shook drops from the tree above down onto the porch roof, some so large they almost thudded. The downspout still gurgled into the rain barrel. Inhaling the fragrance of clean air through leaves turning gold, she stared out across the harvested fields.

The garden was nearly all picked and in except for the late potatoes and the carrots. The carrots would be safe in the garden until the ground began to freeze. They stayed fresher that way than down in the cellar. When they finally dug them, they would cover them with sand in a bin next to the squash.

She spent the rest of the day cutting out a jumper for Emmy and stitching it up on the sewing machine in her bedroom. She'd moved it in there when Haakan had spent more time in bed so she could keep him company. As the days grew colder, she would move it back to either the kitchen or the parlor near a stove. The treadle's song was always a conductor of peace.

"Grandma, where are you?"

She smiled at the sound of Emmy's voice. "In here sewing."

Both Emmy and Manny charged into her room with cookies in hand. As usual, Freda had left out a plate for them.

"Grandma, guess what?" Manny leaned on his crutches and swallowed the remainder of his cookie, trying to talk around it. "Dr. Astrid is on her way out here."

"In a wagon?"

"No, walking. She waited for Inga to ask her mor if she could come. That's all right?"

"Of course." She finished the seam and clipped the threads. "Here, Emmy, you need to try this on." She held up the first stages of the red jumper. "There's milk or buttermilk in the icebox, Manny. Please pull the coffeepot to the hot end."

"You want wood in the stove?"

"Ja, good idea." When he headed out, she motioned for Emmy to close the door. "We can pull this over what you have on." After settling it in place, she leaned back. "Good. Turn around and let me see the whole thing."

Emmy's eyes shone. "Really for me?"

"I figured for a deep hem. Then we can let it out as you get taller." She pulled the jumper back over Emmy's head. "You go eat now."

"Dr. Astrid's here."

Ingeborg had long ago realized what sharp hearing Emmy had. Besides, the girl paid attention to things like Patches barking his welcome to announce family. She'd heard that, but it didn't really register. She followed Emmy out to the kitchen.

"Grandma, I'm here!" Inga's cry barely preceded her charge into her grandmother's arms. "You been sewing?"

"I sure have. Emmy's outgrowing all her clothes, so I'm sewing for her."

Inga nodded. "Emmy likes red best of all." She grinned at Ingeborg. "I like blue better."

"Really?" Ingeborg kissed the tip of her nose. "I never knew that."

Astrid stopped in the kitchen doorway. "How wonderful it is to see you sewing."

"Emmy has outgrown everything. It took me a while to realize it." Ingeborg reached for a mug. "Do you have time for coffee?"

"Is the sky blue?"

"Well, it sure wasn't earlier today. What brings you out here?"

"Can't a girl want to see her mother?"

"You're not a girl," Inga said with a frown. "You are all grown up."

"You're right. I'll be more careful with my speech. Actually, I came to see Manny."

"You already saw him."

117

"I know, but I have an idea."

Manny looked up from reaching for another cookie. "For me?"

"Ja, for you. I have something for you to try." She pulled two canes out of a long sack. "Maybe it is time for you to put away the crutches."

His eyes rounded, and a grin split his face. "No more crutches?"

Ingeborg checked to see if the coffee was hot, all the while watching Manny's delight.

"Let's see how you do with these. Maybe one might be enough."

He leaned his crutches against the table and stood straight in front of her. He took a cane in each hand.

"Now, you keep the cane straight with your legs." She studied the canes and watched to see the height of them. "We might need to cut a little off the bottoms. See the angle of the arm? Mor, what do you think?"

"Go ahead and walk with them, Manny, and let's see."

The boy fumbled with them but then got the idea. "One step at a time." He nodded as he talked.

"Do you ever walk without your crutches?"

"Not much. But sometimes a step or two. Like down at the barn when I'm milking."

"I want you to try with only one." She showed him how to hold the cane with his left hand and take the step on his right leg at the same time as the cane. "See, this way your healing leg gets supported."

"My papaw used a cane. He got around real good." Manny walked with the one cane.

"Does your leg hurt?"

"No. It ain't hurt for a long time. Lessen I bang it or something."

"Okay. Sit back down here and let me check some. Can you pull your pant leg up?"

Astrid palpated the leg firmly and watched his face to see if he flinched. She pressed harder along the incision scar, but he looked right at her and shook his head.

"I told you it don't hurt."

"Stand and put your weight evenly on both feet."

He did as she asked.

"Hurt now?"

"A mite."

She could tell he hated to say that, but at least he was honest. "How big a mite?"

He made a face and shrugged his shoulders. "Hard to say."

"Now I want you to walk across the floor using the cane. Take it easy."

His gait was uneven, due to the shorter leg, but he seemed to be putting his weight on it correctly.

She squinted in thought. "All right, Manny, here's what we're going to do. Now, I have to be able to trust you on this. Use the cane, but if your leg starts to really hurt, go back to the crutches. I'm not talking about sore muscles, but right at the break site. And if there is any swelling. Also, I want you to use the cane around here but crutches for school for a bit longer. It will take some time to get that right leg as strong as the other leg."

"Thank you."

"No running. Promise me."

He nodded. "I promise."

Ingeborg smiled to herself. She could see how hard it was for him to say that, but she had learned that Manny kept his word. She looked over to see the two little girls watching everything. That Inga had kept from asking questions was a miracle alone.

"I can walk out to get a carrot for Joker. Did you hear him whinny when he saw me? He thought I already got a carrot."

"You sure can."

He walked slowly to the door, as if not as assured as he tried to be.

"Can we go gather the eggs?" Emmy asked.

"Of course. Throw the hens some of that cracked corn."

The two girls skipped out the door, their self-imposed silence replaced with giggles and chatter, as if they'd not seen each other for a week.

"Thanks for coming out for this. We need another celebration." Ingeborg poured their cups full and refilled the cookie plate.

"Where's Freda?"

"Gone over to help Kaaren with something. How's Elizabeth?"

"Feeling better. She has some color back in her face and wants to come to the hospital. I said no. So she is not happy with her doctor right now. I am not taking any chances. That's all there is to it. She's worried about Thorliff, and he's worried about her, and I might have to go poke a hole in that Anner's head and let all the swelling drain out."

Ingeborg rolled her lips together. Then when Astrid gave her an innocent look, she laughed outright.

"You're laughing, Mor. I've not heard you laugh since . . . for too long."

"It would take a mighty strong needle." Ingeborg barely kept a straight face.

"Are you saying Anner Valders is hardheaded? Along with a swelled-head syndrome?" The two grinned at each other. Oh, the laughter did indeed feel good.

Strange how not many hours ago she was teetering on the edge of the pit and crying her eyes raw but now she was able to laugh. Was this God's comfort and healing in action?

Ingeborg hoped so. She needed it so badly.

CHAPTER 13

I'm sorry, but I am doing what my doctor ordered." The tone was polite but underlaid with glass shards.

Astrid watched carefully as Elizabeth slammed her pillows against the headboard. She had been doing so well. Was this a step backward or just a puddle like those left by the rain yesterday? The lowering skies today hinted at more weather. The thunder on the brow more than hinted at Elizabeth's frame of mind.

"Peace goes a long way toward gaining strength." Astrid kept her tone mild and conversational.

"What are we going to do about Anner Valders?"

Astrid ordered herself not to throw kerosene on the fire. "So that is what is bothering you?"

"One of several things, yes!"

Astrid felt like her mor as she sent her request for peace and wisdom heavenward. *A kind word turneth away wrath*. How many years ago had she memorized that one? True, the correct word was *soft* but she thought *kind* fit too. "I don't have any idea. The men are meeting tonight?" She beat off the nagging thought that women should be included also.

"Yes." Elizabeth sucked in and released a deep breath and

then leaned her head back against the pillows. Eyes closed, she nodded slightly. "One of the things I have always loved about Blessing is that mostly people care for one another here. Sure, there have been minor scuffles and hurt feelings, but nothing like this. First the bank robbery, and now what I think is vindictiveness, bitterness."

"But why? Why would Anner be bitter toward Thorliff? I know he gave a business reason, but you believe it is more than that?"

"Oh, I do. You know how furious Anner was when we wouldn't sell Manny's horse? Well, before that, it was because we took the bank robber boy in. He took that bank robbery as a personal attack on him."

"Well, he was wounded trying to save the money."

"True, and he was given a hero's thank-you by the town. But . . ."

Astrid watched and waited. Was she so naïve she didn't suspect that? After all, she had grown up with respect for the man. He did a good job with the bank and the community trusted him, but he'd never been one of the real leaders of the town. Just Anner Valders who managed the bank, a quiet man. But bitter? Vindictive? Hildegunn had always seemed to be the mouth of the two, the bossy one.

"And he was furious because so many threw in money to pay the fifty-five dollars back to the bank so Manny could keep his horse." She nodded, aware she was thinking out loud. "But why Thorliff? Mor put in money too. I don't even remember who else. I thought it was a real show of community caring."

"Thorliff started it. He was the one who really confronted Anner."

"But it wasn't even Anner's money." Astrid shook her head in confusion.

"But *his* bank."

"I guess I am having a hard time understanding this. He's

not even one of the town leaders." Her thoughts took off to explore the idea.

The real leaders were Haakan; Lars; Reverend Solberg; and now Thorliff, who ran the newspaper; Hjelmer; Daniel Jeffers, who brought in the machinery company; and Garth Wiste, who ran the flour mill. The real business owners of the town were mostly women: Sophie with the Blessing Boardinghouse; Penny owned the Blessing Mercantile; Ingeborg, the Blessing Cheese Company; Rebecca, the Blessing Soda Shoppe; Tante Kaaren started the deaf school; and now Dr. Elizabeth and herself. Blessing was indeed an unusual place.

The bank was community-owned. Those whose money was there were the owners, and that was most of the town. Astrid thought back, trying to remember how it was set up. She knew she had a paper saying that because she had an account there, she had a vote at the yearly meeting. Other meetings were called as needed.

One was now needed, but who would call it? The annual meeting wasn't until the first of the year. The meeting tonight could not be about the bank situation, because all the owners had to be invited.

Thelma knocked at the half-closed door. "You have a patient here, Dr. Astrid. In room one. From the tents."

"Thank you." She rose. "Don't go away," she told Elizabeth. "I'll be back shortly, so hang on to these thoughts, and we can talk some more."

"As if I dared." Elizabeth's mutter seemed more complaint now than angry.

Astrid knocked on the door and entered the examining room. "Good morning. I'm Dr. Bjorklund."

Two women were waiting for her—one curled up in a fetal position on the bed, the other clutching a bag that might have been a reticule. "Mrs. Sorvito said we had to come."

Astrid listened hard to decipher the heavy accent. What

language were they speaking? She nodded to encourage the woman speaking, all the time her attention on the younger woman. Pale, obviously in lower abdominal pain, since she clutched both arms around herself. Was that blood on her legs?

"Good. Her name?" She pointed to the sick woman. *Lord, please, wisdom.*

"Leona Bach."

"Mrs. Bach?"

A nod and more information that Astrid did not understand.

"What country are you from?" Astrid spoke slowly and enunciated clearly.

"Osterreich. Os—, Os—, Osterreich."

"May I examine her?" She pantomimed as she spoke. If this was Germanic, she should be able to pick up some words. Perhaps it was some dialect. *Think, Astrid.* She stepped to the woman, a girl really, and laid a hand on the one clutching. "How long has she been bleeding? Short time? Long time?" She motioned to the stains on the dress and leg.

"Long." Vigorous nodding and hand waving.

Purple circles under the eyes, skin so pale as to be transparent. So thin, no wonder she shivered sporadically. Hot to the touch. Astrid reached under the table for a sheet and a blanket. She needed to examine her female parts but how to say that? She signaled she'd be right back and went out the door in search of Thelma.

"Do you know if the Geddicks have a telephone?"

Thelma shrugged and shook her head. "Please ask Gerald, and if not, please go fetch Mrs. Geddick for me. Ask her to come right away." She returned to the room, already sure of what she had to do. Get her moved to the hospital, where she could have some help.

She made sure she smiled reassuringly when she returned to the room and checked heart and lungs and pulse. Thready. It felt like forever before she heard Mrs. Geddick talking to Thelma.

Astrid stepped out of the room to greet Mrs. Geddick. "Thank you for coming. I think they are from Europe and maybe you can understand and talk with them. I need to know when the bleeding started and if she is pregnant, and I want her at the hospital as soon as possible."

"Ja, I do that." Mrs. Geddick asked something, then repeated it, listening intently. Even Astrid could tell she was having a hard time.

She turned to Astrid after some back and forth. "Her husband is a carpenter here. She lost a baby early on, a month or so ago, I think, and has been bleeding off and on since then. The older woman half carried her here."

"Thank you. I will find someone to help get her over to the hospital. Please stay with them and find out whatever more you can." She relayed her need to Thelma, who picked up the receiver before she finished. If one needed something done, Thelma was the one to ask.

Astrid stopped in to tell Elizabeth what was happening, and within minutes, Thorliff and Trygve showed up, grabbed a stretcher out of the closet, and carried the young woman to the hospital.

"Easier and quicker than a wagon," Thorliff said when they laid the stretcher on the gurney.

Mrs. Geddick followed along, just in case she was needed.

"Thank you. Talk about a need met quickly." Miriam welcomed them.

Trygve touched his hat and left with a smile for Miriam. The two men were teasing each other as they went out the door.

"Danke, danke," the woman kept repeating. By now they had more information, and Mrs. Geddick answered Miriam's questions for the chart while Astrid and Deborah undressed the close-to-comatose patient.

"Why do they wait so long?" Miriam shook her head while Astrid nodded her agreement.

"I'm going to do an examination, and then we'll clean her up. I fear we have both bleeding and infection here, as if the miscarried fetus was expelled but not all of the placenta."

The woman was dirty as well as malnourished. Not a careless sort of dirtiness, rather the dingy look that comes of not having enough water to wash in.

An hour later Astrid left the hospital and returned to sit down with Elizabeth.

"Call Chicago and ask for their advice," Elizabeth said when Astrid described the symptoms. "How I wish I could assist you." Sitting in the chair by the window, she lifted her cup of tea. "How badly dehydrated is she?"

"That's the least of our worries. We are pushing fluids and have her covered in wet cloths to both bring down her temperature and hydrate her."

Astrid looked up. "Mor, what are you doing here?"

"Thelma called me. Reverend Solberg will come when school is out."

"We've given her something for the pain, and she relaxed not long after that. She is cleaned up, the bleeding is packed, and Gray Cloud is spooning broth while Dawn Breaking keeps changing the cloths. Mrs. Bach's husband has been notified. At least they have no small children for her to worry about." She poured her mother a cup of tea from the teapot kept warm over a candle. "I'm calling Chicago. I will return with their suggestions." She paused in the doorway. "How did the quilting go?"

"Hildegunn wasn't there. She sent a note saying she couldn't find anyone to take over the post office." Ingeborg shook her head. "The rest of us had a blessed and lively time. I just got home a short while ago."

"Wonderful. And your devotions?"

"Would you believe I used Jesus on the Great Commandment, but the person who needed to hear it most wasn't there?" Ingeborg smiled at Elizabeth. "Still a few of us squirmed when we

126

talked about loving our neighbors as ourselves. We all fall so far short on that. It is a good thing we have a merciful God. Lord have mercy on us—it's so easy to say and so easy to forget our need. Like right now. Lord have mercy on that young woman and on each of us who God calls to help her."

"Takk. I needed that reminder too." Elizabeth heaved a sigh. "Right now I am fighting to be merciful to Anner. He shows no mercy, but that is beside the point. How do we do this and yet make him realize what he is doing?"

"What if making him realize is God's job and not ours?"

Astrid felt her jaw drop. "Mor!"

Ingeborg shrugged. "I don't know. Those words just came out. I am as shocked as you are."

"But Anner Valders is not listening to God or anyone else!"

"And our God is not stronger than Anner Valders?" Ingeborg closed her eyes and slowly, heavily, her head moved from side to side.

Astrid made her way to the telephone, her mind back on the bleeding woman, her steps slow as if weighted by the spring mud, which could stop wagon wheels. The woman's only solution was probably a hysterectomy, removal of the uterus.

She had a lengthy conversation with Dr. Whitaker, the surgeon she had trained with when she went for her surgery rotation before she became an accredited physician. The conference did not give her peace of mind. While he assured her she was capable of performing this much-needed surgery, the thought of it made her shake. So many what ifs. She'd asked him several times about the infection present, but she asked once more.

"I agree with your analysis," he told her, "that when the aborted fetus was expelled, part of the afterbirth remained and festered. My opinion is that you should go ahead. She will most likely die if you don't."

That was not at all what she'd wanted to hear. "But—"

"Dr. Bjorklund, these are the kinds of calls all doctors hate to make, but our goal is to do all we can to preserve life. You can stand by and do nothing, or you can act and give her a better chance. One of the sad things is that when she does recover, she will not be able to have children."

Astrid hung up the receiver and rested her forehead against the oak box. He had recommended doing it as soon as possible, but she would not proceed until she spoke with the husband. She had asked Thorliff to get a message to him to come to the hospital as soon as he got off work. And that could be soon. She told Elizabeth and Mor what Dr. Whitaker had said.

"I'll walk over with you." Ingeborg smiled at her daughter.

Elizabeth smiled too. "And I will be praying from here. God has given you great skill in surgery, Astrid. Trust that He will guide your hands and heal this woman."

"Ja. Thank you. Would you please tell Daniel what is going on? I hope to be done in time for the meeting tonight, but we shall see."

"Have you done this before?" Ingeborg asked as she locked arms with her daughter.

"I have only assisted and closed up. There were never any female cadavers to practice on." When they stepped through the front door of the hospital, she inhaled and set her shoulders and mind. Letting her shoulders relax along with outgoing air, she motioned to Miriam. "I know your shift ends soon, but I would appreciate your staying late to assist with this surgery. You and Deborah both."

Deborah nodded. "Dr. Whitaker said to go ahead?"

"He did. So please get the surgery prepared, along with the patient, and we will begin as soon as I have permission from Mr. Bach. Thorliff sent a message for him to come here right after work." She let out a sigh, praying the weight would be gone from her shoulders. Right now she felt like she was about to sink into the floor because of it.

"Deborah, will you please telephone our other two nursing

students to come in now or as soon as they can get here. We may need their help, and they need this experience."

Deborah assigned jobs to the others, and they all went about their duties as if they did this every day. Astrid sat down in her office and leaned back in the chair. With her eyes closed, she walked herself through every detail of the coming surgery: the blood vessels, muscles, nerves, incising the layers of skin and muscle, tying off both veins and arteries, separating the uterus, lifting it out, and closing the site, leaving in a drain. She pictured the anesthesia. Miriam would be in charge of that, with Deborah assisting Astrid.

A knock at the door and Deborah announced, "Mr. Bach is here."

"Send him in."

A sturdy young man, his hands mangling his hat, stepped into the room, just barely. He moved when Deborah closed the door.

"Please sit down." She pointed to the chair. When he sat on the very edge of the chair, she asked, "How well do you understand me?"

"I say English better than my wife." In spite of a heavy accent, she could understand him. Probably thanks to Amelia's teaching.

"Your wife is bleeding and has an infection."

His brow wrinkled. "What? Bleeding but . . . ?"

"Infection. Very sick. I want to do an operation to help her."

He shook his head and shrugged. "No, uh . . ."

"No to the surgery?"

"Surgery. Uh . . . cut into her?"

"Yes. If I do, she cannot have more children." Astrid paused and rephrased. "I cut—no more babies. I do not cut—she may die."

He stared at her a long, long moment. "Ja, cut." He leaned forward. He pointed to her. "You make her good. Ja?"

"I will do my best."

"Best, ja." He collapsed against the back of the chair, obviously

129

understanding that. He shook his head and pointed at her again. "You do."

"Just a minute." Astrid stood and went to the door. "Is Mrs. Geddick still here?"

"She went home."

Astrid returned to her mission. "I will do my best." If only she could understand him better. "You will wait here?"

"Ja, wait."

"Did Mrs. Geddick learn what country they are from?"

Deborah looked at the chart and shrugged. "Wherever Osterreich is."

"I think it's Austria, so we're probably struggling with German here." Astrid took the chart from Deborah. "Someone show him where he can wait. I sure hope someone else comes to be with him."

"Reverend Solberg will be here. And your mor."

And God. That thought did bring comfort. A quote from Sunday's sermon wandered into her mind. "God inhabits the praises of His people." That brought her more comfort. He would use her hands.

As soon as everyone was scrubbed and the patient prepped, Astrid closed her eyes. "Dear Lord God, I know you are right here with us. Guide us all, our hands, our hearts, our minds. And please bring healing to this young woman. And, Lord, we will give you all the thanks and praise." She opened her eyes and looked around at her team. "Ready?"

They all nodded. Astrid made the first incision on the line she had marked. The lights heated up the room, along with the tension, as she blocked out the world and concentrated on the job at her hands. The muscle layers. Almost no fat at all. Most people had at least some abdominal fat.

Astrid gasped as she reached the uterus. It was red, angry, ready to burst with the poison in it. *Get it out of there!*

Miriam and Deborah followed her instructions well, as did

130

the others. When sweat blurred her vision, Corabell wiped it away without being asked. Deborah was like another pair of her own hands. What a blessing, these women.

Finally, finally, Astrid stood erect. "You close," she said to Deborah when the area was cleared with no further visible bleeders and disinfected again.

Deborah gave her a startled look but went ahead as Astrid had taught her.

"Corabell, you and Vera do the dressing. Miriam, let her begin to come around. But as soon as she comes out of the ether, we will keep her sedated with morphine for at least the next twenty-four hours."

"She is breathing well," Miriam reported. "Heart rate as to be expected."

Astrid watched as her nurses worked. Splendid nurses! When they were all finished, she said, "I thank our God and I thank each of you for doing a fine job. We have done our best. Now we will do all we can to help her recover. Gray Cloud, please bring in the gurney, and we will transfer her. Each of you take a corner of the sheet, and we will repeat what we did in the beginning. Then we'll do the same in her room." They had prepared one of the two private rooms.

Once they had her in the bed, they heaved a collective sigh of relief. "Vera, you and Dawn stay with her now. She is not to be left alone, even for a minute, so we will all do shifts tonight. I am going to talk with her husband, and I am sure he will be in here too."

She fought off the exhaustion that threatened to knock her to the floor and entered the office where Reverend Solberg, Ingeborg, and Mr. Bach all stood at her entry.

"Mrs. Bach made it through the surgery and is now in her room. Mr. Bach, we have a comfortable chair in there for you."

"She . . . she is good?" The fear in his eyes made her take his shaking hands.

131

"Ja, but sleeping."

He nodded. "Sleeping. I see her?"

"Ja, come with me."

Reverend Solberg smiled at her and went with them. Mr. Bach took his wife's hand, tears streaming down his face. He looked to Solberg. "You pray?"

Astrid nodded and kept herself on her feet until the amen. "I will be back."

Back in her office, she collapsed into a chair and leaned against her Mor. "Thank you." *Please, God. Please.*

CHAPTER 14

"Sorry I'm late." Reverend Solberg paused in the doorway to the crowded newspaper office. All the chairs were taken, but there was a bale of newsprint. He sat on that.

"Glad you got here. How is that young woman doing?" Thorliff asked.

"She came through the surgery fairly well. We can be proud of our hospital and those who are working there. They all were pushed beyond what they thought they knew or were able to do. Astrid told me her team did as well in the operating room as any she has worked with. We prayed that God would guide their hands, and He most certainly did, their minds too." He blew out a breath, puffing his cheeks out. "Do any of you know anything about Mr. Bach?"

Trygve nodded. "He's on Toby's crew and a hard worker."

"My mother says he's been faithfully attending her English class," Daniel said. "She didn't realize he had a wife with him. They are sharing a tent with an older couple. They came with the last group of immigrants and had not been in the United States very long before they came here." Daniel Jeffers leaned back. "The four of them have put in for one of the apartments. I have a feeling there might be more than one family in some of those."

"If we can finish the building. I can't carry it much longer without more cash." Thorliff felt the anger rising. "Would you start us with prayer, John? God knows I need plenty of that."

John Solberg waited for what seemed an interminable time before he began. "Lord God, Creator of all that we have and all that we dream of, we praise and thank you that we can ask for your help and guidance, that you have promised us in your Word you will always answer, that you will always love us and be with us. We really need your wisdom here, because ours is too small and too narrow. And, Lord, our feelings get in the way. We want everything to be fair and all your people to be loving. But you know us far better than we know ourselves, so we ask you to guide and guard us. Thank you for your work in the hospital surgery today. Our hope lies in you. In your Son's name we pray, amen."

"Thank you." Thorliff looked around at the men gathered. "You all realize this meeting is private. Please keep the things we discuss tonight to yourself. I cannot say you shouldn't talk it over with your wives, for we all know that they are praying for us as we meet." He sat down, as the others already were. "Any questions, clarifications?"

"You tried to reason with him?" Daniel asked.

"I tried, yes."

"Part of the problem, the way I see it, is that we have given him the authority to make decisions through the years." Lars spoke slowly and gently, as usual.

"But has he ever abused his authority before?" Daniel asked. "I mean, do you know of anyone else turned down for a loan?"

"I don't think so." Thorliff's jaw ached from keeping what he wanted to say under control. "The freedom we have given him has created a tyrant."

"Is there sufficient liquid cash in the bank for the loan to be approved?"

"That's a good question, one we usually get the answer for in January at the bank meeting." Thorliff stared up at the ceiling.

"But the building boom has happened since then, right?" Garth asked.

"Pretty much."

"Are there loans in arrears?" Daniel asked.

"Again, that would be in January's report. I've not ever heard of any."

"It's a shame Hjelmer isn't here. He keeps better track of the bank than anyone."

"I say we ask for an accounting."

"I think we have to call for a special meeting first. And if we do that, this will get out to everyone, and that could be even more divisive."

"The Word says that if you have a problem with a brother, you go to him, and that is what you did." Reverend Solberg nodded to Thorliff.

"No, actually I blew up at the time, and I have not gone back to talk to him. Because he was being so self-righteous and pompous, I was afraid I would talk with my fists. I don't remember ever wanting to hit someone like that before." Thorliff propped his elbows on his knees and scrubbed his hands through his hair. "Elizabeth believes Anner is out to get even with us for taking Manny in and for paying for his horse."

"But he's way out of line on the church issue too. The way he treated Thomas Devlin and then that young nurse. Like he thinks those of us who've been around for a long time are somehow better than the folks who have come here more recently to work and start new lives." Garth sat shaking his head.

Thorliff sat up straight. "We can't afford to stop on that building. Too many people are counting on living there. I'll go to Grafton for the money if I have to, but we have all tried to keep our businesses in Blessing, for the betterment of the whole town. But this is like a cancer that grows unseen until it erupts."

"What are the choices?"

"Fire Anner and appoint someone else to run the bank."

"How and who?"

"I say we follow the biblical way first," Reverend Solberg said. "You go to talk with him, Thorliff, and take me and one other with you. We all commit to praying about this before then, and if God suggests any other way in the meantime, we listen carefully for God's leading. We have to give Him time to work."

Thorliff stared at his pastor. "Do you think I haven't been praying?"

"That's not what I said. There are others praying too: Ingeborg, Astrid, Elizabeth, Kaaren. We pray specifically for Anner to listen to God's Word and to root out the quack grass of bitterness and pride. As our God forgives us, we must forgive others and be merciful, as He is merciful."

"I tell you, I don't think this will work, and after next week, I can't ask those men to work and not get paid." Fury screamed to be let loose. They should be planning for other things that needed doing in Blessing, like a new school, and here they were spending their time on the mess Anner made. He looked up. "Pardon me, my mind got away."

"I said, then we pray for God to provide the funds for wages too. He has unlimited funds, you know." Solberg looked around the table. "Are we all agreed? Or are there any questions?"

Thorliff pushed his chair back so hard that it tipped and crashed to the floor. He leaned over to set it upright again. He shook his head, gently at first and then more emphatically. "I can't do it."

"Do what?"

"Pray for Anner Valders and then go see him." Arms rigid, braced against the tabletop, his head hung and still shook no. "He has caused this and is creating more hate-filled feelings. I don't want to see him, be polite, hear his angry voice." He looked up. "I'm sorry. I can't do it."

Lars pushed himself to his feet and came around the table. He laid an arm over Thorliff's shoulders. "You won't have to. We'll all just watch and pray. Our God has never let us down."

"I'm not so sure about that. Right now He seems to be loading an awful lot on all of us."

"Haakan always said, 'God will provide. He always has, so why would He stop now?'" Lars squeezed and then slapped Thorliff on the shoulder. "Reverend Solberg, how about you close this meeting, and we'll see what God is going to do next."

All the men stood and bowed their heads.

"Father in heaven, we know you are right here, for you said where two or three are gathered together in your name, you will be there in the midst of them. You know our concerns. Thank you that you will make clear to us the way you would have us go. We have agreed to pray and wait, to watch to see the way you will unfold this plan. We trust that you know best. And now we pray together the way you taught us to pray. Our Father . . ."

The others joined in, and at the amen, Solberg added, "The Lord bless us and keep us and give us His peace."

When Thorliff and the pastor were the only ones left in his office, Solberg stepped to his side. "I know Haakan is so proud of you. I'm sure he's bragging to everyone around, 'That's my son.' You see, Thorliff, all these years you've had both of your parents praying for you, and they still are, but now God is treating you like a man, a son He loves dearly and is determined to grow into real manhood, the God variety. Growing is always painful. Come on, let's close this up. I promised to return for one of the praying shifts at the hospital for Mrs. Bach. She's barely more than a child herself."

Thorliff nodded. "Ja, when Trygve and I carried her on the stretcher, we figured that." He stopped at the gate. "I meant what I said, you know."

"I know. Good night, son."

Thorliff watched his pastor and friend go whistling up the street, then turned to head to his own house. He checked on Elizabeth, who was sleeping soundly in her room downstairs, kissed her forehead, and mounted the stairs. He looked in on

Inga. Moonlight fell in window shadows across the floor of her room. She slept with arms and legs flung out as if ready to leap up and charge into the new day. He kissed her cheek and made his way down the hall to the room he used to share with Elizabeth. Until she was given orders not to climb the stairs.

Once in bed, he stared at the moonlight patterning the floor. Maybe he was too drained, but right now he couldn't even be angry at Anner. Instead, he felt empty, like a jar that all the juice had been drained out of. He could still feel Lars' arm on his shoulders.

"Oh, Far, how I need your wisdom and experience right now. I think I understand trust, but . . . Well, I sure don't trust Anner Valders." He paused, waited. And nodded. "Ja, Lord God, I choose to trust you."

CHAPTER 15

*O*h, *please don't die on my watch.* Miriam hoped she hadn't said that aloud as she dipped the wet cloths in cold water and laid them back on the patient. After the surgery, Miriam had gone back to her room and collapsed, sleeping right through supper. Vera woke her when she was getting ready for bed and told her Mrs. Landsverk had saved some food for her, and it would be brought up as soon as she asked.

Instead, she'd dressed and gone down to the dining room, eaten, and returned to the hospital to take a three-hour shift, not leaving the patient's side. At three o'clock she would go back to her room and sleep until her regular duty on the day shift.

Mrs. Bach. It was hard for her to think of the patient as Mrs. Bach. She surely didn't look any older than Mercy, who was now sixteen, she suddenly realized, and working at the Chicago hospital. Oh dear. She had forgotten that Mercy had a birthday last week. She would have to send her a special note.

"We better start using ice. Her temperature is climbing," she said to Corabell, who was on the night shift with Dawn Breaking and had just come in to check on her.

"I get it." The Indian woman left. When she returned a few minutes later with the bowl of ice, she helped Miriam fold the ice into the wet cloths and lay them back against their patient. The next time they would change the pads on the bed again.

"Has she regained consciousness at all?" Corabell asked.

"No. Dr. Astrid said we should keep her sedated."

A snore came from her young husband, who was sound asleep on the cot they had set up for him. He'd stayed awake, taking part in the first round, but succumbed to sleep in the chair. They had promised to wake him if there was any change.

Miriam again slid an ice chip into the girl's mouth. She was not so sedated she didn't swallow. "Thank you, Dawn."

"I watch. You go walk around."

"I will do that, thank you." Miriam stretched and left the room, heading outside for a breath of fresh air. She never ceased to be amazed at the fragrances wafting on the breeze. The sickle moon hung in the western sky, and the chill in the air said fall was fading into winter. But tonight she could see countless stars. So few could be seen in Chicago. She rubbed her upper arms and strode down the street, then shortly turned back and returned to her patient.

"Thanks. Now I at least feel awake again."

A baby cried and was shushed by either the nurse or the mother who lay beside her small son. Someone coughed, and when the man continued to cough, Miriam heard Corabell's shoes click down the ward. All the night sounds of the hospital.

Miriam wrote on the chart that they'd started ice packs at one thirty. She checked the dressing: no sign of further blood loss. Sliding in another ice chip, she watched Mrs. Bach's face. Her eyelids had indeed fluttered. She checked the chart for the time the morphine was last administered. She shouldn't be waking up. Another hour before it was to be given again.

Miriam strode to the kichen where Mrs. Geddick had chosen to sleep on a cot in case she was needed. Miriam explained what was needed as they returned to the room.

Mrs. Geddick leaned close to their patient's ear, speaking in

German. "You are safe. Your husband is sleeping here in your room at the hospital. You just rest and get well." She repeated herself, speaking slowly and softly. She watched Miriam carefully and translated slowly. "If you can hear me, squeeze my hand. Good. Now, if the pain is severe again, squeeze my hand. Pain?" Again a weak squeeze. "I'll bring you something to drink in a few minutes." Miriam asked Dawn Breaking to stay by the young woman as she went to prepare the medication. By the time she returned, Mrs. Bach was sound asleep again, but this time she seemed to be resting, not comatose. Had they had a breakthrough?

Together she and Dawn Breaking wrung the cloths out and put in more ice.

A while later Ingeborg joined them at the bedside, catching a yawn. "How is she?"

Miriam brought her up to date and Ingeborg nodded. "I know I'm a bit early, but since I have the next shift, you go on back to your room and get some more sleep."

"Thank you." On her way back to the boardinghouse, thoughts of Trygve danced into her mind. They had walked these streets together and had a marvelous time at Ingeborg's on Sunday. Yet they were both so busy she'd hardly seen him this week. Other than when he and Mr. Bjorklund brought their patient to the hospital.

His smile had made her heart leap even in the midst of caring for a terribly ill woman. She had been back in Blessing for less than a week, and other than missing her mother, Chicago felt like long ago and on the other side of the world.

She had a feeling her mother's going on to heaven was easier on her with the distance, since she hadn't seen her mother every day for the last years and especially these last months. She needed to write to her brothers and sisters. After all, she was now the head of the family, or the oldest at least. But not this morning. She had to be back at the hospital at seven. One good thing she'd learned in nurses' training: how to sleep any time she got the opportunity.

Ingeborg finished spooning broth into Leona Bach, then wiped her face and hands with a warm wet cloth before drying them. She took a bottle of lotion out of her pocket and rubbed that on her face and hands, then turned at a noise.

Young Mr. Bach staggered to his feet, stuttering an apology for sleeping so soundly. When she told him his wife had taken some broth, he looked at her.

"What do I do? I have to go to work."

She got the gist of what he was saying and answered, "If there is any change, someone will come for you."

"Ja, for sure?"

"Ja. You keep praying for her. But now, you take her hand and lean close to her ear. Then you tell her to squeeze your hand if she can hear you."

"And tell her I come back later?"

"Ja." Ingeborg watched a smile change his face when his wife could hear him and respond. *Thank you, Lord God. You are the reason this young woman is still alive, so please continue with your plan, and thank you for the privilege of allowing us to take part in it. How can we take better care of these people you have sent to us?* This was something the quilters needed to look into. The men were working, but so far the women had little contact with the rest of the town.

There was a language barrier indeed, but they could communicate if they tried hard enough. When Reverend Solberg appeared at the door, she rose and offered him her chair, then brought him up to date.

"I am thankful she is still alive."

"We are fighting the infection with all that we have, and since the offending organ is no longer there, I pray we have a better chance. But as with all those we've prayed for through the years, no matter how good the medicine and care, healing is still His province."

John Solberg nodded. "You are praying for Anner?"

"Of course, and for Thorliff. It is hard, you know, when your son is attacked."

"I know." He took her hand. "And how are you doing?"

"Up and down. The pit yawns, but God pulls me back from the edge. The tears stop eventually, and I feel His presence so strongly at times. I know He is with me, and I know Haakan is with Him. And someday I will get to join them."

"Please don't be in a hurry to go, all right?"

Ingeborg shook her head. "As if that would make any difference. But we can make a difference with these young people." She nodded toward Leona Bach. "Starting right here."

"We have to get that apartment house built. And those three houses."

"I know there aren't very many women there now, but Thorliff said several of the men want to bring their families. Uff da. Who would have thought God had such a plan for our little town?"

Ingeborg said good-bye to Corabell and Dawn Breaking, and using the predawn for light, she walked on home. The cows were already in the barn for milking, the rooster was crowing, and Patches came running out to meet her. Smoke from the chimney told her Freda was fixing breakfast. The thought of a cup of coffee made her pick up her feet and mount the steps to the back porch with a spring in her step. Oh, but it felt good to be home.

"Gud dag." She greeted Freda from the doorway as she unwrapped her shawl and hung it on the wall peg.

"You seem mighty cheerful for nursing half the night."

"I slept for several hours before my shift to stay with Mrs. Bach and then had a beautiful walk home as the world came alive. Is Manny milking?"

Freda nodded. "And Emmy is getting dressed. She already made their lunches. She sure is one capable little girl."

Ingeborg shot Freda a warm smile. It wasn't often Freda paid a compliment, so when she did, Ingeborg made sure to comment on it. "You are so right." She poured herself a cup of coffee. "What do you want me to do?"

"Sit down at the table and enjoy your coffee. The mush is fried and in the oven, the sausage too—"

"From Garrisons'?"

"Ja. And I will do the eggs when Manny gets in here." Just then they heard him on the porch and without the thump of his crutches.

"Mornin', Grandma," he said with a smile, using his cane as if he'd had it for years instead of days. "D'you think I can leave the crutches home today?"

"How does your leg feel?"

"Hurts some at times but no big thing."

"How about using the crutches today, and then try the cane come Monday?"

He frowned but nodded. "I was thinking maybe me and Emmy could ride Joker."

"And where would he stay all day?"

"I know. I thought of that." He went to the sink to wash without being asked. "Be good if I could train him to come home by himself."

Ingeborg shook her head. Leave it to Manny. But inwardly she smiled even more. He'd referred to her house as home. And he'd called her Grandma, like Emmy and Inga and the little ones did. What wonderful changes!

Using hot pads, Emmy brought one of the platters to the table and Freda brought the others. When they'd all sat down, Ingeborg asked Manny to say grace.

"Thank you, Lord, for our food and for Grandma and Freda who cook so good. Thank you for making my leg better all the time. Amen."

Ingeborg heard a buggy and looked out the window. Patches leaped off the porch, barking a welcome, and danced beside Trygve right up to the door.

"Come in, come in. You are just in time." Freda pointed to the plate waiting for him. When Emmy set the table, she always set an extra place.

Trygve seated himself and bowed his head briefly. A whistle sounded and the two kids leaped up and grabbed their lunch buckets, and out the door they went with a chorus of good-byes and thank-yous.

Trygve laughed. "Samuel whistles and they jump. That's good for all of them." He helped himself to plenty of everything.

Ingeborg smiled. "Have you been digging this morning?"

"Ja. Getting close to done with my basement. It's interesting that we're having such a warm fall—an Indian summer, I guess. I wonder why they call it that."

"I don't really know." Ingeborg refilled the coffee cups after motioning for Freda to sit still for a change.

Trygve worked on his breakfast for a moment. "How is Mrs. Bach?"

"I'm thinking she is doing well for it being not even twenty-four hours since the surgery. The problem is she was so run-down from the last month of bleeding off and on."

He nodded thoughtfully. "You realize she'd be dead if it weren't for all of the fine medical staff—you and John Solberg included. Freda, you're amazing. Thank you."

He stood up. "Thanks for the breakfast. I told Thorliff I wanted to dig your potatoes today, so he gave me the day off."

"You all take such good care of me. Thank you, Trygve."

After he headed for the field, she helped Freda clear the table and put the dishes in the pan. When she started to wash them, Freda shook her head.

"You go back to your sewing. I know you want to finish that

145

dress for Emmy. And you should probably take a nap in case you are needed to sit with Mrs. Bach again."

"Freda, thank you. And thank you for staying here so I could be gone."

"You are welcome. That order for cheese should be shipped early next week. Manny put the crates together. The wheels are all waxed and ready—well, almost all. If we get any more orders in the mail, we could ship more."

I should be out there at the cheese house helping her. Actually there were a lot of things she *should* be doing. Baking cookies for one thing. The jar was nearly empty and all the children would probably be here at the farm tomorrow. Saturday seemed to be turning into grandkids' day with Grandma at the farm.

"First I'm going to mix up some cookie dough and put it in the icebox. Then I can sew and not feel guilty."

Freda shook her head. "Guilty for what? Running out of cookies?"

Ingeborg shrugged. "It's been too long since I've baked. You have spoiled me, you know." *Oh, Haakan, how I would love to bake you an apple pie.* She sniffed and went to fetch the ingredients out of the pantry.

～∾～

Waiting is never easy.
Waiting on the unseen is even harder.

Thorliff had resolved on waking that he would just go forward today with what he knew. He knew setting the exterior windows and doors was next to be done on the apartment house. The building would then be ready for a full effort on the interior walls. A smaller crew had already gotten a good start on that, doing one floor at a time.

He could lay out the newspaper, write his editorial column—a rather scathing one had come to mind. He laid out the ads first. Blessing Mercantile's ad gave a discount on winter boots.

Garrisons' Groceries was running a special on sausages. Mr. Garrison had become a sausage maker and was building a name for himself beyond the outskirts of Blessing, thanks in part to the article Thorliff had written about Mr. Garrison and his delicious sausages two editions earlier.

The Friday morning train came and went. He was in the middle of pasting an ad in place when the door opened and Hjelmer entered. "Gud dag!" He must have had a good trip if the grin on his face was any indication.

"Welcome home." Thorliff smoothed the paper precisely in place. "You missed the meeting last night."

"What meeting?"

"A what-do-we-do-about-Anner-Valders meeting."

Hjelmer Bjorklund's blue eyes widened. "Now what?"

Thorliff filled him in on the happenings in Blessing since he'd been gone. "I figured you keep better track of the bank than any of the rest of us, so perhaps you could shed some light on things."

"And Elizabeth believes Anner's behavior is vindictive?"

"She does."

"But why against you?"

"First chance he had was the extension I applied for. You know that has always been a formality. After all, we all own the bank he manages. But he's been different since that robbery, like he took it personally."

Hjelmer wagged his head. "No one ever even intimated it was his fault." He looked up. "And you went to talk with him?"

"Sort of." Thorliff explained what happened.

"And the consensus of last night's meeting?"

"We all committed to pray about it, and pray for Anner, and wait on God to see how He is going to handle it."

"Not easy."

"Enough of that subject. How was your trip?"

"Could have sold more if winter weren't breathing down our necks. The crew is doing well, but I need two crews out there, and we have no more men to send. Anyone off the threshing crew that might work?"

"If I don't get money to finish that apartment house, some of those men might be interested."

"We'll get you the money for that."

"Where?"

"Threaten to rob the bank?" Hjelmer held up his hands, palms out. "Throwing ink pots is not allowed. Let me check into some things at the bank. How much did you ask for?"

"Five thousand."

"Is that enough?"

"It's a good estimate. When we finish up with those houses, I'll be more liquid again."

"I'll drop my bag at home and get on this. By the way, guess who was on the train."

"I'm not into guessing games right now."

"Anji Moen and her four children."

"Good. Gerald and Rebecca were hoping to hear from her soon."

"What do you suppose she is going to do?"

"I just hope she doesn't want a house. At least not anytime soon."

Hjelmer started out the door, then turned back. "I'll let you know what I find. And never fear, there will be money to finish that building. We sure need a long fall to get all the housing ready."

Thorliff went back to work on the next edition. Now to keep his thoughts from Anner. What was that Scripture Solberg had quoted one time? He snorted at the memory. That's right, *Bringing into captivity every thought to the obedience of Christ*. That was one tall order. How did one control his thoughts? Choose to think on something else. Like what? So many verses in the Psalms, especially, talked about praising God.

Setting type was a good way to focus his mind. And relax.

His fingers flew over the trays, and the lines appeared on the setting tray.

Putting together a new edition of his newspaper always challenged him. Time slipped away as the layout took shape in type. Had he invested in a newer printer, he could do this more easily, but newer did not necessarily mean better. *Thank you, Lord, that I get to do this job that I love. Thank you that Elizabeth is seeming stronger. Thank you for such a glorious fall day, and for Hjelmer showing up today.* The rhythm of typesetting, the pungent odor of ink—oops, a misspelled word. He reset that.

What was he doing building houses and apartments anyway? This was what he loved doing. But running a newspaper in a small town like Blessing did not make enough money to support his family. Construction was a solid business, a good investment.

And Blessing was growing. He knew he was doing the right thing. Wasn't he?

CHAPTER 16

Mister Trygve? Lookit here!"

Trygve paused from digging Tante Ingeborg's potatoes and turned.

Manny's bay gelding, saddled and bridled, stood right behind him. And on the horse sat Manny! The grin on the boy's face was wide enough to slide a saucer into.

"Done it myself. Climbed up on him all by myself."

Trygve was grinning too. He leaned on his fork. "That's wonderful, Manny! But where is your cane?"

Manny jammed his right toe forward, poking it in behind the horse's elbow. The horse obediently turned aside in place. "Right here. In this rifle scabbard under my right stirrup. I climb aboard and slide my cane into the rifle scabbard. See?"

"So it's handy that you don't own a rifle."

"Used to have one, but Shack lost his. We backtracked and all, but we never found it. So he took mine for hisself. He said it's 'cause he's the better shot."

"Is he?"

Manny shrugged, grinning. He didn't have to say "No, he isn't" out loud. The grin faded. "Mr. Trygve, I'm beholden forever to Dr. Bjorklund for saving my leg when she didn't hafta.

I can't grip good with it yet, but I can knee Joker aside and use spurs. If I had any spurs."

"A lot of us are beholden to her for one thing or another. It's a fine thing when you can do so much good for so many people."

"Yes, sir." Manny watched him dig potatoes for a minute. "I'm not so sure I could help you fork up taters. Don't know if my leg can do that."

"You could sit on the ground and pick them up as I turn the dirt."

Still grinning mightily, Manny kicked his stirrups free, swung his bad leg over the cantle, and slid off onto his good leg. He plopped down onto the ground beside the potato row.

"Shouldn't you tie your horse up somewhere?"

"Nah. He ground ties real good. 'Bout hafta have a horse that ground ties out here where there ain't no trees." And Manny was right about the horse. Joker just stood there.

Trygve dragged the peck basket in closer and forked up clump of dirt. Manny ran his fingers through it, sifting c potatoes. He got not only the small potatoes but the very sm ones. "Are these too little?"

"Nope. Wait until you taste those little darlings in Ta Ingeborg's potato soup."

"Haven't tasted nothing around here yet that ain't mi good."

"Well, there's spinach." Trygve found himself still grin This was such a different boy from the sullen youngster Tante Ingeborg and Onkel Haakan had taken under their

They worked together well. Trygve dug and Manny sifte fingers working through every inch. Trygve brought out the bushel baskets from the barn and dumped the peck b into them. It had been a bumper year for wheat. Looked was a bumper year for potatoes as well.

Presently Manny sat up straight. "You know somethin Trygve?"

151

"You can call me just Trygve."

"You sure it's all right? Ma said I had to *mister* everybody."

"I'm sure. Call me Trygve."

Manny nodded. "I been thinking about that fifty-five dollars. They took it with them out to that hideout, but when you caught them, they didn't have it."

"We figured they could have buried it anywhere. It's a big prairie."

"Don't think so. Jed's sort of a good worker, and Gabe's a fair worker, but Shack don't use a single muscle he don't have to. Now lookit this dirt." Manny raised a handful and dropped it. "Good garden dirt, but kinda dry and hard to dig. Not like Kentucky dirt. You're really working on your fork there. And the dirt out where you don't plow is hard as rock."

"That's true."

"So Gabe and Jed, and for sure Shack, wouldn't be burying nothing. Too much work. Besides, I mucked out the stalls, so I know all the tools that's in that barn. Ain't any. Just a hay fork. I had to use a hay fork to muck stalls. Hit's a real pain in the backside, trying to take up horse manure with a hay fork."

Trygve smiled. When they left their farm behind, the Hefner family would for sure have taken nearly all their tools and kitchen utensils with them, because everyone who moves on does that. He stopped digging. "So you're thinking they did something with the money besides bury it?"

"Yes, sir. I'd ride out there and look around some, but I can't recall exactly how to get there." He dumped two big handfuls of potatoes into the basket.

Trygve mulled this. He knew how to get there, because Tante Ingeborg had shown them the way, leading them out there to catch Manny's bank-robbing brothers. And Manny certainly knew those three robbers. He had grown up with them.

Trygve turned a few more forkfuls of dirt. "Manny, how do your legs feel, being back on a horse after months of not riding?"

The boy shrugged. "All right."

"I know how to get there. Let's ride out to that place when we finish with the potatoes. Take some food and bedding along, of course. There isn't much out there to eat. Look around a little, spend the night there."

Manny was grinning broadly. "You know the way?" At Trygve's nod he clambered to his feet. "Gabe wouldn't let us cook anything or light a fire because the smoke from the stove would give us away. But you and me can cook. Maybe even some of them little taters, you think?"

"I think. Let's talk to Tante Ingeborg."

By hanging on to his saddle, Manny could stand on his bad right leg, tuck his left toe into the stirrup, and swing aboard. Actually, he did it pretty slickly. He rode over to the house behind Trygve and took his cane with him when he got off. He galumphed up onto the porch and followed Trygve into the kitchen.

Tante Ingeborg was sitting at the table, leaning on it with one elbow and gazing out the window. Just sitting. It was not at all like her. She turned toward them and smiled. "Did you dig the potatoes already?"

Trygve plopped down into a chair. "Not quite. We have one short row to go, but with Manny helping, it's going quickly. Lots of potatoes this year. They're going to pretty much fill up the root cellar. Manny and I have been talking. We want to ride out to the Hefner place, spend the night there, and look around for the money that's still missing. We think it might be out there. And we're hoping you'll put some food in a sack for us because there isn't much out there."

"Except wormy flour," Manny added. "Really wormy. More worms than flour."

Ingeborg stared at Trygve, frowning.

Trygve added, "Manny thought of it. And I thought if we found the money, and he gave it away, that might redeem him

153

in Anner's eyes. Change Anner's mind about him. See if we can lance this boil now and not let it fester any longer."

Ingeborg stared at her nephew. "Trygve Knutson, I am so pleased to be your tante. You make all of us proud. Daniel borrowed the wagon, though. You'll have to wait until he's done with it."

Manny had that big wide grin back. "No wagon, ma'am. Ride."

"Manny here is mounting his horse by himself, and he thinks he can make the trip."

Ingeborg's mouth dropped open. "But your leg . . . it's not ready yet. No. You could break it again, and then you'd lose it, for sure."

Trygve watched her for a moment, trying to read her sad face. "Tante Ingeborg . . ." He didn't know how to say this. "Remember when Onkel Haakan got kind of negative when he started to slip downhill? When he used to say yes, but then he was saying no, it can't be done. Not like him at all." He took a deep breath. "Now you're doing it."

"Yes, but Manny . . ." She frowned, a sad frown wrinkling a sad face that seemed to have gotten much older just in this last month. "But this isn't like that. Manny shouldn't test the leg yet."

"I'm sure I can do it, Grandma. Really sure."

"No. I don't want to be any part of this." She wagged her head.

Trygve nodded. "Well, we certainly won't ask you to do something you don't think is right. That would be wrong." He stood up. "Come on, Manny."

They went outside and Manny clumped down off the steps with his cane, following Trygve. Trygve picked up the reins of Manny's horse and headed for the potato patch.

Manny sighed. "I was sure 'nough wanting to do that."

From the porch, Ingeborg called, "I changed my mind. I'll put together some food for you."

Manny whooped, grinning joyously.

Trygve grinned too, but because he was happy for his aunt.

Manny said, "Finish digging taters, right?"

"Right. What's out at the Hefner place in the way of bedding?"

"Not much. We used our bedrolls. No kerosene either. Lamps were burnt dry, and we couldn't refill them. And there was one kettle and a pot we had with us."

"Good to know. Soon as we finish up here, we'll take off."

"Wait." Manny frowned. "Who's gonna milk?"

"Andrew tonight. Maybe he can bring along someone or start earlier. Something."

Tante Ingeborg was waiting for them on the porch when they finished with the potatoes and rode up to the house. "Manny, if it feels that there might be problems, turn around and come back, will you? Or just sit by the track, and we'll send Daniel out to get you."

"Yes'm, Grandma, I will."

And away they went.

On the long ride out, Trygve glanced over to Manny now and then, but the boy didn't seem uncomfortable. And he was certainly a fine hand with horses. They rode in silence. And rode. And rode.

Manny interrupted Trygve's idle thoughts of building his home and of Miriam in that home. "You sure we should be doing this if'n Grandma don't like us to?"

Trygve almost answered, but as he thought about it, he changed what he was going to say. "No, Manny, I'm not sure. We might get partway and you'll ruin your leg. But if we find the money and turn it in, that will be a big step toward the town accepting you better. Maybe soothing Mr. Valders too."

"Give it back to the bank?"

And Trygve grinned. "Nope. That debt's been paid."

"But I didn't pay it. I just owe lots of people now instead of just one."

"Paid is paid." Trygve thought for another few minutes. "Reverend Solberg will be the first to tell you that we, each of us, owe a debt to God we can never pay for sinning. Jesus paid that debt, and it's paid. We don't have to pay it, not that we ever could."

"Don't seem right to me."

"It doesn't seem right to lots of people, but that's the way it is." Did Miriam understand how Jesus paid with His lifeblood? The subject had never come up. In fact, it seemed that Trygve and Miriam pretty much avoided talking about religion. And if her views were different from his, would that taint his love for her?

He knew the answer to that one. Absolutely not!

"There it is!" Manny whooped and pointed toward a very distant farmstead. "Way out there, but that's it! I recka-nize it! We found it!"

Manny's horse seemed to figure out this was home as well. It quickened its pace even as Trygve's was slowing down.

It was a beautiful farm. The buildings were rather small as farm buildings go. Milking sheds were usually built for ten or twenty cows, even if you had only one or two. The herd was going to grow. This one handled maybe three or four.

They rode into the corral behind the barn and Manny slid off his horse. "Guess I ain't used to riding no more." He arched his back.

"You'll loosen up." Trygve felt stiff too. He usually drove a buggy or a wagon. Saddles were for cowboys. They put up their horses and forked them some of the dusty gray hay from a big stack on the barn floor.

"There's still water in the trough," Manny said, "'cause a-course we was planning on coming back. Not much water, though."

"Enough for tonight. Let's go cook some supper." He felt a lot stiffer than he would ever let on, especially where legs meet torso. And Manny looked about as bedraggled. The boy hobbled into the house using his cane heavily and plopped on a chair at the table.

With that cane, Manny couldn't carry much, so it took Trygve two trips to haul the bedrolls, kerosene, bag of food, and bag of utensils into the house. He left the manure fork they'd brought in the barn.

Trygve plopped the burlap food bag on the table and crumpled up some crackly yellowed newspaper to start a fire in the stove.

Eagerly, Manny unloaded the bag. "She sent us corn bread! And eggs and bacon! And butter. Is this beans in this can? I never ate beans out of a can before. And some of them little taters! And here's syrup!" He wrenched the lid off the jar and tasted. "Real syrup, not molasses."

"I thought we'd have bacon and beans and those potatoes tonight, because it's easy. And eggs and pancakes in the morning. You also need eggs to make good pancake batter. Will you slice some rashers off that slab of bacon, please?"

"Man, we're gonna eat like kings." Manny sat back and pulled out his knife. He sobered. "This here's the knife Mr. Haakan gave me. Onkel Haakan. Sure is a good one." He slapped the bacon slab down on the table and started slicing off rashers with a very sharp blade.

"Tante Ingeborg says he showed you how to sharpen it."

Manny nodded. "And whittle. I sure do miss him."

"We all do."

"And I don't care what everybody says. If I hadn't of fallen asleep, he'd prob'ly still be alive." He sawed viciously at the bacon.

Trygve didn't argue the point. He knew what everyone said, and so far it wasn't sinking in for the boy. Would it ever? Does guilt ever really go away?

He had not brought a can opener. Manny stabbed the can open with his knife. He was going to have to sharpen it again, for sure.

Manny stopped being talkative, and Trygve didn't mind. He tried not to think about Miriam, but she kept popping into his head anyway. Did she feel guilt the way Manny did? And what in the world could she ever feel guilty about? She was right up there next to angels.

He put the potatoes on first, taking away the stove lid and setting the pan right on the open hole. It took the little iron stove an hour to warm up, but once it was hot, it cooked beautifully. He moved the potatoes back and put the iron frying pan on the stove. It heated up in less than five minutes. He laid the thick rashers out in the pan, dumped the beans on top, and listened to the warm, welcome sizzle.

Manny was slicing the corn bread, or trying to. His knife really did need sharpening now. "That bacon smells so good. I wish my brothers coulda ate like this, maybe just once. We mostly ate stuff we caught. Or shot. Ate a coyote once. Didn't do that again."

Trygve slipped a spatula under the bacon. "Almost ready. Do you miss your brothers?"

"Yeah, and that's crazy. It's not like they treated me good or something. Shack would haul off and whack me until Jed would say, *'Do that once more and I'll knock you into next Tuesday,'* and he'd quit. I try to work as much as I can for Grandma, 'cause she really needs me. My brothers made me work just so's they wouldn't hafta. Hit's a big difference." He unwrapped the oilcloth from around the butter and set it out.

Trygve couldn't think of anything to say. He couldn't imagine a family like that, a life like that. He picked up a bowl and scooped bacon, beans, and potatoes into it. "Here you go. I saw salt and pepper in the bag somewhere."

"Right here." Manny scooted himself closer to the table, snatched up a spoon, and paused. He looked at Trygve.

Trygve bowed his head. "Dear God, please give Tante Ingeborg rest and peace. Strengthen Astrid and Elizabeth. Help us find the money, please, and bless this food and our hands to your service. Amen."

"Amen." Manny salted his potatoes and slathered butter on them. He tasted. He closed his eyes. "Mm, mm! Heaven."

And that tickled Trygve. He had just made life a little bit happier for a boy who needed all the happiness he could get. He scooped out his own dinner and settled at the table. As he savored that first flavorful mouthful of baby potatoes, he had to agree with Manny. Heaven.

Manny ate in silence for a couple minutes, then paused and waved his fork. "Been thinking a lot as we rode out here. We're not going to keep watch tonight, are we?"

"I wasn't planning on it. Do you think we should?"

"No, sir. It's just, when me and my brothers were here, we had to, a-course."

"That's why Tante Ingeborg showed us how to get here the back way. We figured you'd keep watch."

Manny nodded. "So I think I have it figured out, how it all happened. They didn't wanna take the money into town when they were goin' to spring me from the hospital. If one of them got caught, that money'd be gone. So they'd hide it here until they came back. Someplace easy to get it if they had to leave in a hurry."

Trygve finished off his beans. "Good so far."

"Now, Shack is all right, I guess. You just can't trust him. Or Gabe either, really. And I know Jed wouldn't trust either of them. So now I'm gonna think like Jed. He and Gabe and Shack hide the money so everyone knows where it is. Then during his night watch, Jed moves it to a different hiding place the other two don't know about. That way one of them can't sneak off with it while the others ain't lookin'."

"Your brothers were that dishonest? Really? And selfish?"

Manny pondered that a moment. "Yeah. I think *selfish* is the perfect word. Dishonest for sure. They robbed banks, right?"

Trygve smiled.

"Shack and Gabe would hide it somewheres right here in

the house, 'cause they're too lazy to go out to one of the other buildings. Maybe tear up floorboards or something. In here. So that means Jed would most likely move it to the barn."

Trygve was grinning now. "Let's go look."

Manny bobbed his head. He started to stand and quickly sat down again. "Trygve, thank you for dinner. It was very good."

"You're welcome." Trygve sat there for a moment, flabbergasted. This boy, who did not so much as string two words together at first, was actually a fairly polite young man.

His ma must have instilled good manners in him well enough that when his hostility, fear, and distrust were all peeled away, the polite behavior surfaced.

Trygve followed Manny out to the barn. The boy was headed straight to that stack of hay. Trygve picked up the hay fork.

Manny kicked at the stack, poked it with his cane. "Jed would know that neither of those two was about to fork hay or do anything else in the barn here that'd look like work. This right here is my first guess."

Trygve lifted off the top of the stack and forked it aside. He lifted off another large forkful. Dry dust poofed and rose, a lot of dust, as he moved the old hay. He sneezed, coughed, and lifted off another swatch. Another.

Manny broke into the most infectious grin. "Bingo! Lookee there!"

On the floor at the very bottom of the stack, toward the back, there lay the satchel with its broken latch. It was still covered with loose hay, but you could see what it was. Manny plopped down beside it, reached in, and brought out a handful of one-dollar bills.

"Manasseh McCrary, you are a brilliant young man."

Manny sat there with both legs out straight, just sat and stared at Trygve's boots. Then he looked up at Trygve. "Your tante Ingeborg and onkel Haakan really had me confused. They were caring about me and doing stuff for me and all that. And

160

the people in town here too, well, excepting the banker, a-course, all caring about me and even paying off the debt I owed. That wasn't like nothing I'd ever seen. Nobody treated me like that."

Trygve extended a hand to help Manny to his feet. "That's a strange thought to think just now."

"No it ain't." Manny lurched up to standing. "Tonight we're gonna wrap up in bedrolls and go to sleep. All night. Don't have to keep watch, right? I can sleep knowing you ain't gonna steal the money from me, and you can sleep knowing I won't steal it either."

"That's true."

Manny wagged his head. There were tears in his eyes that Trygve realized didn't come from the cloud of irritating dust. "I ain't never had that before in my whole life. And now that I got it, I ain't never gonna let go of it."

CHAPTER 17

Y ou found what?" Ingeborg turned toward Manny and Trygve, who were barging into her kitchen.

"Grandma! We found the money, the bank money. My brothers hid it and we found it out at that farm where you went." Manny grinned at Trygve. "Seems she don't believe us."

"Guess you better show it to her, then."

Manny gimped back outside and returned with a satchel that looked to have died and been resurrected more than once. Manny untied the whipcord holding it closed and opened it so Ingeborg and then Freda could look inside. "We counted it. The whole fifty-five dollars. Now we have to figure what to do with it."

Ingeborg rolled her eyes. What was Anner going to think of this?

"I say give it back to the bank. Thataway Mr. Valders can't be mad at me anymore."

Oh, if only life were that simple! Ingeborg exchanged a raised-eyebrow look with Trygve, who wore a smug look that made Ingeborg want to laugh.

"I think this needs to be part of the shareholders meeting," she said.

Trygve frowned. "Is that scheduled?"

162

"Ja. They are pushing to make it Thursday night. Not that everyone will come, but I'm sure the school will be full."

"Another reason for a new school?" The quilting group had discussed the need for a new school more than once. Right now they had a one-room school for the grade school and another nearby for the high school. The grade school needed another teacher and thus another room. The women even had the audacity to dream of offering more classes at the high school, as they did in other places.

She glanced at Manny, who was shaking his head. "What about Mr. Valders?"

"Here's what we should do." Trygve nodded as he spoke. "At the meeting, you bring the bag forward and offer it to Mr. Valders. We'll see what he does."

Ingeborg asked, "But what if he accuses Manny of hiding it?"

"How could he? Manny was in the hospital, and he never saw his brothers again. That's what we remind him."

Oh, I think we are playing with fire here. But right now, the thought of Anner Valders getting his comeuppance made her mother's heart smile. It wouldn't help the situation for Thorliff, but it might help Manny.

"You had a good time camping?" Emmy asked as she came into the room.

"We did." He told her what they had done.

She cocked her head. "You have bad brothers?"

He nodded and hung his head. "They are in prison. In Kentucky."

"Kentucky is far away. I'm happy you are here." Emmy's smile made Ingeborg smile. Emmy too was coming out of another life and making a new one. Blessing was a good place for that.

Trygve glanced out the window. "Sure looks like it's going to rain out there. I better get my horse back home. Thanks, Manny. Let's get Joker unsaddled, and you can let him out in the pasture."

"Thanks. But I can do that now."

163

"Ja, I'm sure you can. But I don't want Dr. Astrid after my hide. Let me help. Okay?"

Manny shook his head, a grin tickling his cheeks.

❧

That evening Ingeborg was stitching the buttonholes on the waist for Emmy with Manny reading to her from his reader. He stopped and looked at her. "Can you help me write a letter to my brothers?"

"Of course. Where will you send it?"

"To the jail, I guess, in Louisville. That's where we pulled the first job. I wish . . ." He let out a sigh.

Ingeborg waited, then asked. "Wish what?"

"To know how they are." His jaw squared. "They're still my brothers." He studied the pages in front of him before looking up at her. "Do you have brothers and sisters?"

Ingeborg laid her handwork in her lap. "Ja, in Norway."

Emmy came and sat at her feet. "Far, far away. Across a big la . . . ocean." She sought and found the right word.

"Ja, that is right. Across the Atlantic Ocean. I came to America when I was young. We came in 1880. Thorliff was just a little boy."

"How come your brothers and sisters din't come too?"

"I don't really know. We invited them. Freda is my cousin."

Emmy leaned against Ingeborg's legs, her dark eyes watching Ingeborg's face. "Grandma has sad eyes."

Ingeborg nodded and stroked the little girl's dark hair, which she braided every morning. "Ja, I know I have sad eyes. But you make my heart glad." She rested her cheek against Emmy's head. She sat up straight, sniffed, and sighed. "Would you like to write that letter now?"

"If'n you don't mind."

"How far until the end of the chapter?"

He flipped through the pages. "Two to go."

"Good. You finish reading that, I will complete these button-

holes, and then we will move to the table and write that letter."
Making a decision, even one this small, felt good. Somehow her
decision-making skills had been drowned in her grief. At least
she hoped that was what it was.

She let Emmy coach him through the rest of the chapter as she
knotted the thread and clipped off, then did the last buttonhole.
She would cut them open when the light was better. She retrieved
paper and a pencil from the drop-front desk Haakan had made
one winter, and the three of them gathered at the kitchen table.

"Cookies?" Emmy asked.

"Of course."

"My writing is not good."

"But it is getting better, and before, you couldn't have written
a letter at all. You can do a practice one first."

Manny gripped the pencil as if it might try to get away. "How
do you spell *dear*?"

"How does it sound?"

"*D* . . ." He sounded the *e*. "*E*."

"Yes, but this is one of those strange words. Instead of
D-e . . ." She looked to him. "The last sound?"

"*R. D-e-r* . . ."

"Take two *e*'s for that sound," Emmy said. "But that's the
animal. The *dear* you want is spelled *d-e-a-r*."

Manny stared. "Whyever for?"

Emmy shrugged. Ingeborg shrugged. "Some words you just have
to memorize the spelling. Don't you have a spelling list this week?"

Manny let out a sigh. "I do. But this ain't on it."

"Don't say *ain't*," Emmy said. "Say *is not*."

He glared at her. "You write it, then."

She smiled at him. "Your brothers. Your letter."

Ingeborg smiled despite her sadness. "All right. Tell you what
we'll do. You tell me what you want to say. I will write it, and
you can write a line at the end and sign your name. How does
that sound?"

The look of utter relief on Manny's face made her realize how hard he was trying. And how far he had come.

She wrote what he said, including *Grandma Ingeborg is writing this for me, but I am learning to read and write. I will write the next letter if you write back to me.*

She slid the paper over to him. "Now you write."

I am good and can walk with a . . . He looked at her. "How do I spell *cane*?" As she waited he rolled his eyes. "Kuh, *k, a.*" He made the sound for *n*. "*N. K-a-n.* Does it need an *e*?"

"Sorry, Manny, but this word starts with a *c*, a hard *c*, which sounds like *k*. And you are right with the *e* at the end."

He crossed out the *k* and made a *c*. "Can I sign my name now?"

"Yes. You've done a good job."

Tongue between his teeth, Manny signed his first name. *Manny.* "Next time I will write my whole name."

"Now fold it and put it in the envelope, and I will address it."

With the letter finally finished, Ingeborg glanced at the clock. How could the evening fly by like this?

"I will mail it after school on Monday." He pushed his chair back. "Thank you."

After both of the children went to bed, Ingeborg got out the inkwell and wrote a letter to her family in Norway to tell them that Haakan had died, along with other news, and reiterated her former invitation for someone else to come.

> *I wrote you this before, but since we have not heard, I am wondering if the letter did not make it to you. Several people here in Blessing are looking for household help, and there is always plenty of work in construction here and farming too. I look forward to hearing from you. Please pass the news on to others.*
>
> *Ingeborg Bjorklund*

She addressed that envelope too and then headed for bed. When the telephone jangled, she stopped to pick it up.

"Hello?"

"Mor, I just wanted to tell you that you do not need to come in to sit with Mrs. Bach tonight. I think the regular nursing staff can handle it. And Mr. Bach is in her room also. She is still sleeping most of the time, but the blood flow has ceased, and we have been able to give her more broth and even mashed vegetables and rice in the soup."

"Oh, how wonderful. Takk for calling me."

"Sleep well."

"I will. Such glorious news." As Ingeborg readied herself for bed, she made sure she focused on God's Word rather than the empty side of the bed. She read and then repeated Psalm 23. "'The Lord is my shepherd.' Father, I miss having sheep. Maybe only two or three ewes, but I like taking care of them. Could you please find me some sheep again?" Pondering that thought, she knelt by the bed and thanked her heavenly Father for the day and the people she'd seen, church in the morning, and her family. She did not ask God to treat Anner the way he was treating other people, and then asked God to forgive her for even thinking it.

"I know this is all in your hands. I want to leave it there. Only you can bring the healing that is needed, and I have no idea how you are going to do so. I know faith is seeing what's not there yet. Please open the eyes of my heart to see clearly and trust you." She thought back to what Reverend Solberg had spoken on. Faith and trust. Both of them were far easier to say than to do. But she loved the picture in her mind of the eyes of her heart. She folded back the blanket and sheet and slid into bed. *Think on the Word rather than . . . than . . .* She took in a slow breath. Than the empty bed beside her.

Lying on her back, tears leaked out of her eyes and meandered through her hair onto her pillow. But at least they were gentle tears, more like a spring rain than a thunder and lightning storm. And like with a spring rain sinking into the earth, peace settled into her heart and she slept.

⁓

There was no pit last night was her first thought on waking Monday morning. *Thank you, Lord, there was no pit.* She could hear Freda in the kitchen rattling the grate. The rooster was trying to wake the dawn, and since the cows were not bellowing, they must have been in the barn already, being milked. How had Manny managed to leave the house without her hearing him? Maybe he was still sleeping? She threw back the covers and, grabbing her wrapper, headed for the kitchen.

"Is Manny—"

"Down at the barn? Yes. Sorry I woke you."

"I just woke up. It was time." Ingeborg stretched and yawned.

"I thought sourdough pancakes sounded good, so I started the batter last night."

"I see that. Let's make extra for raised biscuits."

Ingeborg returned to her room to dress and make the bed. It must have gotten close to freezing during the night, as chilly as the house was.

They had plenty of batter left, so Ingeborg stirred in more flour and emptied the crockery bowl out on a floured board. There was something about kneading bread that settled the soul. The sourdough fragrance tickled her nose and made her smile.

"I think we'll keep some out to fry for when Emmy and Manny get home from school. I haven't done that for a long time."

"Probably since last winter. Somehow that seems like a cold-weather food."

"Trygve said earlier that he would haul the cheese orders in today, right?"

"Ja, but I didn't remind him."

The sound of jingling harness accompanied Patches' barking that someone was there. Ingeborg looked out the window. "Speak of the angels. Do you want some more help?"

Freda slid her arms into her coat that hung on the pegs by the door. "No, we can do it. We have all the invoices ready, right?"

"That we do. And checked against the labels on the crates."

"We'll check one more time." Out the door Freda went, greeting Trygve. She climbed up on the wagon with him, and they drove over to the cheese house.

Ingeborg answered the insistent telephone. "Hello."

"Good morning, Mor. Are you planning on coming into town today?" Thorliff asked.

"Well, I wasn't, but Trygve is here to pick up a cheese shipment. I can come in with him, easy enough. Or do you mean later?"

"If you tell Elizabeth I said this, I will pour sour cream in your coffee, but she needs some Mor time."

"Is she weaker?"

"No. More frustrated with being housebound, I think. Which, on one hand, is a good thing."

"But on the other . . . I will come in with Trygve."

"Takk." He paused. "Did you think it strange that neither Anner nor Hildegunn were in church yesterday?"

Actually I enjoyed the peace and quiet. But Ingeborg did not say that aloud. They all had learned that anything said on the telephone, thanks to the party line, would be around Blessing faster than a horse could run. "They were probably helping Gerald and Rebecca." Thorliff's silence said he wasn't buying that line. "Did you mention your concern to Reverend Solberg?"

"No. See you in a while."

Ingeborg hung up the receiver. What could she take to Elizabeth that might cheer her up? An idea tiptoed in. She gathered up some of her smaller squares cut for a future quilt, looking for the ones with red or blue in them. Then she picked up the extra blue corduroy and folded that into the basket too, all the while smiling at her idea. This would be a surefire way to please both mother and daughter.

CHAPTER 18

Ingeborg met the wagon as it was leaving the cheese house. "Trygve, do you mind if I ride into town with you?"

"Not at all. How quickly can you be ready?"

"I'm ready." Ingeborg raised her basket.

"Then I shall go get some other things done." Freda stepped down out of the wagon and handed her the envelope with all the shipping information. "It is all there. We just made certain of that. I'll make sure there is dough left."

"Takk. Just punch it down again. If I were you, I wouldn't do the wash today, after all."

"Ja, it does look like rain."

Ingeborg handed her basket up and climbed up the wheel into the wagon.

Trygve looked to the north as he clucked to the horse. "That sure is blowing in quick."

"We might be grateful for the roofed end of the train depot. Not that rain could hurt the cheese any, but it sure could mess up the labels."

"I have a tarp in the back if we need it." He sent the horses into a trot as they drove down the lane. With the wind against their backs, Ingeborg unfolded her shawl and wrapped it over her

171

head and shoulders. The trip to the train station passed without discussion, since they needed to shout to be heard over the wind.

Trygve parked the wagon under the roofed section, and Ingeborg climbed down to take the paper work in to the stationmaster.

When she came out, Trygve was looking wistfully down the street to the apartment building. Ingeborg smiled. His face, his hands, his everything betrayed that he would best love to be building right now. He was heart and soul into these building projects, first simply volunteering labor when he should have been working on his own house, then getting paid to do carpentry. Bitterness bubbled to the surface again when she thought about the dispute with Anner.

With this wind, there would be no working on roofs today. At least they had the exterior nearly done, so most of the work now was inside. One of the single houses still had to be roofed, but the others were closed in too. The plan to be ready for fall move-ins needed to speed up. While the tent houses had worked for the summer, it would be too cold in weather like this. And this was just the beginning.

Trygve climbed down and walked over to the station to grab one of the dollies and started to unload the cheese crates.

"Eh, Trygve, might we lend ye a hand?"

They turned to see Thomas Devlin come crossing the street. With him, Silas Nordstrund, grinning inanely, ambled along. The fellow was a head taller than Thomas and twice as wide, but he seemed smaller in a way. A lovely meerschaum pipe stuck out of his ragged shirt pocket.

"If you want, certainly. I never turn down an offer of help."

"Wise man ye be. Ye've met Silas here, I aver."

"I have. Good to see you, Silas." Trygve extended his hand for a shake. "Tante Ingeborg, this is Silas, the night man at the grain elevator."

Ingeborg smiled. "Trygve mentioned you. How do you do?"

"Jus' fine, Miz Tanty." That same silly grin. Ingeborg remembered what Trygve had said: *"Silas makes Manny look like a Harvard professor."*

Devlin grabbed a four-wheeled baggage cart and pulled it over. "With three of us we can stack them on this. Ingeborg," he said, nodding toward her. "Top of the morning to yerself."

"Good morning, Father Devlin." She greeted him with a smile. "And to you."

As the train screeched in, the stationmaster stepped over to the door of the freight car, the paper work all ready.

She watched Mr. Nordstrund. The man was slow of mind, that was for sure. But what a fine worker he was! And strong! He ignored the baggage cart and simply tucked a cheese crate under each arm, strolling into the freight car, hardly noticing his burden. Within minutes they'd transferred the load, just in time to hear the whistle of the train. This time, the train whistle announced its departure, and the train headed for parts east.

The conductor shouted, "All aboard," and the train wheels screamed steel against steel to get the behemoth in motion again.

Thomas stood erect and wiped his brow. "I take it this is from your cheese house?"

"Ja. Our first big shipment this fall."

Trygve smiled. "Thanks for the help."

"Most welcome. We'll be getting back to our jobs." Devlin touched the brim of his hat and strode back across the street and past the post office next to the apartment house, his friend tagging along beside.

"So often he manages to show up at the just right time, doesn't he?" Ingeborg smiled at Trygve. "I'm going over to Thorliff's. What about you?"

"I'll give you a ride."

Trygve stopped the wagon outside the fence and headed for the newspaper office off to the right while Ingeborg climbed the steps to the house.

Thelma met her at the door. "Oh, how good to see you! I know this will help cheer Elizabeth, for sure. You go on in."

"Ingeborg? Am I hearing right?" Elizabeth called. They had turned one of the two rooms where they used to take care of patients into a sitting room/office for Elizabeth, and she slept in the other room, since she was forbidden the stairs.

Ingeborg found her in the sitting room with a shawl around her shoulders, dressed in a simple day dress. The fact that she wasn't in nightclothes meant she was indeed feeling better.

"You have color back in your face, and even your voice is stronger. Oh, my dear, I am so glad for you."

"We can blame it on Astrid. What a tyrant." She waved to the other rocker. "Sit. It has been too long since we had a real visit."

Ingeborg sat and set her basket on the floor.

"So what do you have there?"

"I have an idea for something really special for Inga." Ingeborg picked up the basket and set it on her lap. "I have been sewing for Emmy ever since I realized everything she had was too small. Like far too short and too tight, and I felt terrible. So Miriam and I bought both red and blue corduroy to make jumpers for Emmy. I was sewing the red one, and Inga said blue was her favorite."

"I can guess where this is going."

"So today I had an idea. I don't have enough blue left for a jumper, but I have quite a bit. So what if we pieced these squares together for the bodice, and put a band around the middle of the skirt?" She laid out the squares. "What do you think?"

"I think we'd better start stitching. What a clever idea."

"This way we can make do with what we have."

"We could go buy some more corduroy, you know."

"I know, but I think this will suit her." She laid out alternating blue and red print cotton squares on her lap with several white ones, then laid blues on red and vice versa. She handed one stack to Elizabeth, along with a needle and thread. "Sew them in pairs, and then we'll alternate them on the next row."

"Coffee's ready." Thelma brought in a tray and set it on the low table. "What's this you're doing?" She peered at the pairs. "A quilt?"

"No. A jumper for Inga. Do you want to join us?"

"I could for a while." She poured the coffee, handed the cups around, and they chose their own cookies.

Ingeborg explained the design again, and they sewed the pairs together. Thelma whisked the tray off the table, and they laid them out again. Quickly they had enough for the bodice. "Now I'll lay the pattern on this and cut it out. I'll use white for the facing and possibly to line it. We can sew a long strip for an inset in the skirt."

While they stitched, they caught up and shared what they knew of events in Blessing. Elizabeth's delight was contagious when Ingeborg told of the children and then of Benny's riding Joker, Manny's horse.

"Inga had such fun that day. She bubbled past bedtime."

"I think all the children did. I was so proud of Manny, I nearly busted my buttons."

"You know Inga. She has to have pockets. Ouch!" Elizabeth sucked on her finger.

"True. Let's see. Four squares is too big for pockets for her, and two won't look right."

"Why not cut the original squares in four? We can piece them like we did the bigger ones and then use three across." Thelma looked to Ingeborg, who smiled and nodded.

"I should have brought the pattern with me." Ingeborg rolled out their pieced strip. "But I never dreamed we'd get this far."

"Six hands are faster than four." Elizabeth cocked her head. "You think we've solved all of Blessing's problems too?"

"Short of what to do about Anner Valders, I'd say so." Ingeborg shook her head. "I'm sure grateful that God knows what He is doing, because I most assuredly have run out of ideas."

"I watch Thorliff trying to act as if he is no longer angry, and then I see him lose his temper over some little thing that goes wrong. Like he ran out of shaving soap. He was furious. Over shaving soap! That is not my Thorliff."

"Nor mine. I keep thanking God for the answer, but I have no idea what it will be. The Valders weren't even in church yesterday. Neither of them."

"I've been reading Hebrews, chapter eleven: 'Now faith is the substance of things hoped for, the evidence of things not seen.'" Elizabeth laid her sewing in her lap. "I have never before read my Bible like I have been doing lately. Some of the verses have brought me such comfort and peace. More than that, I'm discovering how much it fits this situation. We have no idea what will happen with Anner, but we know God will deal with him. And that's faith."

"*Hmph!*" Thelma snorted. "The verse in First Timothy is more like it. It says when you put away conscience, you make a shipwreck of your faith."

The rumble of thunder caught their attention. Lightning jagged the western sky. Looking out, they saw bending trees and flailing branches.

"I knew it was getting darker, but we've been having such a good time, I didn't pay much attention." Ingeborg looked around. "Shall we light some of these lamps?"

When the rain hit, it sounded like a roaring train, drenching the world like a washtub had turned over on it.

Thelma returned with some matches. "You light the lamps. I better run upstairs and check the windows there."

"Good thing Freda is at my place. I might have left my bedroom window open a small bit." Ingeborg lighted the two lamps.

Elizabeth and Ingeborg finished the pieced strip and laid it out between two pieces of corduroy.

Elizabeth beamed. "Oh, that is going to look so perfect! All these years I've not had time to join the quilters, and here we are making something beautiful for my daughter. Thank you, Ingeborg. You couldn't have planned anything better."

Slowly the thunder and lightning moved away from Blessing, but the rain poured for another hour or more. Thelma brought in trays of bread and soup and the cucumber pickles she'd made in the summer. Thorliff and Trygve came running in from the newspaper office, and soon they each had a tray in the sitting room too.

Thank you, Lord, for my son, for his calling me this morning. At least he wouldn't have to pour sour cream in her coffee, as he had teased that he would do if she told Elizabeth what they were up to. The thought made her smile.

Thorliff brought up what the women had been ignoring. "Anner is furious that he has to have a report ready in time for the meeting."

Ingeborg shook her head. "Why is that? He has always bragged that he has the bankbooks ready for inspection at any time. Give him an hour was all he asked."

"I know. This caught me by surprise too."

"I could understand if this was right after the robbery, but this is months later. Surely he has things in order again. And it was only that one money box that was stolen, not the whole bank." Ingeborg rubbed her chin. "Has he said he cannot be ready?"

"No, just that he doesn't want to do it. This is Monday. He has three more days. If he gets it to me in time, I will print it out. If he doesn't, he can write it on the blackboard. Always in the past, he brought it over, and I set it and printed it. He never seemed affronted before, not in all the years I've known him."

"But in the past, the date has been established long before the meeting time," Elizabeth reminded them.

"I know. That's probably it. But this concerns me. Maybe running the bank is getting to be too much for him," Trygve said.

"He's done it all by himself all these years." Thorliff shook his head.

I don't think that's the problem, Ingeborg thought, but she couldn't get a handle on what was going through her mind.

"I still think he is trying to get even. Anner Valders does not like change, and you have to admit, Blessing is changing faster than anyone ever dreamed." Elizabeth laid her hands in her lap. "Ever since the robbery. Maybe that knock on the head addled his brains."

"What a horrid thought." Ingeborg looked to her son. Thorliff was staring out the window, but she had a feeling he was not seeing the weather. "Everyone agreed to pray. Right?"

He nodded slowly, barely. The wind rattled the windows, and rainwater sluiced from the drain spouts and into the barrels.

Ingeborg caught Trygve looking at her with raised eyebrows. She shrugged and turned inward to remind God that He had promised to answer. *Where two or three are gathered, I am in the midst.* How often she had clung to that promise.

Thorliff asked, "Do you think God will really answer? I mean, we put Him on the spot, almost like a demand."

Ah, the crux of the silence. "He says to pray, believing."

"I-I'm not sure I believe strong enough. I look at this mess, and I see no good outcome."

"Has He answered in the past?"

Thorliff grimaced. "He did not keep Far alive."

And your wife is pregnant, dangerously so. "I know. Oh, how I know." Tears didn't leak, they spurted and, like the rain drenching the windows, soaked her cheeks.

He looked stricken. "Mor, I am so sorry."

"Don't be. We need to talk of these things, and my tears cannot be a deterrent. I cry and they dry up. We ask God our questions, and we are surrounded by His love. He never lets us go. I was not ready for Haakan to die yet, but no one can ever be ready. Death is part of life, but our lives do not end here. We have a heavenly home, and in that heavenly home, Haakan is waiting for me. Jesus is waiting for us. He is here, all around us.

I do not understand how, but I believe His Word." She mopped and blew. Elizabeth and Thelma did the same, and finally so did Thorliff and Trygve. "And if I know nothing else, I know our Father loves us, far more than we can think or imagine."

Thelma stood up and shook her head. "I left Scooter on the porch. I just realized he is crying." When she left the room, Trygve looked outside. "It has quit raining, at least for now. Shall we make a run for home, Tante Ingeborg?"

"Of course." She gathered up her things. "Were those poor horses out in all this?"

"Of course not, Mor. I put them in the barn, although if they'd been home, they would have most likely stayed right out in it." Thorliff pushed to his feet too.

Thelma returned, the little dog grinning up at her. She picked up the conversation. "Right, and gone to stand under a tree and been struck by lightning." She gathered up the trays and dinner things.

Elizabeth walked with them out to the kitchen and hugged Ingeborg good-bye. "Thank you for coming. You have no idea how low I was feeling."

"I think God gave a gift to both of us. As you saw, the tears sure well up easy, so often triggered by the slightest thought." She inhaled a deep breath. "So I thank you and God too." *And Thorliff, whom I will thank later.*

The rain drifted back in as Trygve drove her home. "Your mail is in the bag there."

"Takk. Uh-oh. Manny planned on mailing his letter after school. He took it with him."

"I'll go pick up all the kids after school. They can tent under the tarp in the wagon. We can go by the post office too."

"Trygve, you are so good to us. What would I do without you?"

He grinned at her. "You might invite Miriam out to your house for a meal someday. And me, of course."

"I will gladly have you both. You go ahead and invite her, and just let me know which day she can come."

"Thank you, Tante Ingeborg."

"Oh, and I wonder if she'd like to come out early and do some sewing with me. Why don't you ask her about that too. And is there anything special you'd like me to fix?"

"An apple pie?"

"Good idea."

At last, something positive to do.

CHAPTER 19

I will keep this meeting on track. Thorliff repeated his order to himself.

Anner glowered from the front row to his left. He had brought the report to Thorliff late the day before, and Thorliff got it set and printed, finally making it to bed by midnight.

He stood waiting for the hubbub to settle down. When quiet almost reigned, he raised his voice. "The meeting will please come to order." He waited before repeating it a bit louder. When he had their attention, he continued. "Reverend Solberg will open our meeting with prayer." He nodded to the pastor sitting in the front row with his wife, Mary Martha, on one side of him, Thomas Devlin on the other.

That Father Devlin was there caught him by surprise. Since these were all bank patrons, the father had to have opened an account at the bank too. Thorliff stared around the room. More of the recent additions to Blessing were there than he had expected. But all anyone had to do was open an account. He wasn't sure if there was a minimum deposit or not.

Reverend Solberg stood. "Heavenly Father, we thank you for your great love and tender mercies. We thank you that you care about every part of our lives, that you promise to give us wisdom

181

whenever and however we need it. Lord, you have made us a community, a family. We count on you to resolve any issues that we have, to take care of all our people, your people, that you have brought us. No one is here by accident. And now we ask you to bless our meeting and bring us to agreement and understanding, always keeping in mind your instructions to love one another, to forgive one another, and to always seek your will. Give us ears to hear and eyes to see. In the mighty name of your son, Jesus Christ. Amen."

John sat down and Thorliff pushed himself to his feet.

"Anner Valders, I ask you to present your report of the Community Bank of Blessing, North Dakota." *Lord God, help us.* He nodded to Anner and moved away from the podium, sitting in the front row beside his mor.

Anner settled his papers on the podium, which was really a wooden music stand. "Good evening. Do you all have a copy of the report? If not, raise your hand." Several people raised their hands, and Hjelmer brought them the ten-page report.

"Thank you all for coming. It is good to see new faces here. You, who have chosen to become part of our little town."

Thorliff turned to see that Ingeborg appeared as shocked as he felt. "His words and eyes don't match." Ingeborg nodded.

Thorliff clenched his jaw. Anything to keep the peace.

"Not so little anymore." The comment made a flutter of laughter pass through the room.

"That is so true. As many of you know, our annual meeting in January is when we have looked at the bank report in the past, but this *emergency* meeting was called, which apparently is the way we do business now, so here we are."

Thorliff felt the barb, the inflection on *emergency*, but he ignored that too.

"My big concern is that you all realize there has been no wrongful activity in our bank. We were robbed in June, as you know, and we retrieved all but fifty-five dollars of the stolen money. Three of the four robbers were apprehended and properly tried, and are now confined to prison in Kentucky."

Thorliff gritted his teeth. Ingeborg laid a hand on his arm, and he covered it with his other.

"Mr. Valders? Sir?" The voice came from the rear of the room. Thorliff shot a look at his mother. "What is . . . ?"

She squeezed his arm.

Thorliff twisted to see Manny on his cane come thumping toward the front along the wall. Trygve followed behind him and stopped off to the side.

Manny handed a dusty old valise to Anner. "This, sir, is the money my brothers took. We found it—Trygve and me—out at the farm where my brothers was hiding out. It belongs to the bank, so I wanted to give it back to you, even though Trygve and Gram—I mean Miz Ingeborg—said I needn't."

Anner's mouth dropped open. He just stood there and stared. Thorliff closed his own mouth, which had dropped open as well.

And then Anner exploded. "You little wretch! You knew where it was all along! You figured you would just—"

But Astrid leaped to her feet. "Anner Valders! When Manny's brothers escaped, he was lying on the ground, and they never saw one another again. He couldn't have known anything!"

"They told him when they came to kidnap him at the hospital! You know that! You were there! You heard them. So you've known where it was all along!"

Astrid continued. "I know exactly what happened that day because I was witness to it. Manny was completely doped with morphine, hearing nothing, and his brothers mentioned nothing about money. Don't you tell me what happened in that room, Anner Valders, when you have no idea what took place!"

Anner roared, "You are mocking me! Trying to embarrass me! You're all in this together! You, Thorliff, all these yellow-bellied bleeding hearts who think it's quite fine to coddle a bank robber just because—"

But he didn't get to end his sentence. Trygve had stepped up behind him. He grabbed Anner by both ears, holding them tight like a teacher would discipline a rowdy child. He moved Anner sideways and plunked him in a chair.

Then he let go and leaned over, facing Anner nose to nose. "You will never, and I mean *never*, speak to a woman in that tone of voice again." He stood erect and backed away.

John Solberg was on his feet too, but it was Thomas Devlin who stepped between Trygve and Anner. Very quietly, very soothingly, he said, "Peace be unto ye, Trygve. Peace be within ye." And he marked a little cross with his thumb on Trygve's forehead. He wheeled around to Anner. "And peace be unto ye also, Anner. May it settle in yer poor sore heart and give ye rest."

He reached out toward Anner, but Anner snapped to his feet so fast, he dumped the chair backwards on the floor. "You're a charlatan! You're not a true man of God!" He looked about wildly. "You've all been taken in by this mountebank! And by a bank robber! You are fools! All of you! What is the matter with all of you?" He stormed down the narrow aisle and out the door. Even his flaming ears shot off sparks.

No one moved or spoke. Silence. Astrid sat down.

Thorliff was chairing this meeting. Now what? He got up and walked over to the music stand.

Manny was saying to Trygve, "I'm sorry. I'm so sorry. You were right. I was wrong. I shouldn'ta tried to give him his money back." He started to walk away, but Trygve stopped him, holding on to his arm.

Trygve looked around the room. "I don't know how many of you knew Manny here when he first arrived. Those of you who did, you know he was a sullen, scowling, obnoxious pain. And look at him now. Here is a young man brave enough to step forward and try to do the right thing. Try to do the honest thing. Thorliff, Astrid, Elizabeth, Tante Ingeborg, we all see his value. That is why we took him in. He is an honest, caring young man."

Thorliff asked, "Manny, what shall we do with this money you found, since Anner doesn't seem to want it?"

Manny shrugged. He looked so sad. And frightened.

Reverend Solberg suggested, "Finders keepers. Let him open his own account with it. The first step toward a responsible adulthood, a good citizen of Blessing."

A voice called out, "I so move." It sounded like Mr. Sam.

Another said, "I second."

Thorliff nodded and looked around. "It's been moved and seconded. Discussion?"

Manny was about to become fifty-five dollars richer. Instead of happy, he looked near tears.

Trygve asked, "What would you prefer, Manny?"

"I don' know. But it ain't mine. Never was. I don' want it if'n it ain't mine." He was studying Trygve, looking intently at him. "Can Blessing buy something with it? Does the town need something? The town all paid my debt. Maybe they can think of something."

Thorliff looked at his mor. She was beaming with pride. He looked at all these many people, shareholders in a struggling bank. "We can all think of something, that's for sure. The town needs everything. Anyone have suggestions?"

"I do." John Solberg stood up. "For years we have been talking about being prepared for sudden emergencies. What if a prairie fire really got going and threatened the town? What if a drought started wiping out farms and farmers? The river flooded? Tornadoes? Let's consider what we might need in that area."

Jonathan Gould stood. "And we have no law enforcement. We have to rely on others. But what if they cannot get here when we need them?"

"Manny," Thorliff asked, "do you think we should spend this money on something like that?"

The boy smiled. "Yes, sir! That'd be right fine."

"If you wish, sit over there in the chair beside Mrs. Bjorklund—

Ingeborg—and we'll pick a worthy project to use your money on."

Andrei Belin stood. His English was halting but a lot better than it had been a short while ago. "Perhaps we hire more workers, finish houses sooner. Getting cold."

Trygve nodded. "We are already hiring every able-bodied man who shows up. Not enough are showing up."

Daniel stood. "I highly recommend purchasing some fire apparatus. If a house catches fire, we form a bucket brigade. But that isn't going to work well here in town. We need a pumper."

Andrew stood. "It won't work in this part of the country. There's no barn warm enough in midwinter to keep a fire pumper with any water in it from freezing solid."

Thomas Devlin stood up. "I happen to know a wee bit about fire apparatus as it be used in St. Louis. I worked there a few years ago. Andrew is right. So ye store the pumper drained in wintertime. In the event of a fire, ye run it down to the river shore, break a hole in the ice if need be, and draft out of the river. Fill yer tank. Douse yer fire. Drain the pumper again before putting it away."

Joshua Landsverk stood. "In Fargo, I hear, they keep their equipment in a barn that's kept warm in winter, above freezing. And horses that are harnessed and ready to go. Of course, that is a big city. Here, though, we have enough building to do before we'd think about building a firehouse. Draining it in winter would be a good plan."

Thorliff asked Thomas, "Do you have some idea how much fire equipment fifty-five dollars would buy?"

Thomas stood up. "How many fires do ye have in a year, about?"

"Say two or three. Usually a barn. And it's usually ashes before we get there."

Thomas turned to face the audience. "Then ye'd not be needing a fancy rig such as a steam engine. Ye'd have to keep a fire going in it, and that be a lot of wood or coal to burn to put out two or three fires a year. I suggest a hand pumper. It operates as a bilge pump operates aboard a sailing vessel—a seesaw pumped up and down by two men. The pump draws water into a large tin holding tank, which ye then squirt on the fire."

"Like a handcar on the railroad?" someone asked.

"The very thing. And ye need not buy a new one. When large cities get bigger equipment, they ofttimes sell the old. The older apparatus would work well for our purposes. Fifty-five dollars ought to set ye up in the fire-extinguishing business just fine, including the shipping to get it here."

Manny was grinning. "I'd be right proud if you bought a fire engine with the money. I truly would!"

Thorliff was grinning too.

Toby Valders was not. He stood up. "It's a waste of money in a town this small. We've been getting along just fine without it. We need a lot of other things before we need fire equipment."

Jonathan rose. "The town is not small, and it's not going to get any smaller. Blessing is growing. They have quite fancy pumpers back East, as Mr. Devlin described, and he's right about a hand pumper for Blessing. You don't even need horses with a small rig such as the city neighborhoods back East use. The volunteers pull it with a T-shaped shaft. I move we set the money aside and buy a fire pumper for town use. House it in a tent until we can build a firehouse."

Thorliff shook his head. "We already have a motion on the floor."

Mr. Sam called, "I withdraw my motion. Can I do that?"

Thorliff frowned. "I don't know." He looked at Thomas, at John. "Can he?"

They shrugged.

"Anybody have a copy of *Robert's Rules of Order*?"

Apparently no one did.

Thorliff was running this meeting. He'd just have to make

a snap decision. "If the motion is withdrawn, we'd have to withdraw the second as well, and—"

"I withdraw my second."

"The standing motion and its second have been withdrawn from the floor. Jonathan?"

"I repeat my motion."

John Solberg nodded. "And I second."

"It's been moved and seconded that we spend this money on a fire pumper appropriate for the town's use. Discussion?"

"And the tent," Jonathan added.

"And a tent. Discussion?"

People were nodding.

"In favor?"

Many hands went up.

"Opposed?"

Toby Valders and a couple of others raised their hands.

"Do we need a count?"

Toby frowned but did not request a count.

"Motion passed." Thorliff licked his lips. "I had one other item on the agenda when we came, the reason I called the meeting, but now there are two. The first is that a loan extension to complete our building projects has been denied. Now we must come up with some other way to keep the workers paid. The second item—new business—is what should we do about the bank manager, if anything. Discussion?"

Mr. Sam rose again. "Who would deny a building loan extension? It's community money for community projects."

"Anner."

"He can't do that!"

Thorliff shrugged. "Last night I went down through the bank's operating agreement, section by section. It doesn't say anything about either granting or refusing a loan or extension. I guess we didn't imagine it would ever come up."

Joshua Landsverk stood. "Then we can solve both items on

your agenda with one motion. I make a motion that we fire Anner Valders and hire someone who understands what this town needs."

Instantly someone called, "I second!"

Thorliff sighed. "Discussion?"

Reverend Solberg stood up and turned to the people. "Anner is very upset, and now we all are. This is not the time to fire Anner, as you put it. Not when we are angry and have not had time to consider our action. I beg you all to insist your head rule over your heart and your anger, and everyone cool off before we decide what to do. Garn, can you file for a loan? You own the grain elevator, and you've been talking about adding on to it. Ask for perhaps half of what we need, and Gerald, would you file a loan application for the balance? I have reasons for asking this, but I don't wish to reveal them just yet. With money in hand, we can take our time making serious decisions."

A lot of rumbling and mumbling went on, with people talking to each other.

Thorliff let it ride a few minutes, then raised his voice. "Order, please!" The rumble quieted. "We have a motion on the floor. Further discussion?" He waited. "Those in favor?"

It looked to be about half, so he called for a count.

"Opposed?"

Again, a count.

"The nos outweigh the yeses by four votes. Motion defeated. Reverend Solberg, was that a motion you made?"

"It is now."

"Second?"

Someone seconded.

"Discussion? . . . Those in favor? . . . Opposed? . . . Motion carried. If there isn't any more business, I ask for a motion for dismissal."

"So move." That was Gerald Valders.

"Second."

Thorliff rapped on the music stand podium. "Dismissed." He gathered up his copy of the bank report.

Thomas was grinning as he stepped up. "Well done, lad. Ye'll be the president of the United States yet."

Thorliff laughed. "Can't. I was born in Norway."

"Eh, lad, don't let that stop ye! We need yer ilk."

Half a dozen men, Mr. Sam among them, came over to Manny, shook his hand, and thanked him. It must have been difficult to look happy and nonplussed at the same time, but Manny managed. Ingeborg too was thanking him.

Thorliff asked Reverend Solberg, "What was that all about? Asking Garn Huslig and Gerald to file for loans?"

"For some reason Anner has it against some of us, especially against any Bjorklunds. Men who are not closely associated with the Bjorklund clan stand a better chance of obtaining a loan. So I asked them. Gerald says he's going over to the bank tomorrow."

Trygve, who had joined them, said, "I felt so much like slugging him! Never felt more like striking someone. I guess he's lucky I only grabbed his ears."

Reverend Solberg gently shook his head. "I understand how you felt, but that was not exactly the best way to bring an enemy over to your side."

Trygve sighed. "Probably not. At least he's not injured." He rubbed his fist. "Me either."

Thorliff took the satchel from Manny, who had picked it up and was hugging it close. "Should we start a separate account for the fire equipment?"

"Let me do that." Reverend Solberg held out his hand, so Thorliff gave him the bag. "Then you don't have to go to the bank."

"Good." Thorliff smiled at Manny. "The soda shop is closed now, but tomorrow we're going out for ice cream. To celebrate."

"Celebrate what? I was dead wrong. I thought he'd like me if'n I gave him back his money. Instead, he hates me worse."

"How he sees you is not your problem, Manny. It's his. You did what you hoped was best, and that's all anyone can do." *God help us all to do what's best.*

CHAPTER 20

M iriam, will you please work closely with Mrs. Bach today? We need to get her up and moving and eating more too." Nurse Deborah was assigning responsibilities for the shift.

"Of course."

"Dawn Breaking and Gray Cloud, you will be training with Dr. Bjorklund until it is time to serve dinner."

They both nodded.

"This afternoon, Dr. Bjorklund will be training all of us on disaster procedures, so be thinking on that. You are all dismissed. I'll be working on the charts and checking supplies."

Miriam headed for the private room where they had kept Leona Bach, since they hadn't needed the bed for anyone else. Helping this young woman want to get well was proving to be a big order. "Mrs. Bach, Leona, good morning." She laid a hand on the young woman's shoulder, studying her face as she did so. Skin so translucent the bones and muscles shadowed it, purple wounds under her eyes, so thin and losing even more weight.

The woman's eyes fluttered open.

"We need to go for a walk so you can get stronger." She knew the young woman did not speak English, so she mimicked each action as she spoke. "Can you sit up by yourself?"

"Hurts." One of the words she had learned.

"I know, but moving around will help that." Miriam hoped she wasn't just making that up. "Come, take my hands and I will help you." She helped the patient to a sitting position, then swung her legs over the edge. "Are you dizzy?" Once she had Leona on her feet, she waited for her to stabilize, then began walking her out the door and down the hall. When the woman sagged against her, she sat her on a chair they had placed there for just such a need. When she seemed stronger again, they walked back past the room and into the ward. They stopped again at the end of the hall. "Good. You are doing good." She smiled and nodded as she spoke.

Leona walked even more slowly on the way back to her room and, when they got there, sat down on the bed with a big sigh, her smile tremulous.

Miriam helped her lie down. "I will bring you something to eat." She made spooning motions. "You must eat more."

Leona nodded but her eyes drifted closed.

Miriam headed for the kitchen. "Mrs. Geddick, I need something more solid but easy for Mrs. Bach to eat."

"I have soup, and bread just out of the oven."

"I see. It smells so good in here. Do you have cheese for the bread?"

Mrs. Geddick said yes and turned to get it.

"Let's put the soup in a cup so she can eat it more easily. She needs to eat every two hours, she is so weak." But when she returned with a tray to the room, Leona was sound asleep. Which was more important, sleep or food? Miriam leaned over and shook her patient gently first, then firmly. When Leona opened her eyes, her nurse motioned to the tray.

"You have to eat."

"No."

"Just a little. I'll help you sit up." *You'll eat even if I have to feed you.* After propping pillows and getting her situated,

193

Miriam set the tray on her lap and sat down on the edge of the bed. She pointed to each item as she named them. "Soup. Cheese. Bread. Milk." She picked up the cup and handed it to Leona, who shook her head. But she did pick up the bread and cheese and, while slowly, ate half of it. "Good." Nods and smiles.

"Now the soup." Miriam held the cup for her, then switched to a spoon and fed her. When the woman shook her head, Miriam smiled. "You did well. You can sleep now for a while." She removed the tray, then the pillows, and by the time she reached the door, the woman was asleep again.

"How did it go?" Deborah asked.

"We have to get someone to talk with her. Can someone talk to her husband and help him understand?"

"We'll find that woman who took her to Dr. Bjorklund. Did she eat?"

"Some bread and cheese, and I fed her half a cup of soup. I'll do it again in two hours. She had to sit down at both ends of the hall, then collapsed on her bed."

Deborah smiled and nodded. "That's better than yesterday. Keep it up."

That afternoon Astrid handed out three printed pages to each of them, listing the procedures they would follow. "Once you've read through this, I will answer any questions you have. Two things are primary: If an emergency occurs, I need everyone to come to the hospital immediately. If you have to help somewhere else, we will send you from here. We have to know where all of you are at all times, for your own safety and in order for us to work efficiently. That rule does not apply, of course, if you are in the middle of an emergency and are needed on the spot. But people will be bringing their injured to the hospital, so this is where we must be.

"The other thing: Keep calm and do not panic. We will take care of the injured as quickly as we can and in an orderly way, the worst first."

Miriam read through the pages. They looked so much like

the instructions she'd practiced in Chicago, only on a much smaller basis. They had one department here rather than four.

After turning Leona's care over to Corabell and making sure all her bookwork was up to date, Miriam pushed open the front door to find Trygve leaning against one of the columns holding up the portico. Her rebellious heart, ignoring her former admonition that he was only a friend, skipped a beat.

"Don't you ever work?" Her mouth wasn't behaving either.

"Of course. In fact, I now have a paying job as a carpenter." His smile added to the reaction. "I am free for the moment, and I figured you might like to see a face not of the hospital." He fell into step beside her. "If the soda shop were open, I would ask if you wanted a soda, but . . ." He shrugged.

What to say? Why did she feel so tongue-tied?

"Also, I have a mission. Tante Ingeborg has invited us to join her for dinner sometime. Can you come tomorrow?"

His aunt's good Norwegian cooking! As lovely as the meals were at the boardinghouse, Ingeborg's cooking appealed. Everything was always so fresh and delicious. *Let's see, tomorrow is Saturday* . . . "Why, thank you! Yes, I would love it."

"I can come for you and bring the buggy if you'd like."

"Or we could walk?"

"That we could. Oh, and Tante Ingeborg said I was to tell you that you can come early if you would like to help with some sewing."

"Then yes, if you want to. I mean, I do know the way." Even her eyes did not behave, sneaking looks at him. Small and short as she was, he made her feel even shorter. And she was afraid her bush of hair must be absolutely wild—she'd not looked in a mirror recently. When his arm brushed hers, a shiver shot to her head, taking a swipe at her middle too. They made the steps to the boardinghouse porch in perfect match.

"I'll see you tomorrow, then?" he was smiling broadly.

"When?"

"Uh, say ten thirty?"

"See you then."

She'd read of eyes locking but thought it a silly saying—until now. And yes, definitely, eyes could talk. And . . . no! She stepped back, whirled, and almost threw herself through the door. She took the stairs at a run and, once in her room, leaned against the closed door. Had he really wanted to kiss her? Had she really wanted him to?

Hearing her name called, she crossed to the window. Trygve stood in the street, looking up at her. Opening the window, she leaned out, just a bit, of course.

"I'll bring a buggy. We could go for a ride."

"No. I am going to sew." *Go for a ride, you silly girl.* "And I want to walk. I love to walk here."

"Not like Chicago, eh?" He touched the brim of his narrow-brimmed hat. "Walk it is, then." Hands in his pockets, he turned and headed off down the street. She could hear him whistling a cheerful tune.

Closing the window, she looked to the bed. How delicious it would be to lie down for even a little bit, but instead she crossed to the table and laid out paper and a pencil. A letter to her family was at the top of her mental list of things she needed to do. She'd just written the greeting when a tap on her door broke her attention.

"Yes?"

"It's me, Vera."

"Come in." She'd finish the letter after supper.

"Oh, I am so glad to have you back." Vera hugged her and then whirled her around. "Oh, Miriam, I have news. I have met a man."

Miriam nodded. Should she say she had already heard? No. Vera was obviously too eager to share her news. Miriam would never want to spoil it. "And how did you meet him?"

"Right here in the dining room. He asked if he could sit beside me one supper, and I said yes. We talked and talked. We even went from the table to the parlor so we could keep talking."

196

"I see. And what does this man who loves to talk do for a living?" Miriam already knew, but she loved to see the glow on her friend's face.

"He is the dentist here in Blessing."

"Ah! Dr. Deming!"

"Yes! Miriam, he is *so* nice! He is having a house built here in Blessing, he likes it so much here."

"So that means that you will be returning to Blessing when we complete schooling?"

Her neck turned pink. "Well, it certainly hasn't progressed so far yet that I need think about that. But . . . well, you know . . ."

"Yes, I know." *And would I return to Blessing for Trygve?*

Miriam would. The answer rang in her head clear and strong, so definite it startled her.

The supper bell sounded.

"Let me wash my hands, and then we'll go eat. Or would you rather eat with Dr. Deming?"

"He won't be eating here tonight."

"I see." Miriam smiled at herself in the mirror above the sink. Life here in Blessing was making an impact on all of them.

After supper, she finished her letter to her family, telling of her invitation to dinner tomorrow.

I know you would all like it here. Mother would have loved it. How are things going for you at the hospital? In school? And Tonio, with your job? There is so much construction going on here as they try to finish the buildings before winter sets in. As I told you, those people who live in tents need warm places by winter. They say winter here makes winter in Chicago look like spring or fall. But I am sure they are exaggerating. I love you all and miss you.

Your big sister,
Miriam

She folded the letter, slid it into the envelope, and addressed it. Never again would she send a letter to her mother. The thought hit her like a sledgehammer. She sank down into the rocking chair and let her tears run, not even bothering to mop them away. When the tear spring ran dry, she changed into her nightdress and crawled into bed. Grief certainly had a way of hiding and then sneaking up on one.

She spent the next morning reading one of her nursing manuals about making home visits and about the prenatal care of the mother. These were major programs at the Chicago hospital, and from the looks of Mrs. Bach, there were people here needing the same thing. Thoughts of Trygve kept intruding.

At ten thirty, she went on downstairs and saw Trygve coming up the porch steps. Her treacherous heart did a replay of the day before. This had to stop. She would be going back to Chicago when her year here was finished, first to complete her training and then to work at the hospital. That was the way she'd planned her life, after all.

After all.

Stupid plan. There was another silly thought she hadn't anticipated.

"You ready?" Trygve interrupted her thoughts.

The thought of *after all* went right out the door before she could reply.

"I hope you don't mind, but after I walk you to the farm, I'm going to go visit my family for a little bit. See if Pa needs a hand with anything."

"But you'll still be joining us for dinner?"

"I wouldn't miss it!"

All the way out to the farm, Trygve entertained her with stories of the places they saw, of the people who lived there, and of life growing up in the area. He had lived in an entirely different world than she had.

"Have you ever been to a big city?" she asked.

"I was in Minneapolis for a few days. That's a real city."

"I have a feeling Chicago is different, but then I've only seen Minneapolis from the train and in the train station. It looks a lot cleaner, not with tenements like Chicago has."

He gave a little shrug. "I'm not sure I know what a tenement really is."

"The one we lived in was seven stories tall, with ten flats on each floor, the largest ones having only two bedrooms. Many families have more than five children, and often families share a flat, or several generations do. Often there is no water or heat. And if people do not have jobs, they don't have food. *Slums* is another word I've heard used for these areas in Chicago. Jobs are scarce because there are so many people needing work. Crime of all kinds is rampant." When he didn't say anything, she turned to look at him.

"And you want to go back to that?"

"My family is there. I have to finish my training at the hospital."

"But that doesn't mean you have to spend the rest of your life there. Your family either."

Patches ran up, yipping and dancing, so she leaned over to pet him. The bay horse named Joker nickered from the field.

"Oh, how good to see you." Ingeborg met her at the door. "Thank you, Trygve, for delivering her here."

"I'll be back at noon. I'm going to go over to the deaf school."

"Will you please give this basket to your mor?" She motioned him not to leave and handed him a full basket. "Tell her that's the quilting squares we are working on."

"Anything else?"

"Not right now."

He left, whistling.

Miriam watched him go. "Does he always whistle?"

"Only when he is happy." Ingeborg took her arm. "Come with me and I'll show you the latest thing. You know who Emmy is?"

"Yes, the little Indian girl who lives with you, the girl you bought the fabric for."

"Ja, and for the last two years her uncle has come in the spring and taken her back to the tribe for the summer. This year he said he would not be back for her. I made her some new clothes, and she was sad one night because her cousins don't have nice clothes like that. One of her cousins came here last year but not this year. So anyway, some of us decided we would make jumpers and waists in various sizes to send up to her tribe. We searched through all we had and found some things that we can cut down. And I bought some more fabric from Penny—oh, and Penny donated some too. Now we need to cut them out and sew them. Do you want to help?"

"I most certainly do. Is Mrs. Jeffers in on this too?"

"Ja. We do quilts to give away also, and that uses up all the smaller pieces."

"What do you want me to do?"

"Cut out."

By the time Freda called them to dinner, they had a stack of jumpers ready to sew, each one rolled with all its pieces.

Miriam smiled at the beautiful pile of love. "I could sew at a machine on my next day off, and I could also do handwork when it's slow at the hospital."

Trygve came through the back door. "Something sure smells good." He set a basket back on the counter. "Mor sent this to you. Guess I am just the errand boy."

Freda shook her head and pointed at the set table with her wooden spoon. "Just set yourself before we find another basket."

Miriam tried to smother a grin, but it crept out anyway. When he winked at her, she laughed and sat down where Ingeborg indicated.

Freda set the last bowl on the table and sat down.

"Trygve, please say grace."

"Do you want English or Norwegian?"

"I'd like to hear the Norwegian." As all three of them spoke together, Miriam bowed her head. She had grown up speaking and hearing grace in English. But still, this reminded her of the home she grew up in. A warm place swelled around her heart.

A warm place, in this foreign country so unlike the home she knew. What was changing inside her?

CHAPTER 21

A strid signed the last chart from evening rounds and stood up to stretch. It was getting dark already, the days growing shorter and shorter. Now to go home and relax for at least a little while. She was so weary.

Boom!

The whole hospital building shook, even the floor beneath her feet! Her reference books tumbled off their shelves. Someone screamed. Astrid headed for the door, since her office had no windows. What happened? *Lord God?*

Out in the hall, she saw Corabell, white-faced, running for Mrs. Bach's room. Were the patients safer left inside, or should they be evacuated immediately? She looked to the left. The window at the far end lay in shards on the floor. Thick smoke was rolling in.

Mrs. Geddick charged out of the kitchen. "What to do? What to do?"

Lord, what do we do? What happened?

Mr. Bach came running out of his wife's room. "I help?"

Dear God, please guide us! "Everyone! Gather in the long ward. Bring all the patients there—it's the farthest end from the

202

smoke. Keep everyone together so we don't miss anyone. I'm going outside to see if we are burning."

A thunderous explosion, building rocking, glass shattering, screaming, shouting.

Miriam picked herself up off the floor. She'd been sitting in the chair in front of her desk, writing a letter. Good thing it had been in pencil, or ink would be all over the place. More screaming. She scrambled to her feet, mentally checking herself for any injuries. None.

Smoke! Was the boardinghouse on fire? What had blown up? Out in the hall someone was banging on doors. She crossed the room, now strewn with pictures from the walls, anything not nailed down. Instead of the hall door, she headed through the bathroom to Vera and Corabell's room. She didn't bother to knock. She barged right in.

"Vera! It's me."

"I'm getting dressed."

The window had shattered in this room, and smoke was pouring in the window. "Are you all right?"

"Just shaken. It threw me out of bed." Vera grabbed a handful of hair and stuffed it into a snood. "Let's go see if anyone needs help."

"We are supposed to head directly to the hospital."

"I know." They ran out into the hallway. The far door slammed open, and a man came staggering through it. Blood was pouring down his face, covering it so that they couldn't recognize him.

Vera screamed.

The man lurched against the wall and slid gracelessly to the floor.

Miriam could not tell who he was.

Vera could. She wailed, "Dr. Deming!"

Astrid ran out the front door. To her left, a crackling fire raged, a column of flames and smoke that was engulfing the whole grain elevator! The heat seared her face. She stepped out far enough to see the hospital roof. No, they were not on fire yet, but the elevator was a fountain of flaming brands, and the burning fragments littered the ground, so they must be raining down on the roof too.

She ran back inside. All the hospital windows on the elevator side had imploded. Glass littered the floor halfway down the hall.

"I get buckets!" Mrs. Geddick ran off.

"Corabell! Stay with the patients. Gray Cloud, Mr. Bach, come with me." She ran up the stairs and through the door onto the roof. Burning brands littered the shingles.

"We need buckets of water!" If only she could throw the burning pieces off the building before the roof caught fire. She could kick the ones close to the edge off onto the ground, but all these others . . .

The clanging school bell told her the call for help had gone out. How long until someone would show up here?

Gray Cloud was here with a broom. Clever girl! She swatted burning brands to the ground, but she could not sweep away the ones near the roof peak. Mr. Bach and Mrs. Geddick formed a line to pass up buckets of water someone was filling from the sink at the end of the ward. Astrid doused a burning brand, splashed the next. The next.

"Astrid!" Daniel's voice.

"Up on the roof!"

Daniel and Thorliff came running up the stairs, bringing more buckets as they came. "You go work the line and let us do this."

"No!" She splashed another burning scrap.

"Yes! We need a longer line."

Several more men came up the stairs and the line lengthened, so they worked their way down the roof. One spot was burning into the shingles and spreading, so Astrid splashed water on it, more and more. She emptied her bucket and Daniel gave her another. Hand over hand, bucket by bucket. More people arrived. Someone brought a shovel and scooped burning pieces off the roof, flinging them out into the nothingness.

Beside them, the grain elevator howled and crackled, the flames hidden by black smoke one moment, illuminated brightly in the night the next. Below, men were throwing water on the hospital's siding, which was scorching and blackening. If the side nearest the elevator became hot enough to burst into flames, the hospital would be lost.

People crowded out into the hallway in front of Miriam's room. They were all shouting at the same time, "What happened?" Vera and Miriam had dropped down onto their knees beside Dr. Deming. He was barefoot and in shirtsleeves. A huge, burly fellow clad in long underwear staggered out of another door on the same side.

Smoke was pouring in through the shattered hall window now.

Miriam felt frantic, but she knew she couldn't show it. She stood up. "Listen to me!" She shouted it louder. "Listen to me!"

Suddenly the man in long underwear bellowed "Quiet!" with a voice that could shake trees.

The panicky voices paused.

Miriam shouted, "Listen! Get out until we know this building is not on fire. Take anyone who is injured over to the hospital. The doctors and nurses will be there. We are trained to help you."

She caught the burly man's eye. "Thank you, sir. Now, can you go room to room and make certain everyone is getting out safely? We nurses were told to report to the hospital, so we will take Dr. Deming with us."

He grunted "Yup" in a voice so deep it rumbled.

Babbling people were rushing for the exit doors. The big man began pounding on doors and opening them with a shout.

The Great Chicago Fire was thirty years ago? Thirty-four. So many stories the old-timers had told of that terrible fire and of all the lives lost. As Vera and Miriam struggled to get Dr. Deming up on his feet and over to the stairs, Miriam tried to remember the life-saving tips she'd heard, of ways to escape, of ways not to escape. The stories had been etched so deeply into her memory.

Now she could not think of a single one.

✺

Up on the hospital roof, Astrid was coughing. Everyone was coughing. *What is happening downstairs? Do we get the patients out? Am I still needed up here?*

She paused to look west toward the main part of town and could see other fires now, easy to spot in the night darkness. Buildings were burning; embers had fallen. Smoke and flame here, a column of thick smoke and a ruddy glow there. What about her house? Other houses? Roiling black smoke, illuminated on its underside by red flame, was spreading across the other side of the tracks. The tent city was burning, the fire spreading out from several scattered places. They were going to lose all of it!

Where had Gray Cloud gone? Here she came with a great armload of blankets. The men spread blankets and quilts out across the roof, throwing water on them, protecting the roof with a fragile skin of wetness.

"You told Elizabeth to stay put?" she asked her brother.

"I did. Thelma is off helping somewhere. Inga was asleep."

"You go. We can handle this now." Daniel, his face sweaty and soot-blackened, nodded Astrid toward the stairs. "We'll let you know if you need to evacuate."

Astrid headed for the stairs and down past the line of bucket passers. "Thank you. Good job. Thank you," she kept saying as she passed. She closed the door behind her, trying to keep the smoke away.

In the far ward she nodded and smiled. Terrified patients and a frightened Corabell all watched her enter. "Please just stay where you are. We are safe here for the moment."

Corabell was trembling. "Miriam and Vera are here. They brought two injured people into the examining rooms."

Astrid nodded and hurried out. The front door opened and a mother in a babushka rushed in with a child in her arms. "Burned. Burned."

She held the ward door open for her and stepped aside. "Please come into the ward. Corabell, get some ice and do what you can for her."

She entered the first examination room, surprised to see Dr. Deming.

"Window blew in. It's just superficial cuts, I believe, but they look terrible. Bled a lot." The dentist sat on the examining table while Miriam removed the towels they had applied to stanch the bleeding.

Dr. Deming's head jerked. "Ow!"

"Glass shard. Get the tweezers, Miriam." Astrid looked over his injuries carefully. "I agree with your diagnosis. Some will need sutures. Miriam? Can you handle that?"

"Yes, ma'am."

"Press against each cut before you close it and dress it. He'll tell you, I'm sure, if there's still a glass splinter in it. I hate to say this, but the quicker the better, but not so hasty that you make a mistake, of course. Where is Vera?"

"Next door with another patient. A heavy bleeder. It might be an artery."

Astrid left that room and stepped into the next. Vera looked up from the man's arm that she had pressed firmly against the table. "The facial ones look worse than they are. This is the bad one."

"Then let's go in and fix it right now." *O Lord, how I wish Elizabeth were here. But we will deal with each case as it comes. If you would send Mor, it would sure be a help.*

207

"Vera, bring dressings, sutures, and carbolic acid. Sir, I'm sorry," she told him, "we don't have time to prep properly or give an anesthetic time to take hold."

"Just get it done."

She did so. He did not wince, but she did. She stepped back when she was through. "Most of those will probably leave scars."

"I'd say right now, that's the least of my worries. How can I help you here at the hospital?"

"I have no idea. Perhaps they can use you to throw water out there. No. I take that back. Your arm might begin bleeding again. Do not use it for any heavy lifting whatsoever."

The fellow nodded and hurried out.

Deborah MacCallister arrived, very much out of breath.

"What is happening out there? What is happening to Blessing?"

Astrid gathered up the bloody rags and tossed them into a corner. "The bank and post office are burning. Tent Town is lost. Most of the men are in the bucket lines, and now women and children are passing buckets also. They are dousing roofs and walls, trying to keep other buildings from catching on fire. So far the hospital here is all right. The burning debris from the elevator started little fires all over, but most are sheds and barns."

"How about the houses?"

"We lost some. As if we needed more people without homes. Most were lucky, though. All that rain we've had recently soaked the shingles."

"Excuse us, please. We be coming through." The Irish brogue announced the speaker before Thomas Devlin could get through the door. He and three other men were struggling with a blanket that carried a wounded man. Everyone was wearing black smoke like an ugly mask.

"Over here." Astrid beckoned him to the examination table. "What do we have?"

"A ladder collapsed and dumped this poor fellow. Sure and the

leg be broken and maybe more besides. He took a wicked fall."
They lifted the man onto the table. The three others hurried out.

A terrified woman with three equally frightened children huddled in the corner.

"His wife and children there. Arlen and Helen Nyland of Detroit. Came to Blessing where they heard there might be work." He hesitated. "Their tent be gone."

As they spoke, Astrid probed the leg. "The fibula is broken but apparently not the tibia. That's the shinbone. Excellent. We needn't worry about traction."

Corabell hovered nearby. "Doctor, we're running low on ice, and there are four more burn casualties." The door behind her opened. "Five."

"Use ice until it runs out completely, then use clean cloths soaked in cool water."

"Yes'm." Corabell hurried off.

Astrid pressed around a knot on her patient's head. His eyes opened.

She smiled. "Oh good. You're back. Where do you hurt besides your leg?"

"Right arm and shoulder."

"Ah, I see. Your shoulder is dislocated. The pain is going to be severe when we put it back in place, but then it should feel much better." She turned to Father Devlin. "Have you ever helped reset a shoulder before?"

"Can't say that I have, but I be muckle fine at following instructions."

"Good." She showed him how to hold the arm, told him what to do, and got her hands in the right positions. "Three, two, one, now." The shoulder slid back into place as their patient yelped. Father Devlin heaved a sigh of relief. The fellow wasn't going to be standing up soon with that leg, so she stabilized his arm with a swathe instead of a sling and turned her attention to the leg.

She motioned to Vera, who had just come back in. "We're going to set this broken leg temporarily and look at it more carefully tomorrow. I need splints and bandages. We'll ice it and see if we can get the swelling down before we cast it, assuming there is ice. No, save the ice for burns. We'll use cool cloths."

Between Father Devlin, Astrid, and the two nurses, they set the leg, splinted it, and moved him to a bed in the other private room with his leg lined with cool rags. His wife and children settled on thin pallets on the floor by his bed. The children instantly fell asleep.

There were more burn victims, mostly from Tent Town. And more lacerations from imploding windows. They were seeing mostly women and children, and Astrid belatedly realized why. Their men were out in the streets helping fight the fires.

❦

Astrid looked at the clock. Six forty five. What was happening out there? She had to know.

She walked through the hospital, her hospital. The glass had been cleaned up at the end of the hall and in the room where Mrs. Bach was now sleeping soundly. In the first ward, the glass was gone and the beds were cleaned and remade. One of the children who had severe burns was sleeping in one bed along with her mother. Two other children shared a pallet on the floor. She made her way up the stairs and out onto the roof.

The sky was starting to pink up in the east.

"Hello, Astrid, or should I say Dr. Bjorklund?"

"You know what, Toby Valders, I don't care what you call me, but how come you are up here?"

"Daniel asked me to check one more time for any hot spots. I've got a couple extra buckets of water up here just in case, but these are all cold now. We'll have to patch it and pray for no rain, or you'll have leaks for sure."

"Leaks we can deal with. Fire, no. I hear we can bless the rain for so few buildings going up. I was afraid for a while we'd lose the whole town."

"We came mighty close. We saved the boardinghouse, Penny's store, Garrisons', and the soda shop. Steeper roofs made raking burning material off them easier, and the rain had soaked the shingles. We ought to build steep roofs on all the houses. Good thing we had metal roofs on the machinery plant and the flour mill. Almost lost that anyway. Had the flour mill been running, it would have gone up for sure."

"So I have a home to return to?"

"You do, but I'm sure Mrs. Jeffers has taken in a family or two."

"Good for her. How bad is the boardinghouse?"

"The new section is damaged the worst. We'll have to re-side the whole east wall and replace some studs. Repair those upper three rooms. The bottom three have smoke and water damage, I think. As far as we can tell, the night watchman who cleans the elevator is our only person missing, but of course there may well be more. If he was working in there, he's likely gone."

"Thank you for checking our roof."

"Welcome."

The pink was brightening into salmon.

Astrid went back downstairs. The ward lights were dimmed so people could sleep. Miriam, Deborah, and Vera were tidying up the second examination room.

She hoped she did not appear as weary as these three did. "Miriam, Vera, since it looks like things have settled down, you have a choice. Return to your rooms, if they are livable, or sleep in one of the spare beds here. Who is on duty?"

"There are no spare beds, ma'am." Miriam licked her lips. "Corabell's on duty. She's checking on patients now."

"Where are Gray Cloud and Dawn Breaking?"

"Cleaning up the operating room again. We had to do some more suturing."

"Was any kind of charting kept?"

"I wrote down a list of those we treated, but that was all the farther I got. I think I got them all, but I'm not certain. They came in so quickly." Miriam dropped the mop into its bucket.

"I'd say that was doing well. And to think we worked out emergency procedures just a couple days ago." Astrid debated, go home or remain here longer just in case?

"Look, I had yesterday off," Deborah said, "so why don't you go home and get some sleep. If we need you, we'll call."

"No you won't. The telephone company burned down."

"Fine. Then I will send someone to get you."

"Send Gray Cloud and Dawn Breaking home too, as soon as they are finished."

"I'll stay too," Miriam said. "I'm on day shift today."

Astrid nodded. "Thank you." Was Mrs. Geddick in the kitchen? If so, she must thank her on the way out. She stopped at the kitchen.

Mrs. Geddick was stirring a huge stock pot of oatmeal. And who was that slumped over in a chair by the kneading table? Astrid stepped into the kitchen.

Mrs. Geddick turned. Astrid motioned toward the stranger.

Mrs. Geddick waved an arm. "Mr. Huslig, this is Dr. Bjorklund. Doctor, Garn Huslig is the new owner of the grain elevator."

"Oh!" No wonder he looked so utterly crushed.

He grimaced. "Dr. Bjorklund," he said and started to rise.

She sat down in the chair beside his, so he sank back. She remembered seeing him here and there around town. He was usually a bouncing, jovial fellow, always ready with a smile. This man beside her looked haggard and drawn, totally defeated.

"I heard that one of your employees is missing. I'm so sorry to hear that."

"Oh, I know where he is." The man's voice was flat. "Oh yes, I know. So many times I warned him, 'Never smoke your pipe in the elevator or anywhere near it. The dust will explode and burn. Grain dust is flammable. Never do it.' And I would catch him with his pipe out anyway. He was a fine worker, but he had great trouble remembering. I'm sure that tonight he finished his chores, swept up the floor, then sat down to smoke his pipe. He is there somewhere, under all the rubble and the twisted metal. Yes, I know where he is."

What could she say? Nothing. He stared at nothing, a half-empty mug of coffee by his hands.

She laid her hand on his arm, and he did not seem to notice, so she stood up to go home.

❧

"Miriam!" The voice was calling frantically. *"Miriam!"*

Miriam ran to the hospital window, the blown-out empty window frame. "Trygve?" she leaned out to see better. The fire was still burning in the elevator next door, and men were still running about in the streets.

"Miriam!" Trygve came racing around the corner so wildly his feet nearly slipped out from under him. He staggered, regained his balance, and dashed to her window. "Oh, thank God! Thank God!" He reached up to her with both arms.

She reached down to him. He grasped her hands, nearly pulling her out the window as he pressed them to his cheeks, his lips. He must have been running a long way. He was gasping for breath.

"Trygve?"

"They said . . . Thank God it was only a rumor! I heard you were caught by the blast at that end of the hall, you and another nurse. Oh, thank God it was a false rumor!"

Her hands squeezed his. "And thank God you are all right!" Her mind, her emotions were playing tricks on her. She felt something huge and overwhelming but could not identify it. "Trygve, we are all safe here. We're treating many injured but are safe." For the first time, she studied his eyes carefully and looked at them without embarrassment or the desire to look away. She gazed into his eyes, and he was gazing into hers. They were wonderful eyes, and there was so much pain in them.

She stammered a little. "I have to get back. So many injured . . ."

He gave her hands a final squeeze and released them. "I love you, Miriam." He turned away even as she was backing up, standing up straight.

What had just happened? Her mind swirled so giddily she leaned for a moment against the window frame, her hand pressed to her sternum. But she had responsibilities, duties. She was needed now. She hurried back to her work.

Outside the hospital doors, Astrid, with Vera at her side, paused to look at Garn Huslig's grain elevator. It was spectacular in a hellish way, a two-story pile of smoldering, smoking, stinking black rubble. The tin siding and roof sheets, hideously buckled and warped, were scattered all about. Was Mr. Huslig right and the night watchman still lay somewhere in that mess? Astrid shuddered.

Several men with shovels stood around, but most probably, the fire was out.

"I'll be home later," Daniel called to her from the ring around the pile of ruins that had been the post office. "Dr. Deming is staying at our house. My mother has been helping your mother find homes for all those displaced."

"Have you seen Thorliff?"

"He just went home."

Astrid debated with herself. Go check on Elizabeth or go to bed?

Daniel added, "He said to tell you Dr. Elizabeth obeyed orders, much against her desires."

Thank you, Lord.

Vera turned aside toward the boardinghouse. Astrid walked home and trudged up her stairs. She had a house to come home to, a husband who made sure she was all right, and a bed to fall into. What more did she need?

CHAPTER 22

Tonio so often accused Miriam of wanting all her soldiers to march in an absolutely straight line. He would say it as if it were a bad thing. Well, just now it was an impossible thing. No matter how she tried, Miriam could not get the hospital running in a halfway orderly manner. As soon as she got one area organized and operating smoothly, another fell apart.

The front doors slammed open. Again. Two men brought a third man in, pressed between them, steadying him. He staggered drunkenly.

"He vomited and collapsed on the bucket line, like he can't get his breath."

"Bring him in here." She pointed them to the examining table. At least she'd had time to clean this room up since the last bandaging. She listened to his heart, which was beating steadily.

"We have to get back." The two men left.

She called after them, "Thank you!" but they were out the door.

She pressed the stethoscope to his side. The air whistled but did not seem to get into the lungs much. He was gasping.

Dawn appeared beside her.

"Get me some pillows, please. We have to get him sitting up."

Dawn returned shortly and they propped the man up. "The smoke got him?"

"Right. You watch him. Don't let him fall off." Miriam headed for their medication supply. Oil of something . . . she'd read about it back in Chicago. Something that helped clear airways. Menthol? Eucalyptus. That was it. She found it in the cabinet Mrs. Bjorklund rummaged in so often. She drew the bottle out and, taking a square of muslin from the drawer, dampened it and added a couple of drops to it.

She returned to the man and laid the cloth over his mouth and nose so that he was forced to breathe through it. He tried to push her hand away, but in a couple of breaths he started to cough. Violently. Dawn stared at her, but Miriam pointed her to the other side of the bed and put an arm around his shoulders to sit him up straighter. When the coughing eased, his eyes fluttered and opened. He sucked in another deep breath, and she felt his shoulders relax.

"Just try to breathe normally now," she said softly. "You stay with him. I'll check the front."

She left them and quickly checked the front. What she needed was a few minutes to think. Minutes? Hours! Days!

And she realized one big thing: She had not taken time to eat. Suddenly she was very hungry. She turned aside to the kitchen. "Mrs. Geddick? Do we have any soup available? Or something?"

"Ja, dear child. I was wondering when you would finally slow down enough to eat. Sit."

Miriam sat.

Mrs. Geddick plunked coffee, milk, and sugar on the table.

"Thank you. Who is that helping you?"

"Mrs. Moen, Anji. She came back here to live. Asked if I needed help. She beckoned the woman over and introduced them. Miriam hoped she smiled.

After they returned to their work, Miriam took a deep breath and immediately thoughts of Trygve bombarded her. Trygve. He loved her. He'd said so. But then, she'd already known that full well. What were *her* feelings? That was what she must sort out.

A bowl of soup appeared in front of her.

"Beef and barley," Mrs. Geddick announced, "and plenty for seconds if you want more." She set the butter dish beside the bowl, along with a plate holding three thick slabs of fresh bread. Very thick soft slices with a heavenly aroma.

Miriam picked up the soup spoon and stopped to simply look at all the food in front of her. Rich food, nourishing food, and so plentiful. She thought about her brothers and sisters in Chicago. Their meals were scant and expensive by comparison and not nearly so fresh. She buttered a piece of bread and sipped the hot soup. Delicious. But then, nearly all the food she'd ever tasted in Blessing was delicious.

Whatever had made her think that her family could do as well by staying in Chicago? Trygve said there was ample work here, and indeed there was. And ample food. And ample opportunity. Why was her mind so set on living in Chicago? All the while she kept spooning in the soup and enjoying the fresh bread.

Because that had been her plan. Finish school and then work where the family was. Once a plan is in place, a goal, never deviate from it. But she had choices now she hadn't then.

For the family didn't have to be in Chicago. Indeed, they would be better off here. Why must she adhere to a plan that was no longer even the best plan?

She almost laughed out loud at herself. She had sat down here just needing food and a bit of a breather, and here she was thinking about her feelings toward Trygve and concern for her family. And her plan pounced on her, all because of Trygve and his declaration of love.

So what about her feelings, feelings that seemed to want to run and hide behind . . . behind what? The catastrophe here—right now, that was what. But he had taken time to come and see how she was. And to say again that he loved her.

218

Attraction? Yes. Caring? Yes. Love? Yes. But did she feel the kind of love between a man and a woman? How did one know for certain? He was so certain. But her feelings?

They were intense. They were uncontrollable. They were frightening. They did not march in a straight tidy line. And that terrified her.

❧

Astrid awoke to a bedroom window full of bright sunlight. What time was it? Nearly noon! She should have gotten up hours ago. Wait. She *was* up hours ago. The whole town was. She rose, dressed, and walked downstairs.

Daniel, at the dining table with a pile of official-looking papers, twisted around. He stood up, took her hand, and kissed her cheek. "You should have slept longer. You have circles under your eyes the size of serving platters."

She sat down at her place. "Perhaps tonight we can get back to regular hours. How is it out there?"

Daniel sat back down and laid aside the papers he'd been working on. "Still some hot spots, and there was a grass fire out by Ingeborg's, but Lars managed to put it out by himself. No threats of new fires anymore. Tent Town is gone and everything in it. We think everyone had a place to stay last night. How did they do at the hospital?"

"Lots of burns, lacerations, and smoke inhalations. When a patient came in, his family, or hers, usually came in as well. We released as many as we could, but where would they go? When I left there were no beds available, all the pallets were in use, and some children were sleeping on the floor. I suppose Thorliff is crazily trying to get a paper out."

Daniel chuckled. "You know your brother. The news is all important. Oh, and that general bank meeting is still on as scheduled. Financing was important before. It's paramount now. We'll almost surely have to go outside for loans."

Astrid sighed. "The grain elevator was full of our farmers' major source of income. It's gone."

Daniel nodded grimly. "A good portion of the wheat harvest had not been shipped out yet. At least the flour mill can get wheat from the surrounding area, so it can continue operating."

Astrid stared at nothing. "I remember Mor and Far's stories about when they arrived here so many years ago. Even before there was a Blessing, the farmers built the grain elevator so that they could ship their wheat. In a very real sense, it helped build this town."

"And now it tried to destroy it."

Astrid stared at him, opened her mouth, then closed it. She smiled. "Yes, but Blessing is smarter than a grain elevator and more resilient too."

He laughed out loud.

Amelia entered with the coffeepot, paused in the doorway, and came over to the table. "You're awake earlier than I thought you would be. Breakfast is coming right up."

"Thank you." Astrid turned her attention back to Daniel. "Like so many other buildings in town, the hospital is going to need windows. And scraping and sanding on the elevator side. There is probably some charring there. Toby thinks the roof should be patched before it rains. A week ago if I heard the roof might leak, I would have leaped into action. Now? Who cares about a little water?"

"One's priorities do change, don't they?"

Amelia brought out a bowl of oatmeal and the brown sugar. "We have half a dozen people sleeping on floors in the parlor and upstairs, and we'll feed about fifteen or twenty people here at dinner. I have a pot of stew on the back of the stove and bread in the oven. We can serve folks as they show up."

"Wonderful!" Astrid picked up her spoon. She smiled at Daniel. "I did say resilient. We'll all come through this just fine."

An hour later, Astrid threw a shawl across her shoulders and walked to the hospital. She looked again at the elevator side of the building. The siding was blistered and scorched in places, but someone had tacked bed sheets over the blown-out windows. So close. They had come so close to losing everything. And if the hospital had burned down, no doubt it would have ignited other buildings around it. How blessed of God they were!

She entered, but she did not go straight to her office. She did rounds first, stopping at each patient. The place still reeked of smoke and charring. Sleeping people sprawled everywhere. Many, many injured. But look how beautifully they were bandaged. What a superb staff she had: nurses and students stretched beyond their abilities, coping so powerfully. She climbed up the stairs and out onto the roof. Men were talking and calling to each other in the street below, but this was so quiet compared to last night. Wisps of smoke still rose from the elevator rubble beyond the roof. She went back downstairs and walked through the ward.

They'd need to order more supplies immediately. She stopped at the nurses' station. "Corabell, could you take charge of counting and ordering supplies today? Have Gray Cloud help you. We need to be prepared immediately for another catastrophe."

"Yes, Doctor. We don't have a telephone anymore, you know."

Astrid shook her head. "Well, we got along without one for years. I guess we can again. I'll be at Dr. Bjorklund's for an hour or so, and then I'll return."

"You think the laundry ladies will be in today?"

"Good question." Both of them had lived in Tent Town. "I hope so, and if not, we'll try to find out where they are staying. Give them a while yet. They may just be sleeping. Go ahead and set things to soak. We will do it if they can't." She stopped at Corabell's grin.

"You've already done that?" Another nod, eyes twinkling. "You have all done wonderfully well. I am so proud of you."

She took a few moments to check the shelves and cabinets.

Were there any supplies that needed to be replaced immediately? What was this standing out on the counter? Oil of eucalyptus.

She carried it back to Corabell. "Who had this out? My mother?"

"Miriam did. She and Gray Cloud used it to help one of the fire fighters breathe more easily. He had smoke in his lungs. I saw it on the chart when I did rounds."

"Thank you." Astrid stopped by her office long enough to write herself a note to give Miriam a special commendation. Using that oil of eucalyptus was brilliant. Astrid herself had not thought of it. Then she picked up her bag and went outside.

Did her hospital smell smoky? The whole town smelled smoky. She walked down to Thorliff's and let herself in. Elizabeth was sitting at the window in her bedroom.

She took one look at Elizabeth's face when she arrived and shook her head. "Back to bed, my friend. Where's Inga?"

"They are having school today, after all." Elizabeth dutifully climbed back in bed. "I just couldn't sleep last night. I'm certain that's all that's wrong."

"Nobody slept last night." Down inside, Astrid thought, *I sure hope that is all it is.*

"I need to do the ordering today. I know you must be running low."

"Yes, we are, but no, you'll not be doing it. I already have the job assigned to others." Astrid applied the stethoscope to Elizabeth's heart. Erratic? She held her breath and listened intently. Should she try digitalis? But would that endanger the baby? She listened for the fetal heartbeat. Strong and sure. *Please, Lord, please.* If only the mother's sounded as strong as her baby's.

Elizabeth propped herself to half sitting. She smiled broadly when Astrid told her about Miriam's oil of eucalyptus. "You know, if we're not careful, some of this smoke inhalation could turn into pneumonia."

"That is another blessing. We had a little breeze last night.

Trygve knew, as did everyone else, that Anner was always the last one out of the bank. If the safe was "accidentally" left open, you could lay the accident squarely at the door of Anner himself.

Daniel started, "The man who died—"

Anner interrupted. "You mean the one that blew himself to kingdom come and almost took the whole town with him?"

"We're not sure what happened, you know."

"It was that dimwit, that fellow Huslig hired. Never should have hired the dolt. He probably lit that meerschaum pipe of his. Or started a fire in the stove. Fool didn't even notice all the *No Smoking* signs all over the place."

Except he couldn't read, Anner. Trygve decided keeping his thoughts to himself was the better course of action. Since he had stayed up all night on fire patrol, he fought back a yawn. Talk about aching in muscles he didn't even know he had. Like the others, his hands were raw from blisters in spite of leather gloves. He figured he'd stop at the hospital to be tended to—salve and maybe bandages—on his way home to bed.

Thomas Devlin raised a hand. "Forgive me for being so brazen, but let me mention here that Reverend Solberg and I be talking about a worship service to give thanks for all the lives saved, buildings too, and God's protection in general. We thought perhaps at the schoolhouse, so as to have room. Or outside. Somehow a bonfire did not seem a good idea." His raised eyebrows brought forth a smattering of chuckles.

Anner shot Father Devlin an angry why-are-you-still-here? look.

If Tommy Devlin noticed, he ignored it. "John had a thank-you meeting at the schools with all the children this morning. Those children, so quick to volunteer things they were thankful for! 'Twould have been good for all the adults to hear them. More than one mentioned their whole family was still alive, especially those children from Tent Town. One little girl said some man grabbed her kitty on the fly and gave it to her later, then showed her the scratches from said ungrateful cat."

While there was a lot of eye blinking going around those at the meeting, it could probably be attributed to the smoke. Leave it to children to remind the adults what was really important. "I think a service is more than just appropriate—it is a must. We have a lot of people to thank too." Trygve blew his nose.

Daniel Jeffers nodded. "Thank you, Trygve. By the way, Dr. Bjorklund said to remind you all that blisters need to be treated so as not to become infected. Spread that news among all those you work with today. And if anyone with smoke inhalation starts coughing badly, or his cough gets worse, trot him right over to the hospital. Anything else we should know, Toby?"

He shrugged. "My crew is on the grain elevator, and Joshua's is on the bank building until the hot spots die down. As soon as we're done here, we need to assess the damage to other buildings, especially the boardinghouse and the new construction."

Daniel nodded. "Ingeborg said the women are meeting at the church this evening to figure out housing for our burned-out people, as well as getting bedding, clothing, and other things people need. Father Devlin, can we put you in charge of finding what those needs are?"

"Aye. Good! For I know many of the Tent Town people."

Jeffers turned to Anner and Hjelmer. "We need you two to assess how the bank can help and report with estimates in two days. If we have to go outside of Blessing to get funds to rebuild"—he scowled at Anner—"we will do that, because we all know winter is breathing down our necks."

Toby added, "I already inspected the hospital roof. Like others, it will leak if we don't fix it immediately."

"I sure am grateful for the metal roofs on the flour mill and the machinery plant. When I think how the flour mill could have gone up too . . ." Hjelmer wagged his head. "If I didn't believe in God's providence before this, I would be a believer now."

Trygve thought of cleaning out his ears. That was Hjelmer talking. Hjelmer of the Midas touch. Ah, Onkel Haakan, if only you could be here now. All those prayers of yours and Tante Ingeborg's, Mor's and Far's, John Solberg's, and all the others. Perhaps that was one of the benefits of a catastrophe. It brought people to work together, to let go of personal differences, and if you looked, you could see the hand of God in action.

Since when did he become a philosopher?

He asked, "Shall I do roof inspections, then?"

"Yes. Thank you, Trygve. All the roofs that we cleaned burning material off of. That's pretty much all of them within a few blocks of the elevator. We need estimates of supplies to replace shingles and things, and how much time that will probably take." Jeffers looked around to the rest of the group. "Any other suggestions? Questions? No? Then I'd like to suggest we meet again tomorrow evening."

Everyone nodded their agreement. The grating of chairs being pushed back and the murmuring of conversations filled the dining room.

"Does Thorliff need help getting the paper out?" Father Devlin asked him.

"He hoped to be here, but as you can see . . ." Trygve picked up one of the tablets on the table and several pencils, stuffing them in the chest pocket of his shirt.

Father Devlin nodded. "Think I'll be dropping by there for a bit." He left.

Sophie met Trygve at the doorway to the dining room. "Did I hear Daniel appoint you as estimator for the roofs?" At his nod, she continued. "Do you want to start here?"

"Might as well, since I'm here."

"Do you want Garth to help you? He investigated the damage to the east wing of the boardinghouse. He and a couple of men are tearing off the damaged siding now. That wing really got hit, but it didn't burn."

"I'll ask him to go up with me, then." He smiled at his sister, who looked a bit worse for the wear, like all the rest of them.

Instead of one of her stylish dresses, which she usually wore, today it was a black skirt, light waist, and an apron. Her hair was fighting to escape the restrictions of the snood, and like all the others, she could probably use some sleep. The thought of that reminded him that he'd not slept either. So far, the repeated cups of coffee were carrying him along.

He asked as casually as possible, "Have you seen Miriam lately?"

"She came in, had dinner, and went up to sleep. The poor girl was completely exhausted. I think this all caught up with her at once. She's a sweet lady, Trygve."

He smiled. "Glad you think so too."

"Oh, and I put Dr. Deming in another room until we get his window boarded up or replaced. The poor man's face is a mess. He has three roofers sleeping in there with him. In fact, all the rooms have a couple extra Tent Town people. I hate to see any stand empty."

He nodded. "Every job is the first job we have to do. If only winter weren't so near." He patted her arm. "I'll go up on the roof."

"Thank you."

He had just stepped out onto the shingles when Garth joined him.

Garth said, "We're going to have to replace a lot of the siding on that east wall. So let's start there."

Together they measured and made notes. The roof had not actually caught fire anywhere, but many shingles on the east side were scorched or had been blown off by the blast. When they finished the boardinghouse, Garth stayed with him. They assessed the Blessing Mercantile and Garrisons' Groceries, and ended up at the new construction. A section of the apartment house was damaged. How they had gotten the fire out was a miracle indeed. The roofs on the three houses had minor damage.

Garth went back to tearing off siding on the boardinghouse, and Trygve sat down at the newspaper office, now empty, to put together the report for each building.

∽

"Trygve, wake up." A hand was shaking his shoulder.

Trygve raised his head. "What?"

"We've been looking for you, thought you went home to sleep." Thorliff grinned at his cousin. "You went to sleep all right. Your cheek looks mashed to the table."

"What time is it?"

"Five thirty. Come on in and have supper."

Trygve blinked again and yet again. The sand cart had surely driven through his eyes. His neck felt like a board, and his stomach growled viciously. "I didn't finish the reports."

"Eat and then finish. Jonathan came looking for you, since he and Grace thought you'd be home for supper. Amazing how dependent we've become on the telephones." Thorliff turned back at the doorway. "Are you coming?"

"Sure. Just trying to unkink myself." He gathered up his papers and joined Thorliff. "You got the paper out?"

"I did. It's short but done. I heard it was a rather interesting meeting this afternoon."

"It seemed strange to have Jeffers leading and not you." The reminder of Anner made him almost smile. "You missed a bit of a circus between Anner and Daniel."

"I heard. It's a good thing I wasn't there."

"Trygve!" Inga bailed off her chair and threw her arms around him. "You were lost!"

"No, I was sound asleep."

She gave him a sideways look. "On the newspapers?"

"No. At the table."

"You have ink on your face."

"Guess I'd better go wash."

When he looked in the mirror, he saw a man with the same purple slashes under the eyes as most of the other people he'd seen. But the others did not have a smear of ink and several smoke smudges. He scrubbed his face and hands and, straight-arming the sink edge, let his head fall forward to stretch his neck. He heaved a deep sigh. "I am tired." He'd been hoping to see Miriam, but he was guessing she would be back at the hospital again by now.

%%%

"I would have invited someone to stay at my house, but as you know, we have Rebecca there and Benny." Hildegunn Valders stated her piece before anyone could ask, then stared at her hands clasped in her lap.

"No matter, Hildegunn. We had enough homes or rooms for everyone to have a place to sleep." Amelia Jeffers nodded with a gracious smile.

Ingeborg and Kaaren did a raised-eyebrow glance. Why had Hildegunn started out like that? Ingeborg had moved Emmy in with her and Manny to a pallet on the floor so that a family with two children and an uncle could sleep upstairs. The children went to school, the men to work, and the woman to the hospi-tal, where she worked in the laundry. They had nothing but the clothes on their backs, so Ingeborg dug out some of Haakan's clothes for the men and gave the missus a dress and a sweater. All those people would need winter clothing, and bedding as well, once some housing was ready.

"We could just send them back where they came from." Was Hildegunn parroting her husband?

Penny barked, "We invited these people to Blessing for a new life, just like all of us who already came here. If some of them want to leave, that is their choice, but for us to act like that would be unconscionable! Whatever are you thinking, Hildegunn?"

"I am just being practical." Her voice dripped self-righteousness.

"Look, if you don't want to help, that is your choice, but I think most of us take our town and our people as part of our family. This can be a tragedy or a chance to show others the love of God that we have all lived with these many years." Penny's voice grew louder, and she glared across the table. She surged to her feet. "I'd better go take a walk before I say something I might be really sorry for."

"All right. That's enough." Mary Martha spoke softly and gently. "Penny, walk around the building and then come back in."

Hildegunn shoved back her chair and snatched up her sewing basket. "No need to leave on my account. I know when I am not wanted." She leaped to her feet and stormed out the door before anyone else could get their mouth shut and feet in motion to stop her.

For a long minute, no one said a word. They all studied the table like they had never seen it before.

"I'm sorry," Penny offered. "I must learn to keep my mouth shut."

"You only said what the rest of us were thinking. Between Hildegunn and Anner, they've managed to offend most of the rest of us." Ingeborg, who was sitting next to her, patted her hand. "I suggest we continue our discussion of how to help those devastated by the fire. We need a plan. We have several quilts we were going to send to the Indian reservation, but now we will need them here. If anyone has any pieces or tops, let's get them finished as quickly as possible. I was going to cut Haakan's coat down for Manny, but a grown man will need it. We need to gather up as much as we can."

"What about writing to some other congregations to ask for help? John and I talked about that last night. Or was it this morning?" Mary Martha wagged her head. "It is all mushing together."

"We could gather the clothes we have and bring them here. Let people come and help themselves," Penny suggested.

Ingeborg added, "Miriam and I started jumpers for the girls on the reservation but girls here can use them, if we have any the right size."

"I have an idea. Why don't we make a list of all the people, and as clothes come in put family names on them. Start a box for each?"

Mary Martha nodded. "We have a box of outgrown clothes at the school. I keep it to pass things on as needed. We can start with that."

"Bedding will be needed, but not until there is housing. Clothes are necessary now. Anything else?"

"Mostly we need clothing for men."

"True."

Everyone agreed to bring in what they could find, and Sunday after church, they would open it up for their refugees to choose from.

Mary Martha clanged a spoon against her coffee cup. "Let's close with the Lord's Prayer. Oh, wait. John and Thomas Devlin have been talking about a gratitude service for all the town. They decided on Saturday night at the schoolhouse. John is going to give Mr. Nyquist, Kaaren, and Miss Rumly notes to send home with all the schoolchildren. We can post signs in town and tell the men at work. Anything else?"

"What are we serving?" Kaaren asked.

"Why do we need to serve anything?"

"Makes it more like a party. If we call it a party rather than a service, more people will want to come, especially the Tent Town people. We can have music and throw a real celebration." Kaaren smiled at everyone. "We need a celebration, ladies. We have so much to be thankful for."

Penny nodded. "Then we need dancing too. So we will make punch and coffee and everyone can bring desserts, cakes, pies, cookies, whatever you want. Just bring plenty."

Mary Martha's grin brought out returned ones. "I knew I

could count on all of you to dress this thing up. Not a service. A celebration! I'll tell the men."

Ingeborg chuckled on the way home. "Did you notice that Mary Martha did not say she would ask the men? She said she'd tell them."

"I did." Kaaren swung her basket. "Please, Lord, hold off the winter for us."

"I suppose someone should go talk with Hildegunn," Ingeborg said with a sigh.

"Not yet. Give her a chance. Perhaps she'll see what is truly happening."

"True. So back to praying for the Valders senior. And that the two of them do not take out their bad feelings on Gerald and his family. Maybe Benny will be a softening influence. Besides, maybe repairs to their house and a real cleaning will soon make it liveable again."

Please, Lord, let it be so.

CHAPTER 24

The meeting the next evening started at seven o'clock on the dot with an opening prayer by Reverend Solberg. Daniel Jeffers calling the meeting to order.

"The purpose of this meeting is to better understand our financial resources available right now and to develop a plan to seek outside assistance if we need it."

Astrid sat at the back of the room to make it easier to leave if she needed to. Her mor was sitting beside her, and Penny, the Garrisons, Sophie, Kaaren, and Mrs. Jeffers were there too. Astrid was surprised Hildegunn wasn't present. She turned her attention to the front, where a table was set up. Daniel, Hjelmer, Thorliff, and Mr. Valders looked out over those assembled.

"We asked Anner Valders and Hjelmer to prepare a statement of the bank funds." He nodded toward Anner Valders, who stood up.

Anner cleared his throat. While the worst of the redness from the burns had left his face, he still looked rather strange—hairless and patchy. His right hand was covered in a bandage.

Astrid wondered how bad his hand was burned. Daniel said he'd injured it slamming the safe closed. It was a miracle the man had gotten out of the burning building in such good shape.

"Understand this is a preliminary report." Anner cleared his throat again and looked like he would rather be anywhere than standing before this group. "As you know, most of our bank cash is reinvested in local loans, so because of that, our liquidity is kept low. When more money comes in, it becomes available for loans. Sometimes, when we have a sufficient surplus cash flow, I invest in other worthwhile ventures so that our money is always earning more money for us to use." He looked up from the paper he was reading. "Any questions?"

Daniel leaned forward and waved his hand. "I assume that seasonally, then, our cash flow is affected. Like with all the wheat harvest, we would have considerable extra cash at this point."

Anner's tone of voice sounded like a schoolmaster correcting a child. "Remember, much of the harvest was still in the elevator, now lost, and is therefore not going to give us income. Only the wheat that was shipped."

"Of course. But—"

"Also, we have been investing heavily in the construction projects here in Blessing, and until they are complete, there is no return on the money invested except for loan payments. They may well dry up."

Daniel stood. "You mentioned outside investments. Outside of Blessing?"

"Yes."

"But this is a locally owned bank intended to provide local investment funds."

Anner was growing more and more tense. "The outside investments are short-term ventures, promising a fifteen percent return or higher."

Daniel's mouthy dropped open. "What kind of investment would promise that kind of return so quickly?"

"How short?" Thorliff too was scowling.

"Let's say the investment has not met our initial projections for profit. However, the time frame on this sort of thing is never exact. You have to expect a few months either way."

Astrid caught Hjelmer in an eye-rolling response. Uh-oh. This didn't look good. She looked at Thorliff, who was studying the paper in front of him, his jaw tight.

Either the heat in the room had gone up or the tension had. Maybe they needed to open a door.

Ingeborg reached over and took her hand. Between Ingeborg and Reverend Solberg, prayers were going up for sure.

"What kind of return have you had on those investments so far?" Daniel kept his voice steady but firm.

Amelia Jeffers hooked her arm through Astrid's from the other side.

"You must be patient," Anner insisted. "We will realize one thousand five hundred dollars at any time now."

Astrid almost felt sorry for Anner. Almost but not quite. But she was certainly glad she was not the one being questioned. She'd not seen this side of her husband before. She knew he was a good businessman, with a great deal of knowledge. Right now she was so proud of him she could have jumped up clapping.

Thorliff dropped his papers on the table. "So that accounts for the fact that our citizens' recent requests for funds have been turned down."

"If any of us needed to withdraw from our savings, there is none available?" Sophie asked, standing up.

Anner looked at Sophie. "These two are trying to paint an unnecessarily dark picture. We have operating cash in the safe, preserved from the fire. And as members pay their loan payments, that will increase the fund. We are not in arrears."

"But we do not have ready cash to assist with the emergency repairs needed right now." Thorliff said it as a statement, not a question.

"True, but the suppliers will no doubt extend credit, as they always have, and by the time the bills come due, we will have sufficient liquidity to work with again."

"In other words, we must depend upon the largess of suppliers to whom we will owe a great deal of money. So we pray there is no run on the Blessing Bank." Thorliff sounded grim.

At Astrid's side, Ingeborg stood up and looked around the room. "Why would there be? It is our bank. If any of us needs something, someone else will help provide it. That is the way we have always done things. We take care of our own."

"Including all those people who have come here to work." Penny shot Anner a dirty look. "We *will* take care of our own."

"Look!" Anner slammed his papers down. "You hired me to manage your resources. I have done so. Now you are questioning my management after the fact. I do not accept that. You people are not professional financiers. I am. When I make an investment, you will not question it. I believe I am finished here."

And he walked out, his jaw set, his back straight.

Hjelmer stood. "I think we need a point of clarification here. Anner did nothing dishonest. He made a poor choice, but in investing, that happens. He's invested before, and his investments have probably paid off. Instead of castigating him, I suggest we need a board that will take part in decisions like that. We as a community have been remiss in leaving these decisions solely up to Anner Valders. Even with a board, the same thing could happen."

Except to Hjelmer. He'd been known to have a Midas touch. In fact, he was often teased because of it. Within the family, anyway. Astrid heaved a sigh of relief.

Daniel nodded. "Which leaves us back to the question: Do we have the funds to both finish construction and repair fire damage?"

A person Astrid did not know stood up, coughed, and spoke. "If a town gets strapped like this down in Mexico, the province it's in—no, I guess those are states, like Sonora or Colima—the states issue chits. Promissory notes. You get a chit for every dollar. Peso. You can spend it in town on rent or groceries and things, and then when the state gets more cash, you can exchange the chits for real dollars. I suggest we try that here."

Hjelmer scowled. "You mean anyone can issue their own money?"

"No. Just the bank. Only the bank. Like a bank note, only different."

Hjelmer wagged his head. "Doesn't sound very good to me."

Thorliff nodded toward the fellow. "We will consider it as an option, though, sir. Thank you. We need all the options we can muster. Other discussion?" He looked around. "If there is no further discussion, I suggest we close with prayer. Reverend Solberg?"

"Lord God, we thank you for guiding us, your people, to live and do business according to your Word. Your Word reminds us over and over to love one another. Sometimes we are not easy to love, but you always promise to lavish us with your great mercy. We can do no less for one another. Help us to remember who and whose we are. In Jesus' precious name we pray. Our Father . . ."

After the prayer, he lifted his hands in the benediction. "The Lord bless us and keep us. The Lord be merciful unto us and give us His peace. Amen."

"Thank you all for coming. If you have any further questions, please feel free to ask them." Daniel smiled graciously, as if he'd been hosting a party.

Astrid feared she might just pop with pride. She grinned at her mother-in-law, who looked like her feet were no longer touching the ground.

Astrid turned to kiss her mother's cheek. "Thank you."

"For what?"

"For helping keep my feet on the ground and for all the hours you spend praying."

"Oh, Astrid." She started to say something, but sniffed and smiled instead. "I pray you will sleep well."

"I know. All will be well."

"Ja, it will."

Astrid watched her mother walk off, her arm locked through Kaaren's.

Thorliff stopped beside her and leaned in to whisper. "You married a good man, and right now I am so grateful for the way he ran this meeting that I am almost out of words."

Astrid turned to him, wide-eyed. "You, Thorliff Bjorklund, out of words?"

He nudged her with his elbow. "Thanks for helping Elizabeth feel better. I think I could sleep for a week."

Daniel joined them. "Am I ever glad that is over. Let's go home, Dr. Bjorklund Jeffers." He tucked her arm through his and latched on to his mother on the other side. "Sure makes you wonder how God is going to clean up all this mess, doesn't it?"

"Where do you think we'll find the money we need?"

"I have no idea, but I truly believe God does. After all, He brought Mother and me to Blessing in the middle of a horrendous nightmare. I heard Him say 'Trust me,' and I've been trying to do that ever since. I was so pleased with Hjelmer's comments."

"I was shocked. Something has changed with him too."

❦

The next morning Jonathan Gould, accompanied by Thorliff, knocked on their door before Astrid even headed for the hospital. "Do you have a few minutes?" he asked when Daniel opened the door.

"Well, of course. Come on in." Daniel stepped back. "I think Mother has the coffee ready. Have you had breakfast yet?"

"No, but I wanted to catch you before anything else happened." Daniel and Thorliff looked at each other and shrugged.

Astrid paused on the stairs, watching the men. "Good morning. Is something wrong?"

"No. I just have a suggestion."

When the men were seated around the kitchen table with coffee before them, Jonathan looked at each of them. "I was at the meeting last night, so I do understand what is going on here. I know my father would be pleased to loan you any amount of money you need. He will offer you a better repayment plan than banks here can afford to."

"We aren't looking for a handout."

"Well, a handout and a hand up are two different things," Jonathan said. "Investing in Blessing is good business. My father has always said so. I am confident he's ready to do that. I suggest that since the telephone system is out and will probably be so for some time, you send him a telegram if you need money quickly, or a letter."

"There is no rush, and we might be able to manage without his assistance." Daniel looked to Thorliff for confirmation. Thorliff nodded.

"As long as the lumber yard will continue to ship to us, for we have a long list to send them. I have Trygve's report on the roofs, and we haven't counted the windows yet. Thirty minimum. I'm not sure where Sophie is with the boardinghouse. I know the new wing was a big investment, and now it will need a lot more." Thorliff nodded slightly as he took a drink of his coffee. "I think we are probably more stable than it felt like a few days ago. And I have to admit, I have no idea why I'm thinking that."

"Amazing what a good night's sleep can do to clarify our thinking."

"That and deciding that booting Anner out of town was probably not the best way to handle things. When a real crisis hits, you kind of get a better perspective."

Mrs. Jeffers slid a plate of cinnamon rolls she'd just taken out of the oven onto the table. "To help you think better."

Daniel smiled at his mother. "The day is looking better by the minute. Help yourselves, gentlemen."

Just as Astrid was about to head for the hospital, another

knock came on the door. She answered it to see a large group of people, both men and women, gathered around the front porch. "How can I help you?" she asked.

"Ve come to help clean up Blessing." In spite of the heavy accent, the message was clear. There they stood, all the people from Tent Town, even older children. "This is our town too."

"Wait, I'll be right back." She hurried to the kitchen. "Come quick, all of you. This you have to see."

She wished her far were there to see it. He always said if you do unto others the way you wanted to be treated, God would see to the ending.

The man repeated what he'd said.

Daniel stepped forward. "This is wonderful! Thank you. There are many jobs that must be done, such as getting all the debris out of the streets and alleys. From the burnt and heavily damaged buildings, we must salvage any wood that can still be used for repair."

Thorliff added, "We also want to save wood that is partially burned. We can use it for cooking and heating this winter. And haul the ashes out to scatter on the fields. They make fine fertilizer."

The spokesman was smiling broadly. "Ve know ve must take care that there are no nails and metal pieces in these ashes. A grazing cow picks up a nail, it causes problems in her stomach. Ja!"

Daniel was beaming. "I'll round up all the rakes and shovels and wheelbarrows I can find, and we'll bring around a couple hitches so you have horses to pull apart big piles. Thank you!" And he repeated, "Thank you."

Astrid stepped back and watched as Daniel sent a group in this direction, another in that.

She was watching faith in action. God takes care of his own.

Blessing was being blessed.

CHAPTER 25

Astrid, at her desk, sat back in her chair. "That about covers it. We've talked about plans for dealing with any other crisis, and everyone is up-to-date about our patients. Any questions?" She looked at the nurses around her desk.

Miriam nodded. "I have one but not about that. You know the man who died at the elevator? Does he have any family to notify?"

"I asked Mr. Huslig. He had no idea. And we've heard of no one." Astrid rubbed her temples. She had a headache again.

"Oh. One other thing." Corabell, who had stood up, sat down again. "I am going to take Vera's shift tonight so that she can go to the thanksgiving celebration with Dr. Deming."

"Thank you, Corabell." The thought of the celebration tonight, put together by the quilt club, was not appealing. Worse than simply not appealing, Astrid dreaded going. She so wanted to do nothing but sleep for a week or two. She did not want to celebrate anything, even though there was so much to be grateful for. But it was necessary that she at least make an appearance, even if she didn't want to dance. The hospital had been spared, and she wanted to publicly thank the people who were involved.

She tugged her shawl over her shoulders and headed for the door. She stopped as Dr. Deming came in.

"Could I have you look at this?" He indicated his bandaged face. "It doesn't feel right."

"Of course." Astrid pulled off her shawl, motioning him to the examining room, and beckoned Gray Cloud to come and assist.

Carefully, she and Gray Cloud removed the dressings. With the lines of stitches across his forehead, two down his cheek, and another on the side of his neck, he looked rather intimidating.

Astrid smiled. "You really don't want to look in a mirror yet."

"Will I scare little children?"

"Probably not. Our children are strong. Most of these will fade away, but it looks like we have some infection here." She probed carefully around a swelling. "We'll start a hot pack here, and I might have to take out a couple of stitches to let this drain." She turned to Gray Cloud. "Please go ask Mrs. Geddick for some vinegar and hot water."

"Vinegar?" Dr. Deming frowned.

"Yes. It is a good antiseptic, and we're running low on carbolic acid. We can also try a bread-and-milk poultice, or an onion one. Are you attending the party tonight?"

"Oh yes. I asked Miss Vera to accompany me. She doesn't seem the least put off by all this carnage."

"I should hope not. She's a nurse. You lie back, and Gray Cloud will change the pack in fifteen minutes or so. You need to do this four times a day. And I want to see it tomorrow morning again. I'm sure Nurse Wells will be delighted to help you." Was that a blush she saw rising on his neck? She kept her smile to herself and turned as soon as Gray Cloud tapped on the door and entered. Was she matchmaking? She knew Vera wouldn't mind assistance in the romance department. After all, Astrid had heard the others teasing her about coming to Blessing to find a husband.

She left Gray Cloud changing the packs to keep them warm. The room smelled like someone had been making pickles. She'd not had time this summer to help with making pickles, something she enjoyed helping her mor with. Mrs. Jeffers had done it all. If Astrid allowed herself to follow that line of thought, she knew she could make herself cringe with guilt in short order. While she knew the reasons she could not be home more, being the only available doctor one of them, sometimes she had to speak firmly to herself about trusting that God knew what He was doing. Most likely her mor was right when she said that learning to trust God, really trust Him, was a lifelong process.

Picking up her black bag, she again started for the door.

A very sorry-looking couple was coming into the hospital. The Munros! Poor Izzie Munro looked wan and harried. She was carrying a fussy bundled-up baby.

"Mr. and Mrs. Munro! How do you do?" Astrid put down her bag. She would not be leaving yet.

"We're doing fine. Fine." Mr. Munro looked awfully grim for someone who was doing fine. "We brought in little Annabel. Maybe something wrong."

Astrid took the baby from Izzie's arms into her own and was shocked by how little the bundle weighed. "Let us go to the examining room." She led the way.

Mr. Munro explained, "Baby Annabel cries, doesn't sleep well."

Astrid unwrapped the little bundle on the examining table. Clean blanket, clean baby sacque. Obviously the infant was well cared for. But look how thin the tiny arms and legs were. And how bloated the abdomen. Astrid stood erect. "Mr. Munro, the child is not getting nearly enough milk. She is starving."

Mr. Munro wagged his head. "She'd suck all day if we let her." He pointed to his wife. He was obviously a modest man. He did not point specifically to her breasts.

Astrid held aside the woman's shawl. The front of her blouse hung straight down. Flaccid breasts, certainly not filled. She dropped Mrs. Munro's shawl back in place. "Mrs. Munro—may I call you Izzie, please?—you're not eating much. Why?"

"Food costs too much money. We have no money."

"Do you not earn the same pay as everyone else?"

Mr. Munro nodded. "Same pay, aye, but I must give half of it to the bank. So we do not have much."

Astrid's jaw dropped. "Why?"

"The bank man. Mr. Vedder. Valler."

"Valders?"

"Aye, the very one. He gave us a loan, and we must pay it back."

"A loan."

"Aye! Soon as we pay the loan, then we'll have money like everyone else."

Fury rose up so wildly, so quickly, Astrid had to breathe deeply for a moment just to get her voice back. "But half your paycheck? No! You do not have to repay at that rate!"

"Aye, we do. Mr. Valders will ship us back to Scotland if we do not."

"What?" Of all the . . . Three people starving, and Anner . . . "Come with me." Astrid marched to the kitchen. "Mrs. Geddick? There you are. I'm sorry to make more work for you, but these people are very hungry. Mrs. Munro cannot make enough milk for her baby. Feed them a big meal, please."

Mrs. Geddick stared for a moment openmouthed. "Oh ja! Oh ja!" She hustled toward the stove, muttering something.

Mr. Munro shook his head. "No. We'll not do this. We cannot pay for—"

"We would not let you pay. Now please listen carefully, Mr. Munro. You do *not* have to give the bank half of your pay. Really. You do not. You will buy food for your family—"

"He will send us away. We spent everything to get here. We will have no job, no home at all."

"No!" She grasped both of his arms. "Anner Valders cannot get you deported. He will not send you away. Feed your family."

"But . . ." Fear clouded his eyes, intense fear.

Mrs. Geddick came marching over. "Mr. Munro. Do you trust your doctor?"

"Aye, but . . ." His eyes darted from face to face.

"She says you do not worry. Do you trust her?"

And an amazing thing happened. The fear softened. His sad gray eyes met Astrid's. "Aye. I trust you. I do not trust him. I will not give the bank more money. When you say I should, then I will give him some."

"Good! Now please sit down, both of you. You will eat dinner here. Tomorrow you will come to the kitchen and eat dinner again. Mrs. Geddick, is that all right?"

"Ja! Oh ja. They must eat dinner here every day until she makes more milk. She did not dry up yet?"

"No. I think we caught it in time. I hope so."

Mrs. Geddick wagged her head. "Look, the baby. The poor, hungry baby." And she hurried off to fill two plates and warm some milk in a bottle for the baby.

Astrid said good-bye to the Munros, gathered up her shawl and black bag, and again headed for the door. She managed to get through it this time, out into the bright afternoon sun.

Although the sun was warming, the nip in the air reminded her that fall was in full swing. Golden cottonwood leaves whirled and danced to the ground in the breeze. While far fewer, the maple leaves glowed red against the yellow carpet. Look at this beauty! She must put aside her anger. It was doing no one any good, herself especially, and it was spoiling this God-given beauty.

Astrid turned into the gate at Elizabeth's. She knew how terribly Elizabeth wanted to go to the celebration and finally made a decision that she hoped she would not regret. While Scooter greeted her, the silence of no Inga made her shrug.

"Where's your girl?" she asked the bouncing dog as she mounted the steps.

"Coffee's ready," Elizabeth called when Astrid opened the door. Soon the isinglass-covered winter door would replace the screen doors of summer. While she loved fall, she was not ready for winter, not by any stretch of the imagination.

"She'll be right here," Thelma said, pointing to the chair by the round table in the corner. The geraniums from outside already graced the windowsills, blooming as if they had not so recently been moved.

"Is Inga out at Mor's?"

"Ja. She spent the night with Emmy." Thelma finished pouring coffee and studied Astrid before walking back to the stove. "You look terrible. Tired."

"Don't we all?"

"Sorry for the delay." Elizabeth came through the arched doorway. "I was hoping we could have coffee outside, but it's too chilly."

Astrid lifted her cup and blew on the rising steam. "I was just thinking the same thing."

"I have been contemplating something." Elizabeth sat down across the table and leaned forward. "I truly believe I can attend the celebration tonight for at least the program. I wouldn't stay for the dancing, of course. I really want to hear the children do their part."

Astrid wagged her head. "You did it to me again."

"What?"

"Read my mind. I decided the same thing, but you have to promise you'll come late and leave early."

Elizabeth reached across the table to take her hand. "Thank you. I didn't really want to fight you on this, but I am feeling so much better, and this is a once-in-a-lifetime experience. I promise to be careful of germs. I'll even scrub my hands with vinegar when I get home."

Should she mention Anner's shabby trick with the Munros? No. If she described it, she would just become irate all over again. Instead she caught Elizabeth up on all else that had transpired at the hospital, concluding with the lacerated Dr. Deming. "He will smell like pickles at the party tonight, but I have a feeling he won't be dancing much with anyone other than Vera." The two women chuckled together and shared a smile over their cup brims.

"We better enjoy moments like these. They don't come very often." Elizabeth turned to Thelma. "Did you hear that? You need to come sit down for a minute too."

"I will." Thelma paused. "Later."

Astrid stared at the woman, who was taking two pies out of the oven. Thelma actually made a joke. When she looked back at Elizabeth, they both fought to keep the laughter from bubbling out.

Miriam hurried back to her room at the boardinghouse after she finished the day shift, wishing she could just eat her supper and spend the evening writing to her family. Tired did not begin to describe how she felt. *Bone weary* was closer to it.

"You have mail," Maisie Landsverk said, reaching into the numbered cubbyholes behind the front counter, where she kept mail for the boarders. "You hit the jackpot with two envelopes." She set the mail on the counter. "Do you have your dancing shoes all shined for the party, or rather the celebration?" she corrected herself.

"Everyone sure is excited about it." Sometimes not answering a direct question was a good thing.

"We need to thank people. That we still have a boardinghouse and any other buildings in Blessing is so miraculous. I'm glad this celebration is for thanking God also."

Miriam nodded and smiled. "Will you be able to attend?"

Mrs. Landsverk nodded emphatically. "We are putting up a sign that if someone needs something, they can find us at the schoolhouse. I won't stay for the dancing, but Sophie and I will be some of those doing the thanking." She cleared her throat. "So close." She shook her head slowly, as if still in shock. "So terribly close. I thank Him every day that no more lives were lost. Or even horrid injuries. Reverend Solberg reminded me of that the other day when he and Mr. Devlin were having coffee in the dining room." She half smiled. "We need reminders, you know."

"That we do. Thank you." She turned away and looked up the staircase. Right now that seemed like a lot of stairs to get to her room.

"Do you want me to send up a tray?"

Miriam turned back. "You would do that?"

"Of course. Give you a chance for a short nap at least."

Do I look that tired? "Thank you." After a comment like that, somehow the stairs did not look so intimidating.

She set her things down, cut open the envelopes, and lay down on the bed to read. One from Mercy and, surprise of surprises, one from Este. She read his first.

Dear Miriam,

We are all doing well here. I like my job. Joy and Truth are doing very well in school. We are happy at the hospital. We miss our mum bad, but I know she is in heaven with Father and they are both happy again.

We miss you too.

Fall is here.

Your brother,
Este

Miriam laid the thin paper down on her chest and stared at the ceiling. He wrote to her. Este wrote to her. In spite of hating writing. It wasn't that he couldn't. After all, he had completed eighth grade with high marks, but that didn't mean he liked to write. Or read, for that matter. He did not mind reading as much as writing. She remembered his saying that one time.

The room was growing dim, due to the sun setting so much earlier. Instead of reading it again, she made herself get up and light the lamp beside her bed. Lying down again, she reread it.

Unbidden, the words tiptoed through her mind. *Thank you, God in heaven, that Este wrote to me.* Did God really care for her so much that He made Este write to her? That was an even more shocking thought. What would Father Devlin have to say if she happened to mention such silliness to him?

Now *that* caused a snort to erupt. *Miriam Hastings, how you carry on.* She folded the first letter, slid it back in the envelope, and drew out the second. From the differences in penmanship, she knew her sisters had collaborated.

Dearest Miriam,

I have a feeling you are going to be mighty surprised to be receiving a letter from Este. I wish I could be there to see your face. I want you to know we did not even force him to write. He is so grateful for his job and loves the garden better but does well in the kitchen too. Our Tonio is such a hard worker and hates laziness, as you well know. He's still at his job loading railroad cars, and his boss notices how hard he works. Perhaps one day you'll even hear from him.

Nurse Korsheski said that she wants me to go into nursing school. I don't believe for a minute that I could pass the entrance exam, and I told her that. So you can guess what she has done. She has given me copies of the past tests so I can find out where my weaknesses are. Then I will know what I need to study the most. Is she not the most amazing of women? She speaks so highly of you and promises me I shall become a nurse like my sister. O Lord God, would that I could.

The others are doing well. I will let them tell you. Don't you be worrying about us, you hear? As Mother said, God is taking care of us, like He said He would.

Love,
Your sister, Mercy

Dear Sister,

Thank you for your last letter. We like hearing from you. Mother saved all your letters so sometimes we read them all again. That makes you seem closer somehow.

Este said to tell you he will write another time. He loves working in the garden, and Mrs. Korsheski says he is a natural gardener. Like our mother. Remember how she loved her gardens?

I like being back in school again, and I help Mercy with the mending at night. Right now we have a stack of mending to catch up on. Truth reads to us as we sew in the evening. Este reads books on gardening that he gets from the gardener. Oh, he is learning how to keep that furnace going at the hospital too.

Sometimes I wish Tonio worked at the hospital like we do. Mrs. Korsheski said again that she will have a position for him if he ever needs one. Don't you think that learning plumbing and repairs would be better than having a strong back, especially when winter comes?

Truth says I am being long-winded.

We love and miss you.
Joy

Dear Miriam,

School is going good. I like my classes but arithmetic is hard. Tonio said he would help me, but he works too late.

It is getting dark early, so we need the lamps almost as soon as we come home. I feel bad using up the kerosene so I can finish my lessons. I try to do it while it is still light by the window.

But Tonio told me not to worry. This winter will not be like the last one. We have money to buy oil for the lamp and fuel for heat.

Do you need any more of your winter things?

I love to read your letters,
Truth

Like the other, Miriam reread this letter too and sighed. At least they were all doing well. Mrs. Korsheski had indeed lived up to her word to provide so that Miriam could stay here in Blessing and finish her contract. Eyes closed, Miriam let herself think what seeing her family again would be like. The others would grow taller. The boys stronger.

Another sigh escaped into the silence of the room.

A knock at the door jerked her upright.

"Miriam, it's Maisie. I brought your tray."

Oh no. She'd fallen asleep. For how long? She called, "Thank you!" and opened the door.

Mrs. Landsverk handed her the tray. "Your Trygve was by, but he did not want you disturbed. He asked me to tell you he will come by for you."

"Why would he . . . ? Oh, the party. I'd forgotten about the party."

"You will so enjoy it! He is a fine young man." Mrs. Landsverk closed the door on her way out.

Miriam set the tray down by the window. Nearly dark already. She must eat quickly. Trygve would be there soon.

So she would enjoy the party, eh? Hardly. What she wanted to enjoy was sleep. And that would probably not come for long hours yet. She sighed and picked up her fork.

CHAPTER 26

She wasn't waiting in the vestibule.

Trygve paused. Hadn't that been their agreement? And no one was behind the desk either. He checked in the dining room. No, not there either. For some reason he felt a bit uncomfortable going up and knocking on her door.

Maisie descended the stairs and smiled at him. "If you are looking for Miss Hastings, she'll be down shortly. I just took her up some supper."

"Thank you. Do you take such good care of all your guests?"

"I try to. Some are just easier than others. Can I get you some coffee while you wait?"

"No thanks. How are the repairs to the building coming along?"

"Wisely, they took care of the roof first, so we are weather tight again. That east wall will take some time. But we have only two rooms that are not habitable, and we have windows boarded up. It's not pleasant to live in a room that is constantly dark, but our guests are being so patient while waiting for the windows to be replaced. No complaining to speak of."

"Glad to hear that."

"And we are grateful for every day the bad weather holds off."

He heard a door shut upstairs and watched as the shoes and

skirt descending the stairs quickly switched to Miriam's smiling face. As always, his heart kicked into a faster pace. Lovely, graceful, desirable—words that danced through his mind. Would that she could feel the same way he did. Crossing to the bottom of the staircase, he held out his arm, bent at the elbow for her to accept. When she did, he grinned down at her.

Another door closing and a conversation up above caught their attention. When Dr. Deming and Miss Wells descended, the four greeted one another. "Are you walking over?" Trygve asked.

"Of course." Dr. Deming smiled down at his partner. "That's all right with you, isn't it?"

Vera nodded. "We could all walk together."

Once they were outside, Dr. Deming commented, "I didn't want to miss this, but if you think all these bandages will make others uncomfortable . . ."

"No. You will not stay home. It isn't like anyone can ignore what happened. There are other bandaged people in town too." Vera shook her head. "Call the dressings your badges of honor."

"Trygve?" The voice down the block sounded like Daniel's. Trygve stopped and turned.

Daniel didn't come over to them at a jog, but he walked fast. He was covered in soot and grime, and he smelled like a fire. "The ashes are cool enough now that we've been poking around in the rubble where the elevator used to be. Good evening, Miss Wells, Miss Hastings."

Trygve realized what Daniel was saying. "Find anything?"

Daniel nodded.

Vera frowned. Suddenly her mouth dropped open and she clapped her hands over it. "You were looking for the hired man at the elevator! And you found him."

Miriam wagged her head sadly. "Is there enough that we can give him a proper Christian burial?"

Trygve almost had to smile. Leave it to Miriam—clever, sensible Miriam—to go directly to the important things.

"I think so. He was where we suspected—well, the little we found of him—on the ground beneath the debris. Enough to bury. And we could include that meerschaum pipe, what's left of it. The blast shattered it." Daniel looked at Trygve. "Thorliff and I have to get cleaned up, obviously, and then we'll be there. Will you tell the quilting ladies, please, that Thorliff and I will help Thelma bring over the rest of the party food?"

"I shall."

Vera still looked upset. Dr. Deming laid his arm across her shoulders and guided her gently off toward the party.

Trygve fell in beside Miriam as she began strolling in the general direction. "I'm glad they found his body. It'll be good to give him a proper burial."

She nodded. "Most of the people in this town are decent. They value the right things. I find that quite comforting."

"I keep hoping you will realize that Blessing has so many advantages, it would pay you and your family to live here. There is plenty of work and plenty of friendliness."

"And you keep forgetting that I signed a contract. I must go back to the hospital." She stopped and turned to face him. "Trygve, I care for you. I do! I really do. But a contract is a promise, and when I make a promise, I will keep it. Do you understand?"

"Completely. But that doesn't mean you cannot come back after your contract is completed." They resumed walking. And down inside, he was singing. Of course she would honor a contract. A woman of immense integrity does that. It was just one more reason why he loved her. And she'd admitted she cared for him! Praise God!

They were arriving about on time, but the room was already crowded. Almost all the chairs were filled by the ladies, which was proper, and the men stood about in clusters. Trygve delivered Daniel's message to two quilting ladies by the food table, and they thanked him. He did not reveal that Mr. Nordstrund had been found. Well, parts of Mr. Nordstrund. That was Daniel and Thorliff's news to announce.

Then Reverend Solberg called the program to order and opened with prayer. The men gathered mostly at the back. Miriam settled into a chair on the edge, and Trygve moved close to stand beside her.

Trygve didn't hear exactly what John had prayed, for his mind was still firmly riveted to the sweet young nurse. She'd said she cared for him! She'd insisted, in fact! What a glorious thing! There was hope.

The two doctors entered and were immediately given chairs at the front. Good! Her swollen belly aside, Elizabeth looked more or less like her usual self, with a pink complexion and a ready smile.

But Astrid's appearance slammed him. She looked ten years older than she was. Haggard. Drawn. A sort of twitchy nervousness, but not exactly. Were he to have to describe her, he would not have the exact words. But she was obviously hurting. And tired. Yes, that was it—very tired. It showed in her eyes. In the way her shoulders drooped. Did Daniel realize how tired she was? When you live with a person day after day, you don't always notice the changes as they happen.

Why shouldn't she be tired? She lost her father only two months ago, and did not have any time at all to grieve. None of them did. It was early harvest, and every hand was needed in the fields. With Elizabeth sidelined, Astrid was carrying the full burden of the hospital and the nurses' training. And now the fire. It had consumed far more than just wood and grain.

But look at her, soldiering on. The Bjorklunds were like that, though. No matter how shattering the blows, they kept going, kept doing, kept serving. But then, just about all Norwegians were good at maintaining life in the face of crushing loss. Trygve was proud of his Norwegian heritage and its stalwart women.

Several children stood up front now to recite the thanksgivings they had offered in school. Trygve clapped when everyone else clapped.

Miriam was like Norwegian women in so many ways. Industrious. Energetic. Efficient. Capable. She had just lost her dear mother, yet here she was, back in harness. She was separated from her beloved family by seven hundred miles, yet she continued on. And she'd admitted she cared about him! Insisted she did!

More children came forward, spoke—most of them in singsong, obviously having memorized their essays—and sat down to applause.

What a contrast: Astrid so harried, and Miriam sitting here beside him looking so youthful and fresh. In fact, she seemed more hale, with better color, than she did back when she had first arrived. It seemed long ago. He had loved her even then, the first time he saw her. And she'd said she cared for him!

Some of the immigrant workmen stood up. They had lost their tent homes, yet how grateful they were for life and for their neighbors. Trygve had a great deal of difficulty understanding the heavy accents, especially the Russian, even though he was around them every day.

Maybe he should travel to Chicago and sit down with this Mrs. Korsheski, or whoever she was. If he could adjust Miriam's contract or perhaps even cut a new one, she might be more inclined to move to Blessing.

Several others, including some of the women, stood up to say the same thing everyone else was saying. Gratitude in the face of loss. Apparently women were allowed to speak at this gathering.

As far as Trygve was concerned, they ought to have a voice all the time, including at business meetings and meetings of bank members. After all, they were the ones who *really* controlled the money in this town, and that included his dear tante Ingeborg.

Sophie stood up and thanked the many families who had

taken in the now homeless people from Tent Town and given them a roof over their heads as winter came at them with freight-train speed.

Trygve nodded to himself. That was definitely the thing to do. Take the train to Chicago, talk to this Mrs. Korsheski. She obviously valued the whole family, not just Miriam, and would almost certainly agree to whatever would be best for them. Maybe while Trygve was there, he could recruit more workmen for Blessing. Put an ad in the papers or something. He had heard of the *Chicago Tribune*. There must be other newspapers in a city that large. Blessing could certainly use all the labor they could get, especially with the massive setbacks the fire had created and winter so close.

But where would they live?

Should he mention this idea to Miriam, or just go?

What's this? Garn Huslig, owner of the grain elevator, was coming forward. Like Astrid, he had aged a decade in the last week. And more than just about anyone else here, he had just lost everything. He'd lost his elevator and all the grain in it—a whole year's profit, for a lot of the grain had not shipped yet. But he was not knocked flat by this horrific loss either. He still stood straight.

"My friends. I have no words. Like the others here, even our precious children, I am grateful to God for the brave men who fought the fires and the men and women who stepped up immediately to help their neighbors. As terrible as this tragedy is, you all kept it from being far worse than it could have been. We could have lost the whole town, every building. We could have had many deaths. But we didn't, because of our dedicated men. Thanks be to God.

"And what do I see when I look around? Strong men and women. Strong children. People who will rebuild our town. Dear friends, we will rise from the ashes and restore Blessing. God willing, it will be the best town in the Dakotas. I give thanks most of all for you, our friends and neighbors, because we stand by each other, and you will bring us back again!"

Sophie's husband, Garth, leaped to his feet. "Amen to that, Garn! We'll come out of this bigger and better than ever!" He started clapping. Half a dozen more men, agreeing with him, applauded enthusiastically. Trygve watched Miriam. She was caught up in the general mood, nodding and clapping. Yep, she would fit right in to Blessing. She'd said she cared about him!

Now Dr. Deming came around to the front, bandaged face and all, to thank God and to praise the personnel at the hospital and the medical treatment he'd received. "Our medical care," he boasted, "is the best!" More enthusiastic applause.

Uh-oh. Anner Valders was standing up. And Trygve noticed that instantly Miriam, who had been so loose and cheerful a moment ago, even slightly embarrassed that the hospital was garnering such praise, suddenly turned stiff. Frowning. Her hands clenched into fists.

"As far as I'm concerned, Deming, your praise is misplaced." Anner looked angry. But lately, he always seemed to look angry. "Whatever that was they gave me for my burns, the sores are still open. They're not healing. I wouldn't call that good service."

Miriam gasped. "Second degree burns, and if they don't heal in a few days, it's our fault?" Her neck had turned red.

"Mine aren't healing yet either, Anner." That was Garn, now standing toward the back. "But that's the way with burns. They take a long time." He pulled his sleeve up enough to show the bandage on his own arm.

Anner didn't seem to hear. "When a man puts his life on the line for the community, he deserves good medical care! And I notice when you were doling out thanks, Huslig, you failed to mention me. If I hadn't rushed into that burning bank to close the door to the safe, this town would have no money! Do you understand? Every dollar gone. Burned up! And all the books."

Apparently now even Dr. Deming was irritated. "Right! And

if you hadn't been so careless as to leave the safe standing open when you went home, you wouldn't have had to come hustling back to close it."

"I am getting sick and tired of being disregarded by this community!" Anner's voice was almost shrill, he was so furious. "I do my best, and all I get is criticism. Besides, Dr. Deming"—he put a nasty slur on the title—"my Hildegunn went to the hospital today for headache powder. She has been suffering for days with a headache, and the doctor would not see her! Would *not*! Flat out said she didn't have time for her. You call that good medical service? She said she didn't have time to see a suffering woman."

Astrid leaped to her feet. "You blathering, mean-spirited—" She caught herself. "Do you know why I did not have time? I was treating a family who is starving, literally starving, and their poor baby is near death. Because of you! You loaned the husband a modest sum of money, and now you are sucking out half of his paycheck every payday! Half! That family has no money for food, you leech!"

Reverend Solberg strode forward from his place at the back of the room. "Enough!"

Anner stood before her nose to nose. "You will *not* malign my sound business practices, you who are ignorant of finance!"

Trygve expected Miriam to gasp or something. Instead she jumped up and stomped over to the furious pair. She pushed between them, facing Anner. "Don't you dare address the doctor in that manner!" She had her hands up, her fists solidly clenched.

Trygve started toward them. Elizabeth looked stricken. Astrid and Elizabeth, of all people, did not deserve this. Not now, not ever.

Astrid was still shouting, her fists white, her face and neck red. "You even lied to the man, saying you would get him deported, knowing full well you can do no such thing. You *lied*! Just so you could milk more money out of him. And his poor baby is starving to death. For some reason, you have turned into a despicable . . ." She stammered for a word. "If I could, I'd get you run out on a rail!"

But now Anner was scowling in rage at Miriam, Trygve's Miriam. "So even the little bushy-haired guttersnipe gets to yell at me. This town has gone mad!"

"Guttersnipe!" Astrid looked ready to punch the pompous excuse for a man.

Anner was not quite finished. "And this incompetent little fool is no more a nurse than you are a doctor!"

But Astrid didn't have to punch him. Miriam hauled off with a fist and knocked Anner Valders back so hard he stumbled two paces before he met the floor, rear first.

CHAPTER 27

Miriam sat quietly shaking, the only person in the schoolroom, her eyes locked on the floor in front of her. Her right hand hurt like everything, but she ignored it. How could she have lost her temper like that? Whatever had possessed her? And in front of Trygve. That hurt even more than her hand.

She heard the music out in the other room, so they must be dancing yet.

The door opened and Thorliff Bjorklund entered. Behind him came Anner Valders, Trygve, Reverend Solberg, and Thomas Devlin. She was really in for it now. She watched Mr. Bjorklund's face. She couldn't bear to look at the others, especially Trygve. Whatever must the man think of her?

"Miriam."

She pushed herself to her feet. "Mr. Bjorklund."

He looked grim, but then, they all looked grim. "As you know, Miriam, our town has no law officers and no jail. You committed an assault, which is punishable by jail, if we had one."

"Yes, sir." She barely spoke it. She went back to studying the floor.

"So we've been discussing what to do about this. For one thing, the hospital is short-handed, and Elizabeth says they cannot afford to lose you for thirty days if we sent you up to jail, which would be the appropriate punishment. Anner agrees that if the reverend and Thomas levy an appropriate punishment, a spiritual punishment, you might say, he'll consider it sufficient. We feel first off you should apologize."

She raised her head and locked eyes with Mr. Valders. This was so very difficult, a punishment in itself. "I apologize with all my heart, Mr. Valders, for losing my temper with you, for hitting you. I am very sorry."

He bobbed his head slightly, turned on his heel, and marched out. The door didn't slam exactly, but it closed firmly. In a very nasty way, she was sort of pleased. Already his cheek was bruised and swollen, his eye turning purple. If she must suffer the consequences, at least she'd gotten in a good, solid punch.

And now she would pay the price, pay handsomely for a moment of foolishness. She looked over at Trygve. *Please forgive me.*

He walked up to her, grabbed her head in both hands, and kissed her on the forehead! "You wonderful woman!" A public display of affection! What?

Father Devlin was laughing. He grabbed her left hand and pumped it up and down enthusiastically. Reverend Solberg was laughing too and pumping her other hand, squeezing it so hard it hurt worse.

Even Thorliff was grinning. "Miss Hastings, you cannot imagine how much all of us have wanted to do exactly that! *Yearned* to do that!"

Reverend Solberg let go, still grinning. "We are all assuming you won't do it again. Right?"

"Too right! It will never happen again."

Father Devlin made a hasty sign of the cross. "Then ye're forgiven yer transgression, and we'll assume yer promise to be penance. 'Twill be hard enough to refrain from punching him again. But tell us, lass, how have ye developed such a powerful punch, a wee slip of a lass like yerself."

She still felt a bit stunned. "Well, er, you don't grow up on the streets of Chicago without learning a thing or two about fighting and defense."

Thorliff stepped back, still smiling. "Don't forget to look very contrite as you leave."

"As I leave?" This was it? Her punishment was to look contrite? Suddenly she was grinning so hard she couldn't quit. "Thank you, all of you. And if I dare admit it"—she ducked her head—"it was the most satisfying thing I've done in years."

 ❧

Astrid remembered Daniel bringing her home, barely.

She stared up at the ceiling and around the room. She was in her own bed, in their bedroom, not the places she'd been to— the horror of the dark and the noises and the tears. Always the tears. What had happened to her? Was it dusk? How long had she been in bed? Her eyes burned as if walking through smoke. Had something happened to her? An accident or something?

Nothing made sense. A picture, a memory. Far smoking his pipe in the kitchen at home. Immediately tears tried to drown her. Using the sheet to wipe her eyes, she turned over and tried to muffle the sobs with the pillow. An explosion that rocked the walls. Flames. How could memories be so real? The night that threatened to burn Blessing to the ground. People screaming, the hospital overflowing. No, that had not happened. Had it?

When she threw back the covers, her feet searching for the rug, she pushed herself to sitting, slowly, as if the entire state of North Dakota were grinding into her shoulders. Staggering to the bathroom, she clung to the doorframe, the wall. Whatever she was suffering from, she must have been terribly ill to be so weak. So weak she felt nauseous.

Her memory flashed back in bits and pieces. Tears. Tears that would not stop. What started them? She focused as hard as she was able, but nothing came to mind. Other than she couldn't quit crying. And now here she was again, mopping the overflow away as she made her way back to bed.

She went back to bed. Sleep. Go back to sleep, she told herself. There is safety in sleep. Or was there? Would all those horrifying dreams return?

Daniel. Perhaps Daniel had some answers for her. She tried to call his name, but instead she spiraled back down into the abyss.

The next time she woke, the birds that had not flown south were heralding the dawn. They must have slept in too. Sunlight whitened the sheer curtains. Someone had said they should have drapes to keep out the light, but she had said no. She needed the light to wake in the morning. Their bedroom had an eastern window for that very purpose.

Back to the bathroom and this time a drink of water too. Anything to soothe her throat. It felt as if she'd been coughing and swallowing sand. But moments later, the nausea returned with a vengeance, and she lost the water. She must drink it more slowly.

Back sitting on the bed, she checked the other pillow. Yes, Daniel had slept there. But she'd not even been aware of him in bed with her. Surely she had missed out on Sunday, since she vaguely remembered waking in the dusk. Was it Monday? Had he already gone to work? She listened closely, surely that was voices she heard.

Steps on the stairs, and to her relief, Daniel came through the doorway. "Good morning." His smile didn't quite make it to his eyes. Was something terribly wrong?

"What day is it?"

"Tuesday." He sat down beside her and took her hand. "Mother wants to know if she can bring you a tray."

Astrid thought about food, and even the thought made her stomach shudder. "Tea maybe?" The words took effort. "What is wrong with me?"

"Your mother called it a breakdown."

The tears started again, only a drizzle this time. How could one body have so many tears? Shoulders curved, she huddled into herself. The warmth of his arm around her shoulders felt like a lifeline.

"I . . . I'm so tired." Even those few words took effort.

"You don't have to get up." He kissed the top of her head.

Waves of weariness threatened to take her under again. "Heavy, so heavy." Her head dropped to his shoulder as if unhinged. "Takk." Did the word get spoken or not? Grateful for his help, she burrowed back into the pillow. Surely if she slept a bit more she would feel like getting up.

"Her vitals are all normal, heart a bit slow, but . . ."

Astrid focused on the words. Elizabeth? Whose vitals? The pillow felt wet beneath her cheek. Had she even been crying in her sleep? How long had this been going on?

"I think exhaustion, accentuated by grief." Her mor's voice.

"I hope so. There are no symptoms of anything else."

Astrid opened her eyes. Halfway was all they would go. "I'm awake."

Her mother's hand of love smoothed back her hair. She'd know that hand anywhere, anytime. "Good."

"The bathroom. I need . . ." She needed it for the usual reason and because the nausea was back. Astrid ordered her hand and arm to remove the covers. Strange, as if she had to tell her body to do the things it usually did without attention. Instead of swinging as usual, her feet crept to the edge of the bed and over the side. When she sat up, the room tilted but righted itself when she was sitting up. "I am so weak." The words croaked.

"Let me help you." Ingeborg wrapped an arm around her daughter and, after helping her to her feet, walked beside her to the other room, assisting her all the way.

Back in the bedroom, she saw Elizabeth sitting in one of the chairs by the south window. "How come you are here?"

Elizabeth smiled. "I am your doctor, you know." She nodded to the tray on the table between the chairs. "Tea?"

Whatever happened to her ability to make instant decisions? After sinking back on the edge of the bed, she nodded. "I guess."

"You want to go over there, or we can prop the pillows behind you here?" When Mor smiled like that, the sun came out.

"Here." This time the pause was almost not noticeable. Instead of sliding back under the covers, Astrid waited until her mother finished.

"We should help you over there, and then we could change the bed."

"Later." Scooting back sucked her energy, but with only a little help, she could relax against the pillows.

"Oh good. You are up." Amelia Jeffers smiled at her from the door. "I'm heating the chicken soup Ingeborg brought." When Astrid started to object, she raised a hand. "Sorry, I'm not listening. You need to eat something." With that she turned and headed back down the stairs.

Elizabeth first grinned, then chuckled. "Now that's a side of Amelia I've not seen before."

"She's so very capable." Ingeborg picked up the washcloth from a basin of warm water and, after wringing it, sat on the edge of the bed and washed her daughter's face, then hands.

"Oh, that feels so good." Astrid tried to sniff back the tears that welled without her permission but failed, so Ingeborg handed her a handkerchief.

"Tears are healing, you know. God even promises to store all our tears in a bottle."

"He must have a bottomless jar."

"Our Astrid is still in there." Elizabeth picked up her teacup and inhaled the fragrance. "I think Amelia put rose hips in this tea." She poured another cup from the teapot snugged inside a quilted cozy. "Do you want honey?"

"Ja, she does." Ingeborg ignored Astrid's almost refusal.

Astrid ordered her eyes to stay open, but like the rest of her, they did not obey. The fragrance of chicken soup brought her back. She watched her mother sit back down on the edge of the bed and proceed to spoon soup into her mouth.

After a few swallows, Astrid moved her head. "No hurry."

"More in a bit, then. You do need to get some fluids into you."

"I know. Let this settle." She listened to the other two talking about the celebration on Saturday, but that seemed like such a long time ago, she barely remembered it. At least the nausea did not come on strongly, and she could keep everything from coming back.

"I don't think Miriam will ever live that down. Imagine her taking on Anner like that." Amelia laughed as she spoke.

"It sure shocked everyone there," Elizabeth said. "Including herself, I am sure. I wanted to applaud, but the shock was too great. If only Anner would get the idea that he is mistaken about so many things."

"Whatever is the matter with him?" Amelia asked. "This is just not like the man I first met."

"Ever since the robbery, he's been different."

Astrid nodded when Ingeborg raised the soup cup. She knew what she needed to do, but somehow even thinking took effort. She drank some of the now cooled soup and let her head fall back against the pillows. So heavy. Everything felt so heavy.

She thought she'd only slept a short while, but when she returned from the bathroom, the sunset was already fading too.

"Welcome back." Daniel sat in the chair where Elizabeth had been sitting. That meant the others had left and hours had passed and still she'd slept. How could a body sleep so much? It wasn't as if she'd only dozed, floating in and out of consciousness. She'd never heard a thing.

"Takk." Should she go clear across the room to sit by him?

"Mother said you finally ate some soup."

"I guess." *Good. That had not been a dream, then.* Strange how she wasn't sure what was real and what was dreams. After all, Elizabeth wasn't supposed to be here. She was supposedly still on medical orders to stay home and take it easy.

"Elizabeth came up our stairs."

"So?" He leaned forward slightly.

"She has orders not to go up or down stairs."

Daniel smiled at her. "She said she is feeling almost back to normal and grateful for that. Short of shooting her or tying her down, there was no way to keep her from coming to check on you."

Astrid blinked and rolled her eyes up, but still the tears flowed. All she did was sleep and cry.

Daniel crossed the room and took her in his arms, murmuring an apology for making her cry again, and with that she cried harder. "Dear heart, what is it?"

"I-I want F-Far to come back." The broken words caused her tears to stop. She leaned her head against him, wondering at what she had said. She didn't mean to say that.

"Ingeborg said she thought that grief from Haakan's dying was finally catching up with you."

"Really?" Leaning against him felt so good.

"I remember when my father disappeared, my mother was so lost. She kept hoping we would find him and then despaired that he had died. She said she was so tired of crying. I'll never forget those days."

"So when you finally found out what had happened?"

"She cried for a while longer, but nothing like the early days. Ingeborg and Elizabeth both agreed that exhaustion would be expected after all that has transpired here."

Astrid thought she nodded but wasn't sure. When he helped her lie back down, she slipped again into her inner darkness.

❧

Several days later, Astrid pleaded with Elizabeth not to come check on her again. Even once a day was pushing things.

"But I feel good again."

"You're not tired?" The pause before Elizabeth confessed "some" said more than the answer.

271

"But all women get tired in pregnancy. I take naps. I put my feet up, Astrid. I am not a fool. I am an accredited physician, and I am being careful." Her eyes narrowed and her jaw tightened. "I have done what you ordered for several months now, and you were right. It has worked. I promise that I will stop if I feel any changes at all."

Astrid heaved a sigh. It was time for her to get going again. There was no question about that. Why had she never heard how disastrously grief could affect the body? She understood exhaustion, but . . . "I should be over this by now." A huge yawn caught her before she could disguise it.

"I can tell." Elizabeth leaned forward. "Astrid, I am not climbing the stairs at my house. I am resting in between anything. I am eating right, like a horse actually, and I am thanking God for making all this possible. Miriam and the other nurses are doing a fine job at the hospital, and since we've had no new patients admitted, they are more than capable enough to see to things."

"Have you been doing rounds?"

"I am curtailing everything I can. Thankfully, there have been no babies in a hurry to come into this world, so no night calls. I sleep soundly."

The dark heaviness lurked just beyond Astrid's sight, the lack of oxygen always a forerunner, announcing the return of her nemesis.

"And with that, I am going home to take another nap," Elizabeth said. "On doctor's orders—mine."

"I will do rounds in the morning." Astrid spoke softly but firmly.

"We shall see."

In spite of her determination to be up and moving around, Astrid fell asleep in the chair.

CHAPTER 28

Tears had drenched her pillow. Again.

Ingeborg sat up and stripped the pillowcase off the goose-down pillow. She'd thought she was over deluges like that. Was that what had awakened her or was it something else? She listened carefully. Someone was rattling the grate, and dark hadn't even begun to think about leaving. Who could be up already?

She blew her nose and felt with her feet for the moccasins Metiz had made her all those years ago and she still used as slippers. A lamp glow glimmered between the floor and the door. Sliding her arms into her robe sleeves, she shrugged it on as she crossed the room, as always pausing a moment to listen for Haakan's breathing. When would she ever stop these senseless actions? Habits died hard. Robe belted, she opened the door. "Manny, what are you doing up?"

He turned to her with a grin. "I woke up and couldn't go back to sleep so thought I'd start the stove for you. I was trying to be quiet."

"What time is it?"

"Five. The other milkers will be down at the barn soon."

Ingeborg trapped a yawn and shivered. "I'll fill the coffeepot

273

while you get the fire going. You want something to eat before you go out?"

He dipped his head toward the table, where one decapitated and one whole gingerbread man lay. "I already raided the cookie jar."

Ingeborg dumped the coffee grounds in the compost bucket and pumped the hand pump until icy water gushed into the coffeepot. She rinsed it out and filled it with water.

The crackle of flames in fine kindling raised the scent of pine resin in the room. Manny's shavings were the perfect fire starter.

That thought brought another memory: all the years Haakan had supplied the shavings as he carved spoons and ladles, coat hooks, a train for Carl, doll beds for the little girls that Ingeborg created the stuffed bodies for. Through the years he'd created furniture for the house too, her rocking chair being one of his first gifts to her. Another tear leaked over. If she closed her eyes, she could see him sitting in his chair, busy knife in hand and the shavings box beside him while she read aloud.

And now Manny, Haakan's pupil and protégé, was making shavings as well. He was whittling something—peg legs for Benny, he'd said. If that was it, they needed a lot of work yet.

"You want anything from the springhouse?" Manny asked.

From the back porch, Patches announced the arrival of the men for milking.

"A jug of milk, please." She checked the number of eggs in the basket on the counter. "You better bring some eggs too. Takk."

He grinned at her as he shoved his arms in his jacket. "Vaer så god." And out the door he went.

She stood there a moment openmouthed.

Ingeborg heard the men's greetings outside. Strange that Freda wasn't up yet. Shortly after the Rasinovs had moved in after the fire, Freda had suggested that they have her house and she'd sleep here. Usually she was the first one up.

With the coffeepot on the front of the stove, Ingeborg fetched the can where she kept the ground coffee and measured what she needed. That too was running low. She'd set Emmy to grinding coffee when she got home from school. Today the women were meeting at the church again to get more winter coats sewn for those whose belongings had burned. They'd received a big box of wool coating material from a church in Minneapolis that had heard of their need. Another box held winter coats. Reverend Solberg had put out the word of their needs, and other churches had responded.

"'Morning, Grandma." Already dressed, Emmy joined her by the stove. "Should I set the table?"

"Did you hear Freda?"

"She's coming. Can I sew with you after school?"

"On the sewing machine, you mean?" Ingeborg set the flour tin on the counter, along with the buttermilk, soda, and bacon grease can from the stove. *What a good idea!* Teach Emmy to sew. She was not too young. For that matter, even Inga was getting old enough.

"Biscuits?" Freda tucked the ends of her braids into the knot at the base of her head as she came into the kitchen. "Why didn't you wake me up?"

"Never entered my mind. You're always up first."

"I don't know what came over me, sleeping like that. Why, I didn't even hear you start the stove." She tied her apron in back. "Did you slice the meat off yet?"

"No."

Freda fetched the smoked venison haunch from the pantry. Trygve and Samuel had gone hunting and brought in two young bucks. They'd smoked the haunches and shoulders and ground some for sausage. As soon as the weather turned colder, the butchering would start, replenishing their meat supplies. Four steers were being grain fed in the corral to fatten them. They would butcher two at a time and then the others after the meat was processed and distributed among the families. The hogs were ready to be butchered too. The smokehouses would be in use full time for a while.

A memory of the last time she'd gone hunting made Ingeborg smile, at least inside. Thorliff had challenged her as to who could bag the first deer. He had been utterly shocked when his mother won. Would her aim be true anymore, since she'd not shot a rifle in years?

"Are you going sewing with us today?" Ingeborg glanced at Freda.

"How about if Thelma and I bring the dinner over? How many might be there?"

Ingeborg shrugged. "I'm hoping some of the tent people will come. Everyone who has a sewing machine is bringing it. We'll leave everything set up and sew every day until Sunday."

Freda settled into a chair. "I'll hem Manny's coat here while the stew and dumplings are cooking. You've marked both hems. Right?"

"Ja, and I left plenty deep hems so we can let them out. He's starting to sprout up. His pants are already getting short, just since school started."

"Probably 'cause he is getting good food for a change."

Ingeborg ignored Freda's rancor against the way Manny had been raised. Someday he might tell her more. Right now he only let little bits of information slip out during a conversation. For a boy who at first didn't want to go to school, he now hungered after knowledge. Which brought up another memory, this one of Haakan teaching the boy as much as he could, the two of them sitting on the porch carving or repairing whatever needed fixing. This must be a morning for memories, and thusly tears.

When Manny returned from milking, carrying eggs in his pockets and a jug of milk, he laid the eggs carefully on the counter. "That cow caught Andrew this morning. He was some mad."

"Because everyone else laughed?"

"That too, but he's like you. Hates to see anything go to waste. They don't make me milk her. I'm glad."

Ingeborg stilled the desire to hug the boy. So far he'd pulled away whenever she'd attempted a hug, but one of these days . . . His volunteering a story like this was coming more often. She motioned to the table, and as soon as the bowls were on the table, they all sat down. "Would you please say the grace, Emmy?"

She nodded and closed her eyes. As always, the pause lengthened before she began. "Heavenly Father, thank you for our house and all the good food we have to eat. Please make sure my other family has food too. And help Manny do good on his test. Amen."

"You prayed for me!" He stared at her, mouth open.

"You said you were scared of this test, so Grandma says to always ask God to help."

Ingeborg could see the ideas ricocheting in his mind. Emmy, all of them really, caught him by surprise every once in a while.

He stared at Ingeborg. "Do you pray too? For me, I mean?"

She nodded. "Of course."

Patches barked, announcing company.

Manny tore his gaze away from her to check the clock. "Might be Trygve. Samuel wouldn't be this early."

"Breakfast sure smells good," Trygve announced as he came in and hung his hat on the rack by the door.

"You've not been here for breakfast in a long while." Freda got up to refill the serving bowls.

"Grace was in a hurry to get to the deaf school and Jonathan hasn't gotten back from Minneapolis yet. Thorliff sent me to make sure all you need is done here too."

"Minneapolis?"

Trygve nodded. "Jonathan took the train to Minneapolis to talk to an architect about the addition to the deaf school. His father recommended the firm, so now that the farm chores are slowing down, Jonathan is working on that dream." Trygve smiled at Freda. "Thanks for cooking extra. I figured you'd want some help getting that next cheese order ready to ship."

"Help is always good. Manny has built a bunch of crates already."

"I'll help more when I get home."

Manny, Ingeborg noticed, was well into his hungry stage. She also noticed that this time he didn't suggest he should miss school in order to work in the cheese house. Whoever would have dreamed this boy could come this far so fast?

After the kids were out the door, Ingeborg gathered up the remainder of supplies she had collected for the sewing marathon. She had sharpened her scissors the night before, something else that Haakan had always done for her. Sharpening scissors was a bit tricky, but she had persevered. So many things he had done that she had come to take for granted. She clamped her jaw against the welling tears. *You will not feel sorry for yourself*, she ordered. *Start thanking God right now, before you get trapped. Thank you, Lord, for the fabrics provided, for good food, for Manny helping, for our warm house, for Trygve always so willing to help, for the cat that caught that mouse in the pantry, for sun and the changing seasons.* Her spirits lifted as she found more to be grateful for, and soon she found herself humming.

"You sound happy." Freda returned from dumping the dishwater on the rosebushes by the front porch. She rinsed the dishpan and hung it on the hook behind the stove. "Good. You've been weepy lately."

"I know, but I reminded myself that praising God is a way to drive those tears away."

"Not easy."

Ingeborg heaved a sigh with a small nod. "Ja, but I like it better than the pit." They had talked through the years of the death of Ingeborg's first husband, Roald, and how she and Kaaren fought both the pit of despair that nearly overcame Ingeborg and the struggle of proving up the land for their children.

The jangle of harness brought her to the window. Trygve had the team harnessed to the wagon. She stepped out onto the porch.

He called, "I'm going over for Mor and her things, then I'll pick you up on the way back. That way I can help haul those sewing machines into the church."

"Tusen takk." She waved and turned back inside. If it didn't warm up plenty today, they would have frost for sure overnight. It was about time. Back in the kitchen she glanced at the oaken box on the wall. "We sure got used to having telephones, didn't we?"

"You might bring that up while you're sewing. I know it will be a while before a separate building will be built again, but the post office and the telephone switchboard . . ." Freda shook her head. " What if the town rented the soda shop building for the winter as soon as that is repaired and put the post office and switchboard there?"

"Surely someone already thought about that."

"I've not heard any such scuttlebutt. I know Daniel offered a space for the post office. Bring it up to the ladies." Freda started peeling the potatoes for the stew. "I'll go dig a few carrots." At the sound of harness music, she stopped. "First I'll help Trygve with the machine. You go ahead."

Ingeborg picked up several baskets, and Freda picked up the box to load in the wagon.

Kaaren waved and called cheerily, "Gud dag."

"Gud dag!" Ingeborg climbed in.

Trygve came out with the sewing machine, put it at their feet, and clambered up into the box. He flicked the reins, and the wagon lumbered off.

"You're awfully quiet today," Kaaren remarked as they neared the church.

"Just thinking."

"Dreading that Hildegunn might be here?"

"Not really." They could hear the children out for recess at the school, and when the wagon stopped at the church steps, chatter from the ladies came from inside.

Ingeborg heard Hildegunn's voice loud and clear, giving instructions, of course. "No, I think it would be better over there." Ingeborg froze to the wagon seat. Trygve helped his mother down and waited to do the same for Ingeborg.

She couldn't move.

"Tante, are you all right?"

Ingeborg swallowed in spite of the tight feeling in her chest. She ordered herself to breathe. *Answer him. I can't.* She swallowed again, but her mouth had gone dry.

"Mor, come here." Trygve's whisper brought his mother from the rear of the wagon.

"Ingeborg, what is it?" Kaaren put a foot on the wagon wheel and hauled herself up before Trygve could help her. As always in the heat of a pressure, she switched to Norwegian. "Ingeborg, can you hear me?"

Ingeborg nodded, at least she hoped she did. Her heart raced. She closed her eyes.

"Any pain?"

"Let me take her to the hospital."

Ingeborg shook her head. Forcing herself to take a deep breath slowly and puffing it out, she squeezed the hand that had taken her own. "Nei." This time when she breathed deep again, her shoulders settled back into their normal place. What had happened? But when she thought back to Hildegunn's voice, she shuddered. She turned her head carefully, as if it might fall off. "I . . . I don't want . . ." Another breath, this time easier. "Hildegunn. I cannot abide the thought of having another . . ." She searched for the word. "Argument, uh, confrontation, uh, mess with her. I think the sound of her voice— This is crazy, but I froze." Her head wagging, she swallowed and frowned.

"Let me take you home. You and I can sew just fine there." Kaaren too sighed. "Maybe your mind is trying to tell you something. I mean, who in their right mind wants an argument or to be bossed around?"

"We've always been able to laugh about her shenanigans. What happened now?"

"Perhaps grief has made you more sensitive to problems, along with all the other things going on in Blessing. Or Anner."

Amelia Jeffers opened the door. "Do you want some help out here?"

"I need another hand with this sewing machine." Trygve glanced at his mother, who nodded to him.

"Let me get one of the younger girls, then." She disappeared back into the church.

"What do you want to do?" Kaaren asked.

Ingeborg took a deep breath. Another. She straightened. "I want to go right into that building with a smile on my face, counting on our Father to smooth the way. If Hildegunn gets out of line, I will come outside until I calm down, and then we will keep on sewing. Those people need warm coats."

"You're sure?"

"I am. A momentary problem." She returned Kaaren's studying gaze and nodded.

Miriam came out, smiling.

Ingeborg smiled back. "You had today off. How wonderful."

"I truly enjoy the sewing I've been able to do. I must say I'm glad we're not doing all the embroidery and lace we had to do on the dresses my mother sewed. Especially tatted lace. Lovely trims, but they take far too much time."

Trygve picked up the heavy end of the sewing machine, the end with the flywheel.

Miriam took the other, which was heavy enough, because the machine was housed in an oak cabinet with cast iron legs and treadle. "You forget how heavy these are."

"Just clumsy for one person to carry. Especially down stairs." Trygve glanced behind him.

Penny appeared, so she held the door for them. "Better you than me. And to think I used to heft these around in the store."

"Tante Penny, if you are saying you are getting old, I'll bust out laughing and possibly drop the machine."

"I'll be careful, then." She picked up a box and followed them downstairs.

"Not to worry," Ingeborg whispered to Kaaren.

"But you would tell me?"

"Ja, I promise." They both knew that Ingeborg never promised lightly.

"Where do you want these machines?" Trygve asked.

Penny pointed. "Under the windows for more light." The kerosene lamps were lit all around the room already. Ever since the pews had been installed in the sanctuary, they'd held the sewing gatherings in the basement. Sawhorses held up tabletops that could thusly be taken down or moved easily. Still, hauling sewing machines up and down steps was quite a chore.

Kaaren watched Miriam start upstairs for another load. "I'm so glad she could come. She loves to sew and is so good at it."

Ingeborg smiled. "She would be a lovely addition to our family."

Kaaren laughed. "True! I think I'll ask Trygve to take care of that." They both laughed. A few minutes later Kaaren stopped Hildegunn on her way by. "We will open with a Bible reading and prayer, won't we?" Kaaren asked gently.

"Of course. Anji Moen said she'd be a bit late. And I know a few more who are coming. I thought we'd wait for them and get set up in the meantime." Hildegunn nodded to the two front tables. "We're sorting there." She turned to answer another question.

Ingeborg shook her head, inside at least. Hildegunn was back in her usual bossy form, but she was good at getting things in order. Ingeborg returned to the wagon for more. One more armful, and it was unloaded, but another wagon pulled up with more to carry in.

The driver stepped down. Miriam began dragging boxes out of that wagon.

"Miriam, I'm glad to see you again."

"I met you at the hospital."

"Yes, Anji Moen. I used to be a Baard. Rebecca is my baby sister." She reached for two baskets, and the two walked in together.

Mary Martha arrived last, bringing her house guest with her. The seamstresses settled in a circle of chairs.

Mary Martha looked around. "I know most of you know Mrs. Sidorov here, but if you will all please say your names, she'll get to know us better too. Her husband calls her Wren, a pet name, and she says she likes it, so let us do so as well. Mrs. Sidorov—Wren Sidorov—is one of those who lost everything."

"Welcome," Amelia said to Mrs. Sidorov. "Mrs. Sidorov is coming to lessons in English and doing quite well," she said slowly and distinctly. "So please give her time to repeat your name. And Alessandra Sorvito here, same thing. It is easier for them to understand us if we slow down some as we talk." So all around the room, the women introduced themselves. Then Kaaren stood with her Bible and read from John, chapter fifteen, where Jesus explained the importance of remaining connected to the vine. "Shall we pray? What if we each prayed the Lord's Prayer in our own native language?" She bowed her head, and when quiet descended, she started gently, "Our Father, which art in heaven . . ."

Ingeborg paused her Norwegian to listen. English, Norwegian, German, Italian perhaps, and Wren Sidorov, while she could speak fair English, recited in Russian. At the amen, silence stretched.

"I think that is what heaven will sound like—all languages speaking together, just like we did. How beautiful." Amelia Jeffers gave a contented sigh.

"And we shall all be able to understand one another, like when the disciples spoke on Pentecost," Rebecca Valders added. "I never have been able to understand if the disciples spoke in all languages or those listening heard their own language. Either way, it was a miracle." She glanced around at the women. "Kind of like we are now. That's a good thing."

Bless you, Rebecca, Ingeborg thought. *I'm so glad I did not go home like Kaaren suggested. Lord God, I don't know what is happening sometimes with me, but you do and I trust you.* She paused and smiled inwardly. *At least I am working at it.*

"Would you mind if I sewed on your machine?" Miriam asked Ingeborg as the group scattered, everyone to her assigned job.

"Oh, please use mine." Kaaren stepped in beside them. "I'm doing handwork at the moment."

Miriam smiled brightly. "Thank you, Mrs. Knutson."

"For pity's sake, child, call me Kaaren. Please. Blessing is not a community so much as it is one big family."

"Is that why Mrs. Landsverk prefers to be called Maisie?"

"Exactly. Come on over to the sorting tables. We'll pick out a project you'd like to work on." And off they went.

Ingeborg watched for a few moments. It took great courage for that young woman to come here today after the way Anner Valders had treated her. Surely Hildegunn would not bring up such an ugly incident here. Would she?

Heads together, Kaaren and Miriam sifted through projects on the table, chatting the whole time. Kaaren laughed. Moments later Miriam laughed just as gaily. What a delight to watch those two hit it off so well!

She also noticed that Hildegunn frowned in disapproval a lot. She frowned at Wren Sidorov and Alessandra Sorvito, as if they should not be there, and she seemed to save her severest scowls for Miriam. Did she really believe, as Anner did, that you had to be Norwegian to live in Blessing?

And what was their disapproval going to do to the delicate fabric of Blessing?

CHAPTER 29

I wish I had not come. That woman makes me want to scream. Miriam knew she'd not scream. Her mother had taught her that one only screamed, and then at the top of her lungs, if she were being attacked. This attack was mental, not physical. She kept her attention on the child's coat she was sewing. But it seemed every time she looked up, she caught Mrs. Valders looking at her disapprovingly.

The buzz in the rest of the room sounded friendly, women having a good time working together, communicating even if their languages didn't match. After all, a needle, thread, and wool coating fit any language. Two of the tables were being used for cutting and another for sorting and pinning, and the four sewing machines thumped like kettledrums, only not in unison.

Ingeborg stopped at her shoulder. "Do you want a cup of coffee?"

"I can get it."

"I know, but I am up and you are in the middle of a seam. Cream or sugar? And a cookie?"

Miriam laughed. "That would be lovely."

Miriam watched her leave. Now, if everyone were as gracious

as Mrs. Bjorklund—oops, not Mrs. Bjorklund, but rather Ingeborg—life in Blessing would be pretty close to ideal.

Miriam Knutson . . . Instead of rejecting the thought the moment it popped up, she paused for the first time to consider it.
Her grandparents, both in various parts of England, had married persons their parents chose for them, arranged marriages.
They were, her mum had said, as happy as anyone else. But her
mother and father had married against everyone's wishes, and
her mother's marriage was just as happy. Perhaps even more so.
Her father had abandoned the Catholic church and embraced
the Anglican tradition, so he was considered a disgrace by his
parents, even without the marriage issue.

What if Trygve had to give up his religion for her? Would he?
Surely so. What if Miriam should have to give up her religion to
marry him? She didn't have a religion anymore. Give up something else very important. Her family. Her nursing. Would she?

"Ouch!" She caught the very edge of her finger with the
needle. *That could have been worse*, she thought as she sucked
the blood out of the needle stab. At least she didn't break the
needle when she yanked her hand away.

"Do you need a bandage?" Ingeborg asked as she set down
the cup and a napkin holding two cookies.

"No, thank you. It will stop. Teach me to keep my mind on
what I am doing." She pressed another finger against the hole.
"Thank you for the coffee."

"You're welcome. I have no idea how many times I have done
that." Ingeborg went back to her work.

Idly, Miriam picked up a cookie. She nibbled. Sugar cookie
with a hint of almond. As far as she could tell, there was not a
bad cook in all of Blessing.

One thing for sure: She had to return to Chicago next fall to
complete her training. Then what? She had already been offered
a job at the hospital in Chicago when she was done training,
but there were lots of staff there. And here? They needed help

of the lining. The ticking clock made her want to hurry, but she already had one hole in her finger and didn't want another.

"How is it?" Kaaren stopped to ask.

"I was hoping to get the lining sewn in, but I'm on duty tonight. I have the night shift for three nights."

"I can finish it. And we are leaving the church open, so whenever someone has time, they can come and keep going. I know some of the others are taking handwork home with them. How about I get the lining sewn in? We figured we'd have a trying-on session after school for the children's things. We'll mark the hem, and you could do that when you can."

Miriam stood up. "Thank you for asking me to help."

Ingeborg chimed in, "Trygve said to tell you that he left something for you at the boardinghouse. He hopes you'll say yes."

"To what?"

Ingeborg smiled. "I have no idea. He didn't tell me. I'm just the messenger, since our telephones are no longer working."

"I'd better go get ready for work." She waved good-bye to some of the others and strode back to the boardinghouse. What could Trygve have left for her? Curiosity made her hurry even more than did the chill of the day. She should have worn her coat instead of just a shawl.

"I have something for you," Maisie Landsverk announced before Miriam could even ask. She withdrew a pretty little box with a blue bow from under the counter and handed it over with a knowing smile. "From Trygve. That man sure is sweet on you."

"I . . . uh . . ." Miriam could feel her neck sending heat clear up to her cheekbones. She must have been redder than a radish. "Th-thank you."

"Don't be embarrassed. I think it is wonderful. He is such a fine man, and you deserve only the best."

"You know I'll be going back to Chicago at the end of July."

"Of course. You go finish your training, and then you get back on the train and come home."

You make it sound so simple. "I-I better get ready. Thank you."

When Miriam turned away, Mrs. Landsverk called her back. "Oh, I got so excited, I forgot to give you this. It came in the mail today." She handed a letter over this time. "Two things in one day. I hope the letter is good news too."

"Thank you." Miriam hurried up the stairs. What could it be? Once inside her room, she hung her shawl on one of the hooks by the door and set her bag on the bed before sinking into the rocking chair. She held the package in one hand and the letter in the other. Which to open first? Almost laughing at herself, she laid the letter in her lap and untied the blue yarn bow. Unfolding the paper, she stared down at a delicate hand-carved heart with a raised cross. An attached narrow purple ribbon could be tied to fit whatever length she wanted. Had he made this himself? She stroked the smooth wood with a tender fingertip. When would she see him to tell him thank-you? Was it even appropriate for him to give this to her? After all, it wasn't her birthday or Christmas or anything special. Yet here it was, warm, as if waiting for her.

She picked it up by the ribbon ends and walked over to the mirror before looping the ribbons around her neck. The golden hue lay against her dress, making the simple garment look elegant. With a sigh she tied the ribbons in a square knot and laid it back in the package. Nurses did not wear jewelry with their uniforms.

Back in the chair, she slit open the letter.

Dear Miriam,

I am sorry it has taken me so long to write, but at least I am doing so now. We are all well here. The fall has been cold and damp, but trains keep needing to be loaded, so I have a job. I am grateful for that. The others are keeping very busy. Mrs. Korsheski has lived up to her promises to us. Now that it is getting dark so much earlier, I worry about Mercy and Este coming home after work, but I insist that they take the trolley rather than trying to walk that far and through the streets here. You know what they are like.

Do you ever think about returning to Blessing after you finish your training? Your letters make it sound like such a good place to live. I have heard how severe the winters are, but still, I dream of a real home with a garden, and perhaps we could even have chickens. I guess I take after our Da and Mum in that way, more than I ever thought.

I will close with love from all of us. We talk about you so much and think about you even more.

With love,
Your brother Tonio

Miriam laid his letter on her lap so she had her hands free to wipe her tears and blow her nose. She'd never dreamed Tonio would write something like this.

Tonio and Trygve, consorting without knowing it, both of them wanting to mess up her tidy plans for her life. She laughed through the tears.

Life was suddenly so complicated, and she hated complications. But what if?

What if?

CHAPTER 30

D r. Bjorklund, I know it is none of my business, but you don't look too well. I'll do more of the paper work tonight. You should go on home."

Astrid looked up, realizing she was rubbing her forehead again. Most likely because she had a headache. "Thanks, Miriam, I think I will." *Tired* sat on her as if it had been sewn onto her shoulders. Surely she should be getting her strength back by now. Yes, she'd had some sort of a nervous breakdown, but that was some time ago. It seemed the better Elizabeth felt, the worse she felt.

Now, where had a thought like that come from? Doctors were not allowed to be tired. At least if she was tired there should be some good reason. And why did all her staff think it was their job to watch out for her? She should be watching out for them. When had she last done any planned teaching for these nurses in her care? After checking to make sure the charts were in alphabetical order, she rose and blew out a breath. Surely a good night's rest would get her back in working order.

Ever since the telephones had gone out, she'd been catching herself worrying about the hospital, as if she were miles away rather than a few doors. Maybe they should set up a bell to ring if she was needed. Similar to the fire bell. Sure, let everyone in town worry about who is sick or got hurt that the doctor is needed at the hospital.

She hung her apron on the hook by the door, took her shawl from another, and stopped. She set her black bag up on the desk and searched through, mentally checking off her necessities. She, Elizabeth, and Ingeborg all kept pretty much the same supplies in their bags, not that her mother was called on to use hers much anymore.

Bag in hand, shawl around her shoulders, and hat pinned in place, she headed for the door. "Good night."

Miriam nodded and smiled, as did Gray Cloud. One more month and the two Indian nurses in training would be returning to their reservation to assist Dr. Red Hawk. That would give him four nurses with at least rudimentary training in patient care.

She paused and inhaled the crisp air. It wasn't freezing yet but would be before dawn. Each night was growing colder. The moon cast her shadow as she headed up the street.

"Astrid!" one of the four men coming toward her called out.

"Trygve? What's happened?"

"Oh, we need some stitches, I think." He was probably trying to sound casual. It wasn't working.

"What happened?" Even in the moonlight she could recognize that one of them was limping, one man was holding an arm to his chest, another was holding a bloody head as his buddy helped him along, and four had bloodied faces, which included Trygve's, and swelling eyes.

"Just a disagreement."

Astrid turned and headed back into the hospital with a sigh.

As they entered, Miriam strode toward them. "What happened?"

"Divide them between the examining rooms. You two go in there, please." She opened the door to the examining room. "Trygve and you, sir"—she motioned to the fellow clutching his arm—"in here. Gray Cloud . . ."

"I get basins and soap." The round little woman rolled her eyes as if this were nothing new to her.

"Bring a bowl of ice too, please." Astrid frowned at Trygve. "Sit in the chair there. You'd better tell me all that happened. No one was drinking, were they?"

"On the job? Of course not." Even Trygve couldn't glare well with one eye rapidly swelling shut. His split lip had quit bleeding.

"We'll ice you and go see to the others. Are you injured anywhere else?"

"No. Not unless pride counts."

"You're not dizzy or having trouble breathing?" He shook his head and winced.

She heard a snort behind her. Miriam held a pan of ice and a couple of wet cloths. The girl should be looking as if she were worried about her loved one. Instead, she looked either bemused or mildly disgusted.

Astrid crossed to the other fellow and pressed around his shoulder briefly. "I thought it appeared dislocated. Let me examine the other two, and I'll return to tend your dislocation. Miriam, prepare some ice packs for Trygve and this man. Then come over to the other room."

She stepped into the next room. "Can you both speak English?" The man in the chair nodded. She recognized the other fellow stretched out on the table, but she could not remember his name. *Check for further bleeding and then ask for necessary information.* As always, her mind went into doctor mode as she crossed to the examination table and removed the dirty handkerchief that had failed to stanch the bleeding from the man's forehead. "Mr. . . . ?"

He mumbled his name.

His companion repeated it. "Dmitri Rasinov. Razzie."

That was it. Now she remembered his wife was Marina. "Do you normally bleed easily with a cut? Is it hard to make it quit bleeding?"

He nodded but kept from flinching when she washed the gash in his forehead.

"I'm washing this with carbolic acid to get rid of any dirt and germs. Nurse Hastings will close it with several stitches. The gash is deep, and we don't want it to break open again, particularly if you bleed easily. That could happen from something as simple as smiling." While she talked, she washed the wound, the red blood welling up immediately. It seemed to be slowing some, or was she just seeing things? Suddenly, she was uncertain of her own observations. "I'm putting this pad on, and I want you to hold it in place, with pressure. Can you do that?"

He nodded. But when he raised his hand, she could see swelling on two fingers. "Was that injured in the fight too? Broken?"

He shrugged and had the grace to look sheepish. "I am not a good fighter."

"I should think not. What is your wife going to say?"

"Plenty," the man mumbled from between swollen lips.

"Your residence?"

"Post office box 3."

"You'd never fit into it. Where do you live?"

"Cannot remember. Brain is foggy. Mrs. . . . uh, that house near your mother." He sucked in a breath when she probed his fingers.

"We'll splint these fingers. That means using your hand is going to be difficult."

"I have to work."

"I know." *What I really want to know is what in the world happened.*

She asked him the standard questions, all the while probing for further injuries, including right around the gash. Was it mushy regarding the bone or just swollen? She couldn't be sure. She would check again in a day or so once the swelling had abated.

Miriam sutured the head wound as Gray Cloud assisted. She

was using tiny stitches to minimize scarring. She did better than Astrid could have, at least now, as bone weary as Astrid felt.

"Good job. Gray Cloud, would you please bandage him up while Miriam splints the fingers? Miriam, in the position of function, I trust you know." She watched as her two nurses calmly and efficiently did what they were asked, as if they'd been doing this for years, not just months.

"Now, if you feel dizzy, sit down before you fall down and get your head down between your knees. I'm sending some pain pills home with you, since you'll probably have a raging headache. If you start to see double, or anything else unusual, come back in here. We'll take the stitches out in ten days to two weeks. Keep your forehead clean."

"We change the bandage?" Gray Cloud asked.

"You're right. See you back here in a couple days for a clean one."

Except for a huge black eye, the fellow's companion in the chair seemed to have survived well enough. She prescribed more ice packs and returned to the other room with her nurses.

Dislocated shoulder. Usually they turned out all right, but sometimes, if a blood vessel or nerve was pinched, they could be terrible.

"I live at the boardinghouse." The man on the table answered her question. "And not married."

"You lost a couple teeth?"

The fellow nodded. "Doesn't happen very often."

With Trygve's help they were able to lever the shoulder back in place. Miriam coached Gray Cloud as she applied a sling and swathe.

Three eyes, already purple and swollen, would announce to the world they'd been in a fight.

Finally, with the others gone out the door, Astrid and Miriam returned to Trygve. "You want to tell me the whole story now?"

"Not much to it really. You know the pressure those guys

have been under to get the apartment building done. They've been working by lantern light, and when one guy accidentally dropped something, it hit another and a fight broke out. I tried to stop it." He slipped his tongue across the swollen split lip. "Ran into a fist."

"I didn't know you were working even after dark."

"Just this week. There's so much work, Thorliff would hire women, if they knew how to use a hammer and saw."

Miriam's eyebrows shot up. "You think women can't build too?" she asked, and there was a sharp edge on her voice.

"I . . . uh . . . I don't think they are trained for it. I know my tante Ingeborg can use a hammer and saw pretty well. But then, she does everything well."

Nice save. Astrid smiled at him. That was certainly true about her mother.

He flinched when Miriam poured some carbolic acid on a cloth and cleaned his lip. She refilled the ice pack and waited for him to hold it on his eye.

"That sure is cold."

"Ice generally is." There was no mercy in the young woman's voice.

Astrid said, "Once you get home, you might want to chip off some ice and pack that eye again."

"I will." Trygve stood. "Can I walk you home, Astrid? Or are you staying longer?"

"I'll take care of the charts," Miriam said. "I got enough information, and we can get more if we need to."

Trygve grimaced. "Ja, you know where to find us."

Astrid threw her bloody apron in the laundry, repinned her hat, and wrapped her shawl around her shoulders. "Thanks, Miriam, Gray Cloud. You both did a fine job. Next time we have a laceration, I'll expect you to suture it."

Gray Cloud widened her eyes but nodded at the same time.

They'd just gotten to the door when Miriam caught up with

them. "In all the blood and mess I forgot to say thank-you." She spoke directly to Trygve. "It is so beautiful."

"You are welcome. I was hoping you'd be happy with it."

"I am. Oh, I am."

Astrid couldn't hide her grin, didn't even try to. She knew what Miriam was referring to, for Trygve had asked her if she thought Miriam would be happy with his handiwork. She'd been so surprised at the detail on such a small piece. If those two didn't figure out the depth of their caring for each other . . .

Once they were finally out the door, Astrid blew out a breath and glanced up at the moon, silvery and without warmth. "What a night."

"She really likes it, huh?" he asked.

"I'd say so. How could she not?" His shrug reminded her of when he was a boy and he'd brought flowers he'd picked to her. Profuse thanks always embarrassed him.

They walked a bit before he said, "I should have known better than to get in the middle of that fight."

"Well, this was one way to have some time with Miriam."

"That's one way of looking at it." He smiled down at Astrid. "I am going to marry her, you know."

"I know she has a commitment to the hospital and her training first."

"I'm not in a hurry. I just wish I was sure she loves me like I love her."

"Ask her." The cold was beginning to seep through her wool shawl, in spite of their walking quickly. How could he doubt after the look she'd given him? Surely sparks had nearly lit the hospital entrance.

"Easier said than done."

"Don't tell me you're shy. Trygve Knutson shy?"

From the distance ahead of them came a cry of "Help!"

They both stopped. Astrid stared forward. "What was that?"

The call came again from the road to the Bjorklund farm.

Trygve took off running with Astrid right behind him. The black bag banging against her side was slowing her down.

Mr. Rasinov lay crumpled on the ground at his companion's feet.

The man was kneeling beside him. "He just went down. I can't carry him by myself, and I was afraid to drag him."

Astrid knelt beside the man with the stitched gash in his head. He was breathing, and his heart was fast but not racing. "Stay with him, please. I'll run back for a stretcher and help." Since her house was closest, she raced up the steps and burst through the back door. "Daniel, I need you now!" She shouted in spite of puffing for breath.

"What?" He burst into the kitchen.

"Get some blankets and a quilt. We have to carry a man back to the hospital. He's out on the road to Mor's. I'll go get Thorliff too." She ran across the street and up on that porch. The light was on out at the newspaper office. Hollering for her brother, she headed there.

"What is it?"

"A man down on the way to Mor's. Trygve and Daniel . . ."

He was gone before she could finish. *Go help them or get to the hospital to prepare?* It had to be that head injury.

"Astrid, were you calling for Thorliff? What is it?" Elizabeth stepped out onto the porch.

"I just treated and released a Mr. Rasinov after suturing a laceration near his temple." She sucked in a breath. "I should have kept him for observation, but he appeared fine. Thank God one of the other men was walking him home. He collapsed and is unconscious."

"Possibly bleeding in the brain. Or a blood clot. Were his eyes all right?"

"Ja, in the hospital. It was too dark to check on the road. What can I do? I should never have let him go."

"Put him to bed and watch for swelling. Did you palpate the site of the gash?"

"Ja, but it was swelling, and I was trying to stop the bleeding. Maybe it was a bit soft, but I wasn't sure." Astrid shook her head.

"Let me get dressed and I'll come too."

"No. Get a message to Reverend Solberg, please. Send Thelma. And look up head injuries like this. Get me as much information as you can."

"I will. Go with God, Astrid. You know He is right beside you, within you, and all around you."

"Thank you for the reminder." Astrid headed for the hospital at a dog trot. She repeated "Please, Lord" with each breath. If only they had the telephones back up.

"What is it?" Miriam asked as soon as Astrid burst through the door.

"Mr. Rasinov collapsed on the way home. Ready the private room for him."

While the two rushed to prepare for their patient, she lighted the first examining room, then went to the front door just in time to open it for the panting men. "Put him in room one." She helped them lift the comatose man up on the table and started an examination all over again.

Swelling at the wound site. Need ice for that. There was no way she could tell if any bone was broken. She asked her patient questions, even pinched the skin on his arm, but she received no response. "Let's get him out of these dirty clothes, clean him up, and we'll move him to the private room, where he can be more comfortable." She turned to his companion. "Will you go out to Freda's house and inform his wife? And if you could, please, stop at the farmhouse and tell my mother what has happened."

"Of course. He'll be all right, won't he?"

"I pray so. Thank you." When he left, she felt Daniel's arm go around her shoulders and hug her close. She wagged her head.

The headache was back. "I should never have let him leave. I should have known better."

"We'll undress him and clean him up. I just heard someone come through the front door." Thorliff squeezed her shoulder. "This is not your fault. I am certain Reverend Solberg is going to remind you that no matter how good a doctor you are, you are not God, who sees all and knows all."

"Takk." *Why did I not err on the side of caution? Because I am too tired to make good decisions? Lord, please don't let this man die because I made a mistake. Please, Lord!*

Gray Cloud brought a basin of hot water, a washcloth, and towels. Miriam brought in an ice pack, and the three women left the room. They met Reverend Solberg and Thomas Devlin coming in the door.

"Thelma sent us to Elizabeth, and she brought us up to date." Solberg stopped in front of Astrid and gripped her upper arms with comforting hands. "Before you go any further, think on this. That Mr. Rasinov collapsed is not your fault. I know you. You gave him the best care possible."

"Ye know the difference 'twould make, lass, had he remained here in bed? He would die for certain. With a head injury, a bleed is invisible inside the skull. Ye'd not see the problem, and he would die unattended in the night, for he would appear asleep." Devlin spoke with quiet authority, just like Reverend Solberg.

She heaved a sigh. "You're ganging up on me?"

"No, lass, we be here to help ye and pray for the injured."

Astrid nodded. "This is one of those times when the telephone would have been such a big help."

Miriam asked, "Will you perform extreme unction, Father?"

"Aye. Just to be on the safe side, since no one seems to know what his preference might be."

Reverend Solberg knocked on the door, and the two men went inside to assist.

"We had something like this happen in Chicago," Miriam said, "a head wound that became an internal bleed."

"What did you do?"

"The same as here. Made him comfortable and prayed for God's mercy. I remember reading about drilling into the skull to allow the blood to drain out and reduce the brain swelling. But you have to know where to drill, and I've never seen it done."

"And you need an auger and bit. We don't have one here at the hospital. I could send one of the men home for one. I assume we would drill near the temple, where the wound is already. He said he always bled easily. That would have been an indication it could happen again."

"But not always, is that so?"

"That is so."

They had just moved him to the private room and settled him in bed when Mor and Mrs. Rasinov came in the door. Gray Cloud showed them to the room.

Marina Rasinov took the chair by the bed and, clasping her husband's hand, held it to her tear-streaked cheek. "Please, Dmitri, please don't die."

Ingeborg put an arm around her daughter.

Reverend Solberg put one hand on the wife's shoulder and the other on the patient. "Let us all pray together. We know God is right here, because Jesus promised that wherever two or three are gathered in His name, He is here." The silence, other than the woman's sniffing back sobs, seemed to stretch until Solberg continued. "Lord God, our Father, Jesus our savior, and Holy Spirit, thou who dwells within us, you know what is happening with this man. We know you bring life and healing, and we ask that of you right now in this place. Cleanse us of any wrong thoughts and fears. Bring your peace and healing, and Lord God, we will give you all the honor and glory, for we know that life and death are in your hands. Amen."

"In the name of the Father and of the Son and of the Holy

Spirit." Thomas Devlin made the sign of the cross from the end of the bed.

Reverend Solberg leaned close to the wife, who had laid her husband's hand back beside him and her head on his hand. "We will keep praying, but if you'd like, we could wait in the hall."

"No. Please don't leave us."

"We won't." Ingeborg moved another chair next to Mrs. Rasinov and kept a hand on her shoulder. Father Devlin commenced mumbling his litany.

Miriam and Gray Cloud left to tend the other patients, and Astrid leaned against her husband. She should send him home. He and Thorliff needed their sleep too. It made her feel guilty to want him to stay, but right now, his presence was such a comfort to her.

Should she try the drilling? What if she only made matters worse? She nodded to Daniel and Thorliff and led the way out to the hall. "Miriam said she knew of a procedure of drilling through the skull to release the blood that is putting pressure on the brain. I seem to remember reading about such a thing, but—"

"You have no bit and auger. I will go get one if you want. You can sterilize it," Daniel offered.

The thought of drilling into the man's skull made Astrid feel weak in the knees. She should have been keeping up more on the latest treatments. So many things she should have done, should have been doing. *Should* was such a horrible word.

"Dr. Bjorklund." Reverend Solberg beckoned her. "Come."

Astrid went back to her patient. There seemed to be no difference. Fingers on his pulse, she leaned closer to listen. Had his breathing changed? His body stiffened, relaxed, and he stopped breathing. "He's gone."

She'd lost another patient. Slowly she turned to the widow. How could she help this poor woman? *Lord God, dear God.*

"In the name of the Father and of the Son and of the Holy Ghost. Amen."

CHAPTER 31

Miriam completed the charts at the nurses' station, hung up her apron, and headed toward the door, her duties completed for another shift. She could not forget the scene as Mr. Rasinov died last evening. It was too fresh, too vivid. It weighed on her.

She stopped cold outside Dr. Astrid's office. The woman looked drawn, ragged, harried. And Miriam knew why. She stepped inside. "He would have died either way."

Dr. Astrid stared at Miriam. "Shouldn't you have gone home by now?"

"Yes. I will, but I saw you and knew you were blaming yourself. We all do that, I think, blame ourselves when it's not our fault. Why would you be different?"

"Why indeed." Dr. Astrid shook her head. "You are wise beyond your years."

"You were the one who impressed that on me when the tuberculosis case died on my shift."

"I never cared much for eating my own words."

Miriam smiled. "Your mother has said that God does not hold us responsible. He's the only one who makes those decisions. And He loves and forgives us."

"And you believe that?"

Did she? Completely? Miriam shrugged. "I suppose I do now. I have learned of God's love through all of you. And Father Devlin, and the reverend. Everyone here in Blessing."

"In spite of the Valders?" Dr. Astrid rubbed her forehead.

"What is that saying about one bad apple can spoil a barrel? Hate and anger are frightening things. I heard Inga tell that to Manny out at the farm one Sunday. Mr. Valders is letting his anger eat away at him, and I know he and his wife are not perfect. The next time he lays into me, I might not be able to still say this. But today I can say that there are far more people like the Bjorklunds and the Knutsons in Blessing than like the elder Valders. In fact, there are only two of them."

Vera stopped beside them. "I thought you two were going home."

"I . . . we are." Dr. Astrid heaved a sigh. "If you need anything . . ."

"I will call Dr. Elizabeth. She said that you are to go home and sleep. She is now on call if we need a doctor today." Vera finished with a dip of her chin as punctuation. "If that's all right with you."

Astrid started to say something, but then shook her head slightly and nodded. "I'm feeling ganged up on, but you are all right. All of you. Thank you." She smiled again. "But if there is a really big emergency, don't leave me out."

Miriam felt herself relax. Vera had handled that well.

"Reverend Solberg said the funeral will be tomorrow, so they are coming for the body sometime this morning. Mrs. Rasinov asked that she be allowed to sit with her husband's body overnight, like their tradition says, and Reverend Solberg offered the church." Dr. Astrid stood up. "I feel so sorry for his widow and the children, in a new land with no immediate family around."

Dr. Astrid and Miriam walked out together.

"You are on again tonight?"

"Yes, ma'am. And tomorrow."

"Then you will be off on Sunday. Good. Mor is planning on folks for dinner after church, so please keep that in mind."

But I've not been invited. Or was that not necessary? Maybe not. She shivered in the wind. "I think I'd better get my winter coat out."

"We could have snow any day. Butchering will probably start tomorrow. It is finally cold enough."

"Oh." So many things she was learning about the world beyond the big city. Miriam paused at Dr. Astrid's gate. "Sleep well." She continued on.

Late that afternoon, when she was ready to leave for the hospital again, she came downstairs with her wool coat over her arm to find Trygve leaning against the desk. His one terribly black eye was still slightly swollen, as was his lip.

"Well, you look much better than the last time I saw you." She felt like patting her chest to make her heart settle back down where it belonged.

He gave her a lopsided grin. "May I walk you to work?"

"Of course you may."

She heard a snicker from the archway into the dining room. Maisie Landsverk joined them. "The coffee is ready and a sandwich for you, Miriam. You didn't have dinner, you know. Do you have time?"

"I believe so." She'd been planning on going in early, but plans could easily be changed. She was finally learning that. "Thank you." Sitting across the table from Trygve, she could see several other bruises on his face. "I thought you would be working at the apartment house."

"I was, but I left early and will go back." He nodded to Mrs. Landsverk, who set a sandwich in front of him too. "Thank you."

"Now I can tell you thank-you properly. I've never had anything as lovely as the carved heart. I am grateful."

"I'm glad you like it. I know you said once that you did not care to go to church again, and I don't blame you, but . . ."

She laid her sandwich down. "I know what I said, but I have changed my mind, thanks to your aunt Ingeborg."

"She manages to change lots of people's minds at times. Anner Valders, well, what can I say? I have no idea why he decided to make you an example in church that day, and I can see how embarrassing that was. I ask that you not hold that against the church."

She smiled. "I'm a little better prepared for Anner Valders' shenanigans now, I think."

"He took me by surprise too. I won't let it happen again. So. Would you join us at church this Sunday?"

"I would be happy to." *I would be happy to join anything anywhere with you. I am confident of that now, even if I have not told you yet.*

He beamed like a child with a new toy. "Thank you!" He took a bite of sandwich. "Did you hear the other news?"

"Probably not."

"Mr. Nyquist, the other teacher at the school, has turned in his letter of resignation, and Reverend Solberg suggested they hire Thomas Devlin, at least for a temporary fill-in until they can find someone else."

"That is wonderful." *So now Mr. Valders can holler about that.* She cut that thought off as not fitting for her change of mind. "I wish my oldest brother and sister, Tonio and Mercy, could go back to school."

"They can as soon as we move them here."

She felt her mouth drop. "What are you saying?"

"I am saying that we'd better get you to the hospital so you are not late."

"Trygve Knutson, what do you have up your sleeve now?"

"Just thinking ahead." He stood up, plucked her coat off the table, and held it for her. When she had both arms in the sleeves, he paused to clasp her shoulders.

Oh, how easy it would have been to lean back into his chest. She jerked herself upright and, with shaking hands, buttoned her coat. Attraction, sure, but was this love? She was going to have to sort out what man-woman love really was. She knew it when she saw it, but how did it feel? Like she was feeling?

Anner Valders was not in church that Sunday, nor was Hildegunn. Miriam felt herself relax and enjoy the warmth of Trygve's shoulder right next to hers. Dr. Astrid sat on her other side.

After church, Inga joined them, taking Dr. Astrid's hand and Miriam's as well. "I like seeing you here with all the family, Miriam," the little girl said. "You belong to us."

Miriam blinked and smiled back. "Why, thank you."

"You are coming to Grandma's for dinner." It wasn't a question. "Emmy and me . . ." She paused, thought, and started again. "Emmy and I have something to show you."

"What?"

"It's a surprise."

Miriam could tell the little girl was dying to tell her, but she held firm.

"You can ride with us. We got room in our buggy."

"Leave it to Inga. It must be nice to be able to say whatever you want." Trygve did not bother to go over and join the circle of men, instead remaining right beside her. Was he making sure nothing bad happened this time? He leaned closer. "We could walk, if you do not mind the cold."

"Cold? You have never walked along Chicago's lakefront when the wind is coming in off the water. Thank you for the offer, Inga, but we will walk."

"And you will ride with us, Inga," Thorliff said firmly.

They waved as the others loaded into their buggies and wagons, then strode down the street, where he took her hand and did not let go. Why did hand in hand feel so right, so easy? So warm. Was this part of that man-woman love?

"Do you have a scarf to protect your face?" he asked. "You're going to need it soon."

"I do. I just haven't taken time to find it." She'd just pulled her coat out of mothballs a couple days ago. When she turned her face, she could smell the odor. She should have aired it out. "I was on duty and couldn't leave. How did the funeral go?"

"Sad, but the Tent Town people gathered around Mrs. Rasinov and her children, as good friends do."

"I know how hard it was for my mother when my da died."

"How long ago was that?"

"It seems so long ago. Truth was just a wee one."

"I'm looking forward to meeting your family."

"When will you meet them?"

"At your graduation, if not before."

She stopped and turned to him. "Trygve, that is the second comment you've made that—"

"That shows I am planning our life together?"

"Well, yes."

"By the way, Tante Ingeborg agrees that we will be getting married."

She stopped and turned to him. "What is going on? Has the family voted or something?"

"No. You know how I feel and the rest of them agree. That is all."

Miriam sucked in a deep breath and continued on. No, this family did not have to vote. They all knew each other completely. One day they would know Miriam as thoroughly, and she would know them.

He began to whistle softly, a strange little tune. His sister and others all said he whistled when he was happy. But she had not revealed her change of heart yet. This was getting so confusing.

"Oh look, all the children are coming to meet us."

"Great."

They were running down the lane and laughing. Emmy and Inga led the pack, of course. They seemed to be playing a game of tag, for when Inga drew abreast of Emmy, she swatted her and cried, "You're it!"

Miriam stopped again and turned to him before the kids met them. "What would you say if I agreed? If I admitted I love you?"

"I'd shout hallelujah."

"Then you'd better start shouting before we get mobbed."

Trygve grabbed her around the waist and swung her in a circle. "Hallelujah! She loves me!" Then he stopped swinging and kissed her right there in front of all the children and the cows lined up along the fence.

He was so unpredictable. *What have I gotten myself into?* A sense of peace settled around her heart and her mind. The right thing, the right season. The season to mourn was over, and the season to love was upon her. She had a feeling her family would be happy too. And if this thrill in her breast was joy bubbling up, she never wanted it to stop.

CHAPTER 32

I don't want to do this. I truly do not want to do this. I can't! Thorliff stared at his coffee cup.

Across the table from him, John Solberg watched him. "I cannot make you do it. I cannot insist. I can only advise you of the right thing. The scriptural way."

"And I know you're right. But, John, he's not . . ." Thorliff sighed deep enough to air out his boots. "I can see that he'd feel uncomfortable with all the changes around here, with people who don't have Norwegian roots or culture. Or religion. The times change, and Anner doesn't want to. But when Astrid told me how that family was starving because he was demanding half their pay every week . . . I'm sorry. That's criminal. Just plain criminal. He should be in jail."

"Do you want to call in Clyde Meeker? If it's criminal, the sheriff is the person to handle it. Of course, it could be that the Munros simply misunderstood."

What a dilemma! Thorliff's thoughts were bouncing off walls in his head, all tangling in each other. "Right now, Anner doesn't like anyone associated with the Bjorklunds. He doesn't like anyone who goes to the 'wrong' church or speaks the 'wrong' language. Certainly not Father Devlin or the like. If I went over

311

to the bank to talk to him, who would go with me? I can't trust myself to be nice to him. The last time we were face-to-face, I nearly punched him."

"I was thinking the dentist, Arthur Deming. He doesn't have a dog in this fight, so to speak. He's a neutral observer, but he attends our church. And I would go along gladly."

Thorliff grimaced and wagged his head. How could he ever do this?

John said gently, "I understand, Thorliff, but Matthew eighteen is clear. You confronted Anner, and he refused you. The next step is to talk to him with a couple brothers present. If he still won't listen, we take it to the church. Jesus did not mention the sheriff, you know."

"I know." Thorliff lurched to his feet. "I guess I just have to do it."

John stood. "Thank you. I appreciate how hard this is for you."

Thorliff slogged along behind John to the hospital to the dentist's office, his heart even heavier than his feet.

Maybe Arthur Deming would be busy with a patient. Thorliff hoped. But no, the dentist had no patient in his chair. The receptionist, one of the wives from Tent Town, confirmed that there were no appointments in the next hour. Yes, Arthur said, he knew about the dissension, and he'd be glad to help out any way he could. Thorliff was doomed. At least that's what it felt like.

The three walked to the bank.

What is wrong with me, anyway? Thorliff wondered. He tried to imagine his father disliking a man this much, any man. He could not. Haakan had depended on prayer and common sense. He'd tended to see only the best in people, although toward the end of his life, he was a little more negative. But being negative and wanting to punch a man were two very different things. Thorliff must put aside his own thoughts and adopt his father's.

He doubted he could. He'd never felt this way about anyone in his entire life.

The sky had clouded over, and a brisk breeze was starting. The gray chill reminded Thorliff all over again that the new housing *must* be finished soon. And Anner stood in the way. Thorliff found himself detesting the banker even more.

The one cage had a teller in it today—Mr. Odell—and he had no customers. The safe stood open, as usual. Everything seemed so normal. Except Thorliff. He was all churned up.

John rapped on the office door, and Anner called, "Come in." The three entered.

"Hello, John," Anner said. Then he froze when he saw Thorliff and Deming, and his face turned from pleasant to angry, instantly.

"Hello, Anner." John sounded relaxed and friendly.

Anner stood up. "If this is another inquisition—"

"Nothing of the sort. There are problems with financing in town here, and we'd like to sit down with you to work them out."

"I do not negotiate with men who would threaten me." Anner glared at Thorliff.

"I apologize." It killed Thorliff to say that, but he knew it was the right step. "I apologize for losing my temper."

"May I sit down?" John motioned toward a chair. He did not wait for Anner to say yes. He sat.

There was only one other chair in the room, so Thorliff stepped back to give it to Dr. Deming.

John's voice purred. "Anner, Garn Huslig told me that he came to you for cash to clean up the elevator mess, and you refused him the loan."

Thorliff gasped. He had not heard about that.

Anner sat down. "Prudence, John. It is not prudent to loan a substantial amount of money to a man with no collateral. Mr. Huslig's collateral, the elevator and its contents, burned."

"But that is why he needs the money."

"I repeat, prudence. If he had hired a reasonable night man, he wouldn't need the money, the fire would not have happened, and we'd still have our year's harvest of wheat. So it's his fault! By hiring that worthless Nordstrund, he showed his true colors. Imprudence."

"I find that rather uncharitable, Anner. I'm sorry."

Anner raised his voice. "I am paid to protect the financial interests of this town. I'm doing it. Now, I beg you, John, to take care of spiritual matters and leave the financial matters to me."

A wicked thought slammed into Thorliff's head. Could it be? He turned on his heel and walked smartly out into the bank lobby. He climbed over the little wooden fence that divided the lobby where customers came from the part where the bank's officers operated.

Behind him, Anner screamed, "Get out of there, Bjorklund! Now you're going to rob the bank?" He charged out of the office, the other two behind him.

Thorliff stood in the doorway of that thick safe. He had to duck to look inside. He scanned the shelves, then stepped inside to look more closely. He turned away and came back out. "There's no cash here, Anner. Usually you keep a few stacks of bills handy. There has always been cash here." He pointed. "Right there. The shelf is empty."

"I moved it. I—"

"And that shelf there is empty. Where is all our money, Anner? Not in the safe."

"Bjorklund, I do not answer to you!"

John was keeping his voice soft. "But you do answer to the citizens who hired you. We also came to talk about the Munros, Anner. Their baby was starving while you recovered his debt. I want to hear your side of that."

Thorliff was furious now. More than furious. "How many more people are you gouging when they borrowed money? Where is the cash?"

Arthur Deming held up his hand in a gesture asking them to stop. "Wait! The conversation is becoming too heated. Anner, how about you go sit down with John in your office, and Thorliff and I will wait outside? You two can iron out the problems better without us."

That was certainly not the way Thorliff wanted the meeting to go, but John was nodding enthusiastically. "Good idea, Arthur."

No, it was not a good idea at all! Thorliff was putting Anner on the carpet and John and Deming were getting him off it. But what could he say?

Thorliff let Arthur lay a hand across his shoulder and lead him outside. "Deming . . ."

Grinning, Dr. Deming headed for the alleyway. He murmured, "His window's open."

Of course. Anner's office window was open six inches. Thorliff had not noticed that. Silently, they moved up until they were close to the window. They could hear everything.

Not that Thorliff wanted to. Listening to Anner only made him more furious.

Anner was practically shouting. "John, Munro is one of those foreigners. He misunderstood. That's all."

"I doubt that. He speaks the king's English, literally, and if he says you threatened him with deportation, I tend to believe it. He is terrified of you."

"I will husband the bank's money. I will—"

"But making money unethically never pays, Anner. It's like the Haggai Scripture says: 'He that earneth wages earneth wages to put it into a bag with holes.' The bank cannot prosper unless you maintain the highest ethics."

"There is nothing unethical here! John, you can't trust them, any of them. They're all dirty foreigners! They'll steal you blind if you let them! I was just getting the bank's money back before they skipped town or reneged or something! You know I wouldn't do that to somebody local."

John's voice now sounded just plain sad. "How many, Anner? How many loans have you made to the Tent Town workmen?"

"A couple. That's all. A couple."

"If I or someone else asked for a cash loan just now, could the bank provide it?"

Silence.

Thorliff stared at Arthur. Arthur stared back.

Then Anner said quietly, "No."

"Anner, I'm beginning to see that you are so desperate to get some cash that you will go to any lengths. Unethical lengths."

"*Not* unethical! I just told you—"

"Unethical. If, as you say, you would not treat a local borrower thus, you know it is unethical. Anner, believe me. I am not here to judge or condemn. I'm here to work out a solution."

Anner sounded impatient. "There is no solution, John. Can't you get that through your head? The money in this town has completely dried up."

"Back when we set up the charter, we agreed to hold ten thousand in reserve against an emergency. The fire was an emergency."

"It's gone. Invested in properties and instruments that did not bring the return I was hoping for. I expected returns by now that would replenish our resources. You cannot just build, build, build with no cash coming back in, as from rents. And now, with the whole wheat crop lost, the situation is even more dire. There is no money."

"So what is Blessing going to do?"

"Trying to put her banker on the spot is certainly not the answer."

"I am not trying to put you on the spot. I'm trying to—"

"Well, you're doing a mighty fine job of it!" Anner's voice was rising. "I do the best I can, and everyone's against me. I see no reason to continue this charade when I don't have the backing of the people who hired me."

Thorliff heard a jangly clattering.

Anner roared, "Here are the keys! Find yourself a banker who can make money appear out of nowhere!"

A door slammed.

Thorliff watched Anner stride down the street to his house and slam the door as he went inside. Now what to do? The three men gathered on the front porch of the bank, all looking a bit stunned.

"I never dreamed this would happen." Thorliff kept shaking his head.

"I say we adjourn to the bank office. I think we need to keep things as normal as possible." John Solberg led the way.

"Reverend Solberg?" Hans Odell caught their attention. Thorliff vaguely remembered Hans had been working as a teller for the last few years on a part-time basis.

"Yes, Hans."

"I . . . I couldn't help but hear."

"I know, probably you and half the town."

"Could I speak with the three of you?"

"Of course. Come on in."

Once in the office, Mr. Odell set his cash drawer on the desk. "I have a hundred fifty dollars here. While there are no bills on the shelf, we have some cash in another place—started doing that after the robbery. I'm not sure how much is in it right now, but every other evening the Garrisons bring in their receipts, as do Penny Bjorklund and Sophie Wiste. We do have businesses here that will provide more cash. There is money due the flour mill. You know Daniel Jeffers runs his accounts through here too. It isn't like we are totally insolvent, just cash poor at the moment."

"We all bank here. As cash comes in, we will put it in the bank."

Mr. Odell cleared his throat, hesitating. "You know, Mr. Valders did a good job with investing Blessing money for a long time."

"But he got greedy?"

The white-haired man nodded. "He didn't do it for himself."

"Thank you, Hans."

"I think we can keep the doors open so the town does not panic. Stay open as usual."

"And you can manage this?"

"Ja, I think so. I can do daily records, but I have always been only a bookkeeper, not a banker."

"Do you know the combination to the safe?"

"I do."

Reverend Solberg smiled. "Then, Mr. Odell, I submit that you are now a banker." He laid a hand on Mr. Odell's shoulder. "You know the bank. You know Blessing. We would not ask you to take over if we did not have every confidence you can do it. You are a man of common sense."

Hans Odell seemed to stand a bit straighter. "Thank you, sir."

"Now, gentlemen, I suggest we do as Hans suggests and proceed normally as much as possible." Reverend Solberg looked to Thorliff and Arthur. He handed the keys to the teller, who pocketed them and left to take care of a customer announced by a tinkling bell.

Thorliff stared at Solberg. "How are we going to pull this off?"

"By the grace of God, as always."

CHAPTER 33

Grandma?"

Ingeborg looked up from the sewing machine and smiled at Inga. She knew that tone. "What do you need?"

"Did you know my ma is going to have a baby and that is what is making her big around the middle?"

Ingeborg nodded and kept on stitching the seam, her feet pumping the treadle without her concentrating.

"So do the babies come out in people like the calves do from the cows?"

Oh Lord, give me the right words. She nodded again. "What has your ma told you about this?"

"Not a thing!" Her forehead wrinkled in a thundercloud. "I figured it out."

"Really? Wouldn't you like to go find Emmy?"

"She's helping Freda. Thelma just keeps saying, 'Wait until you are older.' What does that mean? Or, 'You go ask your ma.'" The little girl threw her hands in the air. "How am I supposed to learn things if no one wants to teach me?"

Ingeborg stopped her stitching and drew her granddaughter into her embrace. "Some things just have to wait until we are older to understand." She laid her cheek on Inga's head.

"So will this baby be all wrinkled and squally like Rebecca's baby? Benny thought he was okay, but I thought he was kind of ugly, and all he could do was cry and mess his diapers. How come human babies aren't cute like the chicks and calves?"

"I think they're cute. And they get cuter as they get older."

"True. Benny's baby brother can laugh and play now. He can crawl too, and Benny takes him for rides on his wagon. At least in the house. His ma says it is too cold outside for the baby now."

Ingeborg steeled herself for the questions she could see coming.

"How come God gave all the animals a winter coat, and we have to put on warmer clothes and babies have to be so wrapped up and—"

"You ask good questions, Inga. I don't know why God did what He did. But I am sure He knows. And has a good reason."

"But—"

"How would you like to help me bake cookies?"

"Gingerbread men?"

"If you want."

"How come we never make gingerbread girls?" She took her grandmother's hand, and the two walked downstairs to the kitchen.

"Because we don't have a cookie cutter for a girl gingerbread cookie." At least she had a good answer for that one. Uff da. How to keep ahead of that one, or at least keep up?

"Grandma?"

Uh-oh. Here we go again.

Freda smirked and winked at Ingeborg. "Inga, you fetch the eggs and the lard from the icebox, and Emmy, you help me get the things from the pantry."

After Inga set the things on the table, she got the big crockery bowl out of the cupboard. "How come you don't have the receipt written down?"

"Because it is in my head."

"Any other suggestions?"

Freda looked into the distance wistfully. "I have always wished we could have the Santa Lucia festival of lights, but none of our people are Swedish."

"Well, that was part of the Norwegian traditions too, wasn't it?"

"Not so much after the independence from Sweden. I think no longer celebrating that was kind of a backlash to the Swedish rule."

"Maybe next year we can do that. I talked with Mr. and Mrs. Sidorov first, for the Russian traditions. He said there are so many different countries that make up Russia that they will speak of the ones where they lived. It's hard to believe how big Russia really is." He dipped his cookie in his coffee. "Ah, this is so good. I think I'll keep the Norwegian ones until last."

"For the community party with the school program, I shall ask all the women to bake or prepare foods from their country." Ingeborg nodded as she spoke, her forehead wrinkled in thought.

"Especially the cookies and pastries," Thorliff said with a grin.

Freda checked the dinner and looked to the clock. "You girls set the table." Emmy and Inga jumped up, but when Ingeborg started to rise, Freda waved her back down. "You two visit a bit."

Thorliff shrugged. "She sounds a lot like Thelma. Hey, did Grace or Jonathan tell you they are hiring Mrs. Rasinov to be their housekeeper, cook, and whatever else they need? She and her children will live right there." He looked up. "So, Freda, you can have your house back."

"Is there anyone else who needs my house?" She looked to Ingeborg. "If that would be all right with you?"

"You mean you would stay here?" Ingeborg could hardly believe her ears. Not that Freda had mentioned wanting to move back home, but she had assumed she did.

"With us?" Emmy beamed.

Manny nodded. "Good."

"Well?"

Thorliff grinned. "Of course, I'm not sure which family yet, but there are plenty of candidates. That would take some more pressure off those working on the building. We hope to open the first floor next week, but when the people move in, they have to understand that the construction will go on above them. We got the fire damage repaired, so we are about winter tight. We've not done much on the inside, because the outside and roof needed all the work first."

"What about the Sidorovs?" Ingeborg asked. "Their two sons are in school, and her sister is one of the laundresses at the hospital. The missus is in Amelia's daytime class, and her husband and sister are in the evening. She has been sewing along with the rest of us."

Freda shook her head and shrugged. "There are beds enough. Go ahead and ask them."

Both Emmy and Inga left their table setting and threw their arms around Freda's middle. She leaned over and patted their heads and shoulders.

Ingeborg was sure she saw the glint of tears in Freda's eyes. Had this been weighing on her? Perhaps she did not like living alone, even though her son and family were not that far away. *Or perhaps she is concerned about you.* That thought floated through her mind like thistledown on a breeze.

After dinner as all the others were going about their plans, she and the two girls returned to the sewing machine.

"Now we can work on Christmas, right?" Inga's whisper made Ingeborg nod. She and Emmy dug into their basket, where they stored the gifts they were making. Since both had learned to knit, they settled cross-legged on the floor. After Ingeborg checked their last row and told them whether to knit or purl— and why—silence reigned, other than the whir and thump of the machine and the click of needles.

Ingeborg was finishing up another shirt for Manny. In the evening she had been hemming his wool coat, but that didn't need to be secret. Emmy was knitting a scarf for him, and Inga was working on one for her father. Since knitting was a new skill for them, they couldn't talk and knit at the same time.

Ingeborg snipped the threads and shook out the shirt. She had to do the buttonholes and buttons, and then it would be done. She could hear the men outside stacking straw and manure from the calf pens against the house for insulation.

❧

Like always, time flew fastest when you didn't want it to. She dreaded Thanksgiving, and it arrived long before Ingeborg was ready for it. She found the day to be very hard for her, this first major holiday since Haakan died. But that night she rocked beside the fire with the satisfaction that she had survived it.

Gloom be gone! The Sunday after Thanksgiving was a big day, in Blessing at least. Everyone gathered at the apartment building and Reverend Solberg led a service of blessing and dedication. That afternoon the first-floor residents moved in, which wasn't difficult, since no one had much to move. Everyone in town and the surrounding area donated what they could for tables and chairs, as each unit already came with a cooking stove and an icebox. Wooden boxes were put to use for chairs as well as for storage, and pegs on the walls served for hanging clothes. Families were given first preference. The remaining single men would share the apartments on the second floor when it was finished.

Monday, Miriam spent the day at Ingeborg's finishing up her sisters' dresses on Ingeborg's sewing machine. "I can't thank you enough. Between you and Mrs. Jeffers . . ." She shook out the dress after she tied off the last threads. "All I have to do is hem them, and my box will be ready to send."

"All the sewing machines in town have been humming nearly around the clock."

"When I think of all the hours it takes to hand sew a shirt . . ." She shook her head. "Sewing machines are one of the best inventions ever. When do you get to use your own machine?"

Ingeborg smiled. "Freda and I take turns after the others go to bed."

"How many quilts have you done?"

She shrugged. "We all do different parts, so who knows? We tied off three more last week, and I know of at least four other tops that are ready to tie. All the women who can, meet at the church and put them together. We are running out of batting. I wish I had more sheep. We could card the wool and form it right into batting. Outfitting this many new homes is a huge undertaking."

"It's a good thing other churches are sending boxes. Trygve said three more came in yesterday."

Ingeborg nodded and tried to hide her smile. Did this young woman realize that even the way she said his name showed her feelings for him? How could she have any doubt that she was in love with Trygve Knutson? Why did the course of true love never run smooth?

Miriam folded the dress roughly on her lap. "May I ask you a question?"

"Of course."

"How did you know you were in love with Haakan? I mean, I know it was a long time ago, but . . ." She dropped her gaze to the folded dress, then looked up to Ingeborg again. "Trygve tells me he loves me, and I am sure he does." She fingered the carved wooden heart she wore except when she was on duty. "I . . . I know I am attracted to him, but marriage is forever, and I don't want to make a mistake. I want what my mum and da had and what I saw you and Haakan living out so beautifully. But, Ingeborg, I've seen so many horrible ones too. Marriages that seemed perfect and then dragged both parties down to hell."

Ingeborg swallowed the lump growing in her throat. "This

is such a hard question to answer. My first husband, Roald, died, along with Kaaren's husband, Carl, and their two little daughters. She and I, well, only through the grace of God did we make it through that winter. And then Lars Knutson came along and married Kaaren—that helped. Then one day another Bjorklund man strode across the plains. He was a cousin to Roald and Carl, and his mother had told him some family needed help. He planned on going back to lumber country when winter came, but he never did. I'm not sure how much I loved him in the beginning, but he was so kind and willing to help us, it seemed natural to say yes to marriage. Oh, but our love grew deeper through the years. He was such a man of God, how could I not love him?"

She mopped the tears trickling down her face. "Trygve is a lot like Haakan, Miriam. A fine man who will become even more of a man of God. When I see the two of you together, it is like two puzzle pieces that fit. A glow seems to surround you." She patted Miriam's hand. "I know that is a long story and is not really your answer, but I do know this: God will make it clear to you when you ask."

"But what if you have a hard time believing that God really does exist, let alone cares about the daily things of our lives?"

Ingeborg looked deep into Miriam's eyes, now swimming in tears also, and took her hands. "He will make himself known to you if you just keep asking. I love the verse 'My grace is sufficient for thee.' I have so been depending on that promise these last months. With all my being, I know it to be true."

"I'd like it to be true."

"Just ask."

Patches barked his way off the porch and down the lane.

Ingeborg stood up. "Manny and Emmy are home."

"How do you know?" Miriam stood as well, gathering her gifts to her breast.

"That's his family bark, and it's time."

"Coffee's ready," Freda announced from the kitchen.

Ingeborg hugged Miriam. "All will be well."

That night, as every night, Ingeborg closed her day with a well-worn prayer. *Lord, calm all the turmoil in Blessing and bring us peace this Jule season.*

CHAPTER 34

Miriam was near tears, her eyes hot. She had been this way all day. They were gathered at Ingeborg's home, in the parlor around the candle-lighted pine tree, laughing, digesting a splendid feast, telling tales, relating reminiscences. It was all very enlightening, and Miriam was learning much about Trygve's family. What extraordinary people!

But she was not home. Wonderful food but not the table around which her family gathered. Lovely people, the Bjorklunds, but she wanted to be among the Hastings. This was Christmas Day. She should be in Chicago, not Blessing. What was Truth doing now? Did she miss her big sister the way Miriam missed her little sister? Ah, well. Very shortly now she would complete her training. Next year the family could be together again for Christmas. Whether here or there, it didn't make any difference. Not being with the other Hastings on Christmas Day made an immense difference.

And this Bjorklund-Knutson clan was so close too, so much like Miriam's family in that regard. Late last evening after church, Thorliff had driven the wagon from house to house, gathering up chairs and rockers and bringing them here to Ingeborg's. Now everyone had a place to sit, to be comfortable, with all the children on the floor. He had brought in extra dishes as well, so that all could be served.

This was not at all like Thanksgiving. On that holiday, each household had celebrated separately. Today, they all gathered as one huge happy mob.

Beside her, Sophie asked, "Why so glum?"

She forced a smile. "Sorry. I was thinking about my family."

Sophie nodded, smiling, and patted her arm. "I figured as much. Trygve often says how closely knit your family is. That is one of the many things he loves about you. Family. And loyalty. What would they be doing now?"

She thought a moment and burst out in a laugh. "Exactly what we are doing here! Gathered in the parlor after dinner, chattering and telling stories. There would not be nearly so many of us, of course." At least it was like that in the years before her father died and her family moved to the tenements. This year . . . She could hardly bear the thought of her brothers and sisters alone in that miserable place. She deliberately closed that door in her mind and paid attention to here.

At her other side, Trygve laughed. "We are getting to be quite a clan, aren't we." And indeed the room was about as full as a room can get, and all of them were talking cheerily. His parents and brother and sisters—all the Ingeborg-and-Haakan children, their spouses and children—my goodness. With six Hastings children, Miriam's family would probably expand like this someday. If they were all able to be together again.

Daniel was saying, "I'm glad the phone service is finally back. Sure, we got along without it, but it's a mighty great convenience. Jonathan, your father is talking about investing in a phone company here in Blessing."

Jonathan nodded. "He is certain that investments in this area will bring great returns. So many people are moving here, and there are so many opportunities."

Thorliff smiled grimly. "We can use the development money. That's for sure."

Andrew had been watching out the window. "The weather is

really getting worse. The snow is back, and the wind is rising."
At least they had milked early, so the chores were all finished
before supper.

The phone rang . . . speaking of telephone service.

Ingeborg sat nearest. She got up and answered. Voices quieted
down in the room a little. Not much.

She was grinning as she looked around the room at no one
in particular. "Of course, Mary Martha, I'll give them all your
warmest Christmas wishes. Certainly. And a very blessed Christmas to you all as well."

"Solbergs," Sophie murmured. "Some of her family even
came for Christmas."

Ingeborg listened in silence for a moment. She lost the smile.
Then she gasped and cried, "Oh no!" Everyone in the room
fell silent.

"Yes! Yes, right now! Good-bye!" Ingeborg hung up. "That
little cousin of Henrik Helder just rode into town to the Solbergs'
house. There's a fire out on the Helder farm. He says there are
injuries! John and the men were running out the door as Mary
Martha hung up!"

"So are we!" Thorliff grabbed his coat off the peg and ran
out, followed by all the other men. Even Manny clumped out
the door with his cane.

Astrid leaped to her feet. "Miriam, go to the hospital and make
certain it is ready to receive casualties. I believe Corabell is the
only one on tonight. I'll go out to the Helders' place. It sounds like
they might need me." She ran for the door, scooping up her bag.

Ingeborg called, "I'll be right behind you. We'll bring food
and coffee for the fire fighters!"

Miriam watched in amazement. Everyone just sort of knew
what had to be done and then did it. This small-town living was
so different from city life!

Ingeborg, Kaaren, Sophie, Anji, and Ellie filled baskets with
food, grabbed the coffeepot, and ran out the door.

Elizabeth stood up and waddled toward the door. She pointed toward the coat pegs. "Miriam, my coat, please. And get yours also."

Miriam grabbed the coats and returned to her, holding Elizabeth's for her, helping her slip into it. She shrugged into her own coat. They hurried out into the night.

The only buggy left was Andrew's. In the light from the front window, Elizabeth climbed up over the wheel. "Untie the horse."

Miriam did. She looped the lead line over a place on the harness as she had seen others do and climbed up the wheel. "This should prove interesting. I've not driven a horse before, ever."

Elizabeth smiled. "I certainly have." As Miriam settled in beside her, hanging on for dear life, Dr. Elizabeth flapped the reins and clucked. The horse lurched forward through the snow.

Driving out the lane was easy, for the other sleigh and wagon tracks had broken a path through the new snow. When Elizabeth left that path and continued toward the hospital, the buggy slowed down and the little horse struggled through knee-deep snow.

Blurred by falling snow, the sky out to the west beyond the horizon glowed faintly. The way the fires in town had looked was still fresh in Miriam's memory, and that was not how this fire looked. This one was yellower, and you could not see the smoke. As Miriam's eyes adjusted to the darkness, she could just make out lantern-lit sleighs or wagons in the middle distance driving toward the glowing spot.

"I'm afraid our winter will be very unpleasant compared to what you are used to." Elizabeth was peering ahead, but how could she see? Snow swirled in the frigid wind and near darkness.

"When winter comes screaming off the lake in Chicago, you learn what unpleasant is." Miriam was afraid she would lose her grip and tumble off. The buggy was bouncing a lot, and quite possibly had left the road without their knowing it.

They entered town and Elizabeth drew the horse alongside the hospital. Miriam hopped down. She ran to the horse's head and held it as Elizabeth very slowly and clumsily got her feet over the side. She reached the ground, said "Oh!" and clutched her belly. She stood there for a moment, then slogged through the snow to the door. "Just leave the horse."

Miriam left the tuckered-out horse to its own devices and ran ahead to open the door for Dr. Elizabeth. They hurried inside, slamming the door.

Welcome warmth embraced them.

"Make certain the ward and examination rooms are prepared. We can anticipate burns and smoke inhalation, possibly fractures." Elizabeth headed for the first exam room.

Miriam ran to the nurses' station. Where was Corabell? Dare she call loudly? She might disturb the few patients sleeping. She could not see from the records where Corabell might be, so she ran to the kitchen.

She was at the table, hunched over a cup of tea with a shawl thrown across her shoulders. She yelped and jumped when Miriam burst in the door.

"Come!" Miriam turned and ran back out. She scooped up extra gauze bandaging and dressings from the supply closet. Burns? They would need carbolic acid, plenty of it. She carried the additional supplies into the first examination room and stopped cold.

Dr. Elizabeth was hunched over the examination table moaning, both arms wrapped across her belly.

Miriam dumped her load on the side table, stepped in beside Elizabeth, and laid a hand on her shoulder. "Doctor?"

She was panting. Then she gave a long wailing cry. If people had been sleeping, they weren't now. "Oh, God! No! Not now!" Another wail in spite of herself.

Miriam waved a hand. "Her feet!" She and Corabell gripped Elizabeth's feet and levered her up onto the examination table. She instantly curled up on her side. Her face was grim and ghastly white.

"Her water just broke!" Corabell sounded frantic.

"We'll undress her and wrap her in blankets."

Easy to say, very difficult to do. Miriam so wanted to just cut the dress and petticoats off her, but these were her best holiday clothes. They must not damage them. It took what seemed a terribly long time. They tucked absorbent pads under her to soak up the blood about to be spilled.

Corabell still sounded frantic. "What if the baby is coming right now?"

"I heard her other pregnancy took many hours. So we have time yet. Dr. Astrid and Ingeborg will be here as soon as they can, and they'll take over."

"But what if they don't?"

Miriam didn't want to think about it. She should, however, gauge just how much dilation had occurred so far. She soaked her right hand thoroughly in carbolic acid and carefully began an examination. This was so strange, so frightening. This was her doctor, her instructor, and here was Miriam doing the examination. Cautiously she palpated, probing the cervix, and gasped. Elizabeth was opening right up! Five centimeters at least, perhaps more! Miriam's four fingers barely spanned the cervix.

"Help me! Help!" The voice was a man's, and it was out in the hallway.

Wide-eyed, Corabell looked at Miriam, then rushed out.

And Miriam was alone with a woman who was about to give birth, a woman who had very nearly died during her first pregnancy. And this was the one case of all Miriam would ever treat that she dare not mess up.

She set up the makeshift blocks that served as stirrups and guided Elizabeth's heels onto them. Elizabeth screamed again, flailing her head. The contraction lasted much longer than normal.

Miriam grabbed Elizabeth's hand in both of hers. "Please remember that God is in control. You know what Dr. Astrid and

Ingeborg say. God knows the situation." Many times Miriam had heard Astrid's mother use that promise.

"Yes." Elizabeth squeezed her hands and relaxed a little. Her face softened. "Yes. He is in control. It is so easy to forget that."

God is in control. Oh, how I wish that were true! But Miriam could not accept that.

Not after so much suffering and loss.

He was vindictive, or He had a malicious sense of humor, or He was not there at all.

"I need Ingeborg! Astrid! Oh, God!" Elizabeth arched in another contraction.

"They said there are injuries. They'll want to stay with the patient and get to the hospital quickly, so they will be here any moment." Through snow. Of course. Any moment.

Was the baby coming? Miriam must check. She released Elizabeth's hand and looked. Her heart nearly stopped! God in control? Hardly!

For a tiny foot had presented. A foot! One foot!

Miriam felt panic rush through her. She had read in a textbook about breech births, but she had never seen one, never been trained for one. And Elizabeth's baby was not only very early, it was breech! She was going to lose them both!

Oh, God, please! Please exist! Please help!

"It's coming! I can . . . Oh! O-o-o-ohh!" Elizabeth wailed, a long endless wail. Her body went so tight and rigid that her hips lifted off the table.

Miriam was quite slight, with very small, delicate hands. She knew she had to act through instinct. If she listened to reason, she would curl up in a corner sobbing. She shoved her right sleeve up to above her elbow. She snatched up a bottle of carbolic acid, the whole bottle, and poured it on her hand and arm, all the way to the elbow, slathering it all in disinfectant. Her arm tingled and burned.

Then she straightened her fingers, drew them together, and

managed to follow that tiny leg up the birth canal to solid, ungiv-
ing bone. The foot disappeared inside. She could not be sure, but
it felt as though the baby was pressing sideways against the floor
of the pelvis. It was not going to go any farther without help.

She could not reach farther. She should not be this far, and
yet . . . was this the other leg? She could not get above the ring
of bone, nor should she. But if this was . . . A forever moment,
a moment that was hours long, and by poking and prodding she
could draw that second leg down. The baby was still positioned
wrong, head up instead of down, feet first instead of head first,
but both feet were now in the birth canal.

Elizabeth was not suffering contractions. This was one single
endless contraction, exquisite pain that did not end, did not
pause. She was bleeding freely now. Oh, if only Miriam could
help her in her agony!

She did not dare tug on the baby either. She remembered being
taught, *"It is so tempting to try to help things along by pulling,
but never ever do it."* She withdrew and washed her hand and
arm in disinfectant again, in case she needed to go back.

The feet appeared. Now a new set of emergencies began. The
baby in the birth canal, especially as it passed down through
the pelvis, was pressing its cord flat. The baby and its cord did
not both fit. No circulation and no air, when a baby normally
would be able to reach air. What did the midwife do in that
case? Miriam had no idea whatsoever.

The tiny buttocks appeared, but they were the narrowest part
of the torso. They presented no problem. The shoulders did.
The head certainly did.

Shoulders. She remembered something. Carefully she forced
her hand in far enough to reach the baby's armpit. Could she
tilt the shoulder girdle so that one shoulder was higher than the
other? Then it would fit better. Yes, it worked. She withdrew.

She grabbed another stack of absorbent pads off the side table
and laid them nearby. They were going to need them.

The shoulders and one arm. Here was the other arm. And then the head slid out.

Elizabeth's baby had arrived.

Instantly, Miriam gripped the tiny ankles and lifted the baby high. She must suction . . . where was the suction syringe? She had forgotten to lay it out! And she could not let go. She was about to scream for Corabell when the baby made a little sound.

She tapped the soles of the baby's feet and began a gentle hum.

The baby cried. It was not a lusty wail that all welcomed. It was feeble, but it was a cry. The baby's ribs heaved, and it cried louder. Yes! And the child was so petite. Of course newborns were always tiny, but this child was tinier than a newborn and scrawnier. And a boy.

Elizabeth was already bleeding heavily, and the placenta had not yet appeared.

Miriam laid the baby, head downward, across Elizabeth's abdomen, up high, because she had to knead the lower area. She had seen Astrid do this. She should tie off the cord, but Elizabeth was bleeding. She kneaded. Her fingers tired and a pinky cramped up. She kneaded. Then a shadow fell across Elizabeth's belly, and Dr. Astrid was there! She began kneading strongly.

Astrid was there! Thank God! Praise God!

Dr. Astrid said, "You keep kneading. Good. Do you see how I am using the heels of my hands? Good. Good!"

"The baby—"

"The mother comes first."

Were they making some progress, or was that Miriam's imagination? Elizabeth wailed again, and the placenta slipped out onto the table, a flaccid purple thing.

Here was Ingeborg! Praise God again! Ingeborg sang her own praise to God as she gently lifted the tiny baby away and took the placenta with her.

"Miriam, replace the pads. We want to know if the hemorrhage is slowing."

Miriam slipped in fresh pads as she yanked the others away and tossed them under the table. Just stopping for that moment helped her pinky loosen up. She went back to kneading.

Astrid relaxed a bit. "I think we're out of the woods."

Now, what did that mean? No one in Chicago ever said "We're out of the woods," and Chicago certainly had more woods than Blessing ever did. The bleeding appeared to be slowing. Yes, it definitely was slowing. It seemed pretty much the normal bleeding expected.

The crisis was past. Elizabeth had slipped into a semiconscious state, and Astrid was taking over. Ingeborg, with the baby at the side table, had tied off the cord and was cutting it. Miriam realized she had also forgotten to set out the string and scissors. Even first-year nurses did better than that!

Her hands were bloody. She looked at her hands, her slim, tiny hands. She should be jubilant! It was over! Success! Rejoice! A baby boy was born.

Her face dropped forward, to be covered by her bloody hands, and she began to sob uncontrollably.

CHAPTER 35

I am having a hard time believing you delivered that baby by yourself. He came early and presented breech, yet you pushed on through." The three of them were in Elizabeth's room at the hospital, two days after that momentous Christmas Day. Astrid automatically checked Elizabeth's pulse while they talked.

Miriam shook her head. "I am still in a state of shock. I panicked more than once, but like your mor always says, 'God is in control.' Up until I saw all this, I could not believe that He cared that much for us—for me. All I could see were the terrible things happening."

While normal color had yet to return to Elizabeth's face, and feeding her tiny son took all her strength, she reached out to take Miriam's hand. "Without you and these small hands of yours, both of us would have died. God told you what to do, and you did it."

"So an idea, a memory, can be God talking?"

"Yes. When we are His children, He communicates with us in more ways than you can ever dream."

"Including dreams," Astrid added. She glanced over to the baby bed, where little Roald lay on fleece and surrounded by

339

hot water bottles, a light tent helping keep the heat in. Usually he was tucked in right next to his mother, but the doctor had ordered her to get some sleep without having to worry about the infant beside her.

Ingeborg tapped at the door. "Is this the gathering of the medical team?"

"Seems that way." Astrid smiled at her mother. "Welcome."

"I brought the baby a sling so that we can take turns carrying him next to our skin so he does not get a chill. And Elizabeth can rest better." She laid the soft flannel sling on the bed and drew a jar of liquid from her basket. "Here is that compound the Metiz taught me about so many years ago. It helps make one stronger and seems to increase milk flow. I mixed it with honey and water. I have also been asking around for someone to wet-nurse him, if we need that."

Astrid checked on Elizabeth, who had fallen sound asleep again. She nodded and motioned them all to leave the room, bringing the baby bed with them and gently closing the door behind them. "So, Mor, show us how this works, please." She held up the flannel contraption.

"Come into the office, and I'll show you."

Within a few minutes the tiny infant was slung tight against her chest, and she buttoned up her sweater, since her waist no longer closed. "Skin to skin is the best, at least that's what Metiz always said. I'd forgotten all about this until last night."

"Don't tell me you had a dream." Miriam's half shrug accompanied a smile. "So that leaves one's hands free to do whatever needs to be done?"

"Ja, and see, it is working." The baby had stopped the little whimpers of discontent at being moved around and seemed to be sleeping again.

Ingeborg patted the bulge of baby. "He already knows when he is hungry, a true Bjorklund for certain." She gently swayed, a mother kind of natural motion.

"Miriam, let's go check on the other patients, and Mor can sit in Elizabeth's room on watch. Not that I think it might be needed, but I am taking no chances."

They checked on the man in Room 1. He'd gone back into the burning barn to get the horses and cows out. A flaming plank fell on him. His son dragged him out. Several others were treated and sent home.

When they had finished seeing to the patients on the ward and were back in the office, Miriam asked, "Do you really think this baby is six weeks or so premature?"

"Good question. Why do you ask?"

"He seems stronger than the tiny preemies I saw at the hospital in Chicago. I mean, he can nurse, and his cry is growing more lusty all the time."

"That we miscalculated the day he was due is a very real possibility. His lungs sound good, and he is digesting his milk. I am in awe that they are both alive. I was so afraid . . ." She cleared her throat. "Elizabeth's last recovery took months."

"Inga?"

"Well, her too, but Elizabeth lost a couple of babies after that."

"Oh, that is so hard on a mother. It happens a lot, doesn't it?"

"Especially with mothers who lack nutrition and women who wear those horrible corsets. The babies have no room to grow." Astrid shuddered. "I abhor fashions at times, so often worn at the expense of the baby or the mother's health."

"Dr. Morganstein often said the same thing when she spoke to the nursing students." Miriam turned to leave when she was needed elsewhere.

Astrid picked up her pen and started working on the stack of charts, something that always got put off. Miriam had taken over much of that, and Deborah and Corabell managed the inventory and ordering of supplies. They had survived another crisis with the fire from the Helder farm and a surprise baby. What an unforgettable Christmas this had been.

❧

I have to see Trygve. The thought zapped Miriam whenever she had a free moment. As soon as she had caught Vera and Deborah up on the status of all the patients at the changing of the shift, she shrugged into her coat. Mother and baby were doing well, considering what they had both been through. Ingeborg had stayed with them most of the day, since Emmy had spent the day with Inga while Freda and Manny were crating up another shipment of cheese. How the lives of the people of Blessing intertwined, leaving Miriam in a constant state of amazement.

I have to see Trygve. The thought kept time with her boots crunching the crusty snow on her way back to the boarding-house. It wasn't like him not to show up, but since all the nurses had been swapping shifts since they were so busy, and all the crews were working to finish the upper floor of the apartment building and to get one of the three houses ready to be lived in, she had to remind herself to be patient. *But I have so much to tell him.*

The sun was already sinking, flaming the sky and sending shadows to blue the snow. As cold as it was, she was grateful the walk was not far. She'd taken Ingeborg's advice and always wore a scarf to pull up over her mouth and nose. Even so, she stopped at the gate to the boardinghouse, just to watch the sun give up and sink beyond the distant horizon line. Oh, how beautiful. She'd never noticed sunsets and sunrises in Chicago. Here one had to stop and stand in awe at such magnificence.

Letting a sigh escape, she trudged up the steps that had recently been swept and pushed open the door to the board-inghouse. Fragrances of fresh bread, cooking beef, and coffee tantalized her to go straight into the dining room, but since no one was at the desk, she unwrapped her scarf and climbed the stairs to her room, half expecting Corabell to meet her with an invitation to have supper together.

A note in the door hanger caught her attention. She pulled it out and read it before she hung her coat in the closet.

May I join you for supper? She smiled at the briefness and his signature. Had he read her mind or what? She sat down in the rocker and read it again. Was this another one of the little things that Ingeborg would say was God sprinkling blessings? After what she had experienced, she gave up and admitted that only God could have put all the people and happenings in the right place and in the right order to save both Elizabeth and her tiny son, and then gave her the knowledge to do the right thing. If she'd not been there, they might have died. Every time she thought of those events, she felt a surge of gratitude. Death had come so close that night. But when she had checked on Elizabeth just before leaving, Thorliff was sitting with her, holding one of her hands while her other arm was cuddling their infant son. Love glowed in that room.

And now she knew for absolute certain. Love glowed in her too. She tipped her head against the back of the rocker and fingered the carved heart she now wore tucked under her uniform. The heart Trygve gave her. He'd said she was in his heart.

And now she knew. She knew. She loved Trygve Knutson the way a woman should love a man, this man that God had given her, another one of His amazing gifts. Now she knew too that God loved her, Miriam Hastings, and that she loved Trygve and wanted nothing more than to be his wife. To share the love that shone from his eyes. That she had just seen with Thorliff and Dr. Elizabeth.

Thank you, Lord, he is coming to supper. How would she tell him? Too many people in the dining room. It was too cold out to go for a walk. Or was it? Do I write him a note? Blurt it out? *Lord, what should I do? I have nothing to give him.* She had embroidered three handkerchiefs with his initials, TK, on them for his Christmas present. She heard the bell calling them to supper. If she went down now, would he be there?

Should she wait? Miriam shook her head. How silly could one get? She ordered the butterflies somersaulting in her middle to go back to sleep. She washed and tried to put some order in her hair, but when the second pin fell to the floor, she leaned on the washstand and stared into the mirror. Her fingers were shaking too much to insert the hairpins. How preposterous. Bundling the mass into a snood, she shook her head at the face in the mirror, pinched her cheeks to bring up some color, and headed for the door.

Just as she reached for the knob, someone knocked.

"Here I am." Ignoring the shock, she pulled the door open to see Corabell smiling at her.

"You have a guest waiting for you." Her eyes twinkled in the lamplight. "I was hoping you would sit at a table with me, but I know you would prefer your guest." Her giggle trailed over her shoulder as she went to her room.

"Aren't you going down?" There went the butterflies again.

"In a bit. You go ahead." More giggles. Corabell was giggling. Ah, yes, so many changes as to seem overwhelming at times.

When she started down the stairs, she saw him leaning against the banister post, looking up at her. His smile widened. Surely he had the most perfect smile she had ever seen. She trailed her hand down the carved wooden banister, almost wishing she could turn and run back upstairs. But not tonight. Tonight she would tell him.

"I was afraid you might have to work late." His voice set her heart to double time. Deep and vibrant, full of warmth. Did he use this warm tone with others, or was this the way he talked only with her?

"I'm glad you came." She reached the bottom step and slid her hand into the crook of his arm. "I wanted you to come."

"Really? Perhaps that was what I was hearing."

344

"What?"

"Your invitation." Together they walked into the dining room, and he pulled out a chair at a table for two, not where she usually sat.

"Maisie said she reserved this just for us." His hand brushed her shoulder after he pushed her chair back in. "Tonight we are not going to hurry, so no one better have an emergency of any kind."

How do I tell him? What if he has changed his mind? Crazy thoughts chased each other through her mind while they ate.

"Dessert tonight is apple pie," Lily Mae told them when she took their plates away.

"How did you know that is my favorite?" Trygve smiled up at her. "And Mrs. Sam makes pies that you never forget."

"Actually, I baked the pies today, but everyone says they's good. No complaints."

"Then thank you." He looked to Miriam, who nodded. She'd never made a pie in her life. Perhaps Ingeborg or his mother would teach her. Or Mrs. Jeffers.

Slowly the other diners pushed back their chairs and left the room, with some people going to the parlor but most to their rooms. Miriam scraped up the last of the apple juice on her plate.

Tell him now before someone else interrupts.

"What is it? Something is bothering you."

"I have so much to tell you, I don't know where to begin." *Help me, Lord.* How strange it felt to have thoughts like that. And yet . . . how comforting to know He listened.

She leaned forward. "Trygve Knutson, yes, I love you and yes, I will marry you." The words came out in a rush, tripping over each other and her tongue.

His eyes widened, delight started in his eyes and then pulled his cheeks into a smile. "You mean that? You are sure now?" He reached across the table and took her hand, his fingers warm and firm.

She nodded. "I have learned three things since Christmas."

"And they are?"

"That God is who He says He is, and He loves me." She paused, trying to corral the words and thoughts so she could speak without stammering.

"That's two."

"I love you."

"You are sure?" He narrowed his eyes. "Absolutely?" He took her other hand and laid his arms on the table, their hands clasped in the middle, his thumbs drawing magnetic circles on the backs of her hands.

She nodded. "Absolutely. I know it took me a long time to be sure, but if you still want to marry me, I . . . I want to be Mrs. Trygve Knutson for the rest of our lives."

He raised one hand to his face and kissed her knuckles, first one, and then the next.

A thrill charged up her arm and straight into her heart. She wove her fingers through his.

"You are sure you want to live in Blessing, bring your family here, and start a new life? I know you have to graduate first, but . . ." His forehead wrinkled. "That is so far away."

"Not really, not the way time flies."

"Do you want to go for a walk?"

"Now?" Her voice squeaked.

"Yes. I have to kiss you, and I do not want to do that here."

"It's cold out there."

"I know, but I don't think that will be a problem. Get your coat."

When they stepped out on the porch, he pointed to the east. "Look. The moon."

"Ohh. How beautiful."

The moon threw shadows across the snow and seemed to smile right at them. In perfect step they went down the three stairs and turned to look at the moon again, their breaths a puff of mist in front of them. With her arm locked securely in his, she leaned her head against the wool of his coat.

"I want to shout for everyone to hear: She loves me! Miriam Hastings has promised to change her name to Knutson." He laughed and pulled her closer to him, if that were possible. "December twenty-seventh, nineteen hundred and five, will go down in history, our history anyway, as the night she said yes."

She shivered. "We need to walk."

"Or." He turned her around and led her back to the porch and up the steps. But instead of opening the door, he led her off to the side, wrapped her in his arms, and kissed her. Cupping her face in his hands, he whispered, "Are you warm?"

"I am now. Thank you." Even through his thick coat, she could feel his heart beating against her cheek. Fall and graduation were so far away. Fall and graduation would be here before she knew it. Would she be sorry she'd not be nursing at the Morganstein Hospital in Chicago? She would always have a place to work here in Blessing.

An arrow thought struck! She pulled back to look up into his shadowed face. "Will you mind my nursing here in this hospital?"

"Do you mean, must you stay home?"

"Once we are married, yes."

He dropped a kiss on her nose. "Not at first, but once we have children . . ."

"Good." She looked up again. "We have a lot to talk about."

"We have a lifetime."

"Not really. My family will live with us."

"Of course. I hope Tonio decides to go back to school, but I have a feeling he is a man now and will want to work instead."

"He might decide to stay in Chicago." The idea made her shudder. "Oh, I hope not."

"Me too." This time it was a shiver, not a shudder that jolted her.

"You are cold. Let's go in. We don't have to make all these decisions tonight."

"True, but I want you to know what you are getting into."

"Ah, Miriam, my love, you are worth any kind of difficulty. We will work these things out when we need to." He held the door open for her. "Do you work tomorrow day again?"

"I do."

"Then I will be here for supper again."

"Good."

She trailed a hand on the banister going up the stairs, hugging the secrets to her heart. *Trygve loves me. God loves me.* Was this one of the reasons she was brought to Blessing? And to think she'd almost refused to come.

This was indeed a harvest season of change, changes beyond her hopes and dreams. Her mother used to repeat Bible verses about that very thing: *a time to weep, and a time to laugh; a time to mourn, and a time to dance.*

True, but love stayed around forever, in spite of the changing seasons. She had seen it, and now she believed it.

Lauraine Snelling is the award-winning author of over 70 books, fiction and nonfiction, for adults and young adults. Her books have sold over 3 million copies. Besides writing books and articles, she teaches at writers' conferences across the country. She and her husband make their home in Tehachapi, California.